Wish Upon a Cowboy

St. Martin's Paperbacks Titles by Kathleen Kane

The Soul Collector

Still Close to Heaven

This Time For Keeps

Dreamweaver

Simply Magic

Wish Upon a Cowboy

Wish Upon a Cowboy

Kathleen Kane

St. Martin's Paperbacks

ISBN: 0-7394-0807-0

Printed in the United States of America

St. Martin's Paperbacks are published by St. Martin's Press, 175 Fifth Avenue, New York, N.Y. 10010.

To the Ladies of the Lounge, a crazy bunch of writers who made the 1999 Chicago RWA conference so much fun . . . Cherry Wilkinson, Susan Plunkett, Adrianne Lee, Myrna Tempte, Rhonda Harding Pollero, Tina Bilton-Smith, Amulya Rasmussen, Terri Farrell, and Pat Kersten, reviewer extraordinaire.

To the members of the Lowcountry chapter of RWA, who are living proof that Southern warmth and charm are not a myth.

And especially to Amy J. Fetzer, writer and friend, who makes every conference an adventure. Is it my turn for the belt yet?

Chapter one

"**Walnuts** are hard, but rocks are harder. We need some food to fill our larder."

Hannah Lowell kept her green eyes tightly closed and whispered her incantation one more time, just for good measure. Then, with a wave of her hands, she smiled to herself and opened her eyes to look at—the still-empty shelf.

Her shoulders slumped in defeat. An all-too-familiar sinking sensation filled the pit of her stomach. Hopeless, that's what she was. Absolutely hopeless.

For most of her life, she'd been trying and failing to live up to the sterling reputation her family held within the Crafters' Guild. Why, it was a wonder she hadn't been drummed out of the Guild entirely. Instantly, visions of some of her more memorable catastrophes filled her mind. Like the potion she'd blended to help Sally Carruthers catch the eye of the local blacksmith. But even as she thought about it, Hannah dismissed that particular failure. After all, Sally's vision had cleared in only a week, so there'd been no permanent damage. And Peggy Ryan wasn't supposed to use the freckle cream *every* day. No wonder her skin turned red. As for Mr. Carruthers's pig . . . well, he'd been destined for Sunday supper anyway.

Oh, it was mortifying to admit to being so untalented.

It was getting so she was embarrassed to face people. She just knew that everyone in town looked at her and wondered how a Lowell could have sunk so low.

"Maybe it's my rhyming," she muttered desperately, tapping her fingertip against her chin. "For pity's sake, what else could it be?" She had the bloodlines. Heaven knew she'd been practicing magic most of her life. There had to be an explanation for her lack of skill.

Frowning, she lowered her gaze to the yellowed pages of the book lying open on the kitchen table. Running the tip of her finger over the faded printing, she clucked her tongue as she once again read the proper ritual. "It's all right there," she told the little white cat perched on the corner of the table. "It should have worked, Hepzibah."

The cat lifted one dainty paw and began grooming itself, apparently bored with the conversation.

"Why didn't it work?" Scowling, Hannah looked back at the bare pantry. If she couldn't whip up a few sacks of flour, how could she hope to solve the problem facing them all?

"Hannah?" The feminine voice drifted to her from the front of the house.

"In here, Aunt Eudora," she called distractedly. Then to herself she muttered, "it *has* to be the rhyme. Never was very good at poetry."

Sure she'd hit at the answer, Hannah closed her eyes again, concentrated, and tried something different. "Sugar's sweet and vinegar's sour, please send Hannah a bag of flour." She winced slightly and hoped she hadn't sounded as whiny as she thought she had. After all, when you're trying to cast a spell, you should sound confident, not desperate.

Eyes closed, she heard her aunt come in behind her.

"Hannah . . . what are you doing?"

"Almost finished, Eudora. One more minute . . ." Then, just for luck, she repeated her spell.

An exasperated chuckle sounded out behind her.

Eudora was fond of saying that magic wasn't to be found in a book, but in your heart. She had always tried to convince Hannah that her talents would reveal themselves one day. She simply had to be patient.

But there was no time for patience anymore. Hannah couldn't keep on waiting for her abilities to improve. She needed help now.

Concentrate, she told herself. See the flour in your mind. Picture it on the shelf. Another long minute passed. Behind her. Eudora's toe tapped gently against the kitchen floor.

When she couldn't put it off any longer, Hannah sucked in a deep gulp of air and slowly, hopefully, opened one eye. She gasped and clapped her hands. "I did it!" she shrieked and stared at the single ten-pound sack of flour as though it were a pirate's treasure. Spinning around, she grabbed her aunt and swung her in a wide circle. "My spell worked!"

"Well, of course it did, child," Eudora said as she lifted one hand to hold her red velvet hat down on her head. "You're a Lowell, aren't you?"

Grinning now, Hannah released her aunt and reached up to push her long, blond hair back from her face impatiently. "I am indeed! Although," she added with a wry grin, "I was beginning to wonder if maybe the Lowell blood had thinned out in my case."

"Nonsense," Eudora said, giving her niece a pat on the cheek. "I've always told you that your magic would come, given enough time and patience."

"At least it worked today. Just look at that flour, Eudora," she went on, walking closer so she could stroke the cloth bag reverently. "Enough to make a dozen cakes at least!"

"Yes, dear," Eudora said and took a seat at the table. "It's very nice."

Something in the older woman's tone finally caught Hannah's attention and she turned from the scene of her triumph to really look at her aunt. At sixty, Eudora was as beautiful as ever. Although her once-black-as-midnight hair was mostly silver now and even her soft blue eyes seemed somehow faded, she had an innate dignity and elegance that could never be touched by the years.

At least she had until recently.

Worry slithered up Hannah's spine as she watched Eudora take off her hat and set it down onto the scrubbed pine table. "What is it?" she asked. "Bad news?" Heavens, she hoped not. It seemed as though in the last year all they'd had was bad news. Starting with the arrival of one Blake Wolcott.

The Englishman had oozed his way into every corner of life in Creekford, up to and including the Crafters' Guild. For more than a hundred years, the tiny town of Creekford had been a haven, a sanctuary for witches and warlocks. Founded by a handful of crafters running from the witch trials and ignorant outsiders, Creekford drew crafters from all over the world. It seemed that all witches were interested in finding a safe harbor in which to practice magic without fear.

Not that Creekford's citizens were unsociable. There were dances and county fairs and barn raisings to attend in neighboring towns. But there were no nonwitches living in Creekford. Hannah wasn't sure if the people in the surrounding areas actually realized that witches and warlocks were living in their midst, but there'd never been any trouble.

Until recently.

Now their pleasant little town was no longer their own. Wolcott made the decisions these days. Since he arrived, Hannah's friends and neighbors, shoulders hunched as if expecting a blow, scuttled fearfully along the village streets. Outsiders were banned. And socializing with the neighboring towns was cut off.

At first, Creekford had welcomed Blake as it had all witches and warlocks before him. But soon enough, the man had made it clear he wasn't there to make friends.

What he wanted was a kingdom, and he didn't care what he had to do to get it.

And no one was strong enough to stand against him.

Eudora sat down, stared at her clasped hands for a long minute, then glanced up at Hannah. "You remember Mr. Tewkesbury?"

Instantly, the man's cherubic face rose up in Hannah's mind. A traveling tinker. Jasper Tewkesbury had been stopping in Creekford to sharpen knives and repair pots and pans for as long as she could remember. "Of course I do," she said. "Is he here?"

"He was," Eudora said and lifted one hand to cover her mouth.

A flicker of foreboding rippled along Hannah's spine. "Was?"

Steeling herself, Eudora inhaled sharply and said, "Jasper refused to leave when Blake ordered him out of town. Claimed he'd been coming for years. It was his right to do business here."

"It is."

"It used to be."

"What happened?"

"What always happens?" Eudora said stiffly, squaring her shoulders and shooting Hannah a wild look. "Blake Wolcott *removed* Jasper."

Hannah swallowed heavily and dropped into a chair. "He's gone?"

"Vanished," Eudora said, her voice a pale whisper. "Like every other nonwitch Blake's found in town."

Not many outsiders lingered in Creekford, thanks to the protective spell woven around it years ago by the founding fathers. But the few who did had never been in danger. Until recently.

"We've got to do something," Hannah muttered, shaking her head. Glancing at her aunt, she asked a question she'd asked countless times over the last year. "Surely if we all band together . . ."

"No." Eudora shook her head. "Perhaps, if we'd acted

in the beginning . . . but who could have guessed we were welcoming a snake into our little Eden?" The older woman lay both hands flat on the tabletop. "You know as well as I what's happened to the people here."

Yes. Beaten down by fear and by the slow draining of their power, the citizens of Creekford were no match for a warlock bent on enslaving them. Hannah's stomach churned. Even escape wasn't a real option. The last man to try to leave was hunted down by Blake's men and dragged back to the town square, where Wolcott and his small band of supporters made an example of him.

Donald Southern had paid the ultimate price for defiance and his death hadn't been an easy one.

"There's something else," Eudora said quietly, catching her niece's attention.

Hannah looked at her aunt, caught the glint of determination shining in her eyes, and knew.

"You found him." It wasn't a question.

"Yes. Finally."

This was it, then. Hannah would have wished for more time. Time to strengthen her skills. Time to gain confidence. Time to think of another way. But there was no more time to be had. It was now or never and both women knew it.

Eudora had been studying her glass for weeks now, searching for the one man who could help them. But it was as if he hadn't wanted to be found. Clouds of vapor befogged the glass ball and Eudora had had to ease her way through countless cobweblike layers of mist to reach her goal.

"Where is he?"

"On a cattle ranch," Eudora said and reached across the table to take Hannah's hand in hers. "In Wyoming."

"Wyoming," she whispered. The West. Unsettled, wild and open. She gave a quick glance around the familiar, cozy kitchen. "It's so far away."

"Not so far," Eudora told her and gave her fingers a squeeze. "You can be there in just a few days."

"So soon?" Her stomach twisted and Hannah swallowed heavily. She'd known this was coming, but somehow, illogically enough, she hadn't really expected it to arrive. "I can't leave . . ." She let the sentence drift off as she looked into Eudora's determined blue eyes.

"Of course you can," her aunt countered briskly, before adding, "and *must*. Right away."

"How many times have you told me over the years that running from your problems isn't an answer?" There, Hannah thought. She had the older woman with that one.

"If you're running *to* a solution," Eudora said, shaking her head, "it's the only possible answer."

"Slippery, that's what you are," Hannah muttered and leaned back in her chair before crossing her arms over her middle. She was caught and she knew it. She had a responsibility to her family. To the Guild.

To the town and the people she loved.

"Hannah, we've been all through this many times."

"I know," she said. "But there must be another way."

"There isn't."

"We could try."

"We have tried." Eudora shook her head again firmly. "Now we've run out of time. We need help, Hannah. We need *him*."

A flash of irritation shot through her. Heaven knew she was willing to do whatever she had to to protect Eudora, the only family she had left. But at the same time, she realized if her aunt didn't, they had no guarantee that this man in Wyoming would be willing—or able—to help them.

"You mean to fight the devil we know with the devil we don't."

Eudora smiled, transforming her solemn features into the pleasant, loving expression Hannah had known most of her life. "The Mackenzie isn't a devil."

Hannah wished she could believe that. But no one in Creekford had seen or heard about the Mackenzies since the little family had left town more than twenty years ago.

"Then why isn't he here when we need him?" she asked.

"Be reasonable, Hannah. How can he know that the Guild is in trouble?"

She didn't want to be reasonable. Reasonable meant she would have to leave the only family she had ever known and travel halfway across the country, *alone,* looking for a man she wouldn't recognize if she tripped over him.

No. It made much more sense to stay right here and try to find another way.

But before she could say so one more time, the back door flew open with a crash as it slammed into the wall. Hannah jumped up and turned to face the intruder. Eudora kept her seat, only the whitening of her knuckles betraying her emotions.

Blake Wolcott entered the small, neat kitchen and the door swung closed behind him. Tall and broad-shouldered, wearing an expensive, well-tailored black suit, he seemed to fill the tiny, whitewashed room with dark waves of power that shimmered in the air around him.

His brown hair swept back from a wide forehead, his equally dark brows lowered over mud-brown eyes. He graced both women with a tight smile, then turned his steady gaze on Hannah. "I've come for your answer," he said, his voice rich and deep.

"We need more time," Eudora told him as she rose and moved to stand beside the younger woman.

Instinctively, Hannah stiffened her spine, trying unsuccessfully to make her five-foot-one-inch frame as tall and imposing as her aunt's.

Wolcott smiled and waved a negligent hand. Across the room, a copper teakettle jumped from its spot at the back of the stove, sailed across the kitchen, and clattered against the wall opposite. "I understand," he said quietly.

"A bride requires time enough to gather her trousseau."
A slight narrowing of his eyes warned the two women
of his growing impatience. Inclining his head a bit, he
met Hannah's gaze and said, "Until the Summer Solstice, then. At which time we *will* be married."

"I haven't said yes," she muttered, mindful of her
aunt's restraining grip on one of her hands.

"You will," he said pleasantly. "Or Eudora will find
herself greatly . . . changed, shall we say?"

In other words, he would strip Eudora of her powers.
Hannah didn't doubt him. He'd already done the same
to a couple of the Guild members who'd dared try to
oppose his takeover. The fact that he'd also done far
worse made her shiver.

This was all her fault. If she'd been better at her
work, she wouldn't need anyone's help. By the stars and
planets, she was a Lowell. The pride and power of generations long past ran in her veins. If she'd only been
able to master the family craft, she could have dealt with
this interloper and sent him flying back to England. Although, a voice inside reminded her, not even Eudora
had been able to stand against Blake Wolcott. And Eudora's powers were formidable indeed.

So what in heaven made the older woman think a
man who had turned his back on his heritage—his people—could?

"I'll leave you to begin your preparations for the wedding," Wolcott said and gave them each a benevolent
smile that didn't fool either of them.

Still, at least he was leaving.

As he turned for the door, a small white ball of fluff
jumped from the table, streaked across the floor, and
darted between his legs.

"Hepzibah!" Hannah shouted and started forward
even as Blake's balance dissolved and he fell to the floor
in a clumsy heap. Instantly, he jumped to his feet again,
making a grab for the cat.

But Hannah was quicker and snatched the little animal up to cradle against her bosom.

His features flushed a dark red. Blake reached for the hissing cat, but Hannah only tightened her grip and glared at him, daring him to take it.

A moment passed, then two. Blake's dark eyes looked like two empty holes. Hannah wanted to duck her head and run from the room, but instead she stood her ground and only hoped he couldn't see her trembling or hear her knees knocking.

Slowly, the color receded from his face and he gave her a stiff nod. "As you wish," he muttered, giving the cat a look that should have scalded it. Glancing at Eudora, he said, "Forgive my clumsiness," then walked to the door and stood aside as the heavy oak portal opened before him. Without another word, he left, and the door slamming closed behind him echoed in the room like a rifle shot.

"Don't push him like that, Hannah."

"He would have killed Hepzibah."

"Without a thought, yes."

Hannah tucked the little cat up close to her chin and rubbed her cheek against its soft white fur. Hepzibah's heartbeat raced beneath her fingers and Hannah knew that her own was running in time.

Eudora moved to pick up the kettle. Smoothing her fingers across the glossy surface, she glanced at Hannah and whispered, "Well? Is it marriage to that one, or the other?"

The other. The unknown. The man Eudora had seen in her crystal. The man all the members of the Crafters' Guild were pinning their hopes on.

The stranger Hannah would have to marry in order to save everything—and everyone—she loved.

The Solstice was only six weeks away.

A shiver of apprehension slithered along her spine. The thought of marrying Blake Wolcott was enough to

turn her blood to ice. And yet, she worried that she was
leaping from the frying pan into the fire.

Still, there was no denying Eudora was right, as she
usually was. They needed help fast. Even if a blind jump
would land her in the flames, the clean heat would have
to be better than sharing a frying pan with Blake Wolcott.

Hannah drew a shaky breath before turning to look
at her aunt. "I'll leave for Wyoming tomorrow." She
only hoped the Mackenzie was half the warlock Eudora
believed he was.

A Week Later

The longhorn bull tossed its head angrily, then turned a
dark look on the cowboy recoiling his rope for another
try at him. Stamping its hooves against the spring grass
and snorting like a demon, the bull ducked its head and
waved its massive horns in warning.

"That is the damnedest critter I ever saw," Elias Holt
muttered as he rubbed one hand over the gray stubble
lining his weathered jaws. "You'd think he wouldn't
fight so hard against being pulled into the breeding pen."

Jonas Mackenzie shifted in his saddle and glanced at
the man beside him. Years of weather and hard work
had drawn deep lines into the older man's face. Pale
gray eyes narrowed into a familiar squint as he watched
the goings-on. His battered hat covered a head that was
mostly bald, but for a dusting of steel-gray hair. His
hands were like old leather, stringy and brown, and just
as strong.

It was only in the last couple of years that Elias had
begun to slow down a bit. At sixty-five, he'd more than
earned the right, Jonas knew. But it was a hard thing to
watch. It only reminded him that years were passing and
that one day, when Elias was gone, Jonas would be
alone.

Irritated with that train of thought, he brushed it aside

and said, "Maybe he likes to pick and choose his own females."

"Hell, Mac," Elias countered, "he's too old to be roamin' the range now. If a young bull didn't kill him, the next winter would. 'Sides, as mean as he is, he ought to be grateful we ain't shot him yet."

Chuckling, Jonas yanked off his hat and wiped his forehead on the sleeve of his shirt. "He's sired too many good calves for me to shoot him and he knows it."

Mean to the bone he might be, but that bull had helped build the beginnings of a hell of a herd. Jonas glanced around him briefly, letting his gaze take in the log structures they'd worked so hard to build. A bunkhouse, a barn, and two pole corrals, and off to one side, the smallest of the three buildings, the main house. Of course, a stranger might ask why the boss's place was the least impressive of the bunch. But Jonas figured that at this point, all he really needed was a roof to keep the rain and snow off. Later on, when the ranch was as big as his dreams—he figured another ten years or so—he'd build a fine house, with a wide porch and maybe some fancy scrollwork trim. And of an evening, he'd sit on that porch and stare out at the ranch he'd built from the ground up.

If a part of him realized that he'd be alone in that fine house, he silenced it.

He'd had his chance at a wife and family—and he'd lost it. After ten long years, the sting of that failure had become a dull ache that came alive only when an echo of the past rose up to taunt him. He'd buried Marie and their stillborn daughter in the cold, hard soil of Montana, then he'd tucked his heart into that dark hole with them.

He inhaled sharply, reached up, and tugged his hat brim down low over his eyes. He'd build his ranch. Make his mark . . . but he'd do it alone.

Nope. Family life wasn't for everybody and certainly not for him.

Tilting his head back, Jonas studied the clear blue

sky. Good weather lately, and after a hard winter, they'd earned it. Lazily, he shifted his gaze back to study the range.

A handful of mounted men rode slowly through the milling cattle dotting the meadow that stretched out as far as he could see. Roundup didn't officially start for a few weeks yet, but he'd started his gather early, anxious to see how his herd had withstood the winter.

By western standards, his herd was relatively small. Yet every year there were more calves born. A mixture of Hereford and longhorn, his cattle were hardy stock, and in a few years beeves would fill this meadow and beyond. Cattle he'd worked for, sweated over, and worried about. Cattle that would one day make him one of the biggest, wealthiest ranchers in Wyoming. As long as the roundup went well, the weather held, and they were able to get the herd to the trains and a good price for them at railhead.

Any rancher who said he wasn't a gambler was lying. Hell, life was a gamble. One throw of the dice could set you up like a king or take everything you ever worked for. Or loved. It all came down to luck, he figured. And his luck had generally been better than most.

He sucked in a lungful of fresh mountain air and told himself his luck would hold. Everything would go as it should. Didn't everybody for miles around call him the luckiest son of a bitch in the territory?

Mac had come a long way in the twenty-five years since he'd been left an orphan by a stray band of Indians. He had no real memories of the parents he'd lost on the trail west, just the occasional shadowy images that raced through his mind and were gone again.

And that was just as well, he reasoned. A man can't go forward if he's forever looking behind him. Besides, some memories were better left buried.

"What's that?" Elias asked quietly.

Mac blinked and turned his head to look at the older man. Elias was as close to a father as Mac had ever known. Hired by the Mackenzies to guide them west, he had buried them where they fell, then taken on the responsibility of raising their boy. They'd been together ever since. Through good times . . . and bad. To Mac's mind, he'd done a good job of it, too. Everything he knew about anything, he'd learned from Elias Holt.

"What are you talking about?" Mac asked, his gaze straying now.

"That out there." He lifted one hand and pointed.

"Old man," Mac said softly, squinting into the afternoon sun, "you've got eyes like a hawk."

He snorted. "It ain't hard to see what don't belong."

An instant later, Mac saw it too. "What in the hell?" He rubbed his eyes with his fingertips, then stared again, expecting the strange apparition to be gone. But it wasn't. "What's a woman doing out there?"

Elias squinted. "Looks like she's dancin'."

It did indeed, though why some strange woman would be dancing in the middle of a herd of cattle was beyond him.

A yelp of surprise sounded out from close by. Mac swung his head around in time to see the longhorn bull charge the cowhand trying to rope it, then side step and take off at a dead run, its hooves tearing at the meadow grass. Other cattle moved aside as the ornery old beast thundered in the direction of the damn fool dancing woman.

"Son of a bitch," Jonas muttered. So much for luck. He dug his heels into his horse's sides and the big black took off like a shot. The air rushed past him. All he heard was the startled lowing of the cattle around him and the thunder of his horse's hooves against the earth. Guiding the animal with his knees, Jonas reached for the rope coiled around his saddle horn, and, loosening it, swung the wide loop high over his head.

He didn't know who she was or what in the hell she was doing on his land, but he couldn't very well sit still and watch her get trampled into the meadow.

The old bull was still charging, snorting and roaring like it was remembering years past when it had been the most powerful animal on the range.

Jonas would only get one toss at it. Moving as fast as it was, the animal would be atop the woman before she even knew what hit her. She'd never outrun it, even if she tried. He glanced at her. She wasn't trying.

Still hopping and skipping around, the stupid woman obviously didn't even realize what danger she was in. Absently, he noted long blond hair flying in the chill wind and a full red skirt swirling high above her knees.

Then he focused on the bull and stopping the animal's wild flight. Snaking the loop out farther, he widened his swing, letting his instincts take over the familiar motions. The weight of the rope, the rocking of the horse, the high arc of his hand as he let the rope fly, sailing through the air toward a moving target. He watched, unsurprised as the heavy hemp circled the bull's back legs neatly.

Instantly, the big animal dropped. Snorting and roaring its rage, the bull kicked at the loosely knotted rope, giving Mac just a few extra seconds. The big animal would be free in no time and mad as spit on a hot griddle, to boot. Hardly breaking stride, Mac's horse continued on past the fallen bull until its rider was within arm's reach of the woman, who had finally stopped dancing to look up in surprise.

Mac had a brief moment to notice the deep green of her eyes before he leaned to one side, caught her with one arm, and swung her up onto the saddle in front of him. Small and light, she nonetheless landed with a jolt and a grunt, then curled her fingers into his shirtfront for balance.

Expecting to hear tearful words of gratitude, Mac was unprepared when she shoved ineffectually at his chest and demanded, "Let me down!"

Not even a thanks, he thought, more disgusted than ever. "There's a bull over there, just wanting to get another chance at your hide," he muttered, keeping his arm tight around her waist as she squirmed against him.

She threw her head back, tossing her hair out of her eyes. Mac stared into the deep forest-green depths and for one tantalizing moment felt something hard and tight clutch at his chest. Something he hadn't felt in years and didn't want to feel now. Then she shattered the spell by frowning up at him and ordering, "Put me down. I have to get Hepzibah."

He sent a frantic look around the small clearing. Who the hell is Hepzibah? Another dancer? One unlucky enough to be knocked to the ground by the restive herd? He didn't see anything. Next Mac shot a glance over his shoulder at the bull, already kicking free of his loop. The fact that he also saw two of his riders headed for the surly animal didn't give him much ease. One slash from those wicked horns could bring down a horse with no problem, and once the bull was afoot, he and this crazy woman would both be in big trouble.

She went limp in his grasp and attempted to slide free.

"Lady," he grumbled irritably, "don't push me."

"I can't leave Hepzibah," she said, glaring up at him.

If looks could kill, Mac figured he'd be about six feet under right now. He glared right back at her and absently noted the distant rumble of thunder. Perfect. Just what he needed right now. A storm coming. "Who the hell is Hepzibah?"

"My cat," she snapped and pointed.

He looked. Sure enough, a small white cat was mincing its way toward them, delicately lifting each tiny paw from the damp meadow grass as if afraid to get dirty.

"Cats and crazy women," he muttered darkly and nudged his horse closer to the little animal. Swinging down from the saddle, he ordered, "Stay put, I'll get the damn thing."

He figured he'd have to chase the cat, but once again, he was wrong. When he reached for it, the animal leaped at him, digging its claws into his shirt and scaling him like it would a handy tree. In seconds, he had a cat perched on his shoulder. Mac turned his head to stare at it and met the little beast eyeball to eyeball. It meowed once, then dug its talons into Mac's flesh as if digging a bed. Wincing slightly at the needlesharp stings, Mac considered yanking it off and tossing it at its owner. Then he heard the muffled roar and snort of that blasted bull and remembered where he was.

Shoving a steer out of his way, he stepped into the stirrup, climbed aboard his horse, wrapped his arm around the woman again, grabbed the reins in his free hand, and turned the black for safe ground.

From the corner of his eyes, he watched the bull, free now, stand up and amble off in the opposite direction.

Immediate danger past, he gave his attention to the woman on his lap. He looked down into the biggest, greenest eyes he'd ever seen and once again felt that odd constriction in his chest. He ignored it. Her hair fell across her shoulders in waves of a blond so rich it looked shot with gold. The top button of her simple white shirt was opened and her full red skirt was hiked up to the knees of shapely legs covered by pale white stockings. Even as he looked, though, she squirmed on his lap and tugged the hem of her skirt down.

Just as well.

Meeting her gaze again, he told himself that, pretty or not, she was clearly addle-brained or she wouldn't have been dancing in the middle of a herd of cattle.

Blond eyebrows arched high on her forehead and her full lips curved into a delighted smile as she stared back at him. "You're the Mackenzie, aren't you? I can tell by the way Hepzibah has taken to you. She doesn't care for just anyone, you know."

"Lucky me," he said tightly, with a quick glance at the cat, still sitting like a sentry atop his shoulder. Shifting his gaze back to the woman, he continued. "Yeah. I'm Jonas Mackenzie. What were you thinking, lady?

You always go dancing in the middle of a herd?"

"No," she admitted, giving a quick glance around her at the cattle wandering aimlessly across the grass. "But sometimes you just feel so good, you have to dance. No matter where you are. Don't you think?"

"I don't dance." Stupid conversation.

"That's a shame," she said and actually looked sorry for him.

Scowling slightly, he ignored her sympathetic expression and asked, "Who are you, lady? And what are you doing on my land? Besides dancing, I mean."

She gave him a smile so dazzling, his breath caught in his chest. An instant later, though, it left him in a rush as she said, "My name is Hannah Lowell. And I'm here to marry you."

Chapter two

"I don't know who put you up to this, lady," he said, "but I can tell you I don't think it's funny."

"It's not a joke," she told him, clearly surprised that he would think so.

"Lady, I don't even know you."

"In good time," she said and settled herself more comfortably in front of him.

Everything inside him went cold and still. Jaw tight, he stared down into those eyes of hers and tried to guess what was behind all this. But there were no clues to be found in those deep green depths.

Mac inhaled deeply, drawing the cool mountain air into his lungs, and told himself that if no one had sent her on a lark, she had to be crazy as a bedbug. And wouldn't you know she'd find her way to his ranch?

He steered the horse through the meandering crowd of cattle, mostly giving it its head. A fine cutting horse he'd trained himself, the black was as at home in a herd as it was in its stall. After a long, calming moment, Mac said, "Lady, are you lost or something?"

"Oh, I never get lost," she assured him.

So, the crazy woman had a good sense of direction. It still didn't explain why she'd come to him.

"I came as quickly as I could," she said.

"To marry me."

"Well that, too," she continued. "But first to meet you. You could hardly marry me if you didn't even know I existed."

Irritation swept through him. He didn't have time to deal with a feebleminded female. He had a ranch to run. Roundup to prepare for. His temper began a slow boil.

Thunder rolled again in the distance and he looked over his shoulder to see dark clouds gathering over the peaks of the mountains. Rain—or snow . . . you never knew in Wyoming—by nightfall, he figured.

Mac shot a glance ahead to where Elias still sat on his horse at the edge of the herd. The old coot hadn't moved an inch. Sure, Jonas thought. When I need him, he's just sitting there like some kind of statue.

A chill, damp wind swept down on them from the mountains, heralding the coming change in weather, but it sent a ripple of uneasiness down Mac's spine.

"So here I am," she was saying, and he looked down into that dazzling smile of hers. "And if it's all right with you, I think we should be married fairly quickly, all things considered."

All things considered, he thought he should just turn this horse around, drop her back in the middle of the herd, and forget he'd ever talked to her. But since he couldn't do that, he tried to reason with her.

"Lady—"

"Hannah."

"Fine. Hannah."

"Normally, we wouldn't use our Christian names so early in our acquaintance, of course." She gave him a smile that staggered him. "But then, these are not ordinary circumstances, are they?"

"You could say that . . ." Keep her calm, he told himself. No sense getting her all worked up. He wasn't sure how to deal with light-minded people, but he figured prodding her temper could only make things worse. How, he had no idea.

"It's a lovely place you have here," she said. Turning her head to admire the scenery, a soft smile curved her mouth. He watched as she lifted her gaze to the nearby mountains.

Mac saw the same awed wonder he always experienced at that magnificent view shimmer on her features, and felt an odd sort of fleeting kinship with the woman. At the very least, she knew good land when she saw it.

"I like it."

"What a wonderful thing to wake up to every morning." She stared at the Rockies, her voice hushed as though she were in church.

It was indeed, he thought, briefly staring at the snow-capped mountains. This valley, this ranch, was everything he'd ever wanted.

"A man with a home as nice as this needs a wife to care for it."

Old memories rose up, threatened to choke him, then receded again, back into the dark corner of his heart where he'd managed to corral them.

"I could be very helpful," she said, watching him.

"I don't need help."

"Oh, everyone needs help sometimes," she said and let her gaze drift from his to stare into the distance. "Actually—"

"Look," he interrupted sharply. "Hannah, isn't it?"

"Yes."

He looked down at her and silently reminded himself that she was, no doubt, a loon. When he spoke again, his voice was kinder than before. "You don't want to marry me, Hannah."

She laughed gently and Mac found himself enjoying the sound. Oh, no question about it, he'd been too long without a woman. Time to head on over to Jefferson and spend an hour or two with one of Sal's girls.

Shaking her head, the blond finally said, "It's true. I was against the marriage, at first. But Aunt Eudora convinced me this was the only way."

So there was a crazy aunt in on this, too.

"And why would she do that?" he asked, though he had a feeling he'd regret it.

"Well, you are the Mackenzie, after all."

Like that explained anything. And why did she insist on saying his name like she was speaking in capital letters?

"What's my name got to do with this?" Even as the words left his mouth, though, the answer came to him. "It's my ranch, isn't it?" he asked. "Somehow this aunt of yours, if you really have one, has decided that marrying me will get you a piece of my ranch."

For the first time since rescuing her, something made sense to him. The ranch might not be much to look at now, but in a few years it would be a showplace. Why wouldn't a far-thinking gold digger think to stake a claim early?

She inhaled sharply and turned horrified eyes on him. "That's dreadful! What a horrible thing to say about me. And Aunt Eudora, who certainly *does* exist, I assure you."

"Oh, well," he snapped, "sure, I'll take your word on that, too."

She caught the sarcasm and those forest-green eyes narrowed on him. "There is no reason to be so nasty."

"You think not?" he demanded a bit too loudly, and a couple of the nearest cattle lowed skittishly. Good job, Mac, he told himself. Start a stampede. Then his hands would have to spend the next few days gathering the cattle they'd already gathered once.

Lowering his voice, he locked his gaze with hers and said, "I find some strange—and, if you don't mind my saying so, *peculiar*—woman dancing in the middle of my herd and when I save her bacon, not only doesn't she bother to thank me, she informs me she's come to marry me. The only problem being, I never *asked* her to marry me."

She twisted uncomfortably in his grasp, but he tightened his hold on her, trying to ignore the soft brush of the undersides of her breasts against his forearm. Oh, yeah. Definitely time for a trip into Jefferson.

"Naturally," she said quietly, "I had every intention of thanking you . . ."

"Naturally."

"I was simply overcome by the situation."

"Sure."

"Thank you."

"You're welcome." At least she wasn't talking foolishly anymore.

"And now that the niceties are taken care of," she continued, leaning back to look up at him, "I want to assure you that I do not have designs on your property."

"Uh-huh."

"I wish you'd stop saying that."

"Uh-huh."

She gritted her teeth, pushed against his forearm ineffectually, then subsided again. "You are the Mackenzie. It's only reasonable that Aunt Eudora would send me to you."

"Uh-huh." There was absolutely *nothing* reasonable about any of this. Least of all, this aunt of hers choosing *him* to be bridegroom to her beautiful, but apparently dim, niece.

"She sends her best, by the way."

"That's real nice of her, I'm sure." Where the hell was everybody? Why didn't they ride out to meet him? His gaze snapped to the spot where he'd left Elias. There he sat. Still hadn't moved a hair. You'd think the ornery old cuss would be able to tell that he and his passenger weren't exactly out on a pleasure ride.

But no. Just like always, Jonas Mackenzie was left to handle things on his own. And that thought reminded him of a question she still hadn't answered.

"Why do you keep saying my name like it's supposed to mean something?"

"It does," she told him, looking at him through eyes

shining with confusion. Obviously, she figured he should already know the reason.

Well, he didn't, but he damn well wanted to find out.

"To who?" he asked.

"To a lot of people," she hedged. "Myself, for one. I admit," she continued, tipping her head back to look up at him squarely, "the idea of traveling so far to marry a man I'd never seen before wasn't appealing."

Another sensible statement. Was there hope here after all? The cat kneaded Jonas's shoulder, claws digging through the fabric of his shirt and into his skin. He shrugged in an unsuccessful effort to dislodge it. Instead, the damn thing nuzzled his neck, its whiskers tickling his throat.

He gritted his teeth as irritation bubbled inside him. Never had cared for cats. Thunder, closer now, rolled across the sky and clattered high above them. Damn.

"But now that I've seen you," Hannah told him, "I know it's for the best."

"Do you, now," Jonas said, his voice as tight as the smile he gave her. She talked like she believed everything she was saying, so arguing with her wouldn't do him a damn sight of good.

"Too, Hepzibah took a liking to you right away and she's an excellent judge of character."

"Really." He'd never known a cat to care about anything save its own comfort.

"Oh, my, yes," Hannah went on. "She didn't like Blake Wolcott at all. The very first time she saw him, she arched her back and hissed like a demon."

Jonas glanced at the cat again. He had no idea who this Wolcott fellow was, but at the moment, he envied him.

"Look, Hannah," he said, inching backward as far as the saddle would allow, because it seemed important to keep as much distance as possible between them, "why don't you forget about this marrying nonsense, tell me where your folks are, and one of my hands will take you there?"

"I can't," she told him flatly. "The decision's been made. The die cast. Set in stone. Laid out clearly before us both—"

"I get it," he interrupted wearily.

"Besides," she added, "I don't have any folks. Except for Aunt Eudora, of course, and she's in Massachusetts."

Jonas was getting tired of talking in circles. The damned woman had an answer for everything, even if it wasn't really an answer at all. And he was beginning to suspect she wasn't really as crazy as she appeared to be.

Besides the beauty in those eyes of hers, he saw a rare and sharp intelligence sparkling there. But she was wasting her time on him. He had no intention to marrying. Not again. Sure, she made his insides sit up and take notice, but that was lust, pure and simple. That he knew how to deal with, and marriage didn't have a thing to do with it.

Reining in the flash of impatience nudging him, Jonas shot a quick look at the darkening sky. Then, calmly, deliberately, he tried again. "Where are you staying in Wyoming?"

"With you, of course," she said and gave him a look that clearly said she thought *he* was the one whose train had slipped its track. He bit back an oath as lightning flashed.

Hannah's smile didn't falter. Not even when he drew his head back and stared at her as though she'd suddenly sprouted horns.

Of course he was surprised, she told herself. He simply needed a little time to get used to the idea. After all, Eudora had always told her that no man *wants* to get married. Why should the Mackenzie be any different?

However, she hadn't expected a warlock from a family as distinguished as his to be quite so surly.

"Hannah," he said finally in a tone that was almost a growl, "you are not staying here."

"Oh, you'll find me good to have around, I promise you. I'm an excellent cook and I've won first prize at the county fair three years running for my quilts."

"That's real nice," he said, giving her a smile that barely touched his eyes. "But it doesn't change a thing. You can't—"

"Isn't it a glorious day?" she asked, tipping her head back to enjoy the deep, clear blue of the sky and was surprised to see banks of clouds scudding across its surface. She didn't think she'd ever seen a storm blow in so quickly.

"Storm coming," he said shortly.

"I see that." She watched him and could have sworn she saw the storm reflected in his eyes.

She patted the arm he had wrapped around her middle and absently noted the muscular strength of him. Her stomach did an odd little flip-flop and she sucked in a deep breath to steady it. "You'll see, Mackenzie. We'll be good together."

Oh, she would be the first to admit that she hadn't much cared for the idea of marrying a man she didn't know. But now that she'd had a good look at the Mackenzie, she felt much better about the whole thing.

His black hair was a bit too long; it curled atop his shirt collar and poked out from beneath his dirt-brown hat. But his sapphire-blue eyes glittered with intelligence and his hard, whisker-shadowed jaw looked as strong as the arm he kept tight around her.

She could almost feel the power that surrounded him. Surely this was the man who could defeat Blake Wolcott and protect her, Eudora, and the members of the Crafters' Guild. Once they were married and back in Massachusetts, everything would be as it should be.

Besides, hadn't Hepzibah taken an immediate liking to him?

"*We're* not doing anything, lady," he said with quiet determination. "I am taking you to the nearest wagon and sending you back to wherever you came from."

She sighed. Why was he being so difficult? "It's a long way to Massachusetts."

He muttered something she didn't quite catch, and judging by his expression, she should be relieved about that.

"Fine," he said quietly. "One of my boys will drive you into town."

"But I don't want to leave. I only just got here." She tossed a quick look at the row of log buildings they were fast approaching. "Wouldn't it be better if I settled in right away?"

Pulling in a deep breath, he looked down at her. "We are not gettin' married, Hannah, so you can't stay here. You don't need to 'settle in.' "

"I hadn't expected you to be so stubborn," she said and folded her arms across her chest. Leaning back against him, she stared straight ahead, barely noticing the working cowboys and the milling cattle.

He laughed shortly. "Lady, you could give lessons in stubborn."

She'd heard that most of her life and she supposed it was true. But stubbornly clinging to your convictions was a good thing, wasn't it? And if it took every ounce of her fairly formidable will, she *would* marry Jonas Mackenzie.

Too much was at stake for her to accept failure.

Briefly, the image of her town and the frightened people there rose up in her mind. She must succeed. There was no other choice.

With his strong arm still wrapped around her stomach and the solid, warm strength of him pressed to her back, Hannah felt more certain than ever that the Mackenzie was the answer to her problems. The only trouble was in making him see reason.

Frowning to herself, she thought that maybe she'd gone about this initial meeting all wrong. Maybe she shouldn't have announced her intention to marry him right off that way. It really wasn't surprising that he was so against marriage to a complete stranger, she supposed. After all, his family had been gone from Massachusetts for so long, he probably didn't consider himself bound to the old ties.

Nodding to herself, Hannah decided that clearly he was going to need a little time to get used to the idea of marriage. Summer Solstice was still almost two months away. She could afford to be a bit more patient.

Perhaps she should invest a couple of weeks in letting him get to know her. See her in his house. Become accustomed to the idea of her presence. Hannah smiled to herself. Yes. Two weeks should be enough, and that would still leave plenty of time for them to be married.

"Mackenzie," she said.

"Call me Mac," he grumbled. "Or Jonas."

"Jonas, then."

"Fine. What is it?"

"I've decided that we shouldn't get married right away."

He sighed again and his breath brushed the top of her head. "That's real good, Hannah."

"Instead, I believe I'll become your cook." She twisted on his lap to look at him again.

This time he groaned slightly, muffling the sound by clenching his jaw so tight, Hannah was surprised it didn't snap.

"Thanks, but I've already got a cook," he said. "Juana's been with me for a year now."

"Oh, dear," she murmured. "That is a problem."

"Thought you might see it that way."

"But," Hannah added thoughtfully, "perhaps she could use a nice long rest."

He grumbled something again, then said, "Juana doesn't need rest. Believe me."

"Hmmm . . ." Hannah's mind was whirling, looking for a solution to this newest development. How could she work her way into Jonas's house and his affections if he already had a cook who wasn't even interested in taking some time off?

Blast Blake Wolcott and the boat that had brought him from England! This was all his fault. If the British warlock weren't so hungry for power, none of this would have happened and she could be safely at home now.

Jonas pulled his horse to a stop alongside an older man whose gaze locked on her suspiciously. "Elias," Jonas said and swung down from the saddle, "take Miss Lowell back to town."

Back to town? She couldn't leave. Not yet. Not until she'd come up with a solution.

"Oh, but I—" Hannah began.

Jonas grabbed her off the horse and dropped her on her feet. "It's better that you just go, Hannah," he said, his voice low enough that only she could hear him.

Looking up into the clear, cold blue of his eyes, Hannah could only nod. He'd won this round, but the game was hardly finished. "All right," she said, her voice as low as his had been. "But I'll be back tomorrow."

"Hannah . . ."

"You never know," she said, lifting one hand to push her hair out of her eyes. "Juana may change her mind about taking some time off."

"Like I said," he muttered with a shake of his head. "Stubborn."

"Birds of a feather," she pointed out.

His lips tightened and he turned back to his horse.

"What about that?" Elias asked.

"What now?" Jonas demanded.

The older man's gray gaze shifted to the cat still clinging to Jonas's shirt. He'd almost forgotten about the damned thing. But then, who could blame him? Reaching up, he pulled at the animal and then, one by one, released its clawed paws before handing the animal to Hannah.

The little cat yowled its displeasure.

Hannah smiled. "She likes you."

Jonas shook his head again, tipped his hat to her, swung back into the saddle, and turned his horse toward the herd. "Hannah," he said with a half smile, "it's been real interesting." Then, with a jab of his heels, he set the horse into a trot that carried him quickly away.

She watched him for a long moment, studying his easy posture in the saddle and the muscular width of his back. She sighed gently and tried to ignore the tiny ripples of awareness shifting and tugging at every nerve in her body.

The Mackenzie was much more *man* than she'd expected. She only hoped his skills as a warlock compared in kind.

"Ma'am," Elias said, and Hannah tore her gaze from her retreating would-be bridegroom. "You come with me, I'll see you get to town."

"Thank you," she said and dutifully followed him. It didn't matter where she went today. Tomorrow she would be back. Because by then, she vowed—a little guiltily at the thought of the poor, unsuspecting Juana— Jonas Mackenzie *would* be needing a cook.

Her campfire was a small one, just big enough to boil water for the tea she'd purchased in town. Digging into the carpetbag she'd had to ask Elias to retrieve from the field for her, she pulled out a small leather pouch and carefully opened the ties holding it closed.

Instantly, the combined scents of several dried herbs lifted from the pouch and teased her nostrils, reminding her of the home that was too far away. Hannah closed her eyes and brought up the mental image of Aunt Eudora, sitting in her favorite rocker in a corner of their cozy kitchen. She could see the flickering shadows of firelight playing across the older woman's features and could almost feel the serenity that always seemed to surround her aunt.

A long, mournful howl somewhere in the distance

splintered Hannah's comforting daydream and she
opened her eyes to stare off into the darkness just beyond her fire.

Only a few hours ago, she'd been filled with delight
at being free of the almost suffocating atmosphere of
dark power hovering over Creekford. It had been too
long since she'd felt the urge to run or dance in a field.
Wolcott had stolen even that from her. Now, though, as
she looked into the darkness surrounding her, Hannah
wished fervently that she was home again. Evil warlock
or no.

Wyoming was too big. Too . . . *dark*.

Tall trees marched in formation for as far as she could
see. It had rained that afternoon and the smell of the
damp forest floor plucked at her nerves in its strangeness.

Again, that distant animal howled, and this time Hepzibah mewed and curled up on Hannah's lap as if looking for protection.

"It's all right," she whispered, needing to hear the
words herself. "Whatever that was won't bother us," she
hoped aloud.

Shifting her gaze from the black shadows of the trees,
she looked down the short incline to the Mackenzie's
ranch. Squares of lamplight glimmered in the darkness
and lay faint yellow patterns on the ground. She stared
at the light for a long time, relishing the knowledge that
she wasn't truly, completely alone in the darkness.

Down there, the Mackenzie sat in his house, perhaps
thinking of their encounter today and wondering where
she was and what she was doing. What surprised her
was that she was wondering the same thing about him.

Jonas stood up, stretched, and said, "I'm for bed. Need
to get a couple hours sleep at least."

Elias nodded from his chair by the fire. His gnarled
fingers deftly moved in the flickering light as he twisted

and braided a length of rawhide into a bridle strap. "That was a right pretty gal here today."

Jonas shot the older man a look from over his shoulder. Since taking Hannah into town and leaving her there, Elias hadn't said a word about her. Until now.

"Yeah, she was," he agreed, although he thought *pretty* a fairly mild word to describe Hannah Lowell. The words *beautiful, crazy,* and *irritating* came to mind.

"Seems odd," Elias murmured, "come all the way from Massachusetts just to end up here."

Odder than the old man knew, Jonas thought. Apparently his would-be bride hadn't told Elias the real reason for her visit, and Jonas saw no point in telling the other man about her plans for a marriage that wouldn't happen.

She was gone. That's all that mattered.

Rubbing one hand across his whiskered jaw, he thought again, as he had all day, about clear green eyes, shinning blond hair, and a mouth made for kissing. Damn it.

He didn't want to think about her anymore. He wouldn't be seeing her again and that's the way he wanted it. No sense in distracting himself with thoughts of her—or in talking about her to a nosy old coot who would only want to stay up half the night gossiping about the strangeness of her proposal.

"She got lost is all," he finally said, determined not to tell the other man about Hannah's outlandish story. It was late. He was tired. And he just plain didn't want to talk about it.

"Uh-huh," Elias muttered.

"Yeah, lost." Jonas turned for the far wall and the door that led to his bedroom. Already he was trying to figure out a way to wipe Hannah's face from his mind so he could sleep awhile before work began at dawn. "Wyoming's a big place. Easy enough to get lost in."

"Uh-huh."

All right, now he understood why that short phrase

had bothered Hannah so much. In fact, it was downright irritating. "Look, you old coot—"

Whatever he might have said was forgotten in the next moment, when a choked-off scream rattled through the room.

Juana.

Instantly, Jonas was off and running toward the kitchen and the side door, with Elias just one step behind him.

Hannah sprinkled the sweet-smelling herbs onto the fire and smiled when a dusting of sparks lifted toward the night sky. The combined scent of the herbs filled her mind and heart as she closed her eyes and whispered fervently, "Rivers from an ocean, streams from a brook, Hannah needs to be the Mackenzie's cook."

Opening her eyes again, she frowned slightly at the stars overhead and whatever gods were hiding behind their gentle, steady light. "I know my rhyming needs work, but perhaps you could make an exception in this case. Oh," she added quickly, "and please, I don't want anything terrible to happen to Juana, poor woman. It's not her fault that she has the job I need. Perhaps a good, nasty head cold? Just something that will keep her from her work for a while."

Smiling to herself, she thought that had gone fairly well. After all, she didn't mean any harm to a hard-working woman. She only needed to get into the Mackenzie's household long enough to prove herself irreplacable.

And that shouldn't take more than a couple of weeks.

A brief, half-heard scream began and ended again in a heartbeat's worth of time. Hannah sat straight up and looked around her wildly. What sort of beast had a cry that sounded so . . . human? And how close by was it? One minute passed, then another. When nothing leaped at her from the shadows, fangs bared, claws outstretched, she slowly began to relax again. At last, she decided that whatever animal had made that noise was far enough away to not be a worry.

Settling back against the trunk of an ancient pine, she again stared down at the ranch house below. The soft, welcoming glow of the lamplight seemed like a golden path laid out for her to follow. Spirals of smoke drifted up from one of the chimneys, carrying the scent of roasting meat and burning wood.

Hannah sniffed the air wistfully, then took a bite of the apple she'd purchased in town. If all went well, she would be in that house tomorrow and she could begin her campaign to win the Mackenzie's heart.

Chapter three

When the knock on the front door came just as dawn was brushing the sky with soft shades of lavender and rose, Jonas wasn't even surprised.

After all, hadn't she warned him she'd be back today?

He crossed the room in a few long steps and threw the door open in time to be met by Hannah's still-raised fist.

Quietly he jerked his head back out of range. She lowered her hand and laughed gently. "Sorry," she said.

"Somehow," Jonas admitted on a sigh, "I knew it would be you."

She smiled at him, and damned if that smile wasn't even brighter than he'd remembered it to be. He'd been up all night and felt like he'd been dragged behind a running horse through the halls of hell and she looked fresh as a spring rain.

Her cat mewed suggestively. He looked down in time to watch it sashay past him, pausing only long enough to rub the length of its body against his shins.

He'd forgotten about the blamed cat.

"Good morning," Hannah said and followed her feline inside. He watched her jaw drop as she let her gaze wander around the small, cluttered room. "Oh, my heavens," she whispered as she took a good long look.

He closed the door, turned around, and let himself see the place through her eyes. He understood her soft moan of distress. The dark, smoke-stained walls were split logs with white chinking running like wide stripes between them. A river-stone fireplace took up one whole wall and there were two battered chairs and a short horsehair sofa pulled up in front of it. Four narrow windows let in the growing sunlight through filthy panes of glass and everything from dirty clothes to saddle harnesses were strewn across the hardwood floor.

The cat plopped its behind down in a relatively open spot and immediately started licking its paws in an insult obvious even to Mac.

Rubbing one hand across the back of his neck, he scowled at the mess and wondered how it had gotten so out of hand. Hell, he hardly spent enough time in the room to dirty it, yet somehow it looked as though a tornado had set down square in its center. He bent down to pick up a discarded shirt, then realized it wouldn't make much difference and let it lay.

The cat he ignored.

"It's a . . . sturdy-looking place," Hannah said.

A tight smile touched his face briefly. Sturdy. Well, it was that, anyway. The roof was sound and he'd made sure the log walls were fit tight to withstand a Wyoming winter. But he knew she'd had to search her mind desperately to find something nice to say.

A curl of shame unwound inside him until he stiffened his spine against the feeling. What did he care that his house was a mess? Or that Hannah Lowell looked as though she wanted to hike her skirts to avoid her dress brushing against the dirty floor? Or that even her blasted animal seemed to be looking down its nose at him?

He hadn't invited them here, had he? And it wasn't as though he had a stream of visitors day in and day out. As busy as he was, he hardly got into town more than once a month, so he damn sure wasn't spending his time socializing with his neighbors . . . who were just as damned busy as he was anyway.

All he expected out of his house was a roof to keep the snow off and walls to cut the wind that rattled down off the Rockies to drive cold stakes through a man's bones. Later, when he'd built his cattle empire here in this valley, he'd build a fine house. One that people would ride miles to see and admire.

And, he told himself with another glance around the room, he'd damn well hire a woman who would take better care of the place than Juana did. But even as he thought it, he knew it wasn't the older woman's fault. He'd hired her to cook, not clean. And Lord knew, just the cooking for all the men on this place was enough to tire out a much younger woman than she.

While his thoughts were still flying through his mind, Hannah deliberately turned her back on the devastation of the room and faced him. "I came to see if you've changed your mind about offering me a job." Her gaze slid pointedly across the room again. "And it seems that you need more help than you're willing to admit to."

Mac stiffened slightly because he knew what she said was true and didn't want to acknowledge it, even to himself.

"Now, how did you know I'd change my mind?" he asked.

"You have, then?" Her smile brightened considerably, something he wouldn't have thought possible. "Isn't that wonderful?"

"Wonderful?" He reached up and shoved both hands through his hair, squeezing his scalp in a futile attempt to ease the headache pounding inside his skull. "I doubt Juana thinks so." A puny weight settled on his left boot. Jonas looked down and scowled at the cat, which looked to be making itself at home.

"Oh? Is she sick?"

He looked back up at her, his gaze narrowed thoughtfully. The concern in her eyes looked genuine, but she didn't sound surprised that Juana wouldn't be able to do her job. "No," he said, remembering that short-lived scream the night before.

He and Elias had raced outside to find Juana sitting in the dirt, her right foot pulled up into her lap. In the dark, she'd stepped into a gopher hole and twisted her ankle so badly it was swelling to twice its size as they stood there and watched.

After wrapping her injured ankle, Jonas had spent most of the rest of the night delivering Juana to her sister's house, some ten miles away. And there she would stay until she healed enough to come back to work. Which was fine for Juana, but left him up a creek without a boat.

Not only did he have roundup starting in a couple of weeks, but there were twelve hardworking men on his ranch, counting himself and Elias, who would damn well starve to death if forced to eat their own cooking.

Damn, Juana had picked a hell of a time to twist an ankle. And she'd done such a fine job of it, he doubted she'd be in shape in time for roundup.

Every year, the neighboring ranchers took turns hosting the event. Since their spreads were all relatively small yet, it made more sense to work together and complete the job in less time. And, though everyone brought food, it was expected that the host rancher would take care of most of the cooking for the crowd that always showed up.

God knew Juana wouldn't know a broom if it swatted her on the behind, and she'd never find work in a fancy restaurant, but at least her food was plentiful and edible.

He stared at Hannah and didn't know whether she was a gift or a curse. It seemed an odd coincidence that she should turn up in his life right when she was most needed, but then, who was he to say? Stranger things had happened, he guessed. And if she could cook, she was a welcome help at a desperate hour. As long as she was willing to forget all about any talk of marriage and whatnot, he figured they could get along well enough. If she really could cook.

"Jonas?" Hannah asked, her tone letting him know it wasn't the first time she'd called his name.

"Huh?" He gave his head a shake, hoping to dislodge some of the cobwebs mustying up his brain. It not only didn't work, it quickened the throbbing ache behind his eyes. He had a feeling that nothing short of about ten hours' sleep would help him at this point.

"I asked if Juana was sick," she said slowly, carefully, as she would to a dim-witted child. "Is it a cold?"

Who said anything about a cold? Scowling, he said, "No. She's not sick. She turned her ankle last night."

"No." Surprise widened her eyes. "Are you sure?"

"Of course I'm sure," he snapped. "I watched it swell up like a toad myself."

"But that's not right . . ."

Odd way to put it, he thought and pulled his foot out from beneath the cat, who merely moved over to take up its roost again. Mac sighed.

"It's not . . . *serious*, is it?" she asked, taking a step toward him, concern deepening the color of those green eyes of hers. Her gaze shifted to dart about the cluttered room as if expecting to find the injured woman lying beneath a mound of dirty jeans. "Can I see her?" she asked. "Maybe I can help . . . I have to help." Shaking her head worriedly, she muttered, "What could have gone wrong this time? I was so careful."

That last sentence almost slipped past him, since the words had come out in a whispered hush of sound.

"Gone wrong with what?" he asked. "And you were careful about what?"

Her gaze snapped to his and if he wasn't completely mistaken, he thought he saw a flash of guilt in her eyes. But what the hell did she have to be guilty about? She hadn't dug the gopher hole. If anyone should be feeling badly about this, it should be him. But he'd been so busy getting ready for roundup and doing everything else around here, he'd let the ranch yard fall into disrepair, too.

"Nothing, nothing. It's just . . . I don't understand," she muttered as if to herself. "It wasn't supposed to be her ankle . . ."

Oh, he didn't have the time or the patience for this. He was just too blamed tired. "It wasn't *supposed* to be anything. It was a damned accident. She stepped in a gopher hole on her way to the hen house."

"Where is she?" Hannah asked, still looking around the room.

"She's not here," he said flatly, "so you can quit looking. I drove her to her sister's house last night." He scrubbed both hands across his face and sighed wearily. "I'm sure she's fine and probably sleeping like a baby." Dislodging the cat one more time, he turned for the kitchen, waving at Hannah to follow.

God, he needed sleep. And if not that, then at least coffee. Thick, hot, and black. Gallons of it. Grabbing the pot off the back of the stove, he carried it to the sink and set it down again while he worked the pump. A screech of sound split the air as the iron pump handle groaned into life.

A rush of water splashed into the blackened pot and when it was full, he set it aside. Then, bending over, Mac stuck his head beneath the spout and pumped more of the icy well water over the back of his head. A moment later, he came up sputtering, but more awake than before. Frigid droplets of water rolled down beneath the collar of his shirt to snake along his chest and back. He shivered as he turned to face Hannah, just as her cat settled in on his feet again.

"Where's your friend?" she asked. "Elias, is it?"

"Yeah, that's him." He jerked a thumb toward the back door. "He's outside finishing the work on the branding pen."

"He's all right, then?"

"Course he is."

"Just making sure," she said. "I feel just dreadful about Juana," she added in a stunned whisper as she took in the state of the big kitchen.

He frowned at the cat and didn't even bother to look around. This room was in worse shape than the main room because this place saw more action. One or more of the men was continually going in and out of the kitchen for coffee or a quick sandwich. At night, he and Elias sat around the table making plans for the ranch as they ate dinner. And, he was forced to admit, Juana wasn't exactly the tidiest cook in the territory.

The chickens she had been working on the night before still lay across the table, plucked and ready to be sliced up for frying. If Hannah didn't cook them, he realized bleakly, the task would fall to him. God help 'em all.

"No reason for you to feel bad," he said, letting his gaze slide away from the chickens. "Juana's fine. In better shape than me, except for that sore ankle."

She inhaled deeply and released the breath on a sigh. "Thank goodness." Stepping farther into the room, she went on, "I didn't want anything to happen to her . . ."

"Why should you? You don't even know her." He rubbed aching eyes, hoping for relief, and was disappointed.

"True," Hannah said as she walked toward him. Picking up the coffeepot, she carried it to the stove. Then, still talking, she bent down, fed kindling into the firebox, and poked at the hot ash until the slumbering flames caught. "Of course," she said, "I wanted this job, but naturally I wouldn't wish harm on Juana."

"Who said you did?" He leaned back against the pump sink and didn't even try to get rid of the little cat again. What would be the point? Mac watched Hannah as she made her way expertly around the big room. She might talk in circles, but at least she wasn't a stranger to a stove.

"No one," she agreed, giving him a brief smile. "And it was very kind of you."

Kind of him not to accuse a stranger of stuffing Juana's leg down a gopher hole and then twisting it?

She took off her green wool cape and draped it over a chair back before turning to the counter behind her. Opening one crock after another for a peek inside, she finally found the ground-up coffee beans.

"Still," she continued, "since Juana *is* injured, despite my best intentions, you *do* need a cook after all." She gave him another smile as she measured several scoops of coffee into the pot, then set it on the stove to boil.

Satisfied, she half turned, spotted the broom leaning against the wall, and smiled to herself. Standing stock-still, she stretched out her left hand toward it.

Jonas watched, frowning, as she muttered something under her breath and shook her fingers at the broom. His frown deepened as she took a mincing step closer to the thing, clenched and unclenched her fist as if grasping at the air, and whispered fervently, *"Come."*

She stared at the damn broom so long and so hard, even Jonas half expected it to straighten up and answer her summons by gliding across the floor of its own accord. He gave himself a shake as that thought flickered across his mind. Lord, he needed sleep more than he'd thought.

"For heaven's sake!" she said on a disgusted sigh and this time held out both hands, fingers outstretched.

Naturally, the broom didn't move.

He didn't have time for this.

Keeping a wary eye on her, Jonas leaned to one side, snatched up the broom, and thrust it at her. "It works better if you just pick it up."

Clearly disappointed, she ran both of her small hands up and down the thick broomstick. "I don't understand it," she murmured to herself. "It works at home."

Blowing a rush of air from his lungs, Jonas told her,

"It'll work here, too. All you have to do is pick it up and move it over the floor."

She ignored him and continued to let her hands explore the length of that damned broomstick. Up and down, she covered every inch of the thing with a soft, gentle touch that began stirring things up inside him. He sucked in a deep gulp of air and with great effort, tore his gaze from those small white hands and exploring fingers. Distinctly uncomfortable now, he shifted his stance and asked tightly, "What was that all about?"

"Hmmm?" She glanced at him, then lowered her gaze to the broom again. Then she shook her head and said softly, "Nothing. Nothing at all."

Oh, he thought, it was something. He just didn't know what. But it seemed she was through talking about it. As he watched, she took tight hold of the broom and started sweeping the accumulated dust and dirt into a neat pile. It seemed that once she actually held a broom, she knew well enough what to do with one.

But even as she worked, she went on talking, listing the reasons he should hire her and telling him all about her cooking specialties. Her voice soon became a drone of sound ringing in his ears. Words tumbled over each other in her haste to fill any chance at silence, and Mac had the distinct feeling that even on her deathbed, when she couldn't draw a breath of air into straining lungs, Hannah Lowell would find a way to talk.

She was right about one thing, though. He did indeed need help. The question was, did he need it badly enough to let Hannah stay here at the ranch until Juana was up and around again? It could be weeks. By the look of things last night, Juana's sister was in no hurry to send the woman back to a job that paid way too little.

Now Hannah was humming.

An odd tune, one he'd never heard before but almost seemed to recognize. The thread of the melody settled deep within him, plucking strings of memory and then quieting them before they had a chance to raise up fully in his mind.

Tired, he told himself. Too damn tired for any of this.

Mac frowned to himself as he watched her moving around his kitchen. Even in this, the biggest room in the house, he felt as though she were right on top of him while she worked. The rest of the house was so cramped, they'd be living in each other's pockets for however long she was here.

Which brought up a whole new set of problems.

Idly, his gaze slipped to the swell of her bosom and then down to her narrow waist and the curve of her hips. For a tiny thing, she had a form to make a dead man sit up and shout, "Amen." But it wasn't just what she did to his insides that had him worried. There was the other thing, too. A woman who proposed marriage to a stranger and expected brooms to sweep across the floor under their own steam couldn't be fully right in the head.

No doubt about it, Hannah Lowell was trouble. He felt it deep in his bones. Every instinct he had was screaming at him to get her out of his house now. While he still could.

And then he took a deep breath and inhaled the rich, full scent of coffee on the boil. Even the smell of it was reaching into his brain and giving life to a mind so numbed with fatigue it was a wonder he was standing upright.

She finished sweeping, opened the back door, and swished the flour and dust mixture out into the yard. Then she shut the door, turned to look up at him, and smiled again. Really, the way her eyes lit up when she smiled was as devastating a weapon as a fully loaded Colt.

"So?" she asked, meeting his gaze squarely, "do I get the job?"

Mac took another sniff of coffee and rubbed the back of his neck. He had no other choice and he knew it. But at the very least, he could protect himself, and her, from the strangest of her delusions. "On one condition."

A slight frown twisted her mouth a bit and he fought the urge to smooth over that lip with the pad of his thumb. Cocking her head to one side, she asked, "Which is . . . ?"

He leveled his gaze on hers, telling himself to ignore the swirling, rich deep green of her eyes and concentrate on the slightly off-kilter mind behind them. "No more talk of marriage."

She sighed, then gave him a soft, knowing smile.

"I mean it, Hannah." Weary to the bone, he nonetheless stood his ground. He wasn't a man to take advantage of a female light in the head. He wanted her to know right from the start that she wouldn't be changing his mind about marrying her. A job was one thing. If she could cook and make coffee, then it didn't really matter if her mind wasn't all it should be. "Lord knows I can use your help, if you're as good a cook as you say you are."

"I am."

"Be that as it may," he said quickly, before she could get going again, "I don't want to hear any more nonsense about you and me getting married." It was going to be hard enough as it was to be around her in close quarters without having to listen to her talk about marrying all the time. Because to Jonas—hell, he figured, to any man—thinking about marriage led directly to thoughts of the marriage bed. And there was no sense in torturing himself, was there? "Is it a deal?"

Her fingers curled tight around the broom handle, she thought about it for a long moment before agreeing. "All right," she said. "I won't mention the word *marriage.* You have my word."

Hmmm . . . a carefully worded agreement if he'd ever heard one. Mac had the distinct feeling he was being maneuvered; he just wasn't sure how.

Still, he was desperate and Hannah was his only way out of this. He already knew for a fact that no one in town was interested in working for him for the pitifully small wages he could afford to pay. In fact, he never had been able to figure out why Juana had taken the job. Except, of course, for the fact that the woman wasn't much hand at working anyway and probably no one else would have hired her.

The solemn word of a crazy woman wasn't much, he guessed, but it was all he had.

"All right. But there's something else you should know. The pay's not much," he felt obliged to tell her. "Only twenty a month, plus room and board, of course." He looked beyond her to the main room, from which two smaller rooms branched off. "Elias likes sleeping in the bunkhouse, so Juana's been using his bedroom. I guess you can move in there now."

She turned her head as if she could see past the wall to her new bedroom beyond. With her swift movement, her fall of blond hair swung out in a wide arc around her head and shoulders. White, gold, wheat, and honey colors blended in her hair to make it shimmer with light. His breath caught at the sheer beauty of it.

Then she looked back at him and smiled. "It sounds perfect."

Perfect. He wouldn't say that. Looking from that smile, to her hair, to those sparkling green eyes of hers, to the swell of her bosom and the narrow expanse of her waist, a chill of misgiving slithered along his spine.

It was one thing to share a house with a woman old enough to be your mother. It was quite another to know that the female on the other side of the wall from you was a woman who looked like Hannah. The only thing that might save him was knowing that she expected him to marry her. And by God, that wouldn't be happening. Damn it, a part of him already regretted this.

"You won't regret this," she said, startling him by unknowingly echoing his thoughts.

Whether he did or not, the deal was done and he'd just have to live with it. Just as he'd apparently have to

live with the fact that his body was going to be constantly thrown into turmoil just by her presence.

At that disquieting thought, Jonas countered with,
"Maybe I won't, but you might."

"What do you mean?"

Mac glanced down to where the cat was laying across
both of his feet. He nudged it off, then lifted his gaze
to Hannah's worried expression. Here's where he would
find out if she had the guts to stay or not. "In an hour
or two, twelve men are going to be coming in here looking for breakfast. A few hours later, that same bunch
will want noon dinner, and after that, supper."

Her eyes widened as she glanced quickly around the
messy kitchen. Then, as if listening to a stern inner
voice, she inhaled sharply and gave him a brief, determined nod. "I can do that."

Okay, he could give her a point for that. She hadn't
quailed at the thought of feeding a dozen hungry ranch
hands. But the real test was yet to come. He paused
thoughtfully, then went on. "In a couple of weeks,
there'll be about forty hungry people here day in and
day out for a few more weeks, and they'll all be expecting to be fed."

"Forty?" she said on a gasp and reached up to clasp
at the base of her throat as though the word were choking her.

"Roundup time," he said, refusing to be swayed by
the horrified expression on her face. "The first week or
two, we'll be working on my spread. Some of the ranchers' wives will be bringing food, too, but mainly it's up
to us to feed 'em."

"Forty," she repeated, her voice a little hoarse.

"For right now, it's just the twelve of us. Well, thirteen, counting you."

"Thirteen," she muttered quietly.

"If you can't do this," he said, giving them both one
last chance to escape this situation—although, if she
backed out, he didn't know what the hell he would do

about finding another cook—"say so now."

She actually appeared to be thinking it over and Jonas wasn't sure what he'd prefer she decide. If she left, Lord knew, he'd sleep easier at night, though he surely wouldn't be eating well. If she stayed, his stomach might be satisfied, but another part of his body wouldn't be happy.

What in the hell had happened to his legendary luck?

A long moment passed and he counted several heartbeats before she looked him dead in the eye and said quietly, "I can do it." Hearing her own words seemed to put some steel in her spine because she straightened up and lifted her chin. "I'm not leaving until I've finished what I came here to do."

Which brought them right back where they'd started, he figured. Tightly, he reminded her, "No more talk about—"

"I promised I wouldn't say the word *marriage,*" she said firmly. "Not until you have."

He snorted a tired laugh. "Then you'll have a long wait, lady."

"I'm patient, as well as stubborn."

"So am I," he warned her.

She smiled at him and it felt as though someone had slugged him in the stomach. All of his air left him in a rush. Fighting down the feeling, he said, "Keep a pot of coffee going on the stove all day, every day. The men will come in and help themselves when they want some."

She nodded and set the broom down to lean against the wall. At least, he told himself wryly, she hadn't expected it to put itself away. He could almost see the wheels turning in her befuddled brain as she tried to decide where to begin her new job.

Dislodging the cat again, he walked across the room, poured a cup of coffee, and headed for the door. He had to take a couple of pretty fancy steps to avoid the blasted cat, but he managed. Before he went outside, though, he couldn't resist adding, "See you at breakfast."

Then he stepped into the yard, closed the door, and tried to put Hannah out of his mind.

Hannah had never been sorrier that her witchcraft abilities were so dreadful. She'd only meant to give Juana a cold, or some other small malady that she would recover from fairly quickly. She winced, thinking about the poor woman wracked with pain.

On the other hand, she thought as she did a slow turn, inspecting the disaster of a kitchen, perhaps Juana had gotten the better end of this deal. After all, that woman was lying in bed being waited on by a doting sister. While Hannah, on the other hand . . . She groaned quietly and shook her head.

"It's a wonder, Hepzibah," she said on a sigh, "how men manage to run the world when they can't seem to pick up after themselves."

Briefly, she thought about using her powers to help her with the day's daunting tasks. But in the next instant, she recalled Eudora's most frequently used admonition: Witchcraft is not to be used lightly. The older woman herself didn't rely on her abilities in her everyday work, and those abilities were far superior to Hannah's.

Besides, she thought as she tossed a quick glare at the broom, it was obvious that being so close to a powerful warlock hadn't improved Hannah's witchcraft in the least.

Then, because she really didn't have time enough to stand around and complain about the very situation she'd worked to put herself in, she got busy.

Chapter four

Two hours later, she was seriously rethinking her plan.

If breakfast was an example of what life with the Mackenzie would be like, she didn't know if she was strong enough to survive it without killing him.

As soon as that thought presented itself, she wondered absently how one would go about doing away with a warlock. Her musings ended as she became caught up in the unbelievable scene unfolding in front of her.

Hannah stood openmouthed at one end of the long table. She watched as the ranch hands rushed into the kitchen like a swarm of locusts. No one wiped their boots. Her gaze dropped to the veritable parade of large black clumps of dirt and who knew what else tracking across her freshly swept floor. Outraged, she looked at the men again, but they paid as much attention to her as they would have a cigar-store Indian. None of them removed their hats or lowered their voices as they straddled the ladder-backed chairs surrounding the table heaped high with steaming-hot food. Her mouth opened and closed again before she could utter a host of words that would have horrified Eudora. Tight-lipped, she watched a dozen pairs of hands reaching for the breakfast she'd spent the last hour preparing. With disgust, she noted the grime encrusted on their palms and fingers.

Hands at her hips, Hannah studied the features of the people who made up her new world. Whisker-shadowed faces blurred before her as her temper boiled like a thick, hot stew of fury. But no one noticed her toe tapping against the floor. No one heard her when she muttered curses she couldn't bring herself to shout, and she doubted anyone would have cared if they had.

Two of the men were easily as old as Elias. Like that man, they were certainly old enough to know better. Most were somewhere in their thirties, she guessed, and at least one of them—needless to say, the most clean-shaven of the bunch—didn't look old enough to grow a beard.

And not a one of them—including the Mackenzie—gave her so much as a glance.

Had no one west of Massachusetts heard of washing up before eating? Were simple table manners and common courtesy not to be expected on this side of the Rocky Mountains?

Hannah tried to remind herself why she was there. What she'd come for. How badly she needed the Mackenzie's help. But none of that went toward soothing the anger rushing through her like a river about to overflow its banks.

Indignation roared through her veins. Her plan to ease into the Mackenzie's life and make herself indispensable seemed ludicrous at the moment. Rather than appreciating her efforts on his and his men's behalf, it was as if she didn't even exist.

She spared an angry glance at the man she'd come halfway across the country to find and marry. And though he looked handsome in a rough-hewn, dirty, sweat-stained way, his behavior was no better than the men who worked for him. Snatching at a slice of fresh bread, he yanked a jar of preserves from the hand of the man next to him and then grabbed up four strips of bacon in a none-too-clean fist.

This was the man she'd come so far to find? *This* was the great and powerful Mackenzie?

Oh, if Aunt Eudora could only see him now.

Her toe beat an angry tattoo against the floor, sounding, at least to her, like an overwound clock ticking away accelerated minutes. Her heartbeat quickened to pulse in time and she felt a pounding ache begin to throb in the center of her forehead.

Gritting her teeth, she watched as one man poured coffee and sloshed the hot liquid across the platter of ham. She inhaled sharply. Another man laughed, lifted the platter, and, keeping one dirty palm on the meat, tipped the liquid out onto the floor.

"Great thundering heavens!" she muttered.

No one noticed.

Words failed her completely. There were no curses strong enough to describe her feelings. She'd wanted to fit in. Wanted to make herself such an integral part of the Mackenzie's life that he wouldn't be able to get along without her.

Well, she would never belong in this world. And what was more, she didn't want to. Thoughts, ideas, plans chased each other across her mind. She couldn't go home, she knew that. She still needed the Mackenzie's help, so she would still have to marry him.

But . . . she wouldn't spend the rest of her life viewing scenes like this. She stared at them all as they shoveled food into their gaping mouths. Uttered grunts of appreciation made them sound, as well as look, like a pack of hogs.

She'd worked hard on very short notice to see that they all had their morning meal. The scrambled eggs were fluffy, the flapjacks were lighter than air, the bread, though not fresh, had been warmed in the oven, and there was enough coffee to serve an army.

Yet they were all so busy shoving it into their mouths, she was willing to bet they hadn't even tasted it.

She could have served them mud pies and dirty water and as long as there was plenty of it, she told herself, they wouldn't have cared.

Well, Hannah told herself firmly, no more.

One of the men stood up and, completely oblivious to her presence, reached across her for the jar of molasses. The tight leash on her temper snapped. Gritting her teeth, Hannah snatched up a serving spoon and used it to give his arm a hard smack.

"Hey!" The arm's owner shouted, and he gave her a look that said she was crazy for hitting him and if she wasn't a woman, he'd hit her right back.

She stood her ground and met the man's glare with a steely one of her own, lifting her spoon higher, just for good measure.

"What'd you do that for?" the cowboy demanded, cradling his arm as though she'd broken it.

"If you want the molasses," she snapped, "ask someone to kindly pass it to you!"

"Why in tarnation would I do that when I can reach it?" His bellow was clearly meant to intimidate her.

He was disappointed.

"Because it's polite!" she shouted, finally releasing the pent-up anger knotted in her chest.

Silence fell over the room like a heavy blanket smothering flames. She felt the stares of a dozen pairs of eyes and she met them all, each in turn. Riding the crest of her glorious fury, she went on. "I've never seen such a display in all my life! You ought to charge people admission just to watch you eat!"

Instead of the shamefaced expressions she'd hoped to see, they actually had the nerve to look mightily offended. Even a bit angry.

Exasperation flushed her face with color.

One of the older men finally spoke up. "Now, missy," he said firmly, "you got no call to be shoutin' at us like that, and hittin' on Hank when he can't rightly hit you back don't seem fair at all."

Amazing, she thought.

" 'At's right," Hank said, still clutching his arm as if to prove to his friends just how badly he'd been damaged. "A man's got a right to eat I reckon, without no cook poundin' on him."

Hannah blinked at him.

"Sure enough," someone else piped up. "Don't ever recall no cook bein' so durn snippy."

She couldn't believe it. Rather than being ashamed of their behavior, they were trying to correct *hers*.

Hannah shook the spoon at her audience. "A *man* wouldn't be smacked," she told them shortly. "But wild animals invading a kitchen are lucky if they don't get shot on sight."

"Shot?" the young one sputtered nervously.

"See here, missy," Elias said in a low growl of disapproval, "it's a mite early in the day for talk of shootin', don't you think?"

A dark muttering of agreement rose up from the seated men. Her gaze slid over every one of them. Blue eyes, brown, black, they all looked at her in hostile astonishment. When at last she looked to Jonas, she wasn't even surprised to see a flash of anger in his icy blue eyes.

"What's this about?" he asked, tossing his knife onto his plate with a clatter that rang out overloud in the suddenly still room.

One or two of the men gave her superior smiles that let her know they thought Jonas was going to tell her a thing or two. And that they were going to enjoy watching her taken down a peg.

But Hannah was in no mood. She'd traveled days to reach this . . . *outpost*. She'd changed her life, left her family. Risked everything, was willing to marry a man she'd never met, and *this* was her reward?

Anger still churning in the pit of her stomach, Hannah had a few things to say herself. Letting her temper fly, she waved her serving spoon in the air like a knight of old would wield his sword. "It's about you," she said, sparing the rest of the men a quick glance before locking her gaze with the Mackenzie's. "All of you."

"Well, heckfire, what'd we do?" someone at the end of the table muttered before Jonas could speak.

"I've already told you what you did, but by heaven, I'll tell again," she said hotly, her gaze raking each of them in turn. She shook her spoon at them like a wagging finger. "The lot of you ran in here without so much as a 'good morning.' None of you bothered to wipe your boots or use the wash water and soap I left on the porch."

The youngest cowboy ducked his head and hunched his shoulders slightly. Apparently he was young enough to at least *recall* someone, someone, teaching him manners. A couple of the other men muttered comments she couldn't quite catch, but Hannah was in fine fettle now, so she simply raised her voice to drown them out. "Then you fell on the food like a pack of starving dogs fighting over the last bone in the house."

Someone grumbled under his breath, but she didn't care. She wasn't finished. Not by a long shot. Glaring at Hank, still cradling his arm close to his chest, she demanded, "Were you all brought up in caves? Did no one ever teach you simple table manners?"

"All right, Hannah," Jonas said, pushing back and away from the table. His chair legs screeched against the wood floor and she whipped her head around to stare at him. "I think you've said enough."

"I don't," she countered. "I have never seen anything like it," she continued, raking the men with an angry stare again. "Grown men, acting like . . . like . . ." She shook her head, unable to come up with a likely description.

She hadn't noticed Jonas moving around the table. When he took her elbow firmly in his grasp, she jumped, startled. The spoon dropped from her hand to clatter onto the table. Lifting her gaze to his, she was met by an icy blue wall that simmered with banked fires of anger that burned as hot as her own.

"Let's step outside," he said quietly, "to talk."

There was nothing gentle in his grip on her, but at the same time, she knew he was leashing his strength. Though his grasp was firm, he wasn't hurting her. Instead, she felt an odd sensation of heat threading up the length of her arm.

She looked up at him, wondering if he'd felt it, too. For a moment she thought she saw a flicker of surprise flash across his eyes, but it was gone too quickly to be sure.

"You show her the way of it, boss," someone said, and a shutter dropped over the Mackenzie's eyes.

"Come on, Hannah," he muttered, already steering her toward the door.

Warmth still trickling through her body, Hannah fought against the pleasant feeling and gathered up the remaining threads of her righteous indignation.

This time when she looked him in the eye, she matched him angry stare for angry stare. If they were to have a lasting marriage, he'd better learn right away that she wouldn't be manipulated by the strength of his powers. Either his witchcraft abilities or the affect he seemed to have on her pulse rate.

"Fine," she agreed. "There are a few more things I'd like to say."

Someone actually chuckled.

The Mackenzie shot the table a hard look that silenced any further outbursts.

"You fellas go on with your breakfast, then get back to work," he said over his shoulder as he propelled Hannah toward the door.

Her feet flew across the floor, hardly touching the wooden planks. Once outside, he continued walking quickly and her short legs were no match for his long strides.

"Watch out for gopher holes," he muttered as he practically dragged her across the yard.

Dutifully, her gaze raked the ground, but it was moving so quickly, she had a feeling she'd step in a hole before she could see and avoid it.

He stopped beneath an old cottonwood tree. Dappled shade dusted the hard ground, with splotches of sunlight. The breeze rattled the leaves overhead, sounding like harsh whispers. Out of earshot of the house, he released her and took a step back as though he needed distance between them.

"This isn't going to work out after all," he said flatly.

"What isn't?" She rubbed her elbow, but couldn't wipe away the still-lingering traces of warmth.

"You. Being here." He shook his head and went on through clenched teeth, "Never should have tried it. I'll have Elias take you into town. Put you on the stage that'll take you to the train station."

Whatever she'd been expecting, it hadn't been this. Straightening up to her full, less-than-imposing height, she said, "I'm not leaving."

"If I fire you, you're leaving," he said, and somewhere in the distance, the familiar roar of building thunder sounded out.

Another storm? Hannah tore her gaze from his, glanced up, and watched as dark clouds skittered across the sky, obliterating the sun. Shadows fell all around them and the temperature dropped suddenly, bringing a chill to her veins.

She ignored it and faced him.

Hands at his hips, feet braced wide apart, he looked like a man ready for a fight. Well, then, she would give him one. She wasn't leaving. Not until she knew he would help her by defeating Blake Wolcott.

"You can't fire me after one meal."

"I can do whatever I damn well please," he reminded her. "This is my place."

From the corner of her eye, she caught the silvery

flash of lightning pulse against the clouds, and a few moments later, the crash of thunder rolled down the mountainside.

"And who will you get to cook for you and the rest of them?" she asked. She couldn't imagine any woman willingly cooking for that bunch of ill-mannered goats. By heaven, if she didn't *have* to be there, she'd have already left. Yet here she was. It didn't matter what he answered, she assured herself, because she had no intention of leaving.

"Someone who won't yell and make a big to-do first thing in the morning would be my first choice."

She frowned at him. All of this because she'd lost her temper? For pity's sake. Did he prefer the kind of woman who never raised her voice? If so, this getting-to-know-each-other period was going to be more difficult than she'd imagined.

"Make sure your new cook is blind, then," she said with a lift of her eyebrows. "Because anyone who has to watch a performance like *that* every morning is going to make a big 'to-do.'"

He gave her a tight, unamused smile as another flash of lightning sparkled overhead. A clap of thunder followed. Louder and closer this time, it boomed into the tense silence.

Taking the storm as a sign, Hannah used it shamelessly. "Besides," she pointed out with another glance at the sky, "you can't expect me to leave in the middle of a storm."

He shot a look at the heavens, and if God was watching, even He probably wanted to hide from the Mackenzie's expression. Grumbling darkly, Jonas tugged his hat brim down low on his forehead, then narrowed his gaze on her. Waving one hand at the house, he said, "Why don't you just admit it? You don't belong here. You've only been here a couple of hours and already you've caused more uproar than we've seen in years."

Her big green eyes widened in astonishment and

she clapped one hand to the center of her chest. "*I've* caused . . . ?"

"You are the one who hit Hank with a spoon, aren't you?"

"I didn't hurt him." she defended herself lamely.

Jonas sighed and threw both hands wide. Was she deliberately missing the point? "You couldn't hurt Hank if you backed a wagon over him." Feeling the need to move, to do *something,* he started pacing, kicking at the dirt beneath his feet. "I'm talking about how you carried on in there."

"For heaven's sake, Mackenzie . . ."

He stopped in front of her and silently warned himself not to look too deeply into those green eyes. Or how the top of her head reached only as high as his chin. Or how when she was angry, color rushed into her cheeks, giving her skin a glow that made him want to touch it.

Damn it.

He didn't want her here. Didn't need the distraction she dragged along with her like a shadow. The sky rumbled overhead. From the corner of his eye, he spotted lightning flash against the ridge. His morning was quickly turning to crap. And a blond-haired fireball with soft green eyes and a curvy body wasn't helping anything.

Pretty or not, she had to find out right now just who was the boss around here.

"What the hell was that all about, anyway?" he demanded, his voice as tight as his body.

She leaned in close and he caught a whiff of what smelled like lemons.

"How can you even ask me that?"

He pulled his head back to avoid breathing in her scent again. "It's not up to you to teach those men—or *me*—" he added, "manners."

"Someone should—" she started, but didn't finish because he cut her off abruptly.

"They work hard—we all do." Steeling himself, he

met her gaze and still felt a slap of something hard and searing shake him to his boots. Damn it, he wasn't a kid anymore, stirred into a froth over a pretty face and a sweet smell. Gritting his teeth, he went on determinedly. "We expect our meals to be plentiful and hot. We *don't* expect to get our hands smacked for not saying *please* and *thank you.*"

She was simmering. He didn't need to see the flash of indignation in her eyes. He sensed it pulsing around her body like a heartbeat. Anger fairly rippled off of her in waves. He wouldn't have been surprised to see sparks shooting from the ends of her hair.

Well, she could be as mad as she wanted to be. It didn't matter a damn what she thought of him. Hell, it would probably be easier on them both if she couldn't stand the sight of him. Then at least she'd give up on that marrying nonsense for good and all. And maybe if she was shooting daggers at him all the time, his thoughts would quit straying to notions he had no business considering.

"I worked hard, too," she told him shortly.

Hell, he knew that. Breakfast was better than anything he'd had in longer than he cared to think about. Still, *he* was boss around here and she'd better learn that now.

Bracing his feet wide apart, he folded his arms across his chest and looked down at her. "A cook *cooks,*" he said. "Nothing else."

"That explains what happened to your house," she muttered.

His teeth ground together until he thought his jaw might break. And despite the small part of him that enjoyed her not backing down, he stood his ground. "So," he said, squeezing the words past thinned lips, "do we understand each other?"

Her mouth worked furiously as she drew several deep breaths. She clasped her hands together at her waist and squeezed until her knuckles whitened and paled against her dark green skirt.

And still, he waited.

"I think so," she said at last, in no more than a strangled whisper. She dipped her head and looked up at him from beneath impossibly long, dark eyelashes. "You want plentiful, hot meals with no worrying about table manners."

That had cost her. He could see it. And one part of him admired the hell out of her for it. Anybody who could rein in a temper like hers had strength. She had the look of a woman who didn't give in lightly, or often. As that thought occurred to him, he also thought that perhaps he ought to be worried by her surrender. But in the next instant, Jonas decided there was no point in looking for trouble when it came looking for him often enough.

Nodding, he said, "That's right. Think you can do that?"

"Oh," she told him, still giving him that shaded stare, "I think I'll be able to manage."

"All right, then," he said with another nod. Frustration drained from him as he gave the sky another searching look. He smiled faintly. The once-threatening clouds had thinned into misty ribbons of darkness stretching haphazardly across the sun. Lowering his gaze to hers, he said. "Guess the storm's passed us by this time."

"Perhaps," she said, starting for the house again, "but the clouds are still there, so it's too early to be sure."

He watched her go and as his gaze drifted to the sway of her hips, he wondered idly if they'd been talking about the same storm.

Chapter five

Once astride his horse, Jonas put everything but work out of his mind. A cold mountain wind shot past him and he hunched deeper into the folds of his jacket. Tugging his hat brim down low on his forehead, he squinted into the afternoon light. His sharp eye inspected each of the beeves he passed, judging their weights, mentally adding the tally of what he could expect come sale time. Thoughts of Hannah Lowell were put aside as he lost himself in plans for the future.

In his mind's eye, he could already see the ranch as it would be in just a few more years—barring, of course, floods, droughts. Indians, and the price of beef falling.

He half turned in the saddle to look back at the ranch house. His imagination conjured up a tree-lined graveled drive leading to the three-story house with its wide front porch. He could even see himself, lounging in a chair in the shade, talking to—He scowled as the image of Hannah joined his dream self on that imaginary porch.

Damn it. Now she was invading not only his kitchen, but his mind, too.

"She's a pistol, all right," Elias said as his horse meandered toward Jonas's.

Turning his head, he looked at the older man. "How'd you know I was thinking about her?"

Elias snorted a laugh. "Hell, that look on your face meant either thoughts of Hannah or you're fixin' to kill somebody. Since I ain't heard you're at war with anyone in particular, I figured it had to be Hannah."

"She's a thorn in my side," Jonas admitted in a grumble. "I never should have hired her."

"Maybe not," Elias said, drawing his mount to a stop and looping the reins through his fingers. "But she sure can cook. Beats hell outa the slop Juana sets out."

"Yeah." One small consolation. He'd even heard the men raving about the breakfast they'd been served by that hot-tempered woman. It seemed they were willing to put up with her shouts if she kept the grub coming.

"Why's she here, you reckon?" Elias asked, his gaze sliding to the ranch house some few hundred yards off. "A woman looks like her is usually married by now. Why's she want to come out to the middle of nowhere and be a ranch house cook?"

Married.

That word sure was getting a lot of use here lately.

Jonas folded his hands on the saddle pommel and rubbed the worn leather reins between his fingers. No reason not to tell him, he thought. Hell, even though she'd agreed to let the whole subject of marriage drop, he had a feeling she'd start talking about it sooner or later. Might as well let Elias in on it now, so he'd be prepared. Besides, the old coot might even get a laugh out of it.

"She says she's here to marry me," Jonas told him and waited for a smile that didn't come.

Instead, the older man simply stared at him, his face expressionless, his eyes wary. "To marry you."

"Yeah."

"She's from Massachusetts," Elias muttered, his gaze now locked on the ranch house, "and she's come to marry you."

The man's voice, deep and slow, blended in and was swallowed by the muffled roar of hundreds of hooves stamping into the dirt. He rubbed one gnarled hand across whiskery cheeks and swallowed heavily.

Jonas frowned at the man and shifted uncomfortably in the saddle. He hadn't expected the old badger to go spooky on him. "Jesus, old man," he said on a short bark of laughter. "I only told you 'cause I figured you'd think it funny."

"Did you?" Elias asked suddenly, cocking his head to one side. "Find it funny, I mean."

"Funny? No." Jonas inhaled sharply. "Damn strange. Crazy, even. But funny?" He shook his head. Memories, old and cobweb-covered, rose up in his mind like a dust cloud on a hot, still day. Not only did he carry snatches of images of parents he couldn't really remember—but other, more recent memories were always there in the shadows, waiting for their chance to ambush him.

The problem, he told himself, is that he was a man with too much past and not enough future.

Muttering under his breath, he narrowed his gaze, focusing on his herd. The here and now. Hoping to keep his mind too busy to race into the past.

But once prodded into life, those dusty images wouldn't be silenced so easily. As if conjured by his reluctance, the first glimpses of blurred faces flickered across his brain. A man, black-haired, blue-eyed. A woman, with a sweet smile and a dimple he knew he carried in his own cheek. His parents, he guessed, though he couldn't be sure.

He rubbed his eyes with his fingertips, trying to stem the tide flooding past hastily constructed mental barriers. But they kept coming. Images, pictures. A town he didn't know. Lightning. Someone laughing. A scream.

A muffled groan lodged in his throat. Always the same. Bits and pieces. Snatches of a past long gone. Gritting his teeth, Jonas turned his back on the child he'd been and braced himself for the other, more recent images that, even after ten long years, still had the power to tighten his chest and close his throat.

Wide brown eyes, soft laughter, whispers in the night—then one day, a silent house. And red. So much red.

"Mac? Mac, boy."

Elias's voice dragged him from the drowning pool of mind shadows and back to the sunlit range. Opening his eyes, Jonas took a long look around him.

The familiar landscape soothed him. Cattle. Cowboys in the distance. The mountains, caps covered in snow that glistened like quartz crystal in the midday sun. He pulled in a deep breath, letting the cold, crisp air clear his mind and settle his spirit.

This was what mattered, he told himself firmly. The past couldn't be changed. The future couldn't be known. It was this moment, this time he had to concentrate on. Work at. All the rest was no more substantial than the morning mist that clung by wispy fingers to the mountainside and was gone again by noon.

"You all right, boy?"

He slanted a look at the man beside him. Concern etched itself into Elias's lined, weathered face, reminding Jonas that the older man knew what memories drove him, haunted him. And he wondered if Elias, too, was visited by ghosts.

They'd never spoken of it—as if silently agreeing that talking about the past would only serve to keep it alive, fresh in their minds. But Jonas had discovered that silence didn't protect him from the remembering. The pain of knowing he'd failed the one person who'd needed him the most.

"Course I'm all right," he muttered thickly, turning his head away from the too-knowing gray eyes watching him. "Why wouldn't I be? The herd looks good. Roundup's just a few weeks away, and there's only a few days until Saturday."

Elias grumbled something under his breath.

"What was that?" he asked, though he knew damn

well what the man had said. Same thing he said every damn week.

The older man's jaw worked like he was trying to spit out something that tasted foul as sin. "I said," he repeated, "you don't need to be goin' into town every Saturday night."

Yes, just what he'd thought. A flash of irritation shot through him and was gone again. Pointless to get mad over such an old argument. "That's my business, isn't it?"

"With roundup coming, I figured you'd have better things to do."

Jonas tightened his grip on the reins. The rawhide strips bit into his fingers. "You figured wrong."

"I can see that."

Sighing, Jonas turned on his oldest friend. The man who'd been a father to him. "Don't start on me."

"Start?" Elias snorted. "I been saying this for near ten years."

"Then you ought to be about ready to quit."

"Not hardly."

"Damn it," Jonas said, straining to keep his voice even. "I don't need a gray-bearded mama clucking over me."

"No," Elias grumbled. "What you need is a mule kick to the head."

Despite his frustration, Jonas chuckled shortly. "Well, until you find the mule to do the job . . . leave me be."

The dinner bell rang out loudly, pealing across the range. Heads turned toward the house and, as one, the cowboys started their horses in. After a long morning's work, they were eager for food and the chance to sit on something that wasn't moving.

Jonas and Elias, the tension still thick between them, also headed for the house.

"You reckon," Elias asked, "that new girl's settled down some since this morning?"

Jonas smiled, pleased his old friend had decided to

let go of their long-standing quarrel—at least for the moment. "Oh," he said, remembering vividly the talk he and Hannah had had under the tree that morning. "There won't be any more trouble."

"I don't know, seems a hardheaded female to me. One to keep an eye on." His scowl deepened.

"She might be hardheaded," Jonas agreed, giving his horse a nudge to quicken its pace. "But she knows who the boss is here."

That notion dissolved a few minutes later as he stepped into the kitchen. Rather than sitting at the table eating their dinner, the men were still standing in a group just inside the door.

"What's going on?" he asked and got no answer.

With Elias right behind him, Jonas pushed his way through the small crowd, wondering what in hell could be keeping his cowhands from eating. He stopped dead when he got a clear look at the table.

"Your dinner's ready, *gentlemen.*" Hannah announced in a voice that let him know she was well pleased with herself.

Jonas shot her a look that had been known to quell bar fights.

She smiled at him.

"What are you up to now?" he asked, his voice low and dangerous enough to make one or two of his men back up instinctively.

Hannah merely smoothed the folds of her dark green skirt, untied her apron from around her waist, and then turned to hang it on a nearby peg. When she was good and ready, she looked at him, meeting his steely glare with a look of wide-eyed innocence. "Why, I don't know what you mean."

He should have known she wouldn't cowtow to orders. Hadn't he thought it from the first moment he'd laid eyes on her? Hadn't he told himself she was trouble, pure and simple?

His gaze raked over her, from her shining, amused eyes to the lock of honey-blond hair that fell from the knot on top of her head to lay against her cheek. She looked like an angel and apparently had the temperament of a demon.

Who the hell else would have thought of a way to circumvent his orders without *actually* breaking her word? And though a part of him almost admired her inventiveness, he damn sure wasn't going to let her know it.

He tipped his hat back on his head, planted both hands on his hips, and fought to restrain a surge of frustrated fury that was clamoring at his throat. "I mean *this,*" he nearly shouted, waving one hand at the laden table.

She shrugged. "You said you wanted your meals to be plentiful and hot."

"Yeah . . ."

"With no worrying about table manners."

He sucked in a gulp of air.

Someone behind him chuckled briefly.

He didn't see anything to laugh about.

"I believe I've done just what you wanted," Hannah told him, and the amusement in her eyes shifted to something more like satisfaction. "But, if you *gentlemen* will excuse me, I believe I'll clean the main room while you eat. I don't think I can stand watching a second performance."

And then she was gone, leaving them to their meal. Jonas's gaze drifted to the kitchen table. Just as she'd promised, there looked to be plenty of food. It was even his favorite: fried chicken, mashed potatoes, and hot biscuits.

Too bad he'd lost his appetite.

Lengthwise along the center of the table, piled high directly onto the scrubbed pine tabletop, she'd laid out a wall of mashed potatoes. The thick, buttery mass towered into peaks that resembled the Rockies. Crispy-

looking pieces of fried chicken jutted up out of the
potatoes like dozens of scrub trees along a mountain
range. And scattered across the table's surface were
golden brown biscuits.

There wasn't a plate or a cup or a knife and fork
anywhere in sight.

Damned if she hadn't gotten the best of him after all.

She'd called them a bunch of wild hogs, and blast it
if she hadn't set up their food like she was laying it in
a trough.

Slowly, grumbling, the men moved past him and took
their seats. After looking at each other dubiously for a
minute or two, they picked up the biscuits and used them
as shovels to dig out mouthfuls of potatoes.

"Y'know," one of them mentioned, "a plate would be
a handy thing right about now."

"Maybe, but I ain't gonna ask her for one."

"Durn females," someone else said.

"She might be sassy, but she sure can cook."

"Reckon we'd best start mindin' our manners after
all," still another voice added. " 'Cause I sure as hell
don't want to see how she'd serve up soup."

They were eating. It would take a lot more than this
to keep hungry men from food. But change was already
starting, Jonas thought. She'd made her point. From now
on, these cowhands would be a bit more cautious about
their behavior.

Jonas hadn't moved. Frowning to himself, he had to
admit that Hannah Lowell wasn't what he'd first thought
of her. She wasn't crazy—she was too darned clever to
be loco—and she sure wasn't the quiet sort. Already
she'd slipped into his life, making a mark, refusing to
be ignored. And this was just the first day.

"You gonna eat?" Elias asked from beside him.

Jonas swallowed. "No." Watching dirty hands paw at
creamy potatoes was enough to kill what was left of his
appetite. Maybe there was something to what she said
about table manners after all.

"Like I said," Elias muttered, "that's a hardheaded woman there. One to watch careful."

"Yeah."

He flicked a glance at the open doorway where he'd last seen Hannah. He didn't think he'd have the slightest problem watching her. And that worried him quite a bit.

Creekford

"Oh, my." Eudora groaned quietly and shook her head as the picture of the Mackenzie's kitchen slowly faded into oblivion. Trailing threads of mist swirled across the polished surface of the crystal, dimming the images hidden within.

Eudora's eyebrows arched high on her forehead as she reached for the dark blue silk scarf laying just to hand. Draping the fragile fabric across the glass, she then leaned back in her chair. She shifted her gaze to the window and the maple tree beyond, letting her vision swim blurrily until the broad tree with its umbrella of leaves was nothing more than a wash of green.

"Patience, Hannah," she murmured, concentrating despite the rueful smile curving her lips. "You must have patience with him. He is your destiny, child . . . as you are his. And our only hope."

A dark shadow fell across her mind and she shivered, knowing that Hannah and the Mackenzie faced obstacles far greater than their own stubborn natures.

Privately. Hannah decided that the missing Juana was a slattern. For heaven's sake, what did the woman do with her days? The windows hadn't been scrubbed in weeks, the floors were grimy, and there was enough dust and dirt on the tables in the main room to grow a good-sized crop of potatoes. Apparently, since the woman was being paid to cook, that was *all* she did.

Broom in one hand, dust rags in the other, Hannah grimly surveyed the main room before eyeing the door leading to the short hall and two bedrooms. She'd already peeked at them both and knew she had plenty of work to do there, as well. But first, the main room.

Hepzibah stepped into the room, mewed daintily, and then climbed up the back of the horsehair sofa to nest on its top.

Glancing at her cat, Hannah said, "He needs me more than I'd thought, Hepzibah. And once his house is in fine shape, no doubt he'll be willing to admit it. Soon enough, he won't be able to imagine life here without me."

"Is that so?" a deep voice asked from behind her.

She whirled around, startled, and dropped the broom.

Elias walked out of the kitchen, picked up the broom, and handed it to her.

"You scared me," she admitted with a chuckle as her hands folded around the broom handle. It was the first time he'd really spoken to her since taking her into town the day before. And even then, he'd hardly said a word.

"Figured as much." He shot a quick look around the room before letting his gaze come back to meet hers. Those gray eyes of his seemed to look deep inside her, as if he were searching for answers to questions he hadn't asked yet. "You're a bear for work," he said. "I'll give ya that."

"Well," she said on a sigh, "there's plenty to keep a woman busy around here."

"Mac says you came here to marry him."

Hannah blinked at the abrupt shift in the conversation. But judging by the look on his face, this was what he'd come to talk to her about in the first place. "He told you?"

"He did." And Elias didn't look too happy about it, either. His arms folded atop a slightly bulging belly, he planted his feet wide apart and looked down on her. His gray eyes narrowed as he studied her warily. Well, she supposed he was entitled. Most people looked at strangers with a bit of suspicion. And she guessed she seemed more strange than most.

When she didn't say anything, Elias spoke up again. "What he didn't tell me is why."

"Why what?" She knew what he meant, but she really didn't want to explain all of this to Elias before she'd had a chance to talk to Jonas about it. Fair was fair, after all, and she thought the Mackenzie had the right to be the first to hear about their shared destiny.

"Why him?" Elias asked, taking a step closer and staring deeply into her eyes. "Why come all the way from Massachusetts just to marry Mac?"

He wasn't a witch, Hannah thought, but the older man had his own kind of power. The kind of strength that comes from years of living. Of learning to really see people for who and what they were. And she had the feeling that Elias, whether he would admit it or not, knew a great deal about her.

She lifted her chin slightly and returned his stare evenly. "That's between me and the Mackenzie," she said, not unkindly.

He shook his head slowly. "That's where you're wrong. I raised that boy, missy," he said, his voice no higher than a whisper. "I saw him through both hardships and good times. He don't even remember another family but me. From the time he was five years old, it's been the two of us. I figure that gives me some rights."

"He doesn't remember?" she repeated, focusing on one particular fact. Dipping her head to avoid those knowing gray eyes briefly, she let her mind race with this new information. If he didn't remember the Guild or his family or his duties, this was going to be even more difficult than she'd first thought.

Elias inhaled sharply and exhaled in a rush. "He don't say how much he recalls, but he was only a kid when his folks died, so I figure it ain't much."

Which would explain why he hadn't reacted as she'd expected when she'd told him who she was and why she

was here. Oh, good heavens, no wonder he'd looked at
her as though she should be locked away.

"So," Elias said, his voice gruffer now, more impatient, "you gonna tell me what you're up to?"

Hannah could understand his concern. He clearly
cared for the Mackenzie as a father would. But at the
same time, she couldn't let sympathy for his situation
dissuade her from what she knew she had to do. "No,"
she said. "Not until I talk to Jonas first."

"I thought you might say that," he muttered, already
turning for the door. "Told Mac you looked to be a hardheaded woman."

"I can tell you I mean him no harm," she offered,
even knowing it wouldn't be enough to satisfy the man.

He stopped in the doorway and glanced back at her.
"And I can tell you, missy, I won't stand for anyone
causing Mac grief. Not if I can help it."

Then he was gone, leaving Hannah to wonder if she
had enough time to win over not just the Mackenzie, but
the man who stood between them, as well.

"You did it."

Hannah, her hands buried in hot dishwater, jumped
at the sound of Jonas's voice and splashed the soapy
water down the front of her skirt. As it soaked into the
fabric, she turned to face him.

Standing in the open doorway leading to the main
room, he had one shoulder propped against the door-
jamb, his booted feet crossed at the ankles and his hands
stuffed into his pockets. Though his posture looked lazy.
Hannah sensed the coiled tension within him.

He gave her a brief nod and a half smile that sent
tendrils of warmth snaking along her spine to pool in
her suddenly wobbly knees. She took a deep breath,
locked her knees to keep from dissolving into a puddle,
and asked, "Did what?"

He pushed away from the doorframe, pulled his
hands from his pockets, and took two long strides to stop

beside her. "You managed to tame eleven pretty salty men." He glanced at her sodden skirt and reached for a towel, holding it out to her. "Never thought I'd see that bunch washing up and combing their hair before supper."

Abandoning the dishes for the moment, she took the towel and rubbed at the wetness covering her front. But her wool skirt had already soaked up the water like a garden in summer, so she lifted her gaze to his. A strange rippling sensation surged through her stomach and she wondered idly if he would still have that affect on her fifty years from now.

"Only eleven?" she asked. "You're not counting yourself?"

He shook his head and his too-long black hair fell across his forehead. He brushed it back impatiently before she could give in to the urge to do it herself. "I don't tame, Hannah, so I'd advise you not to try."

There was something more behind his words. Something he wasn't saying.

"I'm not here to tame anyone," she said and wondered what he was thinking. Feeling. Now that she knew he didn't remember his heritage, she realized that his questions about her must be legion. But did he also have questions about himself? Did he even want to know his background? Would he thank her for being the one to tell him?

But even as that thought occurred to her, she told herself that of course he'd be grateful. What man wouldn't want to know that he was in fact, a powerful warlock? She nodded to herself. She had to tell him. Had to remind him about his heritage and about his duty.

"Mackenzie—"

"What are you doing here?" he interrupted, his voice low and intimate enough to send shivers of appreciation along Hannah's spine.

"I told you why I was here. Yesterday."

"No." He shook his head again and moved around her, walking in a slow circle, his gaze raking over every inch of her as thoroughly as a touch. "A woman like you doesn't need to come halfway across the country to marry a man she doesn't know from Adam."

She turned, too, keeping pace with him. "But I *do* know you," she said.

Black eyebrows lifted. "How?"

Lamplight wavered as the flame dipped and swayed on the wick. Silence stretched out between them. Inside the stove, burning wood popped and hissed.

She looked up at him, entranced by the play of shadows across his features. A muscle in his jaw twitched under her steady regard. His eyes darkened as he looked down at her, becoming the deep, violet blue of a storm-tossed sea.

Never before had she been so drawn to a man. She hardly knew him and yet, something inside her seemed to . . . recognize him, somehow.

"How, Hannah?" he demanded, reaching for her. His hands closed around her upper arms in a hard, tight grip. "How do you know me?"

She gasped aloud. Pure, undiluted power rushed through her body, streaming from his hands into her very bones. Hot, bright, pulsing with colors she sensed rather than saw, it filled her, making her feel dizzy and strong all at once. If she'd been struck by lightning, she couldn't have been more stunned.

And any doubts she might have had about him and his abilities to help her family and friends dissolved under the sheer flood of his strength. Eudora had said that marriage to her would make the Mackenzie even stronger because he could draw not only on his own power but on Hannah's as well. Yet she couldn't help wondering why a warlock as powerful as Jonas would have need of her pitiful abilities.

Hannah breathed deeply, steadying herself under the

waves of energy still rippling through her. When she felt sure her voice wouldn't crack, she reached up, covered his hands with hers, and said. "I'm a witch, Jonas. Just like you."

Chapter six

"**What?**" Jonas released her as if he'd been burned and took a hasty step backward. Staring at her earnest features and solemn eyes, he told himself she was crazier than he'd thought at first. But as he continued to look at her, searching her green-eyed gaze for hints of madness, he had to acknowledge that she obviously believed every word she said. Which could still mean she was crazy.

If there was a tiny whisper of recognition echoing softly in the back of his mind, he put it down to being tired.

"A witch," he repeated for lack of anything better to say.

"Yes." She smiled at him and heaved what looked like a sigh of relief. "Like you."

Now he laughed. A strained, forced laugh that hurt his chest and scraped his throat. But what else could a man do when faced with a woman like this? "I don't know what you're up to with this story, Hannah, but even I know that witches are female. And ugly," he pointed out. Hell, just looking at her shining face and creamy skin put the lie to her outlandish tale. If she really was a witch, she was the best-damn-looking one he could imagine.

"A nasty lie invented to frighten children," she said

hotly, obviously insulted. "Naturally, not all witches are beautiful . . ."

"Oh, sure," he agreed, already thinking of a way to escape this crazy conversation.

"But," she added, "I've yet to see one with warts on her nose. And for your information, a male witch is called a warlock."

Something inside him shivered. The dark well of his soul opened a crack and the movement was painful. Jonas had the distinct feeling that if he allowed it, memories long buried would come rushing to the surface. But as he already knew, memories were rarely pleasant. So, desperately, he fought the sensation back.

His gaze swept over her and, as if he'd been dunked in ice water, the desire he'd felt only moments ago froze in his veins.

"Warlocks and witches," he muttered and stared around the familiar kitchen as if trying to ground himself in reality.

All right, maybe *she* was a witch. It would certainly explain why his mind seemed filled with thoughts of her. And why he had hired her in the first place. And why she was still here when every instinct he possessed kept screaming at him to send her away.

Now *he* sounded crazy for even considering the possibility that she was telling at least the partial truth.

"Elias told me you don't remember your true heritage."

"So you've decided to make one up for me?" he countered with a snarl in his tone that he couldn't quite contain. "You should have tried something a little easier for me to accept. Like maybe I'm a missing prince, kidnapped from his rightful family as a child."

She clucked her tongue at him in disapproval. "Now you're being silly."

"*I'm* being silly?"

"I didn't make this up," she said and took a step toward him. He backed up from the eager anticipation in her eyes. She may not be crazy, but she was damn sure worked up.

Damn it, he never should have confronted her. He should have left well enough alone. But there was something about this woman that refused to be ignored. It was as if he were drawn to her despite his best intentions. Despite knowing deep in his heart that becoming close with her would signal an end to everything he'd ever known.

But a warlock?

"You are the Mackenzie," she said. "That's why Aunt Eudora sent me to you. That's why we have to be married."

A short bark of unamused laughter exploded from his chest again. "Well, that explains everything," he said tightly.

"You're the hereditary head of the Guild," she went on, as if what she was saying meant something to him.

It didn't, though. He didn't know what the Guild was. And didn't want to know, he told himself as he felt the shadows inside him begin to lift dangerously. His life was here. In Wyoming. On the ranch he intended to make something of.

"Even if you were right—" he said and held up a hand when she looked as though he'd given her a brightly wrapped gift package, "which I'm not saying you are—it doesn't matter. Not to me."

She gasped and pulled her head back, looking at him through wide, shocked eyes. "How can you say that? Your duty—"

"My *duty*," he interrupted her, "is to this ranch and the men I have working for me and the man who raised me." His head was spinning, making him feel as sick as he usually did on a Saturday night, with none of the fun involved in drinking himself into a stupor.

"But you're the Mackenzie," she repeated, as if saying his name in that lofty tone would mean a damn thing to him.

"I'm Jonas Mackenzie," he said. "And that's enough. Nothing you can say is going to change that. My life is here. My everyday, average, *normal* life is here. I'm not a witch and I'm sure as hell not the head of this Guild you keep harping on."

"Search your memories, Jonas," she said, her voice reaching deep inside him to rattle his heart and stir his soul. "Use your powers to recover that which you've lost somehow."

"My powers?" A low-throated chuckle rippled through him as he lifted both hands to squeeze a suddenly aching skull. "Well, sure," he said mockingly, "I'm a witch. Why wouldn't I have powers?" His gaze leveled on her. "What powers are those, I'm almost afraid to ask?"

She reached for him and, before he could avoid her touch, laid one hand on his chest. He felt the warmth of her scatter inside him like a thistle blossom in a high wind. Jonas drew an unsteady breath into heaving lungs and forced himself to stand still. He wouldn't let her know what her touch did to him, any more than he would admit that a few of her words had struck him harder than he'd like to think.

"I feel the power within you," she said, looking up at him. His gaze locked with her forest-green eyes and he felt himself tumbling into their depths. Her voice went on, softly drawing him deeper, deeper into the secrets and shadows she kept hidden in her eyes. And all too close to the secrets he knew were buried inside him.

"You *are* the Mackenzie, Jonas. And the only man who can help me."

The world went still. For a long moment, they stood together in the center of the kitchen, each of them straining to make the other see, understand.

He felt the strength of her belief and it shook him to his bones. Her warmth filled him as she leaned closer, closer. Dipping his head, he kept his gaze locked with hers, losing himself in her eyes. He heard her breath catch just before he dusted his mouth across hers.

A wild, fierce blast of heat rocketed through him as their lips met, and instinctively he pulled back. Staring down at her, he tried to rationalize what had just happened. Tried to pretend that what he'd felt had been nothing more than a simple reaction to a simple kiss.

Damn it.

"Oh, my," she whispered, those incredible eyes of hers glittering in the lamplight.

Then Hepzibah yowled from the corner and the spell was broken. Jonas sucked in great gulps of air like a drowning man breaching the water's surface for the third and last time. He owed that cat a favor, he told himself as he quickly stepped beyond Hannah's reach. When her hand fell to her side, he felt strangely empty. He ignored that feeling and carefully edged past her toward the door.

He needed to be alone. To get away from this woman and her craziness that seemed to be contagious. England ought to be far enough.

Why in God's name had he kissed her?

And what would it be like to deepen that kiss? Stop, he told himself firmly, veering away from that train of thought. He wouldn't be kissing her again. That path would only bring them both all kinds of misery.

"I'm sorry for . . ."

"Kissing me?" she provided.

He nodded and rubbed the back of his neck.

"Don't be," she said, lifting one hand to touch her lips as though she could still feel the slight pressure of his.

His teeth ground together and he steeled himself against the desire to cross the room, pull her into his arms, and kiss her long and deep.

"I'm not what you think I am, Hannah," he said tightly. "So if you're expecting me to shout hallelujah and go along with whatever you've got in mind, forget about it."

"But Jonas—" she started.

He wrenched the door open and spared her a glance over his shoulder. "And for God's sake, don't count on my help for *anything*. I'd only let you down."

In the middle of the night, Hannah went looking for him. She'd waited hours for him to come to the house, but he'd stayed away, apparently determined to avoid her. It was that kiss, she told herself, relishing the memory. All evening, she'd relived that too-brief moment when his lips had touched hers.

Her stomach still flip-flopped just thinking about it. He'd felt it, too, she was sure of it. Otherwise, he would have returned to the house hours ago. As if hiding would help. Didn't he realize he couldn't ignore his destiny any more than she could hers?

And he thought *her* stubborn.

She wrapped a blanket around her nightgown-clad body and stepped out onto the kitchen porch. Shivering slightly, she looked around the moonlit darkness until her gaze landed on a thin strip of lamplight shining at the bottom of the closed barn doors. She smiled to herself, took a deep breath, and hurried across the yard, her bare feet tingling with cold.

Hoping the hinges wouldn't creak, giving Jonas warning of her presence, she pulled on one of the heavy doors and opened it just far enough to allow her to slip silently inside.

She heard him before she saw him. His voice rumbled through the still barn and before she could speak, she found herself caught by his words.

"It's all right, girl," he was saying in a whispered hush. "No need to worry now. I'll stay right here with you."

Hannah sidestepped quietly across the dirt floor until she could see into the far stall, where Jonas stood beside a chestnut horse in a puddle of lamplight. She watched him running his big hands gently over the animal's coat, smoothing along its long, graceful neck, stroking its muzzle with an almost tender touch.

"That cut on your leg's already healing," he was saying in the same calm, reassuring tone. "In a few days, you'll be right as rain."

The horse lifted its head and shook it, sending its mane flying. It moved restlessly in the stall, but Jonas stood his ground, murmuring words of encouragement, letting his hands soothe the animal.

Lamplight gilded his face and hands. Even the tips of his hair seemed to catch the golden glow and shimmer. Hannah watched him, mesmerized by his soft voice, by the gentleness that seemed to flow from him.

She smiled to herself and branded this image of him into her memory. Years from now, she wanted to be able to recall this night and the gentleness in his features, the quiet strength of him. His tenderness tugged at her heart. His compassion for a wounded animal touched her and made her want to go and offer her help. But she knew he wouldn't welcome her.

Talking to him would have to wait, she thought and with one last look at the man in the lamplight, she turned and left the barn as quietly as she'd entered.

Magic didn't help.

Three days later, Hannah was forced to admit that things weren't going well at all. Since their kiss in the kitchen, Jonas had avoided her as he would the plague. She only saw him at mealtimes, and then he bolted his food and left again without a word or even a glance in her direction.

The tenderness she'd glimpsed in him three nights ago seemed to be reserved for the animals in his care.

Even when she followed him about the ranch, turning up at the corral or the barn, he disappeared as quickly as he could.

It was as if he was determined to pretend that she'd never told him who he was. That he hadn't kissed her.

That magic hadn't been born in that brief meeting of their lips.

"Foolish man," she muttered, looking at Hepzibah, who was busy stalking an empty pea pod across the kitchen floor. "Does he think by turning a blind eye to it, he'll change what is?"

The scratch of the cat's claws on the floor was her only answer. Hannah rubbed her upper arms and stared at the clean, lamplit kitchen. All around her, the empty house screamed with silence. Even the usual murmur of voices from the bunkhouse were gone tonight. All but two of the men had gone into town, Jonas with them. She'd hoped to have a moment with him before he left, but again he'd outfoxed her.

"The man doesn't need magic," she said aloud, just to hear the company of a voice, even her own. "But just the same, he'll have it."

All she had to do was make him remember.

Picking up a spoon, Hannah dipped it into the pot on the stove, watching the bubbling pink liquid inside as she stirred carefully.

Hepzibah gave up her hunting to come and rub against her mistress's legs.

But Hannah focused her concentration on the mixture she'd placed her hopes on. Moving the wooden spoon through the potion, she chanted the spell she'd rehearsed earlier. "I've found him, but still he's lost. Return him now, whatever the cost."

She smiled faintly. Perhaps being near the Mackenzie was helping her own pitiful abilities. Her rhymes were much better now, she thought.

Whiskey didn't help.

Neither did the usually comforting noise and stench of the saloon. Jonas squinted into the gray-blue pall of cigar smoke hanging over the crowd, looking from one familiar face to the next. He'd been coming into this saloon every Saturday night for years. But tonight, he wasn't finding the peace he usually did.

Jonas picked up his glass and stared thoughtfully at the amber liquid inside. He'd already drunk half a bottle and it hadn't done a thing to dim the image of Hannah that seemed to be permanently etched on his brain.

In the last few days, he'd done nothing but trip over her. Everywhere he turned, there she was. If he went into the barn to check on the mare, she showed up just a step or two behind him. Smiling that innocent smile. Looking up at him from those incredibly green eyes of hers.

She would stare at him as if waiting for him to kiss her again. Waiting for him to tell her she was right about him. But how could he do that?

For God's sake . . . a witch?

Warlock, his brain corrected, though it didn't matter a damn. Either way it was nonsense. Witches lived only in fairy tales or in minds far drunker than his at the moment.

He took a sip of the whiskey, savoring the liquid fire as it slid along his tongue and down into his belly. But he had a feeling that even if he drank a wagonload of the stuff tonight, it wouldn't bring him the oblivion he wanted.

Still, it was worth a try. He grimaced tightly and tossed the whiskey down his throat. Before it had finished burning a trail down his throat, he was slamming the glass back onto the table and pouring himself another.

Should have gone to Jefferson tonight, he told himself in disgust. A few hours with one of Sal's girls would quench any man's fire. But even as he considered it, he knew it wasn't a solution this time. Not for him, anyway. Because none of Sal's girls was a blond-haired, green eyed . . . witch.

And none of them carried the power of a lightning bolt on their lips.

"Son of a bitch," he muttered thickly and reached for the bottle again. Even if the liquor wasn't helping, it couldn't hurt.

But before he could throw another drink into his already roiling stomach, one of his cowhands rushed up to him, looking back over his shoulder as if being chased by a ghost.

"What's the matter now?" Jonas grumbled. Had it only been a few days ago when he'd been congratulating himself on a long-standing string of good luck?

"Billy's in trouble." Stretch Jones leaned across his table and looked him dead in the eye.

Jonas blinked, bringing the blurry image of the tall, skinny cowhand with an Adam's apple the size of a lemon into focus. "What kind of trouble?"

Stretch pushed his hair out of his eyes, leaned forward, and started talking again, his words tumbling over each other in a rush. "Some cardsharp's took most of his money and Billy's just drunk enough to complain."

Frowning, Jonas looked across the room toward the poker table in the corner. "Complain too loud, he's liable to get shot."

"Don't I know it, boss. That's why I come to get you. You tell Billy to leave it lay and he most likely will."

"He'd damn well better," Jonas growled as he pushed himself to his feet. "I don't need a dead cowhand just before roundup."

Stretch hunched his shoulders. "It would make more work for the rest of us."

Casual talk aside, neither of the men was going to let Billy die over a card game. As he pushed himself to his feet and started for the table in the corner, Jonas thought, at least this was something. Drinking wasn't helping. Maybe a good old-fashioned brawl was just what he needed. Besides, he couldn't just stand there and let Billy get shot, could he?

When he was still too far away to do a damn sight

of good, he saw that he was too late. The gambler drew his pistol and aimed it at Billy.

That corner of the saloon went quiet.

A couple of men scooted their chairs back, getting out of range.

"It's in the fire now," Stretch said from behind him.

Through the haze of whiskey blurring the edges of his mind, Jonas cursed low and long. A careless shout from him might be all the surprise the gambler needed to jerk his finger on that trigger. And Billy would be dead.

Anger rumbled through him and vaguely he noted the distant drums of thunder.

He turned his dark gaze on the gambler's freshly shaved face and cold, empty eyes. Not much hope there. Seconds crawled by, as if the world hung in the balance and time forgot to move.

He shifted his concentration to the small pepperbox pistol the gambler held. An unpredictable weapon at best, Jonas knew it could be counted on to either fire one bullet, all five at once, or none at all.

"All we can hope for," he said softly, more to himself than to Stretch, "is that the damn gun won't work."

Time skittered into life again and the gambler pulled the trigger. Billy jumped in his seat, obviously expecting to feel the slamming white-hot pain of a bullet crashing into his chest.

But nothing happened.

Furious, the gambler jerked the trigger again and the same empty click sounded out in the room. He glared at the gun and tossed it angrily aside.

At the same time, Billy realized he wasn't about to die and lunged across the table, hands outstretched, reaching for the other man's throat. The young cowhand grabbed hold of the gambler's fancy ruffled shirt instead and yanked him off his chair. The two of them went down amid a crashing of chairs and a chorus of shouting voices.

"Luck, boss!" Stretch slapped him on the back. "You always did have the damnedest luck!"

Luck, he thought and for one wild, terrifying minute, he found himself wondering if it really was luck, or was Hannah's story more true than he wanted to know?

Stretch raced past him to join in the fight and Jonas stood stock-still a moment or two longer, asking himself if the pepperbox had failed because it was basically a lousy weapon . . . or had he, somehow, caused the gun to misfire?

A war whoop worthy of a howling Comanche shattered his bizarre thoughts and he ducked in time to avoid a thrown chair as it whistled past his head.

The saloon erupted around him. This was no time for thinking. Jonas eagerly joined in the fight, choosing the closest man to him and landing a roundhouse punch to his jaw. As that same man jumped to his feet and buried his fist in Jonas's stomach, he consoled himself with the knowledge that at least *this* he understood.

Something heavy landed with a thud that shook Hannah out of a restless sleep. Sitting up in bed, she flipped her braid behind her shoulder and listened for another minute before getting out of bed and opening her bedroom door.

Her bare feet tingled with cold against the wood floor and the night air seemed to pierce right through her white cotton nightgown. Shivering slightly, she peered into the darkened main room, wishing she'd left a lamp burning.

The only light came from the banked fire, and its dim orange-red glow only seemed to define the darkness rather than illuminate it.

Then one of the shadowy shapes moved. For one brief instant, thoughts of haunts and demons flew through her still-sleepy mind. But when the shadow stood up, outlining itself against the backdrop of what was left of the fire, Hannah sighed at her own foolishness. Of course it was Jonas.

"Who the hell left that damn sofa in the middle of the damn room?" he muttered and she wondered vaguely why his voice sounded so garbled.

He took another step and every bone in his body seemed to collapse. He folded in on himself and landed with another loud thud.

"Good heavens! Are you all right?" she said as she hurried toward him, her inventive mind drawing up images of a raging fever, or a hideous wound spouting fountains of blood, or . . . She stopped short when the smell hit her.

Wrinkling her nose, Hannah tried to breathe without inhaling.

Whiskey fumes permeated the room like a thick fog hanging over Boston Harbor.

He wasn't sick.

He was drunk.

"Good Lord."

He lifted his head from the floor as though it weighed a hundred pounds. Staring up at her, he blinked, stared, then blinked again. Snorting a laugh that ended in a groan of pain, he muttered, "First witches . . . now angels."

"Angels indeed," she said with a disgusted shake of her head. Still, her lips twitched slightly as she looked down at herself, imagining what she must look like from his befuddled perspective. Billowing white nightgown. Blond hair. The odd light thrown by the dying fire.

His head dropped to the floor again with a smack.

"You're drunk, Mackenzie."

"Shhh . . ." he warned, lifting one finger to lay it crookedly across his mouth. "You'll wake Hannah."

"I'm Hannah," she told him with a reluctant smile.

"She's a witch," he confided, then winked at her. The fact that he had to pry that eye open again with his fingertips rather spoiled the effect.

"Really?" Hannah asked. Wasn't this nice? It had only taken a gallon or two of whiskey to make him believe her. Still, another smile tugged at her lips. He did look ridiculous, sprawled across the floor. Hardly the image of a powerful warlock.

He held up one hand and it swayed limply back and forth in front of him like a flag on a windless day. "Angels are better than witches," he said in that strange garbled tone.

"I suppose so," she granted, already wondering how she was going to get the man off the floor and into his bed.

"Stopped the fight," he told her and waved his hand.

Hannah grabbed it and tugged, trying to pull him to his feet. "Is that right?" A fight, was it?

"Saved Billy." He grunted as she braced her feet and pulled him halfway to a sitting position.

"That's good," she muttered from between clenched teeth. She'd never been so aware of what a big man the Mackenzie was. The muscles in her shoulders were screaming and she'd hardly moved him at all.

"Couldn't save Marie, though," he whispered.

Hannah let go.

His head crashed against the floor. "Ow . . ."

She winced. She hadn't meant to drop him, but . . . "Who's Marie?"

"Dead. Dead and I didn't save her." He shook his head from side to side, groaning slightly with the movement. "Angel didn't save her, either." Jonas glared at her briefly.

"Who is she?" Hannah repeated, but his whiskey-soaked brain was off on another tangent.

"Shhh, Angel," he told her and tried to lift his head again. Apparently, though, that concentrated effort was beyond him at the moment. "If we wake up the witch, she'll put a hex on you . . ."

"Oh, for heaven's sakes," she muttered.

". . . like she did on me," he finished.

"I did no such thing," she snapped and for a moment thought guiltily of the potion she'd spent most of the evening cooking up. Well, she hadn't actually given it to him yet, had she?

"She's lying, angel."

"I'm *not* an angel," she said hotly. "I'm Hannah. And I didn't lie to you."

"Lies," he muttered and turned his head to one side, nestling against the wooden planks as though he were settling deep into a feather pillow. "All lies. Didn't save him. Couldn't save her."

Again, that reference to the mysterious Marie. Hannah's insides tightened up as she realized it would require a miracle to get any more information from him tonight.

"It's not a lie, Mackenzie," she whispered, shaking her head. "You are a warlock."

"Nope," he murmured softly and folded his hands across his chest. "Not."

And people said *she* was stubborn. Hannah sighed and turned around. Going to his room, she grabbed the quilt from his bed and went back to the fallen Mackenzie. She'd never get him off the floor, so she spread the quilt over him and left him there.

As she turned to leave, though, his voice stopped her.

"Hannah?"

"Yes?" She looked back at him. He lay still as death, eyes closed.

"It *is* you, then."

"What do you want, Mackenzie?"

"An answer."

"To which question?"

He paused and Hannah almost convinced herself he'd fallen asleep when he asked quietly. "If I'm really this witch you say I am, how come I can't make you disappear?"

Chapter seven

Sunday morning dawned bright and clear. Not a single cloud marred the lake-blue sky. The snowcapped mountains looked close enough to touch, and a soft, cool breeze ruffled the clothes Hannah hung on the line.

A few of the men had gone into town and the rest, but for those sent to guard the herd, were recuperating quietly in the bunkhouse. Hannah couldn't help but wonder if every Sabbath here was spent in repenting the night before.

This place was so different from home. In Creekford, she would have been attending the local church services, then perhaps gone visiting with Eudora. Here, she handed out liniment and pieces of beefsteak to the men who'd come stumbling into her kitchen sporting black eyes and skinned knuckles.

Snatching up one of Jonas's shirts from the laundry basket, she held it tightly in both hands and realized that as different as this place was, she liked it. Here, she felt useful. She cooked and cleaned and cared for a group of men who were slowly coming to, if not like her, then at least respect her.

Oh, remembering what he'd said the night before, she admitted that Jonas would probably be happier if she'd leave. But he hadn't ordered her off his property, so maybe that was something in itself.

Snapping the wrinkles out of the shirt, she laid it across the clothesline and held it in place with two wooden pins at the shoulders. Thoughtfully, she smoothed her fingers across the worn, blue material. Not only was life different here, *she* was different.

She lifted her gaze to the far mountains and pulled in a deep, satisfying breath of the crisp air. No one on the ranch was judging her and finding her coming up short of expectations. No one here knew about witchcraft. No one realized that she was a complete failure.

As much as she loved Creekford, it wasn't easy living there. An entire town full of practicing witches could be fairly intimidating to a woman whose own powers were so ridiculously paltry.

For the first time in her life, Hannah's pitiful powers didn't mean anything. She was being judged, and approved of, just like an ordinary person.

"Are you *tryin'* to kill yourself?"

Elias's astonished voice lifted Hannah from her reverie and she half turned toward the sound.

"Wasn't last night enough?" the older man asked.

"Leave me alone, you old coot," Jonas complained.

Hannah left the laundry behind and walked around the corner of the house. Across the yard from her, she saw Elias standing outside the corral, watching Jonas tighten a saddle cinch on a black horse that looked mean even from a distance. Hardly realizing she was moving, Hannah started toward them.

The older man half turned as she approached. He nodded at her, then turned his attention back to Jonas. "You don't have to do this today," he said.

"As good a time as any," Jonas told him as he caught a glimpse of Hannah and lowered his head to his task.

"What's going on?" she asked as she stepped up to the corral fence and rested her hands on the highest rail.

"This durn fool's gonna break his neck," Elias muttered.

"What I'm going to do is break this horse before roundup." Jonas tightened the cinch strap, then flipped the stirrup down and into place. Grabbing the reins, he led the horse into the center of the corral.

The big black animal tossed its head and rolled its eyes. Snorting and sidestepping, it looked as though it had no intention of being ridden anytime soon.

Hannah felt a catch in her chest and stepped up onto the bottom railing. In the sunlight, Jonas's bruises looked appalling. His jaw was purple, his split lip still swollen, and his right eye was nearly closed.

"Isn't this dangerous?" she asked quietly.

She felt, rather than saw, Elias's gaze shift to her. "Damn right. Even when a man's got a clear head, it ain't easy." He raised his voice slightly. "A hangover'll only make it harder."

Jonas ignored him.

"Why is he doing this?" she asked herself aloud.

"Because it needs to be done," Elias answered.

"But he's hurt," she said, her gaze locked on Jonas. A part of her admired him for doing his job even when he was obviously in no shape for it.

"Yeah," Elias said on a grunt. "From what I hear, it was a beaut of a fight."

"You didn't go into town, then?" She turned to look at him.

"I got better things to do," he said, then raised his voice pointedly, "even if some folks don't."

Jonas ignored him.

"He came home drunk," Hannah commented.

"Usually does." The older man's gray eyes narrowed as he watched the younger man in front of him.

She shifted her gaze back to where Jonas was stabbing his left foot into the stirrup and grabbing hold of the saddle horn with both hands. Frowning, she asked, "Usually?"

"Every damn Saturday night," he said, his voice thick with concern. "For years, now."

Why? she wondered, but couldn't bring herself to ask. What could drive a man like the Mackenzie to seek solace from a liquor bottle? A man with all the power of the universe at his fingertips. A man who, with the snap of his fingers, could unleash a stream of energy strong enough to rival the white-hot ferocity of a thousand lightning bolts.

She studied him through eyes looking to see beyond the surface and into the soul. The heart. Once again, she remembered the night before, when he'd looked at her and asked, *Why can't I make you disappear?*

The pain of that moment lessened only when she reminded herself that if he'd really wanted her gone . . . she would be.

He pulled himself into the saddle and with his abrupt movement, the horse began a dance designed to dismount him. All four feet left the ground as the huge beast arched its back, lowered its head, and snorted in frustrated fury.

Hannah held her breath and watched as Jonas leaned back in the saddle, straightening his legs, locking his knees as he pitched back and forth with the animal's crazed flight. His left hand high over his head, his right hand kept a firm grip on the reins he'd wrapped around the saddle horn.

Seconds became hours, and minutes, days.

The only sound she heard was the frantic pawing of hooves against hard-packed earth and the whoosh of Jonas's breath rushing in and out of his lungs.

Her own breath was trapped in her chest. She felt her heartbeat thundering in her ears. She felt the man beside her stiffen when Jonas suddenly flew from the saddle to land in a heap, up against the corral fence. And there he lay, still and quiet.

"Damn it," Elias muttered.

Fear tore at her throat, making it impossible to draw

breath. Before she knew what she was doing, Hannah was clambering between the rails of the corral fence, barely aware that Elias was keeping pace with her. She ran across the paddock to Jonas while the older man caught the horse's reins and led the animal a safe distance away.

The sun stabbed at Jonas's closed eyelids, increasing the pounding ache that throbbed in time with his heartbeat. The blinding hangover that had been with him for hours was now joined by the assorted stabs of pain that seemed to attack every inch of his body.

Groaning tightly, he rolled to one side and cautiously opened his eyes. Silhouetted against the sun, she stood over him. Her face in shadows, she seemed haloed by a golden light that reminded him eerily of the night before. Drunk he might have been, but he dimly recalled having a conversation with an *angel,* of all things. An angel that had made him yearn for heaven and suffer in the hell of not having her.

Here, he was willing to bet, was that angel.

Jesus, how had this happened to him? How did one woman show up in a man's life and in less than a week throw everything he'd known into turmoil?

She'd slipped up on him. Made herself a part of the place. Everywhere he looked, he saw her. She'd stepped right up to the challenge of feeding a dozen men three times a day and had managed to tame that same rowdy crew. He knew the men liked her . . . and damned if he didn't, too.

"Are you all right?" she asked and went down on her knees beside him.

He heard the concern in her voice and cringed inwardly. He looked away from the flash of fear he recognized in her eyes. He couldn't—*wouldn't*—be that important to another human being again.

Ever.

"I'm fine," he said. "Just banged up a little."

"Why are you doing this?" she asked with a shake of her head.

"It has to be done," he said and, wincing, tried to sit up.

Instantly, her arms were around him, supporting him until he was leaning back against the rail fence. Warmth rippled from her body into his. The scent of lemons wafted around him and he drew it deep into his lungs despite knowing he shouldn't indulge in even that small comfort. And then the memory of that brief, soul-shaking kiss crashed over him and Jonas nearly groaned aloud.

She must be a witch, he told himself. Otherwise, she wouldn't have such a profound effect on him. His heart had turned to stone too long ago for any ordinary woman to be able to reach it. As for what her presence did to his body . . . hell, even a dead man would take notice of Hannah, he figured.

"There's an easier way," she said softly.

"Don't start with that witchcraft stuff again, Hannah," he interrupted her. "Believe me, I'm in no mood for it."

"For heaven's sake, Mackenzie," she said, her voice filled with the impatience that seemed to flow from her in waves. "This is a gift you've been given. Can't you see that?"

Tipping his head to one side, he studied her briefly. From the flyaway strands of blond hair that swirled about her head in the soft breeze, to her wide, green eyes, to the gently curved lips he'd dreamed of kissing again.

Disgusted with his own wayward mind, he snapped, "What I see is a woman keeping me from doing my job."

"Pretending it's not true won't make it so."

A quick spurt of anger shot through him as he grabbed one of her hands and squeezed it. "I'm not a witch, Hannah."

She shook her head and a few more strands of gold drifted free of her braid. "I don't know how to convince you."

"You can't."

"I have to try," she said and covered his hand with her free one. Heat collected at the spot where they touched and Jonas had to fight against the urge to pull her closer. He suddenly wanted, desperately, to feel her body pressed tightly to his. To surround himself with the warmth and sunlight that seemed to be a part of her.

He'd been so long in the shadows.

Too long, he told himself.

Behind her, Elias stepped closer. Absently, Jonas noticed his old friend, but chose to ignore his presence in the effort to make Hannah understand.

"Don't you get it?" he demanded roughly and snatched his hand free before he could give in to the temptation to reach for more. "I don't *want* to be convinced. I don't want to be who you say I am."

"You don't get a choice Jonas," she said, and he thought he heard a wisp of sympathy laced with the firm conviction in her tone. "You *are* the Mackenzie. By birth. By right. It's not something you can make go away by turning a blind eye to it."

"Watch me."

"But why? Surely anyone would want what you have."

Not everyone, he thought. Not a man who carried around the image of a dead woman. A woman who died because he couldn't reach her in time. Because he'd left her alone when she needed him. Because his own damned ambition had been more important than her safety.

He couldn't believe Hannah's story.

If he did, then he would have to accept that he could have saved Marie if only he'd known.

And he didn't think he could live with that.

Not bothering to answer her, he pushed himself to his feet and stalked past Elias. Brushing himself off, he gathered up the stallion's reins and rejoined the battle.

*   *   *

A few days later, Hannah drove her carriage into the small town of Hat Rock. The long, narrow main street was crowded with weekday shoppers. A bit bigger than Creekford, the mountain town was tidier than she'd expected. Freshly painted buildings looked spruce in the cloud-scattered sunshine and there were even a few flower boxes lining the windows of some of the shops facing the one and only street.

She passed the livery stable, a milliner, a bakery, the mercantile, and a barbershop. From farther down the street, she heard the distinctive ring and crash of a blacksmith's hammer. A few women carrying baskets over their arms hustled along the freshly swept boardwalk, herding small armies of children as they went.

Horses stamped restlessly at the hitching rails and a heavy dray wagon rolled past Hannah on its way out of town. The driver tipped his hat to her and grinned, and she gave him a distracted smile.

Ordinarily, she would have enjoyed this trip into town. A chance to see more of the new world she'd entered, a chance to meet some of the people who would become a part of her life once she and Jonas were married. And they *would* be married, she determined firmly.

However, she had been forced to the conclusion that she was going to need some help in bringing Jonas around to her way of thinking. She'd been at the ranch nearly two weeks and the man was no closer to falling in love with her than he had been the day she'd arrived.

In fact, since kissing her, he seemed more dedicated than ever to keeping his distance.

Gripping the reins tightly, Hannah kept one eye on the road while she searched for the telegraph office. And just before she reached the edge of town, she spotted it, sandwiched between Ellen Kay's Dress Shoppe and Wells Fargo. She stopped her carriage just outside, jumped down from the seat, and tied the reins to the hitching post.

Striding across the boardwalk, she opened the door,

setting a small bell into a clanging dance of welcome.

"Mornin', miss," the tall, thin man behind the counter said as he stood up from his chair. "Can I help you?"

"Yes," she answered, noting the scent of cigar smoke and an out-of-date calendar tacked to the bare plank wall. "I need to send a telegram."

"Then you come to the right place." He smiled at her and slid a stack of yellow forms toward her. "You just fill one of them out, and I'll send it right away."

Thoughtfully, Hannah picked up a pencil and, heaving one last regretful sigh that this was necessary, began to write. In just a few moments, it was done. She'd admitted to failure one more time. Eudora had been counting on her. Creekford had been counting on her.

And not only had her witchcraft failed her this time, she thought dismally, but so had her feminine charms.

Swallowing back that humiliating fact, Hannah paid the man, thanked him, and left the telegraph office. Standing on the boardwalk, she let her gaze sweep across the row of shops and decided to do a little shopping. After all, she thought with a frown, no sense in hurrying back to the ranch just so Mackenzie could ignore her again.

Before she'd taken more than a step, though, a gaggle of voices caught her attention. She turned her head and watched as a beautiful woman walked by, followed by a crowd of men, each vying for her attention. Tall and generously endowed, she wore a lovely red dress that sparkled in the midday sun. Her auburn hair was piled high on her head, and tucked into the fat ringlets were several lovely feathers that waved and dipped in the breeze.

Hannah looked again at the woman's admirers. Smiling and stumbling over each other, they were giving her the kind of attention Hannah had been trying to win from Jonas. Hmmm. She took another long look at the woman, letting her gaze stop on those feathers and the attractive way they swayed with their wearer's movements. A kernel of an idea took root at the back of her mind and blossomed. She smiled softly and told herself that just maybe, by the time Eudora arrived, the problem with Jonas would be solved after all.

Then her happy thoughts dissolved as a hand snaked out of the alley, wrapped itself around her upper arm, and dragged her back into the shadows.

Elias put one hand over her mouth and kept her moving until they were at the far end of the alleyway between the dress shop and the land office. He'd been waiting for days to catch Hannah Lowell alone. But the darn female was always just a step or two behind Jonas. Finally, today, when he'd seen her heading for town, he'd followed, determined to have a little chat with the witch from Massachusetts.

Releasing her, he took a step back and looked down into her wide, green eyes.

She released a pent-up breath and said, "Elias. You frightened me half to death."

"I'm sorry, missy," he said and meant it. He hadn't meant to scare her. She seemed a nice enough girl. For a witch. "That wasn't my aim. Only wanted to talk to you. Private-like."

Nodding, she asked, "About what?"

"About how soon you can leave," he said flatly, a firm believer in not beating about the bush. He figured, if you want something, you say so. Directly.

And what he wanted now was this little female the hell away from Jonas.

She drew her head back and stared at him. Was it his imagination that her eyes looked a bit wounded? He shifted his stance uncomfortably. She had no call to turn those big eyes on him like that. This was for the best, he reminded himself. For Jonas. And for her.

"I don't want to leave," she said at last.

"I dare say," he agreed, keeping his tone firm. "But you've got to go, missy."

"I don't understand," she said. "I haven't done anything to you. Why would you want me to leave? Is it my cooking?"

She was talking so fast, he couldn't get a word in.

"Are you still angry over the mashed potatoes and fried chicken on the table?" She shrugged gently. "I admit that was a bit too much, but really, it was the only way I knew to make all of you see—"

"That ain't it," he interrupted, though it went against his grain. However, in this case, he'd had to. Otherwise they might both be standing in that alleyway for hours waiting for her to wind down. Before she could get up a full head of steam again, he pulled in a deep breath and folded his arms across his chest. "Y'see," he started, "I know who you are and I know why you're here."

"You do?"

She actually looked relieved.

"Yes, ma'am. Jonas told me."

"He did?" She smiled and laid one hand on his arm. "I'm so glad. I really don't like being secretive. It's so difficult."

He imagined it would be hard on a woman who talked as much as she did to keep any kind of secret.

"I've sort of been expectin' you—or someone like you—" Elias said, "to show up."

"What do you mean, like me?"

"A witch."

Her eyes widened even farther. "Jonas told you everything, then. And you believe me."

"Ain't a question of believin' you or not," he told her. Elias glanced around them, as if reassuring himself that they were alone. Stacks of empty wooden crates made a leaning tower at the end of the alley. Stray pieces of paper rustled across the ground as a rogue breeze sent them rolling along the dirt. In the street, people went on about their business, never guessing that here in the shadows, an old man and a young woman were calmly discussing things a sane person would laugh at.

It felt strange, talking about something he hadn't mentioned in twenty-five years. But in a strange way, it was almost comforting.

"When Jonas's folks died, he was just a kid," he said and shook his head at the swift passing of the years. "His pa told me what was what just before he breathed his last. Now, I might not have believed him, either, but for the fear I seen in his eyes."

"Fear?" she whispered and took a step closer.

"More worry, I guess," Elias amended, searching his memory. "Him and his wife both was bound and determined that their boy grow up and have a normal life. That he not be chained to old beliefs and dying superstitions."

"Superstitions?" Hannah interrupted sharply. "Witchcraft is an old and respected art."

"Respected?" he asked wryly. "You think the folks who drowned and burned witches in the olden days respected 'em any?"

"That time's past," she argued.

"Maybe. But people are people, missy, and they don't change all that much." He'd lived enough years to know that human nature was such that folks tended to turn on the things that scared them. "And frightened people can get almighty nasty."

"Elias," she said and patted his arm. "I understand that you're only trying to protect the Mackenzie—"

"And will," he told her firmly, despite the gentleness in her eyes. He didn't have anything against her personally. But that didn't mean he was going to let her stay and work her wiles on Mac.

"But you have to understand that I have people to protect, too," she said earnestly, and he could see the concern glittering in her green eyes. "My aunt. The Guild members back home."

"That's nothin' to me," he said and kept his voice soft to ease the sting of his words. "I'm sorry for your troubles, but I ain't about to let Mac get drawn into something his folks died trying to keep him out of." He patted her hand and shook his head. "I made a deathbed promise, missy. And I won't break it."

"I'm not asking you to."

"Aren't ya?" he demanded, keeping his voice low. "Aren't you here to take him back to the very thing his folks was runnin' from?"

She dipped her head to avoid looking at him and Elias knew he was right. She did expect Jonas to go back to Massachusetts with her.

"He won't go," he told her. "Even if I was to stay out of it, which I won't, he wouldn't go."

"He wouldn't have to stay," she said quickly. "We could return to the ranch once everything was settled."

"We?"

"He and I," she said, as if he should have known all along that was what she meant. "After we're married, of course."

Elias shook his head again. "Jonas said you were talkin' marriage."

"My aunt says marriage is the only way to protect us all—even," she added firmly, "the Mackenzie himself will be safer. She's seen it all in the crystal, Elias," Hannah went on in a rush of words even faster than usual. "It's going to happen. We will be married. We *have* to be."

"Uh-huh."

She frowned.

He rubbed the back of his neck to ease the tension tightening his muscles. It didn't help.

"Now, how do you figure Mac'll be safer if he's hitched?"

"When a warlock marries another witch, his own magic grows. He becomes more powerful, as does she," Hannah sighed and tried to explain. "The joining of lives and powers creates a force that is much stronger than any a witch could claim on his or her own. And a war-

lock as powerful as the Mackenzie would be undefeat-
able once joined with a witch."

"Uh-huh."

"I really do hate that," she muttered, but Elias ignored
her.

He almost felt sorry for her. Almost. His loyalties
toward Jonas ran too deep for him to be completely on
her side, of course, but there was a part of him that
nearly regretted the fact that her plan wasn't going to
work.

Married to her, Jonas might just be able to face the
demons that rode him and start enjoying his life again.
Elias had a feeling Hannah wouldn't allow anything less.

In fact, there was something about her that reminded
him all too well of a woman he'd known thirty years
ago. A woman he'd wooed and lost.

But the chances of Jonas marrying Hannah were slim
to none and he figured she had a right to know it.

"He won't get married," Elias told her. "Not again."

The words hit her hard. He saw it in her eyes.

"Marie," she whispered, lifting one hand to cover her
mouth.

"He told you about her?" Hell. Jonas hadn't so much
as mentioned her in years.

Hannah shook her head. "He said her name. When
he was drunk."

"Ah." He nodded, then added softly, "It ain't something he talks about. Marie died young. A lot of years
ago."

"Oh, my," Hannah murmured thoughtfully, "why
didn't my aunt see that in the crystal, too? Why didn't she
warn me?"

Maybe her aunt wasn't much of a witch, he thought,
but only said, "He ain't gonna marry you, Hannah."

She half turned from him and stared down the mouth
of the alley into the sunshine splashed at the end of the
narrow corridor. "Does he still love her?"

A hard question, he thought. And one he shouldn't

even try to answer. That was something could only come from Jonas himself. "You'll have to ask him, missy."

She nodded.

"But now you see," he went on quietly. "Give this up, Hannah. Go back where you belong."

"I'm afraid I can't, Elias. For his sake as well as mine."

Then she started walking and he let her go. As he watched her step into the sunlight and turn the corner, Elias had to admit that she was pretty hard not to like. She had gumption and she didn't scare off easy. Knew what she wanted and went about getting it. The kind of attributes he'd always thought well of.

Oh, he'd stop her if she tried to scoot Jonas off back East. Massachusetts. It had been thirty years since he'd visited Boston and met Jonas's folks and . . . A twinge of remembered pain settled around his heart as he recalled the face of the woman who still occassionally haunted his dreams.

Then, frowning, he shook those thoughts off and concentrated instead on the here and now. Jonas and Hannah. Maybe, he told himself, she was just what the man he considered a son needed. A grown-up woman, this time. One unafraid to go toe to toe with him. One who knew her own mind but had a tender heart, as well. Not a selfish child unready to be any man's wife.

Oh, Marie might have grown up, if she'd been given the chance. But she'd died the spoiled only child of a too-indulgent father. Elias had watched Jonas try to please the girl and seen him fail at every turn. Marie had simply been one of those people who were never satisfied. The kind who always looked for happiness and never realized that happiness had to be made, not found.

For ten long years, Jonas had punished himself for Marie's death. And damn it, Elias figured that was long enough. He'd lived most of his life alone because the one woman he'd ever loved had been denied him.

He wanted more for Mac.

Oh, Elias figured Jonas would probably kick and scream, fighting every inch of the way.

But something told him that Hannah was just the girl to get the job done.

Chapter eight

Creekford

The surrounding oaks, elms, and maples dappled the street in splotches of sunshine and shade. A soft ocean wind rushed in off the small harbor at the edge of town and tugged at the ladies' hats as they scurried along the busy street.

Eudora lifted one hand to check that her own black velvet hat was still secure, then adjusted the short net veil that stopped just above her eyebrows. Her full gray skirt snapped around her ankles with each of her quick, long strides. A small beaded bag hung from her right wrist, and inside that bag lay the telegram she'd already read a dozen times at least.

Thank heaven there was no telegraph office in Creekford, she thought. If there had been, Blake Wolcott would no doubt have known about the wire from Hannah even before she had. As it was, the message had arrived in Milltown, just an hour's carriage ride away, and had been delivered to Eudora's door early that morning.

She'd had it with her, on her person, ever since. And still, she didn't feel safe. She sensed someone watching and wasn't the least bit surprised by the sensation. Of course Blake would have one of his minions keeping an eye on her. He'd been furious when he'd discovered that

Hannah had managed to leave town and he'd been working on finding her ever since.

Nodding absently to Hattie Smith as she methodically swept her front porch, Eudora kept walking. She'd had to come to town this afternoon, as usual. She couldn't afford to disrupt her routine. But as she walked, she let her mind drift back to the printed words that kept repeating themselves over and over again:

EUDORA   STOP   NEED YOUR
HELP   STOP   THINGS MORE DIFFICULT
THAN I'D PLANNED   STOP   COME
SOONEST   STOP   LOVE HANNAH   END

Difficult how? she wondered and told herself that, as soon as she was home, she would consult the crystal again.

Absently, she noted the husky, deep-throated bark of Jasper Davis's dog, Bear. The hairs at the back of Eudora's neck stood straight up. A usually quiet, good-natured animal, Bear barked only when the scent of danger was near.

"Shopping, Eudora?" a dark, rich voice spoke up from just behind her, and she closed her eyes briefly, gathering her strength. The quick flash of fear that churned in her stomach irritated as much as worried her. Until his arrival, no one in Creekford had really known fear.

Bear's snarling barks were furious now and Eudora wanted to join the animal, snarling and snapping at the warlock who'd invaded their lives. But she couldn't risk showing her true feelings.

"Blake," she said pleasantly and half turned to give the warlock a smile that held only a pretense of warmth. "What a lovely surprise."

He inclined his head in a regal manner that made Eudora want to slap him. As if he could read her desires, his smiling lips thinned. "Any word from my dear Hannah?" he asked over the din of the dog.

She would play his game, Eudora thought, knowing full well that the mail was searched daily for news of her niece. Blake's few friends were all eager to remain in his good graces.

"Actually, no," she said, and to keep him from sensing the telegram hidden in her purse, she mentally surrounded the paper with a protective spell. Just as she used to surround Hannah with an aura of magic. "She's being very thoughtless, I'm afraid," Eudora said, giving the warlock another half smile.

She glanced about them and noticed that the busy street had practically emptied. Eudora tried not to feel abandoned. She understood their fears. She knew what it cost her friends and neighbors to hide behind closed doors and drawn curtains.

And it was all due to him.

"Perhaps," Blake suggested, the darkness in his eyes glittering strangely, "our Hannah is out of her depth in dealing with your unfortunately ill relative."

The story she'd concocted, about Hannah's going to Boston to look after a great-aunt, was wearing thin, she knew. Blake Wolcott expected Hannah to be here. In Creekford. Where he could keep a cold eye on her until their marriage on the Solstice.

"I'm sure it won't be for much longer," Eudora lied without so much as blinking.

Bear howled miserably and Blake shot a disgusted glance at the Davis house. "I do hope not," he said, reaching for her hand and bringing it to his lips. His mouth touched her fingertips lightly and a swirl of blackness swept through Eudora, stealing her breath and leaving her shaken. She was relieved when he released her.

"Well," she said and took a step away from him, trying to distance herself from the shadowy darkness that was such a part of him, "I really must be going, Blake.

I'll let you know when I hear from Hannah."

Turning, she marched quickly away and only stumbled slightly when his voice followed her.

"Eudora!" he called, then muttered, "Damn that dog!"

She gasped and whirled around.

Blake leveled a hard look on the Davis house and instantly a howl of pain splintered the air, then suddenly, abruptly, ended.

Tears filled her eyes.

Then, as if killing a dog meant no more to him than swatting a fly, he turned his even gaze on Eudora again. "Remind Hannah that her anxious bridegroom is growing restless."

Eudora nodded stiffly, turned, and quickly walked away.

Blake Wolcott smiled tightly. Good. Killing that damned dog hadn't done much toward easing the frustration riding him. But on the other hand, it seemed to have made an impression on Eudora.

Raw fury simmered inside him as he watched the tall, elegantly dressed older woman escape him. She knew where her niece was, and it wasn't Boston. The Lowell women were trying to outmaneuver him, but it wouldn't work. Oh, Eudora was strong, he admitted silently. And stupidly brave. Imagine trying to hide the fact of that telegram from him. *Him*. Who knew everything that happened in his adopted hometown.

Everything, he reminded himself with a surge of renewed fury, but the contents of that telegram. He'd tried to glean the message with his formidable strength, but the protective spell Eudora had woven was simply too strong to be broken that easily.

Which was just another reason why he had to marry Hannah. Once he was joined with the last member of the Lowell family and his talents were merged with hers, he would be so powerful that no one—*no one*—could stand against him.

And he would finally have what he'd come all the

way from England to have—the power he'd always dreamed of.

A flicker of movement caught his eye and he glanced at the Davis house in time to see the edge of the curtains fall back into place behind the front window. Jasper Davis should have had more sense than to let a dog annoy him, Blake told himself and casually lifted one hand.

The window glass shattered inward, shards slicing through the curtains to fly into the room like dozens of razor-sharp knives. Jasper shrieked in pain and Blake smiled.

A punishment delivered. A lesson learned.

Feeling better now, the warlock turned toward the harbor and his waterfront home. Soon, he told himself. The man he had watching Eudora would turn up the information he required—or regret the lack of it. And once Hannah was found, he would put her under lock and key until the Solstice and their wedding.

Strolling the empty streets, he noted with satisfaction the curtains that dropped into place over closed windows as he passed.

Hannah paced the small confines of her bedroom restlessly. Her long white nightgown swished against her shins, tangled with her bare feet. Wrapping her arms around herself, she glanced at Hepzibah, curled up at the foot of the bed.

"Why didn't Eudora tell me?" she asked the little cat and paused as if waiting for an answer.

The animal's eyes widened and a soft mew escaped it.

"Do you think she didn't know?" It was certainly a possibility. After all, as Eudora had explained herself, *nothing* in life was a certainty. Not the crystal. Not even magic. "That must be it," Hannah said, answering her own question.

She stopped beside the short chest of drawers and drummed her fingertips against its top. "How long was he married, I wonder," she said, letting her fingers stray to the silver backed-brush lying on the polished wood surface. She picked it up and absently moved her thumb across its bristles.

Moving to the bed, she took a seat on the edge of the mattress and slowly pulled the brush through the length of her hair, letting the soothing tug and pull ease some of the tension from her body.

Remembering her conversation with Elias, Hannah let her mind settle on the one question the older man couldn't—or wouldn't—answer.

"Does Jonas still love Marie?" she whispered, and hearing the words spoken aloud brought a shiver to her spine and an emptiness to her heart.

Her hands fell to her lap and she cradled the silver brush that had been a gift from Eudora in her palms. Why, she wondered, did the idea that Jonas had been married before, *loved* before, bother her so? An ache built up in her chest, making it hard to draw a breath.

It didn't make sense. She hadn't even known him until little more than a week ago. Of course he'd had a life before she'd entered it. It was only natural.

And yet . . . her mind tried to paint a picture of the mysterious Marie. Was she tall or short? Fair or dark? Fat or thin? How had she died? Did he still mourn her?

Was she a witch?

On that thought, Hannah stood up, letting the hairbrush fall to the floor at her feet. Hepzibah, startled, leaped straight into the air and scuttled off the bed, headed for the not-quite-closed door.

"Probably not," Hannah muttered aloud and began to feel a bit better. Surely if the Mackenzie had been married to a witch, Eudora would have been able to see it in the crystal. "Of course," she said on a relieved sigh. The Mackenzie had been married to an ordinary woman. The spirit of a dead witch would have revealed itself to Eudora's searching eye.

At least in this, then, Hannah told herself, she would

be the first. And the last. She could give him the strength and power that came with her name and the long, illustrious line of her family. Theirs would be a marriage that would blossom with the power of the ancients. A marriage that would tie two old, respected families together and bind them forever.

A joining of two houses that would anchor the Guild and banish Blake Wolcott.

The quiet creak of the door opening caught Hannah's attention. She slanted a look in time to see Hepzibah scoot through the narrow opening and streak into the short, dark hallway. Sighing, Hannah went after her.

"Damn it," Jonas's muttered, disgusted voice floated to her from behind his door as it slowly pushed open under the force of a small, determined cat.

Hannah was just a step or two behind Hepzibah, although she at least knocked perfunctorily before opening the door wider.

Jonas sat in a chair on the far side of the room. A lamp burned brightly on the small round table beside him, throwing golden shadows across his face and highlighting the frown twisting his lips. His bare feet propped up on the footrails of his wide oak bed, he held an open book in his lap. His worn jeans hugged his long legs and his work shirt was unbuttoned and lying open, exposing his tanned, sculpted, *very* muscled chest.

"Oh, my," she murmured as the temperature in the room swiftly rose from chilly to downright steamy. Helplessly, Hannah studied that broad expanse of bronzed skin before finally lifting her gaze to his head, where Hepzibah perched like a queen on her throne. The little white cat's long, fluffy tail hung down along one side of his face, and when it twitched across his nose, Jonas sneezed.

"God bless you."

He breathed slowly, deeply, and Hannah was mesmerized by the rise and fall of that magnificent chest.

Jonas shook his head slightly and Hepzibah slid back

and forth like too much water carried in a shallow pan. He winced tightly before saying, "If this is a blessing, I'd sure as hell hate to see a curse."

"Hepzibah . . ." Hannah's eyes widened as the cat slid precariously to one side of Jonas's skull, its claws scraping frantically for a hold on something. She fought down a smile while she watched Jonas's patient response to the little cat's activities.

A long-suffering expression crossed his face and he winced when Hepzibah's claws dug into his scalp. But he didn't snatch at the animal. He wasn't yelling. He wasn't even angry. And Hannah felt another tug at her heart.

"Would you mind," he asked quietly, obviously trying to hold perfectly still, "peeling her off my head before she digs her claws clean down to what's left of my brain?"

"Oh!" Grinning, she muttered, "I'm sorry," and rushed across the room. She stopped directly in front of him and leaned over to reach for Hepzibah.

Clouds of white cat fur fluttered in his face and dusted daintily against his naked chest. Tiny paws and claws scuttled across the top of his head as the damned cat tried to avoid Hannah's grip. The small, stabbing pains went unnoticed, though, as the sweet, unmistakable scent of lemons washed over him.

The minute she'd walked into his room, his breath had left him in a rush that made his head swim. Standing in the doorway, her long hair loose and falling in a soft wave of curls around her shoulders and across her breasts, she'd looked like the answer to a man's prayers.

Or the beautiful doorway to a hell he didn't care to revisit.

He'd spent too much time thinking about her lately, and to see her here, in his bedroom, a thin nightgown the only thing separating her naked body from his hungry eyes . . . well, this was a temptation he wasn't sure he'd survive.

She leaned in farther across him, trying his patience and testing his self-control. Yards of white cotton covered her nudity, backlit by the lamp at his side. He spotted vaguely teasing shadows. Hints of curves and valleys.

His body tightened in response and he nearly groaned with the effort to keep from grabbing her, pulling her onto his lap, and taking her mouth with his . . . losing himself in the taste of her.

When she grabbed at her cat again, one of Hannah's breasts caressed the side of his face and he instinctively turned into her. Inhaling her scent. Imagining the feel of her flesh beneath his hands, her soft sighs whispering in his ears . . .

"For heaven's sake, Hepzibah, let the man go!"

He felt the removal of every claw and told himself it was just punishment for what he'd been considering. Unfortunately, it wasn't nearly enough to keep him from considering the same damn thing all over again.

"There!" Hannah stood back, triumphant. Her unrepentant cat lay cradled in her arms and for the first time ever, Jonas envied a damned feline.

This was a dangerous path and he knew it. The sooner he got Hannah out of his room, the sooner he'd be able to lie down in his empty bed and groan until morning.

"Thanks," he said gruffly, laying his forgotten book flat on his lap to hide the evidence of his response to her.

"I am sorry," she said with a small shrug. "It's just that Hepzibah's taken a real liking to you."

"My own fault," he said. "Should have fixed my door a long time ago. Never did shut right."

"I could put a spell on it for you," she suggested helpfully. "Of course, I could just try to fix it, but I'm afraid my skills with tools are hardly remarkable."

She plopped herself down on the edge of the bed and

looked to be settling in for a nice long chat, God help him.

"Although," she went on, "if I'm to be honest, my magic skills aren't much better."

"Don't worry about it," he interrupted. "I can fix it myself, without the help of magic." He sure as hell wasn't going to get back into a discussion of witches and warlocks and whatever else was running around in her mind.

"That's very nice of you," Hannah was saying, "to be so understanding. But frankly, I don't understand it myself. At home, my powers were much stronger." She stroked one hand down the length of Hepzibah's back and the cat arched into her touch, much like Jonas had dreams of doing.

He linked his fingers atop the book on his lap.

"I'd hoped," she went on, "that by being around you, my abilities would improve."

His gaze locked on the caressing strokes she gave her cat, Jonas's mind wandered. "Abilities?"

"My witchcraft."

"Uh-huh."

She sniffed. "But . . ." she said, her voice a bit stronger, demanding his attention. He tore his gaze from her fingertips to look into her eyes. "It seems that not only am I not improving, I'm getting worse."

"That's a shame," he said, still not entirely sure what they were talking about.

"Even the potion I mixed up a few days ago . . ." She shook her head in confusion. "It separated when it cooled and it's not supposed to do that."

"Sorry to hear that," he said and managed to keep from asking what kind of potion she'd been mixing. He was sure he didn't want to know. Then what she'd been saying actually sank into his head and, sensing a possible road out of this situation, he said. "Maybe you're wrong about me."

"In what way?" Her brow furrowed slightly, drawing

honey-blond eyebrows together over her eyes.

"If your *powers* are getting worse," he ventured, "maybe I'm not the warlock you think I am."

"Oh," she assured him, shattering his hopes, "there's no mistake. You are the Mackenzie."

Her absolute belief was hard to argue with. But he'd keep trying. He had to, he told himself as her gaze drifted around the room. For his own peace of mind, such as it was.

She gasped suddenly and, releasing Hepzibah, scooted off the edge of the bed, drawing the hem of her nightgown up to her knees. Jonas gritted his teeth and held the book on his lap down tight, as if he expected it to be pushed aside by the force of his body's fierce response to her.

The blasted cat raced to his side. Jonas scowled and surrendered to the inevitable. This time, thankfully, the little animal contented itself with scaling his legs. Jonas shifted his gaze to follow Hannah and told himself not to notice the way her cotton nightgown clung to her thighs with her hurried steps.

Crossing to the chest of drawers in the corner, she picked something off its top and turned to face him. Holding the object up for the light to glitter off its surface, she beamed at him as lamplight flashed and winked off the polished brass.

"Here's your proof," she nearly crowed.

"My belt buckle?" he asked, giving her a look that clearly said she'd lost her mind.

But Hannah was used to that. He still hadn't accepted the truth of his identity, so how could he accept the fact that *she* was a witch? And yet, her fingers curled around the cold metal in her hand. She should have thought of the circlet herself. It was only purest luck that she'd spotted it on his dresser.

Or, she thought, smiling, *destiny*.

"I don't know what you're talking about now, Hannah," he said tightly. "But then, that's nothin' new."

"This," she said, moving to his chair and dropping to her knees beside him. Unlacing his fingers, she turned one of his hands up and placed the circlet in the center of his palm. "This is the Mackenzie brooch," she said, looking deeply into the icy blue of his eyes, willing him to believe her. To trust her.

To *know*.

Instead, she watched as his features tightened. His feet hit the floor and he sat up straight, glaring at her. "How did you know it used to be a brooch?" he demanded. "Nobody knew about it but me. And Elias."

"Where did you get it?" she asked quietly.

His fingers closed over the cold metal protectively. Then he stood up, walked past her, and laid the buckle down where she'd found it. "It was my mother's," he said, running his fingertip gently across the brassy circles. "Elias told me she wore it every day." He inhaled sharply. "My father gave it to her—"

"When they were married." Hannah finished for him and stood up, turning to face him.

"Good guess." His expression blank, he refused to give an inch.

She shook her head and smiled at him, hoping to ease the storm in his eyes. "It wasn't a guess, Jonas. Where I come from, everyone knows the story behind that circlet."

"And why's that?" His voice sounded raw with choked emotion.

She walked to his side slowly and stopped in front of him. Her gaze dropped briefly to the gleaming belt buckle. The brassy gold metal shone in the lamplight, defining each of the three, intertwined circles. Nicks and scratches pitted its surface, attesting to the centuries it had survived.

Her eyes misted at the thought. Since the time of the Druids, his family had loved and died and loved again. She wanted him to know the pride she felt in her own heritage. She wanted him to remember all of the Mackenzies who had come before him. All of the faceless people through the ages who had formed him, made him the warlock he was today.

As her family, the Lowells, had survived and prospered, so had his. He had the right to know who he was and to take pride in that knowledge.

Turning back to him, she lifted her chin and looked up into his eyes. "That brooch," she said quietly, "has been passed down from generation to generation in your family. Since the first Druid warlock fashioned it as a gift for his betrothed, it's been given by the Mackenzie to the woman he's chosen for his wife. The brass circlet has belonged to the hereditary head of the Guild—the Mackenzie—for centuries."

He sucked in a gulp of air and shifted his gaze between her and the buckle and back again. The clear color of his eyes darkened as a quick succession of expressions darted across his features. Outrage, confusion, anger, and briefly she thought she recognized fear. And then all emotion was gone from his face and he met her gaze with a studied veil of blank indifference.

But her moment had come and she wouldn't be ignored.

Hannah reached up and laid both palms against his chest, feeling the heat of his body and the warmth of his banked power enter her, surge through her blood, and pool at her center. The time had come. At last. A shiver of anticipation rippled along her spine.

She would need every ounce of courage she'd ever possessed to do what she must do next. A blush stole over her, but she set the warm tide of embarrassment aside. This was not the moment for modesty. It was, instead, the moment to seal their bond and take the first steps into their destiny.

"And now," she said, forcing the words from a suddenly tight throat, "the circlet belongs to *you*. The Mackenzie."

A curl of uneasiness unwound in the pit of Jonas's

stomach. Memory whispered at the edges of his mind. His brain filled with images—half-formed, blurred shapes and shadows of things and people he didn't know. Didn't remember.

But this was worse than anything he'd ever experienced before. Because now he sensed . . . he *felt* . . . that he should know these things. These people.

He groaned tightly and let his head fall back on his neck. It wasn't true. None of it. And she had no business trying to make it real.

"In time, we will give it to our son," she said, "when he's chosen his mate."

Son? Jonas blinked and realized she'd moved away from him toward the bed. She stopped at the edge of the wide oak frame and turned to face him.

"Our *son*?" he heard himself ask and was surprised to find that his voice worked.

"Yes," she said and gave him a smile that rocked him to his heels. Still reeling from everything she'd said already, he barely understood her now as words tumbled from her mouth in a rush of nervousness.

In the soft lamplight, he saw deep pink color flood her cheeks before she dipped her head momentarily. She seemed to gather her strength before lifting her chin and looking at him again. Swallowing heavily, she started talking.

"I'll help you, Jonas. I'll help you remember who you are and what you come from." Her hands twisted together at her waist and even from this distance he saw her knuckles whiten. "When our first son is born, he'll be a strong warlock, in heart and power. He'll care for the sisters and brothers we give him, Mackenzie. The joining of our families will strengthen the Guild for years to come." She gave him a tremulous smile and took a deep, steadying breath before she began lifting her nightgown up her legs. "Of course"—she kept talking, nerves making her words tumble from her mouth in a stream of sound—"we'll have to be married right away, but there's no time like the present to start making our first child."

"First child?" he muttered, his gaze locked on the expanding length of creamy white skin exposed to him as she drew her nightgown higher and higher. Ankles, shins, knees, thighs. His breath came hard and fast. His pulse pounded in his head. He felt the roaring of his blood and his body thickened and hardened until he thought he might burst.

"You are the Mackenzie, after all," she was saying, "so I'm sure if you concentrate all of your will, you should be able to give me a baby tonight." She paused to sigh, with the hem of her nightgown just below the apex of her thighs.

Palms damp, mouth dry, Jonas watched her, unable to move.

"I supose you can tell I'm a little nervous," she said softly. "But this is my destiny. And yours. It's why I'm here. With you."

"Uh-huh."

"A baby, Jonas," she went on, her voice dreamy now, "will seal our joining. Won't it be wonderful? Won't we have a splendid life together?" Humming slightly to herself, as if to bolster her courage, she pulled on the nightgown and he caught a heart-stopping look at the soft, golden curls that lay at the base of her abdomen.

He sucked in air like a dying man.

And still she went on, pulling the fabric up and up and over her head. She shook her hair back from her face as she dropped the nightgown and stood before him as naked as the day she was born.

Stunned speechless, Jonas nonetheless took advantage of the moment to admire her shapely body. Narrow waist, rounded hips, straight, slim legs, and full, luscious breasts topped by pale pink nipples, already erect and calling to him.

"I'm ready, Mackenzie," she whispered and crossed

her arms over the breasts his hands itched to touch, caress.

"Ready?" He reached up and shoved both hands through his hair as she jumped up onto the mattress and edged herself into the exact center of the bed.

From somewhere in the shadows, Hepzibah yowled.

"Ready for what?" he asked, squeezing the words past the knot in his throat.

"To be taken," she said, as if he should have known that already. Then she settled her head onto one of his pillows.

Jonas groaned. Just when he thought she couldn't surprise him again, she managed to make a liar out of him. Heart pounding, body hard and tight, he stared at the tiny woman in his bed.

She looked like a picture he'd seen once of a fancy statue laying atop a stone tomb. Her legs were locked together as if she'd been tied up, her arms crisscrossed her breasts, her eyes were closed, and her lips pursed as if she'd been sucking on something sour.

Like a damn sacrifice, he thought and felt the mad rush of desire that had been crowding him ebb just a little. Then snippets of what she'd been saying began to rise up in his mind and Jonas told himself that he had to start paying closer attention when she talked.

Did she really believe that telling him a story about his belt buckle was going to change his mind about marriage?

Turning, he walked across the room and snatched up his boots. The damn cat scuttled out from behind a chair and he gave it a look that should have scalded it.

"Jonas?"

He didn't look at her. Didn't trust himself to be able to leave if he did. "Go to bed, Hannah."

"I am in bed."

"I mean *your* bed." He tugged his boots on, stamping into them.

The mattress creaked and groaned as she sat up.

Don't look, he told himself firmly and grabbed his hat.

"But Jonas," she said, clearly confused, "I'm ready."

And so was he. That was the problem. He buttoned his shirt, stuffed the tails into the waistband of his jeans.

"Hannah . . ."

All right, one last look. He spun around to face her and regretted it almost instantly. Her creamy skin seemed to glow in the lamplight. Her hair fell around her shoulders and hid her breasts, with only the rigid pink tips peeking from behind that golden, shimmering curtain.

But it was her eyes that nearly undid him. Wide and miserable and disappointed, they stared at him, tugging at what used to be his soul.

"I am *not* going to marry you, Hannah," he said, slowly, carefully. Then, taking one step closer to the bed, he grabbed his jacket off the bedpost and draped it across her, covering her from chest to thigh. His breath came a little easier even as he told himself he'd be damn cold outside without that jacket. Still, better she wear it now. Protect them both from something far worse than the cold.

She clutched at his coat, holding it in front of her, and he thanked her silently for it.

Proud of himself for being able to resist the tempting package she made, he said, "Don't get me wrong. I want nothing more than to make love to you right now. It's taking everything in me to resist the urge."

She smiled, but her eyes still looked wounded. "Don't resist, Jonas," she said softly. "This was meant."

Meant. Destiny. Witchcraft.

His brain raced with everything she'd told him. Everything his gut told him was true and his brain insisted was a lie.

Hannah swung her legs off the bed and stood up in front of him. Her eyes met his as she let the jacket drop to the floor. He groaned tightly and watched a slow rush of color warm her cheeks.

"*We* are meant," she said.

Good intentions or no, he was only human.

Reaching out, he drew her to him, wrapped his arms around her, and lowered his mouth to hers. She sighed as their lips met and he took her breath inside him. This kiss was deeper, more intimate than that first brief meeting of lips. But like then, a flash of white-hot energy erupted between them, sizzling through his veins, humming across his brain. Something inside him trembled as awareness fluttered to the surface of his mind. And then it was gone and there was only this moment. His hands smoothed up and down her spine, learning her curves, feeling the silky softness of her skin.

She leaned into him and when he parted her lips with his tongue, she gasped quietly and trembled against him. Another, stronger shimmer of something he'd never experienced before shot through him and Jonas's soul shook. He wanted to lose himself in her. Dive into her sweetness and submerge himself in the innocence he saw shining inside her.

Yet he realized that if he did, he might stay lost in her forever. Reluctantly, acting against every instinct he possessed, he drew back, breaking their kiss and the strange, almost electrical thread joining them together.

"Jonas?" she whispered.

He didn't . . . couldn't answer. Turning around, he left her, walked through the house and out into the cold, clear—*empty* night.

Chapter nine

The cold night air hit him with a fisted punch.

He sucked in a gulp of the frosty night and hoped the chill would cool the fire in his blood. But somehow, he doubted it.

Jamming his hands into his jeans pockets, Jonas jumped off the back steps and hurried across the ranch yard to the barn. Visions of Hannah dashed through his mind, her bare skin, creamy in the lamplight. Her lips, soft and full and eager beneath his. The brush of her breath against his cheek, the feel of her body beneath his hands. Her eyes, wide and green, shining with passion as she talked about his future—*their* future.

"Married," he whispered, disgusted. "Not me. Not again."

Never again would he be responsible for someone else's life. Happiness. The burden of that one miserable failure had weighed him down for ten years. He couldn't imagine another such burden being heaped on his shoulders.

He yanked the double doors open and stepped into the shadowy barn. Instantly, the scent of horses, straw, and weathered wood invaded him, making his breath come easier.

His bootsteps echoed eerily as he walked down the

center aisle to the stall at the end. The big black horse whinnied a greeting, lifted its head, and stretched out its nose toward him.

"Hope you're feeling up to riding night herd," Jonas told the animal as he ran a still-shaking hand over the horse's jaw and neck. "I need to get out of that damned house."

"Run you out, did she?" a voice from behind him asked in a tone half colored with subdued laughter.

Scowling, Jonas looked the horse in the eye and muttered, "You could have warned me."

The stallion shook its head, sending a long, black mane flying.

"So, what'd she do now?" Elias asked as he stepped out of the stall across the aisle and latched the half door behind him.

Instead of answering, Jonas looked past the older man to the pregnant mare Elias had been checking on. "She all right? Her leg healing?"

Elias tossed a glance at the gray. "She's fine. I was just feelin' a bit restless. Thought I'd sit with her awhile." Turning his gaze back to Jonas, he asked, "What're you up to?"

With only the barest hint of moonlight entering the barn, Jonas saw his old friend as a silhouetted shadow against the darker blackness behind him. "Couldn't sleep. Figured I'd spell Billy on night herd."

"Uh-huh."

Jonas grimaced tightly and turned to snatch the saddle blanket off the stall wall. As he spread it over the horse's back and smoothed out wrinkles, Elias went on.

"Seems a mite cold out tonight to be ridin' without a jacket."

Jonas closed his eyes briefly, trying not to remember the sound of that jacket dropping to the floor at Hannah's bare feet. "I'll take Billy's when I send him in."

The older man chuckled, a harsh, grating sound in the stillness. "She did run you out, didn't she?"

"Nobody runs me out of my own house, you old coot."

"So what'd she do?" Elias prompted, obviously not convinced.

Jonas lifted his saddle and set it down on the black's back. Leaning his forearms on the worn leather, he swiveled his head to look at the man who'd raised him.

"She started talking about getting married. Having babies, for Christ's sake." He wasn't about to tell the other man about Hannah undressing and laying herself down across the bed. Some things a man just didn't talk about.

"Ah . . ." Elias stepped closer to the stall and leaned against the door.

A world of understanding was contained in that heavy sigh and for the first time that night, Jonas started to relax. Elias knew. He'd been a witness to that long-ago night. He knew why Jonas had closed himself off from everything that most men wanted and worked toward.

The tightness in his chest eased a bit. Then the memory of Hannah's face swam in front of him again and his insides coiled up like an overwound watch spring. Gritting his teeth, he flipped the stirrup up and across the saddle. Bending down, he grabbed the cinch strap and threaded it through the buckle.

"I never should have hired her," he said with a shake of his head. "I knew she was trouble the minute I saw her." He yanked on the strap one more time, then secured it and set the stirrup back into place. Leaning both elbows on the saddle seat, he scrubbed his face with his hands. "Damn it, I knew I'd regret it and I hired her anyway."

"You needed her."

Jonas heard the shrug in the man's voice and, turning his head to look at him, said, "I needed her like a bullet to the brain."

"She's a good cook."

"Yeah," he admitted.

"Hard worker, too," Elias went on. "That girl's goin' at a full gallop all day long."

True. Hannah did her share of work and more. The whole damn ranch had been running better since her arrival. The men worked harder because their bellies were satisfied. The ranch yard was cleaned up, laundry done, and he was even getting used to the fresh wild-flowers she left all over the house.

She'd put her stamp on his house and she'd only been there a couple of weeks, God help him.

"I've got no complaint with her work. It's the rest."

"What rest?"

The haunting of his dreams. The unsettling of his soul. The unleashed snatches of the past that seemed to dog his every footstep here lately.

"So," Elias said softly, "what you don't like is her making you think about living again."

"What?" He stared into the blackness, but Elias's gray eyes were lost in the shadows.

"This talk of marriage and children," the man said quietly, "it's makin' you think. Remember."

"Hell, I don't need somebody to remind me," Jonas muttered thickly. "How the hell could I forget?"

"It was a long time ago," Elias said.

"Ten years." Years filled with regret and thoughts of what might have been.

"Maybe it's time you let it go."

"And how do I do that?" he asked, weariness tinging his voice.

"By livin'."

A flash of anger shot through him and was gone again. "You were there, old man. You saw it. You saw her." His voice shook and he cleared his throat delib-erately. "I can't just pretend it didn't happen."

"No one said you had to," Elias said.

"You just said—"

"I said it's time to leave the past in the past." Elias straightened up and shuffled his feet on the straw-littered dirt. "It's beyond time. What's done is done. There's no changin' it."

"Don't you think I know that?" Jonas nearly shouted and instantly lowered his voice again as the black horse sidestepped anxiously and rolled its brown eyes. "Hell, if I could change it, I'd have done it that night."

A long pause stretched out between them. Just when Jonas was hoping Elias would leave it lay, the older man spoke again.

"She would have loved this, y'know."

His fingers tightened around the lip of the saddle, fingernails digging into the worn, buttersoft leather. "What?"

"You bein' miserable. You sufferin' for the rest of your life."

A stab of pain sliced at him and he wanted to argue with the man he thought of as a father. But he couldn't do it. Maybe time hadn't let him forget his failures, but it had sure enough defined the truth about the woman he'd married so long ago.

Back then, he'd been young enough to be taken in by a sweet smile and the promise of heaven on a mattress. But that heaven had become a hell on their wedding night, when his bride had 'done her Christian duty' with a stoic forbearance that still made him shiver to think about it.

But Elias didn't know any of that. What he referred to was the crying, the complaining, the dissatisfaction that had driven Marie to make everyone's life miserable.

"It wasn't all her fault." He felt compelled to defend her, even now. She'd been his wife and he'd failed her. If he'd been a better husband, she wouldn't have been so unhappy. "She was young."

"So were you."

"It's different for a man."

Elias spat. "Jesus, boy. You think all women are like that? Take a look around you." He rubbed one hand across the top of his skull. "Most women out here are

like Hannah. The kind to stand beside their men. Shootin', workin', livin', and dyin'. Just because you picked
the wrong one the first time don't mean you'd do it
again."

Something inside him snapped. "Why are we always
talkin' about me? If you think so highly of marriage,
how come you never got hitched yourself?"

"It wasn't for lack of tryin'!" Elias said just as angrily. "But I let her slip away—just like you're fixin' to
do with Hannah."

Stunned, Jonas stared at him. He'd known the man
all his life and never once had Elias mentioned a lost
love. His whole world was spinning. Nothing was the
same as it had been only a couple of weeks ago. Even
the man he'd thought he knew better than anyone else
had secrets. Jesus. Couldn't he count on anything? "You
never said anything about a woman."

"No point in talkin'—*thinkin'*—" he added meaning-
fully. "about what's done and gone. Like I been sayin'."

But Jonas wouldn't be diverted back to talk of Marie.
Not before he got a few answers. "What happened? Why
didn't you marry her?"

"Was a long time ago," Elias said, his voice quiet
now, as shadow-filled as the barn. He sighed and added,
"Nearly thirty years now. Hard to believe."

He would have been about thirty-five then, Jonas
thought and tried to imagine Elias young and in love.

"Met her on a ship."

"A *ship*?" Jesus, what else didn't he know about the
man?

Elias chuckled. "Don't sound so surprised. I was workin' for a ranch in Texas and the boss shipped a few
dozen head of longhorns to England. I was one of the
cowboys that went along. *She* was a passenger, too." His
voice softened in memory and even in the dim light,
Jonas saw his friend's expression gentle. "Pretty thing,"
he was saying. "Tall and slim, with a smile that lit up
all the dark spots inside me the first time I saw it."

Caught by the other man's story, Jonas silently admitted he'd felt the same way about Hannah the first time he'd laid eyes on her.

"Anyway," Elias went on, his voice rougher now as he eased further away from the memories, "we fell in love." He shook his head as if he still couldn't believe that she'd loved him. "A cowboy and a beautiful lady. Oh, I knew I wasn't good enough for her . . . but no other man could have loved her more."

Jonas wanted to say that no woman could have asked for a better man than Elias, but instead he said, "What went wrong?"

"We were gonna elope our first night in England, since her pa was dead set against her 'wastin' ' her life on a cowboy. Figured we'd just do the deed and then her pa would have to come around." He dipped one hand into his pocket and pulled out a small gold watch that Jonas had often admired. Elias smiled down at the timepiece cradled in the palm of his hand. "She gave me her watch. Said this was one night I *couldn't* be late." His thumb smoothed across the intricately carved metal. "I was on time," he mused, more to himself than to Jonas. "But she didn't come. I waited most of the night. Half out of my mind with worry, wonderin' where she was . . . *how* she was. Then, around dawn, her pa showed up, told me he'd already sent her home and that I should just forget about her."

"Bastard. Didn't you follow her?" Jonas asked, completely caught up in the story.

"Course I did." Elias snapped. "I ain't so quick to give up on a chance at love as you."

Jonas scowled at him, but kept quiet.

Elias tucked the watch back into his pocket, then scraped one hand across his jaw. "I was stuck in England another month, workin'. When I got home, I looked for her everywhere." He shook his head in remembered frustration. "Never did find a trace of her. It was like she disappeared."

Jonas felt the regret in his old friend and was sorry for it. Strange how you could spend your whole life with a person and never really know all his secrets. Still, he pointed out, "So after you lost her, you never tried marrying again?"

Elias glared at him, clearly understanding Jonas's meaning. "It ain't the same thing at all."

"What's different about it?"

"I loved her. She loved me."

Jonas sucked in a gulp of air and shifted position uneasily. "I loved Marie."

"Maybe," the older man agreed. "Leastways, you tell yourself now you did. But did she love you?"

"Why the hell else would she marry me?" he demanded and fitted the bridle over the horse's head. Should have known better than to feel sympathy for the old coot. Hell, he'd probably only told Jonas that story so he could use it against him. Damn it, he didn't want to talk about this. But he knew that wouldn't stop Elias.

"Because she knew her pa would hate it," he said softly.

The simple words hit him like a solid fist.

Jonas had thought the same thing over the years. Wondered if Marie's easy acceptance of him had had more to do with anger at her father's remarriage than it did with her undying love for him.

"She wasn't interested in being your wife," Elias went on. "She only wanted to make her pa miserable and she used you to do it."

True, his mind screamed, but Jonas ignored the voice inside. If that had been Marie's plan, Lord knew she'd paid for it in the end. Shaking his head slowly, he gathered the reins in one hand and turned to face Elias again.

"It doesn't matter," he said. "Whatever Marie was, she was my wife and I failed her. Me. I wasn't there when she needed me most." His teeth ground together. "And *that's* why I won't marry again."

Elias grunted, disgusted. "So you're just gonna let Hannah walk out of your life?"

Jonas swallowed heavily. "She's not in my life."

"If you really believe that, you're a damn fool, boy."

"That's been said before," Jonas told him and swung onto the horse, gathering the reins up in his left hand. Giving the horse a nudge with his heels, Jonas left the barn and headed for the herd, hoping for a little peace.

Creekford

Eudora gripped the handle of her carpetbag and stepped into the night. Closing her front door behind her, she turned and looked into the darkness surrounding her little house.

Moon-cast shadows danced and writhed along the grass bordering the road that led to town. Tree limbs waving in the wind outlined themselves against the starstudded sky, looking like black, thorny arms reaching for her. Their leaves rustled like dry paper and the soft patter of a nearby creek had the sound of low-pitched voices whispering.

She inhaled sharply and tried to ignore the flutter of nerves swirling in the pit of her stomach. But between worry over Hannah and Wolcott and the Mackenzie, and now a train trip to a place she'd never been before . . . well, it was hopeless. It was her own fault. She should have left Creekford more. Seen some of the world. Instead, she'd lived her entire life within the safe boundaries of a town full of witches. Well, but for that one trip to Europe.

Still, it wasn't really the traveling that worried her.

It was her destination . . . and what she might find.

Eudora stared into the darkness and wondered as she had so many times over the years. Old regrets shimmered through her and she wished, not for the first time, that she'd been able to use the crystal on her own behalf.

But seeing into her own future was impossible, and looking into her past, futile.

She sniffed, tightened her grip on the carpetbag, and resolved to keep her mind on the matters at hand. From the corner of her eye, she glanced at the ivy-covered fence to her left. Someone was there. She felt his presence as surely as she could feel her own heartbeat.

Her fingers squeezed the worn leather strap in her hand. Blake Wolcott's man was still watching her, then. Good. A small, tight smile curved her lips briefly as she took the porch steps and moved onto the road. She walked quickly, her long, even strides carrying her toward the tiny train station outside town.

She walked surely, following the silvery path of moonlight. Let her watcher stumble and crash his way blindly through the darkened woods. Let him chase after her as she led him in circles around the country. The longer Wolcott and his minion were concerned with her, the more time Hannah would have to do what she must.

One Week Later

Hannah still felt the sting of rejection.

Oh, she'd gone about her business, cleaning, cooking, talking with the men as they streamed in and out of her kitchen looking for coffee or cookies. She'd already planned what she would cook for the first day of the roundup, due to start in less than a week. And every night, she attempted new spells, designed to weaken Jonas's ability to resist her.

Unfortunately, none of them seemed to be working.

A sudden hot wash of tears swam in her eyes and she blinked them back furiously. She would not give in to tears, despite the temptation.

She'd offered herself to him. Stood before him *naked,* for heaven's sake. He'd kissed her and made her feel all sorts of things she'd never imagined. He'd touched her and shared the strength of his power. Her hands gripped

the edge of the kitchen table and squeezed tightly as a
rush of embarrassed heat swamped her. If he could kiss
her and walk away from her in that situation, what
chance of success did her latest plan have?

"I have to try, though," she said, gritting her teeth
and lifting her chin. Glancing at Hepzibah, she asked,
"How do I look?" When the little cat only stared at her,
Hannah sighed and reached up to anxiously pat at her
hair. "It will work, you'll see," she muttered and wasn't
sure if she was trying to convince Hepzibah or herself.

Turning to the window that overlooked the ranch
yard, Hannah stared out at the lightening darkness.
Dawn was still an hour or more away. Stars shone
faintly in the sky and the moon hung low and looked
close enough to touch.

Even the men in the bunkhouse hadn't stirred yet.
But Jonas was awake, she knew. As he had all week, he
was up and moving long before anyone else. He'd
avoided her neatly every morning and surrounded himself with others during the day. At night, he'd retreated
to his bedroom, closing a now-secure door.

This was her first chance to talk to him alone since
the night he'd rushed out of his room as if demons were
on his heels. But she was ready. Memories of her day
in town and the woman she'd seen filled her mind, re-
storing her confidence. Hannah'd decided that what had
been lacking between she and Jonas was seduction. And
now that she'd figured out how to seduce the Mackenzie,
everything else would fall into place.

He did want her. Hadn't he said so?

But she couldn't wait much longer. The Solstice was
almost upon them. They had to be joined. They had to
have found each other before then.

For everyone's sake.

Footsteps in the main room alerted her to his presence. Breathing deeply to quiet the butterflies in her
stomach, she turned in time to flash him a smile and see
his eyes narrow as he looked at her.

"Good morning," she said and walked past him slowly, headed for the stove. Remembering the woman she'd seen in town and how the men had stumbled over each other to be near her, Hannah desperately wished she owned a red dress that sparkled. Her blue and white calico hardly seemed appropriate to the task. Deliberately, though, she straightened her spine, pushed out her chest, and let her hips sway from side to side as she moved at a snail's pace. She wanted to give him plenty of time to notice the change in her. To be seduced by her.

"Did you sleep well, Mackenzie?" she asked and filled a cup with thick black coffee.

"What the hell . . . ?"

She turned around, offered him the cup, and, hiding a satisfied smile, dipped her head, giving him an excellent view of her hair.

Feathers.

Her head was covered in small white feathers.

Jonas stared at her, amazed. Blond hair piled high on her head, the tight rolls and ringlets she'd arranged so carefully were dotted with feathers sticking up and out at odd angles.

She turned and sashayed across the kitchen, swinging her hips wildly from side to side, and bunches of feathers flew off her head and swirled in her passing like a small snowstorm.

As he watched, dumbfounded, his fingers curled around the cup of coffee and he took a quick sip, burning his tongue and scalding his throat. A moment later, though, he grimaced tightly and stuck his fingers in his mouth, pulling out a limp, wet feather.

The damn things were all over the place, wafting in the air, settling in his coffee, and dotting the surface of the fresh bread she'd just pulled from the oven.

The woman was a constant surprise.

Helplessly, he shook his head and heard himself ask, "What are you doing?"

She turned again and, smiling, headed straight for him, laying down yet another trail of white. "I'm seducing you," she said and stepped up close to him.

Seducing him? Hell, she did that just by entering a room.

"With feathers?" he managed to ask around the sudden knot in his throat.

Her smile widened. "You noticed."

"Hard not to," he pointed out. "Like it's snowing in here."

She patted her hair, sending a puff of feathers flying high over her head.

The scent of lemon surrounded him. Memories of that night in his room crashed down around him, strangling him. A week it had been. The longest week of his life. He kept waiting for the mental image of her, naked in his bed, to fade a bit. To give him peace.

Instead, each day the images were clearer, stronger, harder to ignore.

"Jonas," she repeated, looking up at him from beneath lowered lashes. "I've been thinking about the kiss you gave me that night . . ."

His long-suffering body tightened instantly and he knew another uncomfortable day in the saddle was stretching out in front of him.

"Hannah," he said tightly, "Now's not the time."

"And I'd like another kiss, please," she said as if he hadn't spoken. Then she tipped her head back, closed her eyes, and pursed her lips.

Ah, damn it.

Jonas smiled softly, letting his gaze sweep across her features. What was it about this woman that touched him in so many ways? Innocence, surely. But there was so much more to her than that. Clearly unused to ranch living, she'd slipped into the life here and made herself so much a part of the place that Jonas couldn't imagine his home without her. Couldn't imagine spending a day not thinking of her. Lifting one hand, he grazed the tips of his fingers along her jaw and caught his breath when she turned her face into his touch.

So easy. So . . . *right*.

Her eyes opened. Dazzling green. Gazes locked, they stared at each other for a long, breathless minute. Then she asked, "Aren't you going to kiss me?"

He wanted to so badly he could already taste her. And realizing that made him see that she'd already come to mean too much to him. He couldn't risk letting her mean more. "No, ma'am, I'm not."

The disappointment in her eyes twisted inside him. Damn her for making him feel things again. Damn her for smiling. For having eyes the color of spring grass. For smelling like lemons. For coming into his life and throwing everything he'd ever known upside down.

And mostly, damn her for making him want her.

Need her.

His hand dropped to his side. Setting the coffee cup down, he turned for the door. "I've got work, Hannah."

"You're leaving again?" she asked, following him to the door. "Without even a kiss this time?"

He stopped, his fingers curled around the doorknob. Glancing back at her over his shoulder, he said softly, "If I kiss you again, Hannah, it won't end there."

She touched him. Her hand lay atop his forearm and the slight brush of her fingertips sent warmth scattering through him. "I don't want it to end," she said.

"And I can't let it begin," he told her softly, then stepped outside and closed the door behind him.

Behind him, she kicked the door, then yelped with the pain before muttering, "But I'm wearing feathers!"

He glanced over his shoulder and smiled. At least she was mad, not hurt.

Shaking his head, he jumped off the back step and into the dirt, idly brushing feathers off his shirt. Feathers. What had she been trying to do with feathers? Smiling to himself, he realized that since Hannah's arrival, he'd been doing a lot of grinning. And yelling. And thinking. More than he had in ten years. Maybe Elias was right. Maybe he didn't like the fact that Hannah Lowell was making him live again whether he wanted to or not.

But *feathers*? And where'd she get them?

As he walked into the cool, shadowy barn, that question was answered.

Clucking in outrage, a flock of hens scuttled past him in the dark. Each of them sported a plucked-pink, nearly naked behind.

Jonas laughed out loud for the first time in too long.

"The pen's ready, boss."

Jonas drew his mind away from the thought of Hannah covered in feathers and concentrated instead on the branding pens in front of him. Two small enclosures, side by side, with a narrow opening on each end and fire pits already stacked with wood and kindling, ready for the first match.

He nodded thoughtfully as his gaze moved over the work done by his crew and imagined the scene as it would be soon, when the ranchers came together to separate and brand their herds.

"You want me to ride out and help Stretch with the last of the gather?" Billy asked as he walked to his horse, tethered to the top rail of the branding pen.

"Yeah," Jonas said. "The south pastures clear?"

"Finished yesterday," the young cowhand assured him. "Got some fine spring calves in that bunch, boss."

"Good." This was what was important, he reminded himself, dismissing thoughts of Hannah. This ranch. The cattle. The future he would build for himself with his bare hands.

Witchcraft, warlocks, and green-eyed blonds to the contrary, in the West, a man was what he made of himself.

"You and the boys finish the gather and I'll see you back at the house."

Through eyes gritty with a lack of sleep, Jonas watched the younger man wheel his horse around and take off across the pasture like the hounds of hell were after him.

He squinted into the late morning sun, letting his gaze rake over the herd and the men riding guard over them. Yanking off his hat, he wiped his forehead with the sleeve of his shirt, then resettled the hat low enough to keep the sun from streaming into his eyes.

Sleep.

That's all he needed.

Hell, since that night Hannah had stretched out across his bed, he'd been haunted by so many wild, vivid dreams, he was willing to bet he hadn't had more than an hour or two of sleep altogether.

And it wasn't just Hannah's face and form invading his nights. With her story about his belt buckle, she'd opened a closed door in his mind. And once opened, visions, images raced each other through his dreams, each fighting to be recognized at last.

Scowling, he tried to recall them now and only half succeeded. Snatched glimpses of faces, people he didn't know, places he'd never been. And sometimes, he even thought he heard whispered voices chanting in a language he'd never heard before.

Warlock.

Something inside him tightened, hardened. It wasn't possible, he told himself. There were no such things as witches, haunts, and spooks. And he was too damned old to be swayed by ghost stories, no matter how well told.

But he had to wonder, if Hannah was lying, how had she known about the belt buckle? How had she known it was his mother's?

"Crazy," he muttered thickly and tightened his grip on the reins. Kneeing his horse, he started around the edges of the herd, trying to concentrate on the feel of the wind against his face, the sun on the trees, the distracted lowing of the cattle.

But his brain wouldn't be appeased that quickly. He remembered the fight in the bar and how the gambler's gun had misfired . . . right after Jonas had wished it to be so.

What were the odds, he asked himself, that a gun wouldn't shoot when the trigger was pulled? With a pepperbox, he argued silently, pretty damn good. Those little guns had never been reliable. And yet . . .

"Damn it," he swore viciously at the swirling thoughts in his head. It was all nonsense. Caused by a tiny woman who looked sane and beautiful but was obviously as wild-brained as a horse on locoweed.

If something inside him shivered with anticipation, he ignored it.

Chapter ten

Somewhere in Indiana a Week Later

After a week on the train, Eudora was tired to the bone.

Her clothes were sooty, her silvery hair drooped, and the tiny pink net veil on her hat was smudged and torn.

She turned her face toward the window and watched as the train pulled into the latest station. They all looked alike, she'd noticed. Small clapboard rooms where the station master reigned over his kingdom, and a long, wooden platform with benches placed here and there so waiting passengers could get used to the feeling of a hard, uncomfortable seat before actually boarding the train.

She smiled to herself, picked up her purse, and as usual headed for the doorway at the end of the car. At every stop, Eudora left the train to wander the platform, sometimes buying fresh fruit from an enterprising farmer. But mostly she did it to keep the man following her on his toes.

Approaching the station master's office, she picked up several train schedules and idly thumbed through them.

"Can I help you, lady?" The man behind the counter asked, leaning toward her.

She smiled into brown eyes hidden behind spectacles in thin wire frames. "Thank you, no," she said and threw a glance from the corner of her eye toward the end of the platform.

There he was. Ed Thistlewaite. A slight frown turned her lips. Balding, overweight, he was an instinctive bully who lacked the courage to back his temperament. An unremarkable warlock from an undistinguished family, poor Ed had convinced himself that by becoming one of Blake Wolcott's minions, he himself attained a measure of respect.

Now that she was sure he'd had to disembark and walk around, something Ed avoided doing whenever possible, Eudora reboarded the train. If she was going to be followed, then she would make sure the man following her regretted ever taking the assignment.

Once in her seat again, Eudora picked up her knitting and ducked her head. Winded, Ed huffed and puffed his way down the aisle, holding a newspaper in front of his face in a futile attempt to keep his prey from recognizing him.

As the train chugged out of the station, she lifted her gaze to the trees and farmland passing by. Another week, she told herself grimly. She could stay on the train and travel her roundabout route for another week—two at best. That was all the time she could give the girl. And once Eudora arrived in Wyoming, she knew Ed would send a telegram to Blake, assuring *his* quick arrival.

A pang of worry ricocheted through her, but she fought it down. The Mackenzie would keep Hannah safe, she told herself. And Eudora would be there as well, to add her own power to the confrontation she knew was coming. But everything would be so much easier if only the two young people could be married when Blake Wolcott faced them.

"Hurry, Hannah," she whispered to the rhythm of the train's steel wheels on the rails. "Time is running out."

*   *   *

The first week of roundup passed in a whirl of activity. Hannah had never been so busy in her life.

Streams of people crowded the ranch every day. The other ranchers' families were there and the men who worked for them, of course. But she'd been surprised to see that several of the townspeople turned out as well, making the roundup more of a community affair.

The work lasted from sunup to sundown. The cowhands labored on the range, driving the cattle, separating the different ranchers' beasts, and then giving matching brands to the spring calves found with their mothers.

Jonas worked every bit as hard as his men and had even taken to sleeping in shifts with them out on the open range. So Hannah had had to content herself with seeing him only when crowds of people surrounded them. There'd been no time to talk. No chance for her to try her hand at seduction again—though the failure of the feathers still rankled enough so that she wasn't sure what she'd try even if she had the opportunity.

All she was sure of was that time was passing. Too quickly. Precious time that should have been spent in learning about each other . . . strengthening their bond . . . preparing for the confrontation with Blake Wolcott. Because, whether Jonas wanted to acknowledge it or not, that confrontation *would* come. Wolcott's only goal in life was to become the most powerful warlock in the country. And to do that, he needed to marry Hannah— claiming her hereditary powers—and eventually destroy Jonas.

He wouldn't stop until both goals were met.

She shivered, forcing thoughts of Blake from her mind as she drove the buckboard to the edge of the crowd surrounding the branding pens. Setting the brake, she tied the reins off on the stiff wooden handle and let her gaze move over the scene in front of her.

Sunshine spilled over the range. The distant mountains looked stark against the blue sky. Shouts from the gathered crowd almost drowned out the constant lowing of the cattle. Dust rose up from the milling herd like a small dirt-brown fog, coating the men in a layer of dirt that clung to clothes and skin.

Hannah sat on the bench seat, able to see over the heads of the people into the branding pen where the men worked feverishly in the noonday sun. The fires burned hot, with fresh wood being added continuously. Towers of black smoke twisted in the air before scuttling skyward. Several branding irons, their heads glowing red with heat, jutted out from the flames like spokes on a wagon wheel.

She knew she should be unloading the food she'd brought out in the bed of the buckboard, but she was drawn to the excitement rippling through the air. It was thrilling, she admitted silently. The crush of people. The heat. The noise.

Her gaze raked the faces of the ranchers standing on the edges of the pen, looking for Jonas. But he wasn't with them. Nodding to herself, she realized that he would never be a man to sit on the sidelines while other men did the hard work.

She shifted her gaze to the crowd of people surrounding the branding pens and studied the faces until she found him. A wide smile on his face, he picked up Davey Simpson, a five-year-old son of one of their neighbors, and plunked the boy down onto the top rail of the fence, where he would have an excellent view of the branding.

Hannah smiled softly. Davey had been following Jonas like a shadow for the last three days. Yet the man never seemed to tire of answering the child's questions. Jonas was always patient with the boy and his gentleness never failed to stir something in Hannah.

Davey's fingers curled around the wooden post and still he swayed slightly. Jonas reached out and steadied him until the boy had found his balance. Then, while she watched, Jonas took off his hat, set it on the boy's head, then turned back to work again.

Clearly in his element, he worked alongside his men. His shirtfront sweatstained and filthy, his whisker-shadowed jaw set tight, he looked as though he'd been born for this moment. He moved around the pen with casual ease, and she followed his steps with her gaze locked on his long, lean legs and broad, muscular back.

Something inside her shifted and as she watched him, she realized she was no longer looking at him as *just* the Mackenzie—the warlock she was expected to marry. She was looking at and appreciating the man he was. Hardworking, loyal, kind. Magic or not, Jonas Mackenzie stirred the air around him just with his presence. Even if she wasn't a witch, she thought, she would want to be near him. To be held by him. To be *loved* by him.

But none of that would happen unless the man realized that they were meant to be together and quit fighting her.

Offering herself hadn't worked.

Feathers had fared no better.

Her witchcraft, much as she hated to admit it, was useless.

Hannah inhaled deeply and released the breath on a sigh. Why was he being so stubborn?

As she watched, Jonas shoved one of the calves out of the branding pen and signaled to Stretch Jones to let in the next one.

Another calf was trotted into the enclosure, where a cowhand quickly tossed a rope loop around its hind legs, dropping it to the ground. Then another man grabbed its head and, laying in the dirt beside it, held the animal still while Jonas strode across the grassy pen and snatched up the handle of a glowing-red branding iron in a gloved fist.

He stepped up to the calf and, holding the iron steady, stamped it down hard on the animal's side.

The stench of burned hair lifted over the crowd. The calves bawled and their mothers called back to them from the herd. As the calf was released and went stag-

gering toward escape, Hannah's soft heart twisted a bit
in sympathy.

"It doesn't hurt," someone close by said. "Not really."

She turned her head and looked down at Myra Simpson, little Davey's mother. Soft brown hair pulled back
into a braid that hung down her back, Myra wore a black
skirt with a white shirtwaist that was already marred
with streaks of dirt. She didn't seem to mind, though,
as she usually could be found in the front row of watch-
ers surrounding the pens.

"My Dan says they only make all that noise because
they're scared. Their hides are so thick, the brand
doesn't have a chance to burn down to pain level." She
shrugged and smiled wryly. "Of course, to be sure, we'd
have to ask a calf."

Hannah nodded and smiled before climbing down
from her seat to stand beside the other woman. "I think
I'll just believe your husband."

Myra grinned. "Me, too." Then she stared off toward
the pens. "I see Davey's underfoot again."

Hannah laughed. "Jonas doesn't seem to think so."

"That boy of mine does dote on Jonas." Myra
winked. "Irritates heck out of Big Dave."

"Your husband." She'd seen Dave Simpson often in
the last few days. A tall, muscular man with a hard jaw
and a steely look about him that turned to mush whenever he glanced at his wife.

Myra nodded. "Dave's been so busy here lately with
our older boys, he hasn't had time to spend with Davey."

"Jonas certainly enjoys the boy." Hannah said, letting
her gaze slide back to the man always on her mind. "I
saw him yesterday giving Davey riding lessons in the
corral."

"I know," Myra laughed and laid one hand on Hannah's arm. "The child talked about it all night until Big
Dave promised to get him his own horse if he'd just
keep quiet awhile." Myra cocked her head and grinned

slyly. "I always thought Jonas would make a good father . . ."

Hannah smiled and sighed. "Indeed he would," she
said.

Hiding a smile, Myra steered Hannah to the back of
the buckboard. "What did you bring down today?"

Hannah waved a hand at the load of food. "Ham,
fried chicken, two cakes, and four loaves of bread."

"Dave'll be glad to hear it," her new friend said.
"He's been raving about your fried chicken since that
first day."

Her spells might not work very often, but she'd always been a good cook.

Myra smiled at her again and reached for one of the
baskets. "Between Mrs. Morales's tamales and your
fried chicken, my rabbit stew is coming in a poor third.
You have to give me the recipe or I'll never hear the
end of it."

"I'd be happy to." Hannah lifted another basket from
the wagon and started after Myra as she walked toward
the food tables set up beneath a pair of giant cottonwood
trees.

The other women were standing off to one side, gossiping and waving flies from the food. Rather than joining them, Hannah and Myra turned and walked toward
the pens, where the crowd was still cheering the men
on.

A companionable silence rose up between them until
Myra splintered it with a casual remark.

"I'm glad Jonas's found you."

Hannah stumbled slightly. "I beg your pardon?"

Myra laughed and shook her head. "Dave's always
saying how I don't have any tact. Guess he's right."

Thankfully, the woman didn't seem to expect her to
comment. They edged their way past the group of people
to take up spots along the branding pen's fence. From
their vantage point, they could watch the men in both
enclosures and keep an eye on Davey, still on his perch.

This close, the stench of burning hair was thick and blended with the swirling smoke to make the air almost unbreathable. Hannah looked toward Jonas, her gaze raking him up and down. He would be a good father, she thought—and imagined herself round with his child, secure in his love.

Her thoughts must have shown on her features because Myra leaned in and whispered, "He looks at you just like that when he thinks you're not looking."

Hannah turned to look at her new friend. She didn't bother to pretend that she didn't know what Myra was talking about. "He does?"

"Oh, my, yes." The woman set her elbows on the top rail of the fence and cupped her chin in her hands. "Sometimes I'm surprised you don't just burst into flames on the strength of the looks he gives you."

Heat rushed into her cheeks while a renewed sense of hope leaped up inside her. A moment later, though, that hope was dashed. She already knew that Jonas desired her. But that was a long way from what she wanted from him. "You wouldn't know it to listen to him," she said.

"But isn't that just like a man." Myra shook her head. "There's not a one of them knows what's good for them until we tell them."

"I've tried to tell him," Hannah muttered, and voicing her failure out loud stung more than she'd thought it would.

Myra slanted a glance her way and nodded. "Jonas doesn't strike me as an easy man to know. He's been here several years and we almost never see him. There's always been a sort of . . . loneliness to him." Pausing briefly, she smiled and added, "I haven't noticed it so much this week, though."

Hannah sighed and turned her gaze back to the man she couldn't seem to stop thinking about. Lonely. She'd sensed that in him, too. And maybe that was partly what drew her to him, she thought. The aura of old aches she longed to ease.

"Keeps to himself too much," Myra said quietly. "But then, men are strange creatures, even the best of them."

Watching him at work, Hannah thought again of how at home he seemed in this setting. As much a part of the place as the mountains, the trees, the squalling cattle. And as hard as she tried, she couldn't imagine him in her small, settled hometown.

She drew in a long breath and told herself that the Mackenzie needed this wild, open land. In Creekford, he would be no more than a caged lion. Her thoughts flew through her mind as Jonas worked with the confidence of a person sure of his own abilities . . . his own strengths.

And he did it all without witchcraft.

She shook her head, remembering Blake Wolcott and his casual use of power. He was strong, too. And getting stronger. In a way that would crush Jonas if he didn't accept who and what he was in time to stop it.

The sun pounded on Jonas's back and shoulders. He felt a river of sweat rolling down his spine. His shoulders ached, his arms were sore . . . hell, even his teeth hurt. But by damn they were seeing a lot of spring calves. More than he'd hoped for.

Satisfaction rose up in him, despite his aches and pains. All of the hard work was worth it. The ranch was coming along well. Another few years, and it would be everything he wanted it to be.

Straightening up, he eased the kinks out of his muscles while he quickly checked to make sure little Davey was still safely out of harm's way. He swallowed a grin as he watched the boy tip the brim of the too-big hat out of his eyes.

Then Jonas let his gaze stray across the faces of the people lining the fence rails until he found her. Green eyes locked with blue. He'd known she was there even before he spotted her. Jonas had felt her presence as surely as if she'd stepped up behind him and tapped him on the shoulder.

And that connection worried him.

But he couldn't disguise the small rush of pleasure he felt having her there. Every year, he saw his neighbors' wives smiling and encouraging their husbands. And every year, he'd fought against a twinge of envy.

Until now. For the first time, there was a woman in the crowd whose gaze was meant for him alone. And it staggered him to realize just how important she'd become to him. Seconds ticked past as he stared at her, wondering what she was thinking—planning. Wondering why she'd come to him. Wondering why he'd allowed her to turn his world upside down.

But mostly, wondering why he was torturing himself this way. Hannah Lowell, witch or not, was the marrying kind of woman. She wanted a ring on her finger and a house full of kids.

A cold chill swept over him, despite the warmth of the sun. This was no good. Wanting and needing were two different things, and though he wanted her badly, he wouldn't allow himself to need her. Tearing his gaze from hers, he happened to catch the speculative gleam in Elias's eyes and muttered a curse under his breath.

The old coot's words had been ringing in his mind for days now. Time to let the past go, huh? Well, how could he do that when Hannah was here demanding he remember at least a part of that past?

Elias said the past was merely that. Years gone into dust. Hannah said that the past was who he was and that centuries of tradition had to be honored.

Ahead? Or back?

Which way should he go?

"Damn it," he muttered fiercely and turned away from both of them in time to see young Billy stumble and fall against a man holding a red-hot branding iron.

The kid half screamed in surprised agony and even

Jonas winced at the thought of glowing hot iron searing flesh not protected by a thick hide.

A choked-off scream put an end to her thoughts and Hannah blinked as she stared at the men gathering around Billy.

"Somebody's hurt," Myra muttered darkly. "I'll go find the doctor. He's in this crowd somewhere."

The woman turned and disappeared into the mob of people just as Hannah slipped through the rails of the fence and hurried across the grass to where the men stood in a small, tight knot.

His eyes scrunched up tight, teeth gritted, Billy groaned and held his left arm gingerly. Stretch Jones stepped aside for Hannah and she moved up beside Jonas as he took Billy's arm in his hands to inspect the injury.

"What happened?" she asked, and Jonas didn't even look at her.

"Burn," he muttered. "He fell into one of the irons."

She looked at the young cowboy's features. Face pale, sweat streamed along his cheeks and down his neck. He bit down hard on his bottom lip to keep from crying out again.

Hannah laid her hand gently on his shoulder and angled her head to one side, looking down at the reddened, blistering skin of Billy's forearm. Her stomach pitched and her eyes welled up in sympathy. But as she watched, Jonas began moving his hands over the boy's skin, as if testing the depth of the burned flesh.

"Not too bad," he muttered, and Hannah couldn't help wondering what he would have considered a serious injury. Then she realized he was talking for Billy's sake. Trying to ease the boy's mind. Her gaze softened as she looked at the Mackenzie while he kept up a steady stream of reassuring words.

"I've seen worse, Billy," he was saying as his fingers

dusted the edges of the wound. "This won't earn you more than a day or two off of work."

Billy forced a too-hearty chuckle.

"You'll have a heck of a scar to brag about, though," he said, continuing his careful examination of the wound.

It was working. Billy no longer looked like he was going to faint. But what no one but she seemed to notice was that as Jonas touched the edges of the burn, the injury seemed to lessen. The raw, scarlet skin lightened to a dark pink and some of the blisters flattened out, smoothing into undamaged skin.

"Hell, this is nothing, Billy. Get you a bandage and you can sit under the trees, telling the ladies all about the dangers of ranch work."

"Maybe I should better help him with that, boss," Stretch offered, and several of the men laughed. Stretch was always willing to entertain the ladies.

As his pain eased and his drawn features relaxed, Billy managed to open his eyes and see the wound for himself. Relief shone in his gaze as he said thankfully. "It don't look too bad, does it?"

Jonas shook his head and released him. Glancing past him, he saw an older man in a black coat hurrying toward them. "You'll be all right. But the doc's here, so he can put a dressing on it." Taking the young cowhand by the shoulder, Jonas gave him a shove toward the fence and said, "Go sit down somewhere and try to stay away from fires."

"Yessir, boss," Billy said, wincing slightly.

Over the commotion in the crowd, one loud voice shouted, "All right folks, this seems as good a time as any to stop for dinner. So come and get it."

The crowds slowly drifted off toward the food tables and Jonas and Hannah were alone.

The fresh, clean scent of lemon washed over him and something inside Jonas turned over.

He wasn't sure how it had happened, but in a couple

of short weeks, this tiny blond with her outlandish stories had inched her way past the walls he'd built around himself. Every time she was near him, he felt another brick in the wall tumble free, exposing him to things he never again wanted to feel.

On that thought, he gave her a brief nod and turned away. Leaving her standing in the center of the now-empty pen, he climbed through the fence rails and strode off in the opposite direction of the crowds.

The gathered herd was much smaller today. Though, still a couple hundred animals strong, most of the cattle had been divided and driven to their home ranges. But for the first time in years, his mind wasn't on the cattle. Or the ranch. Or his grand plans for this place he'd carved out for himself.

No, his thoughts were centered on Hannah. Having her. Holding her. Caressing the naked flesh he'd already seen and continued to dream about. Grumbling, he hurried his pace, his long legs carrying him quickly around the edges of the herd, while his mind raced.

"Jonas . . . Mackenzie." Hannah called out from behind him, and he sighed heavily. He should have known she wouldn't let him go. "Wait for me."

If he'd had a horse handy, he might have made a run for it. As it was, he wouldn't let his neighbors see him being chased in circles by a woman he was afraid to be alone with.

He stopped dead, keeping his gaze focused on the far mountains. She came up beside him and stopped, laying one hand on his forearm. The heat of her touch drove straight to the heart of him, sizzling every inch of his body until he felt as though he'd been burned far worse than Billy.

"Jonas," she said, demanding his attention.

Unable to avoid it, he looked down at her windblown hair, flushed face, and wide, green eyes. And in those vivid, emerald eyes, there were shadows of children and picket fences and long evenings of loving.

Lifting his head, he gritted his teeth and curled his hands into fists to keep from reaching for her. "Leave me be, Hannah. For both our sakes, leave me be."

"I can't," she whispered, shaking her head. Then, smiling softly, she added, "And even if I could, I wouldn't."

He stepped back from her touch and his insides mourned the lack of her. He reached up and pushed his sweat-dampened hair back from his forehead.

"Folks are eating," he said finally, hopefully. "Shouldn't you be helping the other ladies?"

"They won't miss me," Hannah said, her gaze locked on his features. "I wanted to talk to you . . ."

"Hannah . . ."

". . . about Billy," she finished.

Frowning, he shifted his gaze back to hers. Obviously surprised, he asked, "What about him?"

"Didn't you see?" Was it possible that he still hadn't noticed his own power? His own strength? Was he purposely blinding himself to the truth?

"Of course I saw." He shook his head, impatient now. "It looked like it might be a bad burn, but it wasn't. He was lucky."

Stepping up close to him, Hannah laid both hands on his chest, feeling the throbbing of his heart beneath her palms. She trembled slightly, then steadied herself. She had to make him see. Before it was too late.

"He wasn't lucky, Mackenzie," she said quietly.

He snorted and held her wrists, pulling her hands from his chest. "Don't know what you'd call it. But that iron could have taken off layers of skin and didn't."

She glanced at his hands, still encircling her much smaller ones, before staring up into his eyes again. "It was you, Jonas. Not luck. *You* helped Billy."

"I kept his mind off the pain until the doc could get there."

"No." She smiled up at him, willing him to believe

her. "It was your touch and your words that kept his wound so slight."

"What're you talking about?" He let her go before taking a step back. "Everyone was there. They all saw it. Hell, *you* saw it."

She nodded and closed the distance between them. "I saw your hands moving over the injury. I heard you repeating. 'It's not bad,' like a chant. And as you talked. Billy's wound healed."

"Stop, Hannah."

"Telling me to be quiet won't change what is."

"So now I can heal with a touch?" He snorted a choked laugh that sounded as though it was strangling him. "Hell, why don't I get rid of the ranch and buy a snake-oil wagon? I could travel the country, selling salvation in a bottle! A *touch*."

Frustration and fury rode him and Hannah felt the anger and something else—panic?—surrounding him. Like a muffled roar from a muzzled beast, thunder rolled in from miles away.

And for the first time, Hannah wondered if Jonas's emotions were affecting the weather. Every time he got mad at her, which was fairly often, thunder crashed and lightning flashed in the sky.

But that was a question for another day. Now she had to concentrate on reaching him. Making him accept who and what he was. Before it was too late for all of them.

"You're only a witch, Jonas," she said, reaching for him again and wincing slightly when he stepped back. "You can't work miracles. But you *can* make a difference. And you did. For Billy."

"I did nothing, damn it." He rubbed one hand across his mouth, swallowed heavily.

"You did," Hannah said, her voice quiet but determined. "And pretending differently won't change anything."

In the distance, thunder growled. His features drawn and tight, he looked like a man on the edge of madness.

"I'm not who you want me to be," he said, his fingers digging into her flesh through the soft fabric of her yellow shirt. "And what's more, I don't *want* to be that man."

She felt for him. His world as he'd known it was gone forever. Despite the fact that he was still arguing the point, she saw a glimmer of terrified acceptance in his eyes and responded to that.

"Fate doesn't often give us the choice Jonas," she said, reaching up to cup his face in her palms. "And whether you like it or not, ours is a shared destiny. One that cannot be ignored for much longer."

"Why won't you give up?" he asked, his whispered voice full of confusion and pain. "Why won't you stop doing this—to both of us?"

"I can't," she said, meeting his gaze and willing him to understand. "For both our sakes, I can't."

Chapter eleven

"**Is** he back?" Hannah spun about, eyes wide, to face the man opening the door.

Hours had passed since Jonas had ridden off. Long after the other ranchers had gone home, she'd waited. Long after twilight deepened into night, she'd waited.

But he hadn't returned and a small corner of Hannah's heart wondered if he ever would. Yet even as that thought niggled and worried inside her, a storm raged outside. Wind tearing at the trees. Thunder and lightning slashing across the sky. And she knew, despite her anxiousness, that Jonas was close—and still angry.

In the hours he'd been gone, Hannah had brought to mind every time she'd angered him in the last couple of weeks—an innumerable amount, she was forced to admit. And each time his temper flared, she recalled, clouds gathered and lightning flashed. Apparently, Jonas's anger was enough to shake even heaven.

So the fact that a storm seemed to be hovering over them almost gave her comfort.

Elias stepped into the kitchen, took off his hat, and pulled out a chair. Soaked to the skin, his movements slow and weary, he looked every one of his years. The cracks and crevices in his face looked as though they'd been carved with a heavy hand. Tossing his hat onto the table, he sat down heavily and peered up at her.

"Yeah," he said. "He's back. Riding night herd. And God help the man who gives him any trouble tonight."

"Angry, is he?" she asked, glancing once at the pelting rain slamming against the windowpane.

A tired half smile curved Elias's mouth briefly and was gone again. "Angry?" He shook his head. "If you'd call a howling Comanche out for hair *angry,* then yeah. I guess you could say that."

"Did he say anything to you about why he's mad?"

Elias's gray gaze narrowed on her thoughtfully. "No, he didn't. But I'm willin' to bet it's got somethin' to do with you."

Only everything, she thought and felt the bottom drop out of her stomach. She'd made such a mess of things. What had gone wrong? Back in Creekford, this had all seemed so simple.

Come to the Mackenzie. Point out his duty. Marry him and conceive a child.

And yet . . . nothing was working the way she'd expected it to. He should have been *happy* to discover his abilities. Anyone else would have been. And if her own magic hadn't deserted her completely, Hannah would be sorely tempted to whip up a love potion or two.

But no. She'd so hoped that being near a powerful warlock would help her abilities grow. Instead, they seemed to have drained from her altogether. Just as, she reminded herself, the witches in Creekford were being stripped of their powers by Blake.

But Jonas Mackenzie hadn't deliberately taken anything from her. He didn't even want his own powers, let alone hers.

"I have to talk to him," she muttered, more to herself than to the man still watching her from the table.

"I don't think that's a good idea," Elias told her quietly.

Her gaze snapped to his, drawn by the warning implicit in his tone.

"When you first came here," he went on, his work-gnarled fingers toying with the brim of his hat, "I thought to get rid of you as fast as I could."

"I know, but—" Briefly, their encounter in the alley leaped into her mind. She'd seen then the depth of the older man's love for the Mackenzie and had understood the instinct to protect him. She still did; she only wished that Elias would see that she meant Jonas no harm.

"Then," Elias continued, raising his voice to drown out hers, "I saw how Mac was around you. Saw a spark in him I hadn't seen in a long time."

Spark was a good description of what happened between them when they were together, she thought. And when they kissed . . . sparks and fires and lightning strikes and the sweet, full rush of his magic swarming over her.

Elias looked at her, saw her eyes go soft and dreamy, and barely managed to swallow back a groan. He was too late to intervene between the two of them. He realized that whatever lay between she and Jonas had gone further than he'd suspected. Reluctantly, he let go of the half-baked plan he'd come up with on his wet ride back from the herd.

After seeing Jonas and the misery the man was in, Elias had thought to scoot Hannah away from the ranch and have her gone and out of their lives before morning. Though he'd become fond of the girl, he wasn't willing to sit idly by while she made Jonas's life a torture.

Should have known it wouldn't work, he told himself grimly. Should have remembered that when a fellow came back to life after being so long closed up inside, there would be pain as well as joy.

Well. However this hand of cards was played out, it would be up to Jonas and Hannah to settle it. Still, he had to offer at least a word of advice.

"You'd best keep something in mind, missy," he said and waited until she looked at him to continue. "Sparks don't just start up a nice, cozy fire in a hearth. They can explode into a wildfire that destroys all it touches."

Hannah nodded and walked toward him. He looked up into the cool green meadow of her eyes as she stopped beside his chair and laid one hand on his shoulder. Smiling, she said stubbornly. "But after a fire, something new and beautiful grows from the ashes."

"Sometimes," he said.

"I have to try."

"I know it, but it ain't goin' to be easy," he warned her.

Hannah smiled. "Nothing about the Mackenzie is easy, Elias."

Then she snatched up a coat from the wall peg, draped it over her head and shoulders, and slipped out the door, closing it behind her as the storm swallowed her.

The cat strolled into the kitchen just then and leaped up onto the table to stare at him. Elias glanced at it, then closed his eyes. "I'm gettin' too old for this nonsense, cat."

Hepzibah yowled.

Another few days, Jonas told himself. A week at the most and his share of the spring roundup would be finished. He squinted into the driving rain and scowled. A damn good thing he'd started his men gathering the herd weeks ago. He'd hate like hell to have to worry about keeping a thousand head of cattle calm during a lightning storm.

The two hundred or so he *did* have to worry about were stamping their hooves and lowing restlessly in the wake of the lights flashing in the sky and the thunder smashing directly overhead. On the far side of the herd, Jonas spotted Stretch Jones and another man from a neighboring ranch. The three of them should be able to contain this bunch, he told himself with a furious glare at the sky, if the damn storm would let up.

Instantly, more rain sluiced down over him and he hunched deeper into the folds of his slicker. Tugging his hat brim down low over his eyes, he let his mind wander from the storm and the cattle, and the goddamned weather.

Once free to think as it wanted, his brain returned to the notions that had swirled through it since he'd walked away from Hannah that afternoon. Walked. He snorted at the word. Hell, he'd *run* from her. From her and everything she'd said. Everything she'd tried to make him believe.

He'd raced his horse across miles of open range and still hadn't been able to distance himself from the thoughts careening inside his head. One after another, they presented themselves and were gone again. Hannah. Billy. The gambler's pistol. The burned arm. Feathers. Big green eyes, looking up at him with quiet confidence. Trust.

And when he finally admitted that running wasn't the answer and turned his horse for the home range, he'd dragged this damn storm with him.

The reins threaded through his fingers, Jonas closed his fist around the worn, smooth leather of the saddle horn and held on as if it meant his life. He needed something to steady him. Something to ground him to this place. This world. Before he found himself swept up into Hannah's.

The cattle nearest him stirred again, their horns clacking together like an old man's store-bought teeth. Jonas shook himself from his thoughts and concentrated on the herd. One thing he didn't need at the moment was another problem.

Hannah peered out from beneath the jacket she held over her head and shoulders. The ground was a soggy mess, the mud grabbing at her feet with every step as though the earth itself were trying to keep her from finding Jonas.

Lightning shimmered from behind the clouds, gilding their edges as thunder rumbled in its wake. The wind pushed at her, driving the rain straight at her even as it pushed her back toward the ranch house. And still she went on, bending her head against the storm, determined to find him. Talk to him.

At the edge of the herd, she stopped, squinting into the gloom. Two silhouetted figures rode past each other as they circled the cattle, but neither one was Jonas. Her gaze swept on, across the backs of the gathered animals churning up the rain-soaked ground. Another man sat his horse on the far side of the herd. Alone. And she knew, without a doubt, she'd found him.

Amid the crashing violence of the storm, Hannah started walking toward him. To go around the herd would take too long and an urgency she couldn't describe refused to allow the delay. A small frisson of fear rippled along her spine at the thought of trusting her own pitiful powers to protect her from the cattle. But then she reminded herself that the man sitting his horse opposite her was the Mackenzie. And whether he accepted that fact or not, the strength and power of his heritage was within him. He would keep her safe. She only had to trust her heart.

And him.

Swallowing back a rising tide of apprehension, Hannah started walking through the gathered cattle, her gaze fixed on Jonas, blacker shadow against the night.

Jonas sensed the change in the cattle and his skin prickled. He sat up straighter in the saddle and tightened his grip on the reins as he studied the herd through experienced eyes. Unsettled, no doubt by the storm, their heavy bodies shifted against each other and uneasiness stirred inside him. He glanced toward the two mounted men, hoping they, too, had picked up on the danger building here.

A stampede was coming. And though it would only be a couple hundred animals strong, it wasn't a thing to be taken lightly.

His mind already trying to work out which way the animals would run when they bolted, his gaze continued moving until he spotted—*her*.

Hannah.

Mouth suddenly dry, he blinked once, wiped a sheen of rain from his eyes, and looked again, desperate to believe that his mind was playing tricks on him. But it wasn't. She was headed straight for him, walking through the center of the herd as though she were strolling down an empty country lane.

Fear, heavy and dark, clutched at his throat. She looked so small. So defenseless, surrounded by thousands of pounds of cattle on the verge of stampede.

Lightning flashed and in the brief stab of light he saw her face, pale beneath the coat she held up over her as protection from the rain. "Go back, Hannah," he muttered as thunder smashed overhead and one of the steers nearest him lowed wildly, its eyes rolling over white.

And then it happened.

He'd been expecting it, but even so, as the restless, spooked animals turned and started moving, Jonas felt his heart stop.

His gaze locked on Hannah. Even through the rain, he could see her turning one way and then the other, dodging horns and hooves. And they hadn't even started running yet.

She'd never make it.

Panic shot through his veins. Terror grabbed him hard and squeezed his lungs until he couldn't draw a breath. She was going to die right in front of him and there wasn't a damn thing he could do about it. Helplessness roared through his body, threatening to strangle him as the scene continued to unfold in front of him.

In another minute, the cattle would be running blindly across anything in their path. Nothing would stop them. He'd seen them crash over chuckwagons, splintering the wood into piles of shavings and the men riding them into nothing more than scraps of tattered clothing.

Even if his horse could maneuver through a crazed herd without being brought down by slashing horns, he wouldn't reach her in time to keep her small body from being crushed and ground into the mud.

Visions he couldn't stop flooded his mind. Memories of his first cattle drive and the stampede that had killed two of the outriders. There hadn't been enough left of the men to bury.

He tasted fear at the back of his throat.

Hannah . . .

Instantly, images of the last two weeks rushed through his mind, one after the other. Once more, he saw her charm the neighboring ranchers and mother his cowhands. He heard her muttering half-baked attempts at spell casting and saw her standing at the stove, smiling a welcome to him as he entered the kitchen.

He'd never be able to walk through that room again without seeing her.

"Jesus," he muttered, and the wind snatched the word from his throat and tossed it into the rumbling roar of a herd on the move. Again lightning flashed, and once more thunder rolled around him. Hundreds of cattle lowed plaintively, sounding like lost souls on their way to hell.

"Jonas!"

Somehow, he heard her. He felt her fear. Tasted her terror as completely as his own.

"Don't you die, damn it," he muttered desperately.

His mind reached out blindly, wildy, groping for something, anything that might help him. And in that instant, somewhere in the back of his mind, a flicker of instinctive knowledge took root.

A day ago—hell, an hour ago—he would have laughed at the notion. Now he didn't question it. Instead, he snatched at it, like a drowning man at a thrown rope. Out of options, out of hope, he put his trust in Hannah's beliefs. In the kernel of truth blossoming in his heart.

He had no other choice.

Dropping the reins, he sat up straight in the saddle, threw his hands high and wide, tipped his face to the howling wind, and yelled, "NO!" with every ounce of his strength.

Instantly, an awesome rush of energy poured into his body, like pumped well water into a jug. His body jerked with the impact as it filled him, flooding every vein, every inch of him until he felt as though he might explode from the force of it.

In that split second, Jonas felt everything around him as he never had before. The wind. The rain. Even the lightning flickering now against the edges of the cloud-tossed sky felt different. Stronger. Sharper.

As if he could feel the heartbeat of the world deep within him. Ancient knowledge tugged at the corners of his mind. Memories long dead flickered into life and sputtered out again like candles guttering in pools of molten wax.

Anger and panic faded, and around him, as if cut off by a heavenly hand, the storm died. A faint, rain-scented breeze and the sting of air burned by lightning were the only reminders of its wrath.

The cattle calmed, their frenzied movements quieting. The danger was over.

"Jonas!"

Still shaken, he shifted his gaze to the woman whose presence had changed everything in his life. As he watched, unbelieving, the milling cattle slowly parted, creating a wide, unobstructed path between he and Hannah.

She walked toward him and even from a distance he saw the smile curving her lips. As she drew closer, the last of the storm clouds scuttled out of sight, leaving a trail of starlight to lead her to him.

From the corner of his eye, Jonas spotted Stretch Jones riding hard in his direction! He ignored the cowboy, focusing instead on Hannah's face and the terrifying realizations still roiling inside him.

He gathered up his horse's reins and held them tightly in a fisted left hand. Hannah stopped alongside him, lifting her gaze to his. In her eyes, he read respect, admiration . . . and a hint of 'I told you so.' His stomach clenched.

"Are you all right?" he asked, his voice raw and harsher than he'd planned.

"Yes, thanks to you," she said and laid one hand on his leg.

He knew that. He knew what he'd done. He just didn't know *how* he'd done it.

But for the moment, it was enough to know she was safe.

Drawing in a long, shuddering breath, Jonas reached out a hand to her and she took it, folding her fingers around his. He pulled her up behind him on the horse and gritted his teeth when she wrapped her arms around his waist and snuggled in close to him.

"You must believe now," she whispered. "You *are* the Mackenzie."

"I don't know what I believe, Hannah."

"Jonas, you can't turn your back on who and what you are," she argued, as he'd known she would.

"I can do whatever the hell I want to," he muttered and nodded at Stretch as the other man pulled his horse to a rearing stop. "I'm the Mackenzie, *remember*?" he finished in a whisper meant for her ears alone.

"You two all right, boss?" Stretch asked, ripping his hat off and shaking the excess rainwater off against his thigh.

"We're fine," Jonas told him and turned his horse toward the house.

"Damnedest thing I ever seen," Stretch crowed. "I always did say you had the devil's own luck."

"The devil has nothing to do with it," Hannah said, "it was—"

"Pure dumb luck," Jonas said, cutting her off and shooting her a look over his shoulder. All he needed was for his men to hear Hannah's wild tales of witchcraft and warlocks. Hell, folks here were superstitious about black cats and spilled milk. Couldn't she see how they'd react to talk of witches? "It's over now anyway, so can we quit talking about it?"

"Quit talkin'?" Stretch echoed on a short bark of laughter. "Hell, I ain't even started talkin' about it. Wait'll the boys hear about this!"

Perfect, Jonas thought. Now everyone within a hundred miles would hear the tale and there'd be no chance of his putting this behind him—where, at the moment, he desperately wanted it to be.

"Did you see that?" another cowboy called as he rode up to join them.

Jonas's jaw tightened enough so that he thought the bone might snap. In the distance, thunder rumbled again and he cursed the thought of yet more rain.

"Son," Stretch told him, "I seen it and I still don't believe it."

Neither did Jonas.

If he accepted what Hannah was saying, believed in what he just did, then he also had to accept that his whole life had been a lie.

Lies told to him by a man he'd always considered a father. And if he couldn't trust Elias, what did he have left?

Inhaling sharply, he jabbed his horse's sides with his heels. Whether he wanted to or not, he had to ask that old man some questions—and hope he could live with the answers.

"I'm taking Hannah back to the house," he said. "You two keep an eye on the herd."

Stretch laughed again. "Hell, boss, I'm fixin' to watch 'em every blasted minute. Who knows what they'll do next!"

"Oh, for God's sake . . ."

"Mackenzie," Hannah said softly, and something inside him tightened up again.

"What?" His horse jumped into a slow trot away from the cattle and the two befuddled cowboys.

"Not talking about it won't change anything."

"Maybe not," he said, fixing his gaze on the square of lamplight glimmering in the darkness ahead. "But I'm gonna try."

Even as he said it, though, he knew he didn't mean it. Whether he wanted to admit it or not, something had changed for him tonight. Something had reached inside him and torn his familiar little world apart.

And he needed to know why.

Creekford

Something had changed.

Somewhere, a corner had been rounded. A difference made.

Blake Wolcott scowled and tried to put a mental finger on what it was. But the feeling was too elusive to be pinned down further than the certain knowledge that a shift in power had happened—and that it would affect him.

He shook off the odd sensation and stared into the fire blazing on the hearth. His gaze blurred and in the heart of the flames he saw Hannah's face. And Eudora's. Smiling. Laughing.

At him.

His gaze narrowed. His teeth ground together in frustrated fury. His fingers tightened on the small glass of excellent brandy he held, just before he hurled the delicate crystal tumbler into the fireplace. Flames leaped at the alcohol, licking at the brick hearth. The soft tinkle of broken glass was lost in his muttered curse as he shoved himself up from the chair to pace the elegantly furnished room.

Urgency nipped at his heels. Impatience rattled his soul. But Blake kept moving because it helped him think. He desperately needed to think clearly. Now, more than ever.

Frustration shimmered all around him and small decorative objects trembled on their shelves as he passed.

"This is their fault," he muttered and stopped dead in front of the fireplace again. Curling his fingers around the mantel's edge, he stared into the gilt-edged mirror facing him. Meeting his reflected gaze, he saw what he'd always seen.

A powerful man, destined for greatness.

A man too big for the English village that had bred him. A man on the verge of snatching up the reins to more power than he'd ever known before.

"And I'll be damned in hell before I'll let those women cheat me out of my rightful place." His voice rumbled into the room, and behind him a small porcelain vase toppled from its perch and landed with a thud on the carpet.

He paid it no mind.

Turning abruptly, he crossed the floor to the front window and stared through a filmy white cloud of lace curtains at *his* town.

Time was passing, and along with it his hold on the Guild members. He saw it daily. They no longer feared him as thoroughly as they had before. With Hannah and then Eudora escaping him, his power over the lesser witches was fading.

"But they're not gone," he told himself. "Not really." The man he had following Eudora was an idiot, but bright enough to know that his life depended on keeping up with the older woman and reporting to Blake when she finally—damn her for stalling and playing games with him—joined Hannah.

Once he knew where the women were, he'd go to them and resolve this entire situation with a brief, but very legal, wedding.

And when he was joined to the last of the Lowells, he told himself, staring hard at a farmer rolling into town atop a hay wagon, his victory would be complete.

Blake lifted one hand, snapped his fingers, and smiled when the neatly bound stacks of golden straw erupted into flames. The farmer screamed and fell from the high bench seat, his clothes afire. Witches and warlocks from all over town ran to help the man and Blake smiled again, sure they'd all understood his little reminder of just who was in charge here.

Chapter twelve

At the house, Jonas reached back, took hold of Hannah's arm, and swung her down from the saddle in one easy motion. He avoided looking into her eyes, because he didn't want to see that shine of admiration for him again.

He felt as though he were straddling a barbed-wire fence and the slightest movement either way could do him a hell of a lot of damage. Already turning the horse's head toward the barn, he said simply, "Tell Elias I need to talk to him."

She grabbed at the reins, forcing him to either stop or drag her along behind the horse. He stopped.

"Don't you think you and I should have a talk first?"

"No." Steeling himself, he looked down into starlit green eyes and felt the wicked punch of desire anyway. Despite the turmoil in his mind and heart, despite not knowing anymore who—and what—he was, he wanted her. Sighing, he leaned both hands on the saddle horn. "Before we talk, I need some answers to questions I can only ask Elias."

"But Jonas," she said, and her eyes glimmered with the emotions she kept too close to the surface, "what happened tonight had to convince you. You have to know now that what I've been saying all along is true."

His insides tightened. *Warlock.* The word shimmered

through him, stirring long-dead memories. Deliberately, he fought them down. He wasn't ready yet. For them. Or for her.

"All I know," he said, squeezing the words past the knot in his throat, "is that you were luckier than you had a right to expect tonight. You could have been killed because you trusted in your supposed 'powers' to keep you safe."

He turned the horse's head again, pleased when she released the reins. As he headed for the barn, though, her voice, carried on the wind, reached him. "It was *you* I trusted to keep me safe, Mackenzie."

Jonas shuddered as her words stabbed at him, tearing at an old wound, leaving it open and bleeding again as it had when it was fresh. Long ago, someone else had trusted him to keep her safe. He'd failed her.

And she died.

As surely as the man he'd been this morning had died a few minutes ago on a muddy field.

Elias walked slowly into the shadowy darkness of the barn, like a man taking the five short steps up the gallows to his own hanging. For twenty-five years, he'd known this day would come. Despite his efforts and the promise made to a dying man, he'd known the truth couldn't be kept from Jonas forever. A man would become what nature and fate intended him to become.

And nothing on earth could stop it.

Sounds, soft and familiar, led him to the stall at the end of the narrow aisle. Squinting into the darkness, he saw Jonas standing beside his black stallion, rubbing sweat from its back with a soft towel. The horse whickered as Elias drew near, but the man caring for it didn't turn, and something inside the older man broke.

Nothing would be the same after this night, he told himself and braced for the confrontation he'd been dreading.

Tension rippled between them. The air fairly sizzled

with it. Still, Elias held his peace, wanting to give the other man the chance to speak first.

"Tell me," Jonas finally asked, his voice hushed. "Is Hannah lying?"

There it was. Flat out and in the open at last. Elias drew an unsteady breath and realized that as hard as this was, there was almost a sense of relief accompanying it.

Sighing, he pulled off his still-rain-damp hat and studied the brim through troubled eyes. "Always figured you'd have to know someday," he said softly. "But I got to say, I never did look forward to the tellin'."

"Damn it," Jonas muttered, not turning around, "just say it. Is she lying?"

"No."

One word, and years of trust and affection dissolved like sugar in strong coffee.

Jonas's chin hit his chest. Then he slowly turned around, fixing his gaze on the man who'd raised him. The man who'd taught him how to hunt and fish. To survive in the mountains. The man who'd been with him when Jonas's world had crashed down around him ten years ago.

The man who'd taught him that honesty and honor were the only truly important things in life.

He looked into gray eyes staring worriedly from beneath drawn-down, bushy gray brows and said the only thing he could. "Horseshit."

"You asked me," Elias said, squaring his slumped shoulders and lifting his chin. "I'm tellin' ya."

"You're as crazy as she is," Jonas muttered. Then, remembering what had just happened, he added. "Hell, we're all crazy as coots."

"I ain't never had a crazy day in my life and you damn well know it," Elias snapped.

"Until now." From a distance, the low rumble of thunder seemed to keep pace with the rising tide of fresh anger rolling inside him. "You're tryin' to tell me I'm a *witch*?"

"Warlock," Elias corrected. "Least, that's the word your pa used."

"My pa." A father he couldn't remember had declared him to be a warlock. Well, hell, who said *he* hadn't been crazy as well? He tossed the towel across the stall wall and shoved both hands through his hair, tugging at it and welcoming the pain. Maybe now he'd wake up from whatever nightmare he'd landed in.

"Your folks made me promise—"

"To raise me," Jonas interrupted, throwing his hands wide. "I know."

"You don't know half what you should."

"And why's that?" His voice slashed at the still air and even the horse beside him shifted uneasily in its stall. Grumbling quietly, Jonas left the small enclosure and set the latch on the gate door behind him. "Why is it that I know next to nothing about my parents? Who I am?"

"Because that's the way they wanted it."

Jonas took a half step backward and narrowed his gaze on the old man watching him. "They *wanted* me to forget them?"

Christ. The whole damn world had gone loco.

Elias took a step closer and stopped at the look on Jonas's face. "It's time you heard it all," he said and started talking, words pouring from him in a tumble.

"Your folks told me they'd got my name from a friend of theirs. Never did tell me who, exactly," he muttered, shaking his head. "Anyhow, I agreed to lead 'em west. They were good folks," Elias said, "you should know that."

Jonas nodded.

The older man rubbed the back of his neck and went on. "We didn't have no trouble at all for weeks. Then one day I took you with me to do some hunting." He smiled wistfully as his gaze locked on a past he seemed lost in. Then his smile died as he said, "When we got back to camp, it was over. Indians had hit 'em hard and fast. Mercifully, your ma was already gone."

Jonas swallowed heavily, almost surprised an event he couldn't remember could affect him so deeply.

"It was quick, boy," he said, obviously reading the expression on Jonas's face. "I doubt she knew what had happened till she got to the Pearly Gates and Saint Peter himself told her about it."

Good, Jonas thought. Good. It didn't matter now, surely, twenty-five years later . . . but he was glad she hadn't suffered.

"Your pa, though," Elias went on, clearly determined now to get everything said at last, "he was still hangin' on. Like he'd waited for us to get back." The older man shook his head in silent admiration. "That was a tough man."

His voice drew a picture and Jonas thought he could almost see it. A lonely campsite, somewhere in the mountains. Two men, one of them dying, a dead woman, and a boy watching his world end.

A part of him *almost* remembered.

"He told me then why they'd left Massachusetts," Elias said. "About that Guild and how they wanted you to have a different life. A life you could choose for your own self. A life not burdened with other folks' 'expectations,' he called it."

Somehow, Jonas found his voice. "He told you he—I—was a witch."

Elias snorted a choked, strained laugh. "He did. Can't say I believed him. Figured if he was, he could've stood off those Indians that had killed him and his woman. But he said how not even magic can defeat destiny." He shook his head again and smiled sadly. "He had a fine way of talking. Even then."

Jonas's heartbeat pounded in his ears. He felt every ounce of blood rushing through his veins. He measured every breath and told himself to hear it all, though all he wanted to do was leave this barn and pretend none of this had happened. He wanted his life back. As it had been yesterday. Hell, as it had been an hour ago.

Elias seemed to sense what he was feeling. His gaze speared into Jonas's eyes, refusing to back down. Refusing to stop.

"He made me promise to care for you, which was no hardship, since I was already fond of ya."

Jonas sucked in air like a drowning man.

"And," the older man went on, "he made me promise not to tell you about them. About who you are and where you come from."

"So you lied." Three little words that summed up the last twenty-five years. "You lied to me my whole life." It was a simple statement. One that ripped the solid floor from beneath his feet and left him floundering in uncertainty.

"It was a deathbed promise, boy," Elias told him, his voice steady and hard as it had been when he was a younger man. "I gave him my solemn word."

Jonas knew the value of a man's word. Elias had taught him that.

Honor.

Honesty.

It was laughable now, considering.

"And what about your word to me, Elias?" he snapped, feeling a fresh wave of anger rising within him. "What about that? You spent my whole life keeping this from me and you can talk about *honor*?"

"You think it was easy hiding this from you?"

"Must've been," Jonas shot back, stalking down the center of the aisle to stare out at the starlit ranch yard beyond. Turning his head, he speared the other man with a glance. "You managed it fine for twenty-five years."

"Your folks made me swear."

"And your word to a dead man was worth more to you than me." He nodded somberly, biting down hard on the bitter taste in his mouth. "That's good to know."

"Damn it boy, that ain't the way it was."

"That's how it seems." Jonas shook his head fiercely,

then marched back to take a stand in front of the man he'd loved for most of his life. Now Elias looked like a stranger to him. How many other things were tucked away in that gray head?

"Don't you see, I couldn't tell ya?" he asked.

"When I was a kid, maybe." Jonas was willing to give him that. "But as I grew older, I had a right to know, damn it."

"Would you have believed me any more than you believed Hannah?"

"Probably not, but you could've tried!"

The older man rubbed his jaw and shook his head. "It wasn't just me keeping the secret, boy."

Jonas loomed over him, forcing Elias to tip his head back to meet his gaze. "Who the hell else knows?"

"You do—or did."

This was way too much, he told himself as he threw up his hands in disgust. "Explain," he muttered, though something inside him really didn't want any more damned information tonight.

"To make extra sure you'd forget," Elias said, his voice suddenly old and tired, "your pa did somethin' to ya."

"Did something?" Jonas's gaze narrowed again. "What? Painted me blue? Had me howl at the moon?"

Elias scowled at him. "No call to get so damn smart-mouthed."

"No call?" Jonas asked, amazed. "I think I'm being pretty damned patient under the circumstances."

"Is that so? Well, I didn't raise you to sass your elders."

Jonas laughed shortly. "You didn't raise me to lie, either. But that didn't stop you any."

"It's easy enough to sit by twenty-five years later and say what should have been done," Elias grumbled. "It was different then. It was just me, left to care for a kid."

Jonas wouldn't be swayed by emotion. Not now. Later, he'd recall how much this old devil had done for him. Right at the moment, all he wanted was to hear everything, once and for all, then put it out of his mind for good.

"Tell me what my father did."

"Wasn't much," Elias recalled. "Laid his hand on your forehead and said—"

"Forget." Jonas finished for him and gasped as a closed door inside him was thrown suddenly, violently open.

He held his head in his hands and groaned as a flood tide of information surged into his mind. Images, vivid and real, staggered him. He saw his parents and wondered how he could ever have forgotten their faces.

And when he'd barely caught his breath from that first, wild onslaught of memories, more came to him, crashing through him, racing across his brain. Knowledge, old and deep. Ancient, centuries-old secrets. It was all there. In his heart and mind and soul. And Jonas had no idea how to get rid of it all.

Realizing that, he felt lost. For the second time in his life.

Moments passed. The throbbing ache in his head and heart eased and finally, slowly, Jonas lifted his head to look at Elias.

"You remember it all now, don't ya?"

Remember? God, it wasn't a big enough word to describe what had just happened to him. It wasn't only his own memories he'd regained. But the memories of hundreds of people. All Mackenzies'. The knowledge of the ages had poured into him in the wink of an eye and he still trembled from the impact.

"Yes," he muttered thickly. "Damn me, I do." Turning, he walked down the length of the barn and into the yard, Elias just on his heels. "And damn you, too."

"Why me?"

"You should've kept lying. Hell, you'd been doing it for twenty-five years. Why not a few more?"

"Now you *want* me to lie?" Elias spat.

"What I want is to be alone."

"Where you goin'?" the old man asked.

"To bed," he snapped, then stopped short, seeing the light spilling from the windows onto the dirt. He couldn't go in there. *Hannah* was in there. And if there was one thing he didn't need at the moment, it was one more witch.

Elias cleared his throat and Jonas realized he wouldn't be able to sleep in the bunkhouse, either. The old coot would keep yammering at him all night.

Making a sharp right turn, he started walking again, unwilling even to take the time to go back into the barn and saddle a horse. He needed some distance between him and the people around him. He needed to think, damn it.

He stalked past the corral and kept walking, rocks and pebbles sliding beneath the soles of his boots. The night wind caught and tugged at his hair and he realized he hadn't even brought his hat with him.

Grumbling darkly, he kicked at the far corral post and winced when his foot exploded in pain. He kept walking, hobbling slightly and cursing himself for a fool as he went.

At the edge of the ranch yard, he stopped and looked back. Elias still stood where Jonas had left him. Light still poured from the house, making a golden splash against the earth.

Everything looked the same, yet it was all different now. *He* was different now.

Just to cap everything off, thunder rumbled, and directly overhead a spear of lightning was tossed across the sky, white-hot fingers scraping at the darkness. Rain, cold and pelting like bullets, fell on him, drenching him in seconds, and he scowled at the sky before glaring at the home he didn't dare enter—not even in this storm.

"Damn it, this is *my* ranch," he muttered. "Why the hell am *I* leaving?"

But he didn't get an answer, so he stepped into the

shadow of the tree line, losing himself in the rainy darkness.

"It's the only way." Jonas said and folded his arms across his chest.

"But you need me," Hannah argued futilely as she stared up into his shuttered blue eyes.

More than she knew, he thought, but his rigid stance didn't weaken a bit. "We'll get by," he said, despite the moan of distress from Stretch Jones, who stepped past him to load Hannah's carpetbag into the wagon.

"Who'll cook?" she demanded and snatched up Hepzibah before the little cat got stepped on.

"Elias," he said. "Or me."

"Good Lord, save us," Stretch muttered, then hurried back to the corral when his boss glared at him.

"But Jonas—"

"Hannah," he interrupted, "I'm sorry it's come to this, but you've got to go."

He didn't look sorry. Just determined.

Dawn was just streaking the morning sky with touches of pale pink and rose. He'd hardly given her time to dress before announcing that Elias would be taking her to the stage, where she could catch a lift to the train station.

Her gaze slipped past Jonas to the wagon, horses hitched and ready to go. Her carpetbag was stowed behind the driver's seat and the horses were stamping in their traces, the harnesses jingling quietly in the still morning air.

Reaching out for him, she grabbed his forearm and drew him to one side. Lowering her voice, she looked up at him and said, "What about last night? What happened with the herd?" They hadn't talked about any of it. And she'd *needed* to. What he'd done . . . what she'd seen . . . even the memory of that one moment was enough to steal her breath away. Oh, she'd known the Mackenzie was a powerful warlock. But knowing something and actually witnessing it were two different things.

And in her heart, she silently admitted to a twinge of envy. She'd realized that she would *never* command the kind of abilities the Mackenzie possessed. No matter how much she practiced, how many books she read, the strength of his powers would always elude her.

With that realization, a long-held dream had died. But she'd reminded herself that she was a Lowell, and so had much to offer him anyway.

If he would only listen.

His jaw tightened even further, something she would have wagered was impossible.

"I don't *want* to talk about it." He shifted his stance, his boots scuffing on the still-muddy dirt. His gaze drifted from the house to the corral and back to her. Eyes narrowed, he whispered "I want my life back, Hannah. The way it was before you came. Before I . . . remembered."

She understood, really. But he had to see that was impossible. "You can't go back, Jonas. We can only go forward. Together."

Hepzibah yowled and scrambled in her arms, trying to reach her favorite man. But Hannah kept a tight grip on the little cat.

Jonas inhaled sharply, gave a quick look around to make sure no one was near, then dipped his head a bit, meeting her gaze with his own. "There is no *us,* Hannah. There can't be. I've already told you that."

Moving quickly, before she could start talking again. Jonas picked her up, marched to the wagon, and plopped her down on the bench seat beside Elias.

She glanced at the older man, who shrugged, then looked away guiltily. Then, turning her gaze back on Jonas, she asked, "Can you let me go so easily?"

He tugged the brim of his hat down low over his eyes and squinted up at her. In those icy blue depths, she read his pain and regret, but it didn't help.

"Nothin' about this is easy," he admitted.

"Jonas—"

"It's been real interesting knowing you, Hannah," he said, cutting her off, and slapped his palm down onto the backside of the closest horse. "Have a safe trip home."

The wagon took off with a lurch and she grabbed hold of the seat to steady herself. "Elias," she said.

"There's no talkin' to him about this, missy," the older man said. "Best if you just go on home and forget about him. And this place."

Forget? About her destiny?

How could she forget, when she knew that this failure would cause harm to so many people? Without her marriage to the Mackenzie, Blake Wolcott would be able to force her to marry him. Then he would simply kill whoever tried to stand against him.

She turned in the seat to look at Jonas one last time. Tall and lean, he stood as he had lived most of his life.

Alone.

And in that moment, as she left him, Hannah realized how much she'd come to love the man who was turning his back on their destiny.

A half hour later, Jonas was drinking his second cup of coffee and enjoying the quiet in the room. He scowled to himself, shifted in the chair and moved his shoulders as if trying to shrug off a discomfort.

Had it always been this quiet?

"Yeah," he muttered and told himself he'd forget about Hannah soon enough. The fact that she wasn't standing at the stove humming to herself wouldn't bother him in a few days.

He looked down at his coffee and his lips twitched as he remembered fishing white feathers out of his morning brew. Another thing he wouldn't miss, he thought.

Feathers. What the hell had that been about? he wondered and told himself that he'd never know the answer to that now. Now that he'd sent her away.

Jonas looked up at the open doorway and his mind conjured her there, smiling at him, morning sun gilding the gold in her hair. She was so real, he almost spoke to her, but then she dissolved like morning fog in sunlight.

She was gone and that's what he'd wanted.

He just hadn't expected to miss her so much, damn it.

"That's enough of that," he muttered and shifted his gaze to the black surface of his coffee. Emptying his mind, he tried to find the peace he needed so desperately.

But in an instant, a strange image rose up in front of him. The wagon, he thought, scowling. Elias driving, Hannah talking, naturally.

Jonas watched a scene unfold before his eyes and told himself he was imagining things, even as his heartbeat skittered and his palms went damp.

Hannah on the stage, then arriving at the train station. A tall man coming up behind her, grabbing her. She spun around, looked up at him, and went pale as a ghost. Jonas's teeth ground together as the man smiled at her fear and half dragged her onto the train. Hannah's frantic gaze swept the station platform futilely, searching for help that wasn't there.

Searching for him, Jonas.

Jaw tight, he rubbed his eyes and shook his head. What the hell was going on? he wondered. Why was that fellow grabbing Hannah and why was she so scared?

He sat up straight, pushed his coffee cup into the middle of the table, and gave it a wary look.

Witchcraft.

Horseshit.

He jumped to his feet.

It didn't mean anything. Just his imagination, that was all.

He stomped out of the kitchen and headed for the barn. Hannah wasn't in trouble. And there was no reason to think she would be. That Guild she'd talked about . . . well, that wasn't his concern. Quickly, he saddled the stallion, then swung aboard riding the black beast out of the barn and heading him toward the road to town at a fast trot.

Didn't mean a damn thing, he told himself as he bent low over the horse's neck. Just a daydream. Too tired, that was all. He probably just needed some sleep. The miles flew past, with the only sound the drum of his horse's hooves against the hard-packed dirt.

When he saw the wagon ahead, a wash of relief doused him from head to foot and he didn't even bother trying to figure out why.

Pulling his horse up alongside them, he noted Hannah's quick smile and the shine in her eyes.

Something inside him sparked into life and that worried him far more than any damn vision he'd seen in his morning coffee.

"What's goin' on?" Elias demanded, still angry over the night before. Though what he had to be mad about, Jonas didn't know.

It was a good question, however. One he didn't have an answer to. What *was* going on?

"Changed my mind," he said flatly, refusing to respond to the brightness of Hannah's smile. "Just turn it around and head on home. We got things to do."

"Then I don't have to leave?" she asked, reaching out one hand toward him.

He shook his head and accepted the inevitable. "Not today, anyway."

"Wish you'd make up your mind," Elias grumbled and tugged at the reins, turning the horses back the way they'd come.

"I have," Jonas snapped.

"So you say."

"Just drive, you old goat."

"Jonas," Hannah said, her voice rising to be heard over the men. "I'm so glad. I didn't want to leave. Not until we've—"

He leaned both hands on the saddle horn, caught her gaze, and spoke up quickly. "Understand me, Hannah. Nothing's changed. I'm not getting married and I still don't want to talk about witchcraft."

The smile died from her features slowly, as a dream dissolves when a sleeper wakes.

His chest tightened at the fading gleam in her eye. A few weeks ago, he hadn't known Hannah Lowell existed. And now he'd give anything if she'd just smile at him again.

God help him.

"You can't ignore this, Jonas," she said patiently. "Pretending you're not a warlock won't change a thing, you know—"

"Stop!" he said and gathered up the reins again, almost regretting keeping her from leaving. Almost. "One more word, Hannah, and I swear, I'll be howling at the moon myself!"

Chapter thirteen

Jonas's gaze swept the open meadow, searching for signs that anyone else might be nearby. Spring grasses rippled in a soft wind. Tree limbs rattled together. From off to his right, a small stream ran swiftly with the recent rains and the water chuckled over rocks worn smooth over the years.

He tipped his head back to look at the sky and watched as the sun slipped out from behind a cloud. Squinting, he sighed, lowered his head again, and focused his gaze on a lightning-struck cottonwood at the edge of the clearing.

As old as time, the tree was gnarled and bent, its trunk split years ago during a storm. Yet the damn thing kept on growing, now looking more like two separate trees than one.

"All right," he muttered and flicked a glance to his horse, the only witness to what he was about to try. "You best keep your mouth shut, or you'll find yourself in a stew pot," he warned. The stallion shook its head, sending its mane flying, then, forgetting about the man, dipped its head to the grass.

Crazy, he thought.

But damn it, he had to know. Had to find out. And this was the only way to be sure. He thought.

Jonas rubbed his jaw, faced the tree again, closed his

eyes, inhaled deeply, and lifted one hand to point at it.

"Grow straight again," he said, and even as the words came from him, he could hardly believe he was doing this.

Suddenly, he remembered that first day Hannah had stood in his kitchen and how she'd held her hand out for the broom and he'd laughed at her. Now, a month later he was talking to a tree.

What kind of fool did that make him?

From behind closed eyes, he saw the shimmering warmth of the sunlight and tried to tell himself he didn't look as foolish as he felt. But he knew what sort of picture he made. A lone man, pointing at a tree, waiting for magic to happen and praying it wouldn't.

He shoved that thought aside and buried it beneath the frustration that seemed to bubble too near the surface lately. Nobody had to know what he was up to. And by God, nobody would.

Focusing his mind on the stupid tree, Jonas imagined it strong and straight, as it had been before that long-ago storm.

If this worked, then he'd have to find a way to deal with this new and startling change in his life. If it didn't, then . . . hell, he didn't know what. He couldn't have his life back as it was. Hannah's presence prevented that. And now that he remembered his parents, his mind would never be free of memories.

Grumbling, he threw a mental blanket across the jumble of thoughts in his brain. Obviously, he was damned if he was a witch and damned if he wasn't. There was no way to win in this mess.

Pulling in another deep breath, he slowly, cautiously opened one eye.

"Son of a bitch."

Opening both eyes wide, he stared at the tree.

Still growing like two separate things, one half of the old cottonwood remained twisted and bent like an old man huddled over a glass of whiskey. But the other half, damn it—stood straight and tall as a new sapling.

His gaze followed the towering tree from its base to the tip that scratched at the gray clouds beginning to scuttle in from the mountains. Jonas shook his head slowly and fought down a flicker of disquiet in his soul.

Then, scowling fiercely, he swung his gaze to his horse. "Now, what's that mean, you figure?" he demanded as the stallion cropped grass. "I'm half a warlock? Or half a rancher?"

The horse didn't give a good damn.

And why should it? It was Jonas's world that was tumbling down around his ears.

Disgusted with himself and everyone else, Jonas swung aboard the animal, gave the tree one last, venomous look and rode off in the opposite direction.

"How long are you going to avoid talking to me?" Hannah asked as he stood up from the supper table to follow his men out the back door.

"As long as I can," he said.

"That's not an answer to our problems," she countered and stood up to face him.

"*We* don't have a problem, Hannah," he reminded her. "It's my problem to deal with as I see fit."

"By ignoring it?"

One corner of his mouth lifted as though he were trying to find something to smile about and couldn't quite manage it. "Sounds a likely idea."

He didn't believe that any more than she did. She could see it in his eyes. But a more stubborn man she'd never met.

Hannah told herself to be patient. To understand what it must be like for him to discover the truth after so many years of darkness. But for heaven's sake, she was running out of time.

"Jonas," she blurted as he turned for the door, "do you care for me?"

He stopped, but didn't look at her.

"Do you?" she asked. "Even a little?"

"That's got nothin' to do with this."

"It has everything to do with it." Rounding the edge of the table, she came up to him and laid both hands on his forearms. The tingling warmth of that connection speared directly into her heart. A momentary flash in his eyes told her he'd felt it, too.

"Oh, Jonas, why won't you see that we're meant to be together?"

He stiffened.

She plunged on, refusing to be swayed by his discomfort. "Maybe it would help if I told you more about why I'm here."

"I already know that, thanks," he said gruffly. "You've made no secret of it. But like I told you before. I'm not getting married."

A kernel of panic nestled in the pit of her stomach, but she fought past it. "It's not just me I'm worried about, Jonas. Or even Aunt Eudora. It's the Guild."

His jaw tightened. "The Guild."

She saw knowledge flicker in his eyes. "You know about them now, don't you?"

"Yeah. I know. Just like I know my folks died trying to get me away from 'em."

She shook her head. That wasn't exactly the memory she'd been trying to prod into life. "Aunt Eudora told me about them—your parents. I mean." Her fingers tightened on his arms, and it felt as though she had a grip on a statue. "She said they didn't want the responsibility of the Guild hanging over them or you. That's why they left."

"I know that."

"But things have changed back home," she said hurriedly.

"This is *my* home, Hannah. Wyoming. This ranch."

He tried to pull away, but she doggedly held on.

"The Guild needs you, Jonas." She paused and locked her gaze with his. "I need you. And you need me."

He took a long step back, pulling away from her grasp. "You beat all, you know that?" Staring at her, he shook his head. "Just how do you figure I need you? Before you came here, my life was damn near perfect!"

Hannah winced at the raw pain in his voice, but stood her ground. At least they were talking.

Pacing, his bootheels slamming against the plank floor, he stomped back and forth across the kitchen, tossing her a glance every now and then as he went.

"I've built this ranch up from nothing." He stopped briefly to raise a hand and point at her. "And I did it with none of your witchcraft nonsense."

"It's not *my* witchcraft," she muttered.

"Well, it's sure as hell not mine!" he shouted, then came back around the table to her side. Grabbing her shoulders, he yanked her close, making her tip her head back to look up at him. "Do you know what I did today?"

"No."

"I tried being a witch!" The words came out in a harsh whisper, as if even he couldn't believe what he was saying.

Hope swirled inside her. If he was willing to try, then he might be willing to do a lot more. "What happened?"

He let her go so abruptly, she staggered backward a pace or two, then came close again, silently demanding that he tell her.

Jonas shoved one hand through his hair, raking it back from his eyes. "It only half worked," he muttered thickly.

What? she wondered, but didn't ask. "You only need practice," she told him instead.

"Practice?" He glared at her. "You think I'm going to try something that stupid *again*? No. Forget it. I've made it this far in my life without magic; I'll make it the rest of the way, too."

"Have you?" Hannah asked, grabbing his hands and

holding on when he would have pulled away. "Have you really lived without magic?"

"Damned right I have."

Snippets of things she'd heard since coming to Wyoming filtered through her mind and she snatched at them like a child grabbing for a stick of candy. "Don't all the men say you're the luckiest man they've ever known?"

Worry flitted across his face briefly as though he'd wondered about the same thing himself. But that expression was gone again in a heartbeat.

"Luck's not magic," he snapped, adding, "I've seen dumb luck save more fools than I can count and not one of them was a witch."

"Stubborn," she muttered, then blew a breath and tried again. "What about the weather?"

"What about it?"

"Haven't you noticed that whenever you lose your temper, it rains and storms?"

His hands in hers tightened slowly, steadily, until it felt as though her fingers might snap in his grasp. Mouth grim, he asked. "What are you saying?"

She looked up into eyes that glittered darkly and had to swallow back a small tide of nervousness before answering. "I only noticed it myself a few days ago."

"What?" He let go of her hands and backed her up against the closed kitchen door. "You noticed *what*?"

Thunder rumbled in the distance and his head snapped up like a wolf on the scent of a fresh kill. Quickly, he dropped his gaze to hers again.

"That when you're angry, storm clouds gather. And the angrier you get, the blacker the storm." She shifted beneath his grip and felt her own temper start to rise. After all, it wasn't her fault he'd been drowning the countryside.

"You're lying," he said, his voice a tightly leashed weapon.

"Am I?" she asked over another slow roll of thunder.

He released her again and jumped back, cocking his ear to listen to the coming storm.

"You really should learn to control your temper," Hannah pointed out, "before we all float away."

He snapped her a quick, disgusted look. "I don't remember having a temper until you showed up," he said, but made a visible effort to calm himself. A moment later, he asked. "Is it only anger that sets off a storm?"

She frowned slightly. "I don't know. It could be any number of things, I suppose. Why?"

"Nothing. Nothing." Jonas stabbed his fingers through his hair and tried to think. To figure this new problem out. But all he could hear was her voice telling him that his temper brought storms. Could worry do the same thing? Regret?

Sweet Jesus, he told himself, if it could . . . then what had happened ten long years ago was more his fault than he'd thought.

"What is it?" Hannah asked, dragging him from the bleak thoughts. "What's wrong?"

"Nothing that can be fixed now," he said past the knot lodging in his throat.

"Jonas." She stepped close to him again and he inhaled the light, delicate scent of lemons drifting to him. "Why did you bring me back here yesterday?"

Instantly, a newer memory—of the vision he'd seen the day before—rose up inside him. Hannah. In danger. Just the thought of it was enough to open a tearing wound inside him. He couldn't let her leave just to walk into trouble, could he? But even as he thought it, he knew that wasn't the only reason he'd gone after her.

Though it was the only one he would admit to.

His gaze fixed on hers. Green eyes swimming with emotion, her features tight, she waited. And he couldn't give her what she wanted to hear.

"Does it matter?" he asked, his voice weary.

"It does to me," she said, stepping closer still.

His gaze moved over her face and he realized again

just how empty the house had seemed when she was gone. It was as if she'd brought a heart—that had always been lacking—to the place. And had taken it with her when she left.

How had she done it? he wondered. Was it the way she treated the men who worked for him? Was it her willingness to help? Was it those damn feathers he hadn't been able to get out of his mind?

"Tell me, Jonas," she prodded gently, her voice dropping to a low, throaty whisper. "Tell me why you brought me home."

Home.

That's what she'd made of this place.

A home.

While that realization still shimmered through him, Jonas reached out and took her hands in his. So small. So smooth. Yet she was no stranger to work. She'd made herself a part of this ranch. A part of his life. Despite his efforts to prevent it.

"Damn it," he said on a long, shuddering breath. "I didn't want you here. Didn't want to care about you."

"I know," she said as he drew her closer to him.

His gaze moved over her as his arms held her tightly to him. He felt the fluttering beat of her heart and watched her pulse jump at the base of her throat. Sparks seemed to fly in the cool green depths of her eyes and a like fire sputtered into life inside him.

"I won't love you," he said because he felt he had to warn her.

"But I *will* love you," she said and knocked the wind from his lungs.

"Hannah . . ." His arms tightened around her reflexively.

"Kiss me, Mackenzie," she whispered, and her gaze briefly dropped to his mouth before locking with his again. "For now, just kiss me."

"God help us both," he murmured and gave in to the urges pounding through him. He dipped his head to claim a kiss and the moment their lips met, he felt the staggering rush of lightning-fed fires blazing through him.

Desire flashed into life and his body nearly screamed with wanting her. His hands moved up and down her back, molding her to him even as his mouth took hers. He parted her lips, tasting her warmth, taking her breath and offering his own.

She sighed and a new sense of strength flooded him, from the tips of his boots to the top of his head. It was as if he were coming alive for the first time. He heard the wood in the stove popping and hissing, heard the keening moan of the wind outside and the groaning from the logs as the house settled into night.

And it was all new. She gave him this. She brought him this.

And he had nothing to offer her.

Humbled and shaken to the core, he broke the kiss and, resting his chin atop her head, struggled for the air his lungs clamored for.

"Jonas," she whispered brokenly.

He would have chuckled if he'd had the strength. Of course Hannah couldn't be quiet for more than a minute or two.

"Does everyone feel that when they kiss?" she asked.

Leaning back against the kitchen table, he held her against him and waited for the hammering of his heart to ease. When he thought he could speak without his voice shaking, he said, "I don't think so."

Lord knew, until Hannah he'd never experienced anything like this.

"Aren't we lucky, then," she said and snuggled in closer to him.

Drawing the scent of her deep into his lungs, he stared through the window into the night and told himself to release her. To take a step back. Before it was too late. Instead, his arms tightened around her and he closed his eyes against the night peering in the window.

Against the memories already racing back into his mind.

In a whisper aimed more at himself than her, he said softly, "Lucky."

Hannah ran to him and Jonas jumped from his horse and opened his arms to her. Sunlight poured down on the meadow grass and sparkled in the fresh layers of snow high in the mountains.

He caught her up and swung her in circles through the meadow grass, relishing the fresh, lemony scent of her, loving the feel of her hands on his shoulders. He looked up into her laughing green eyes and felt love for her swell inside him.

He lowered her slowly, letting her slide down the length of his body, reveling in the fact that she was his. That somehow they'd found each other.

And when she framed his face with her hands and guided his mouth to hers, Jonas held his breath and thanked whatever gods had sent her to him.

Then she was gone and his arms were empty.

"Hannah!" He spun around, letting his gaze slide across the once-sun-filled meadow, now cringing from an encroaching darkness.

He watched it come, sweeping across the ground, obliterating everything in its path, cloaking the world in a black shroud that only seemed to blossom as it drew nearer. The air felt thick, poisonous. The hairs at the back of his neck prickled and he felt eyes on him, watching. Waiting.

From a distance, he heard her voice, strained, scared. "Jonas!"

"Hannah, where are you?" he called, racing toward his horse as it was hidden by the blackness still creeping nearer.

"Hannah!" he called again, reacting to the urgency inside him telling him to find her. Before it was too late. Time was running out. He felt it. Knew it.

"*She's with me, Mackenzie,*" *a man said, and his voice was filled with the dark.*

Jonas turned to face the shadows and watched as they twisted and writhed, shifted and tore. And at last, a man stepped out as if born from the blackness swallowing the meadow.

"*Who are you?*"

"*The man who will destroy you and have Hannah.*"

"*Who are you?*" *he demanded and vaguely heard the distant crash of thunder. But the storm wouldn't penetrate this solid wall of night.*

Nothing could.

"*Blake Wolcott,*" *the man said and stepped closer, smiling now at Jonas's confusion.* "*I've come for Hannah.*"

"*You can't have her,*" *he shouted, shifting to his right, preparing to fight this man any way he could.* "*She belongs with me.*"

"*She belongs to whoever is strong enough to claim her.*"

"*Come on, then,*" *Jonas said and half crouched, arms ready to fight.*

"*You're a fool.*" *Wolcott told him and his finely arched brows lowered dangerously over dark brown eyes.* "*You can't fight me and win.*"

"*Only one way to find out,*" *Jonas snapped and lunged at him.*

Wolcott laughed and waved one hand. As if shot by an unseen shotgun, Jonas went staggering backward. Pain engulfed him and he was falling, falling, tail over teakettle. When he finally found his feet again, he reached for the pistol strapped to his leg. He pulled it, aimed it, and fired.

Nothing happened.

"*You are a fool, Mackenzie,*" *the other man shouted, gathering the dark like a cape and swirling it around him until the entire world went black and only the two of them existed.* "*You can't fight me like a mortal man.*

This is warlocks' business and your time is finished!"

He lifted his hand again and Jonas dropped. His head fell back on his neck and he stared at the emptiness as it fell in after him. The earth gave way beneath his feet and the blackness swallowed him.

"No!" He clawed and grabbed, trying to fight free of the emptiness, but it was all around him and the only thing with him in the darkness was Wolcott's laughter . . . and Hannah's screams.

Jonas sat straight up in bed, gasping for air as he reached blindly for the matches he kept on the table close by. He found one, scratched it, and breathed easier as the flame sputtered, flickered wildly, and then caught, creating a tiny circle of light.

Carefully, he touched the flame to the wick of the lamp, then blew it out and stood up, legs shaking. Shoving both hands through his hair, he walked unsteadily toward the window and threw it wide. Cold air rushed into the room, making the candle flame dance and clearing away the last traces of the dream.

"Wolcott," he said, rubbing one hand across his face and shivering in the breeze racing past him. "Hannah said something about a fella named Wolcott."

Glancing over his shoulder at the closed door of his room and Hannah's beyond, he wondered if he should go wake her up and ask her about this bastard.

But a moment later, he reconsidered. One thing he didn't need at the moment was to be around Hannah in the middle of the night.

Not when he had so many other things to think about.

And consider.

Chapter fourteen

Steam lifted from the washtub, wreathing Hannah's face in a cloudy mist that dampened her hair and left curled blond tendrils on her cheeks and forehead. Positioning the scrub board, she reached into the hot, soapy water for another shirt and, fisting it in her hands, rubbed it across the metal slats.

Her shoulders ached, the small of her back throbbed from bending over the tub, but she was nearly finished and that gave her a sense of satisfaction. From around the corner of the house, she heard the men at the corral working with the horses again. The heavy slap of a body hitting the dirt told her yet another man had been thrown.

Shaking her head slightly, she muttered, "But he'll only get up again, bruised or bleeding, and climb back on the horse."

"Should he quit, instead?"

Hannah gasped and looked over her shoulder at Jonas, leaning against a log wall. One foot crossed in front of the other, his arms folded across his chest, he was watching her through eyes that set off sparks inside her.

"You startled me."

"I know."

She hadn't seen him since breakfast and just the sight

of him now was enough to warm her through.

Breathing deeply, she forced herself to turn back to her task. "It would certainly be less painful if the men would just stay off once they're thrown."

"And we'd never get a horse broken around here, either."

Stilted conversation. Awkwardness colored the air between them and she wished it were different. Wished that they could simply come together as it was destined to be. As she knew it should be.

Love swelled inside her and Hannah couldn't help wondering when that love had taken root. Had it always been there, waiting for him? Had she only needed to be with him for it to blossom? Or was it a gift, handed to her by the same fates that had determind a Lowell should marry the Mackenzie?

And what did it matter now?

She remembered saying the words to him last night. And she remembered clearly that he hadn't returned them.

He walked toward her, his boots scratching against the ground. When he stopped beside her, he went down on one knee and glanced into the washtub. "I told you, you didn't have to wash my shirts."

Washing his shirts was simply another way to be close to him. To inhale the scent of him trapped in the fabric.

She shrugged. "I have to do my own; a few more aren't so much extra trouble." Her fingers curled into the wet, dark blue fabric of his shirt. And her mind painted a picture of him without that shirt. Bare chest, muscles gleaming in the lamplight, and the feel of his arms wrapped around her.

She hadn't gotten much sleep last night. Her dreams had been haunted by the memory of his kiss and the craving for more. Her body stirred with longings she didn't know how to ease and her mind kept the image of Jonas's face before her all through the long, dark hours of the night.

But it seemed, she thought with a quick glance at him from the corner of her eye, that he hadn't slept much, either.

She couldn't help hoping it was thoughts of her and not worries over his newly discovered witchcraft abilities that had kept him awake.

He reached out and scooped one finger across the soap bubbles covering the surface of the water. Lifting his hand again, he watched the bubbles pop as water rolled down his finger to soak into the cuff of his sleeve.

"Who's Blake Wolcott?"

The shirt fell from her grasp and her bare knuckles scraped painfully against the metal scrub slats. He grabbed for her hand before she could react and brought it close to his face. Smoothing one finger across the rubbed-raw skin, he looked into her eyes and said, "You mentioned his name once. You said Hepzibah"—frowning, he glanced around for the cat—"didn't care for him."

A sizzle of heat snaked from her hand to her arm to her chest and settled around her heart. As he touched her, the pain of the scrape lessened and she could almost feel her flesh healing over.

Hannah reminded herself to breathe. "No, she doesn't." Smiling slightly, she added, "You can stop looking for her; she's in the house."

"Good." He released her hand, but didn't move otherwise, watching her and waiting for an answer to his question.

Hannah glanced at her injured knuckles, not surprised in the least to find that her skin wasn't even red anymore.

Instead of answering him, she asked a question of her own. "How much do you remember now about the Guild?"

"Enough to know it has nothing to do with me."

"But that's not true," she said quickly and reached out to him She laid her hand on his forearm and he briefly lowered his gaze to it. "The Guild is important to all witches."

He pulled away from her, frowned, and took a seat on a relatively dry patch of ground. "Tell me."

How to explain? she thought, searching her mind for the right words. The words to convince him just how important he was. Not only to her, but to the witches in Creekford, waiting for his help.

"The Guild," she started slowly, choosing each word carefully, "is an association of witches."

He nodded.

"We banded together centuries ago," she went on with a smile, remembering all of the stories Eudora had told her as a child. "In the days of the witch hunts, we were safer as a group than by ourselves."

"I can understand that," he said. "But that doesn't answer my question."

"I'm getting to that."

He sighed.

"The members of the Guild protect the magic, keep it from being misused."

Still frowning, Jonas pulled a tuft of grass from the earth and studied it as though looking for the secrets of the universe in a few blades of green.

Sighing again, he muttered, " 'The magic.' "

"Yes," Hannah said and moved away from the wash-tub to take a seat beside him. Sunshine spilled across her shoulders and a soft, cool breeze filtered down from the mountains to ruffle her hair and ease the hot blood coursing through her.

Gently, she laid her hand on his arm again, feeling the corded muscles beneath the soft, worn fabric of his shirt. A strong man physically, he was also strong in magic. He simply didn't know *how* strong yet.

"The magic doesn't belong to any one witch," she said, dipping her head to find and meet his gaze. "Magic is . . ." She shook her head, searching for the words and not finding them. "Alive."

His gaze narrowed on hers.

"It's in every living thing on the earth. Grass, trees, rocks, water, wind, fire . . ."

He laughed shortly, without humor. "A *rock* is alive?"

She smiled and shook her head again. "Just because you can't see it breathe doesn't mean there isn't life inside it." Sighing, she tried harder. "The magic lies within all these things. And a witch—or a warlock—is merely a human who knows how and where to look for it."

His fingers plucked at the grass in his hands, shredding it, tearing it into tiny pieces to be carried away on the wind. "Magic grass," he muttered on a choked-off laugh.

"Rocks. Trees."

"*They're* not magic," she said, frustrated because she wasn't explaining any of this well enough. But she'd been raised with this knowledge all around her. She'd accepted it as simply a fact of life and had never before had to try and describe it to someone unfamiliar with it. After all, no witch told her secrets to an ordinary person. "Magic is the life pooled inside these things. Magic is something you can feel but not touch. Sense but not see. It's something you *know*." She reached out and laid her hand on his chest. "You *feel* it. In your heart. Your soul."

Jonas shook his head and tossed the last of the grass aside. Gently, he took her hand from his chest, breaking the connection between them.

Staring at her, he said, "You're not telling me about Wolcott. That's what I want to know. The rest is just—"

"All right," she said quickly, reacting to the impatience she sensed rising off of him in huge waves. "Blake Wolcott is a warlock."

His eyes narrowed again. "Like me."

"No," she said quickly. "Not anything like you." Hannah shuddered at the thought. Blake Wolcott was a vicious, unprincipled warlock who killed for the sake of killing.

Jonas was a hard man, certainly. But the life he led had made him that way. Still, he was hard without being cruel. Something Blake Wolcott would never be able to understand.

"You said he was a warlock."

"He is. But he's not interested in protecting the magic."

"Neither am I," Jonas told her and pushed himself to his feet.

She scrambled up to stand beside him. "But you're not trying to steal the magic for yourself, either, are you?"

"Can he do that?"

"Can and is," she said softly, before strengthening her voice again. "He came to Creekford about a year ago from England."

"England!" Jonas snorted the word. "Yeah, we've seen a few of those Englishmen out here, too. Come looking to be cowboys and usually get themselves killed."

"Blake isn't interested in anything but power."

"Power?"

"It's all he cares about." Hannah went on. She'd longed to tell him this whole story since the first day she was here. Maybe if she had, they would be closer now than they were. Maybe he would have accepted his destiny already.

But regrets wouldn't help her now. She had to trust that everything would come about as it should.

"He's strong," she said, drawing up the mental image of Blake's sharp features. "Stronger than any of the rest of us. And since he's been here, he's only weakened us further."

"How?" Jonas asked, frowning.

How, indeed? If they'd known the answer to that question, perhaps they might have stopped him before he'd gone this far.

"I'm not really sure," she admitted, then shrugged and looked up at him. "But somehow, he's draining the strength from everyone in town and taking it for his own. He grows stronger daily while the rest of us can do nothing to stop him."

Jonas shifted his gaze from her and looked beyond her to the snowcapped mountains. Her words rattled around inside his head and he felt himself stiffening up. He'd never liked bullies, no matter what they called themselves. Sheriff. Bartender.

Warlock.

Jesus, a part of his brain still refused to acknowledge that any of this was happening. Warlocks and witches, for God's sake.

Rubbing one hand across his face, he asked, "Why don't you stand together against him? I once saw a town rise up against a bullying sheriff and ride him out of town on a rail." He lowered his gaze to hers again. "One man alone couldn't do it. But surely a whole town of witches could handle the job."

She inhaled sharply and her mouth twisted down at the corners. "People are afraid. Maybe we could have defeated him," she said. "At the beginning. But back then, we didn't know what he was up to. We *welcomed* him to Creekford as one of us." She wrapped her arms around her waist and squeezed tight. "It wasn't until much too late that we discovered he wasn't there to live as one of us. But to crown himself head of the Guild and rule everything from a seat of untouchable power."

"Why don't you all leave?" he asked.

Her gaze snapped to his. "Quit? Then what? Where do we go? What do we do? Do we keep running from Blake?" She shook her head and pointed toward the corral, where the voices of the men were raised at their work. "You said you couldn't quit when you got thrown from a horse or you'd never have a decent animal to ride."

Jonas winced slightly. He had said that.

"Well, if we quit, what would we have?" she demanded, moving in on him until he took a hasty step back, instinctively retreating from the fire in her eyes. "Centuries of tradition thrown at the feet of one greedy man? Our lives ruined? Our town deserted and dying?"

"What do you expect me to do about this, Hannah?"

"I *expect* you to claim your birthright."

"Which is what, exactly?"

"The leadership of the Guild."

"And do what?"

"Help us," she said flatly. "Help your brothers and sisters rid themselves of a warlock who wants to destroy them and everything they know and believe in."

"What if I can't?" he asked, remembering that tree in the meadow. Half straight. Half nothing changed. Could he stand against a powerful warlock and win when he didn't really believe most of this nonsense himself?

Hell, did he even want to try?

Those people in the Guild meant nothing to him. Oh, he thought, Hannah did. Despite his best intentions, he cared for her. More than he wanted to admit. But could he, even for Hannah, give up who and what he was to fight a battle that had nothing to do with him or his life?

"Can't?" she asked tightly as if reading his mind. "Or won't?"

She gave him one quick look up and down, then stomped past him, the dirty laundry forgotten in her angry frustration.

Jonas moved fast, though, and caught up with her in one or two easy strides. Grabbing hold of her arm, he whirled her around to face him. Her green eyes looked like flashing emeralds, glittering with the sun and the fine, high temper riding her.

Well, he wasn't through yet. He wanted to hear it all. Only then could he decide what to do about this.

"There's more, isn't there?" he demanded, remembering his dream and Wolcott's obsession with having Hannah. "Something you're not telling me."

"Isn't that enough?" she snapped, wrenching her arm free of his grasp.

"He wants you, doesn't he?"

She paled. He watched the color leach from her face, leaving her eyes two brilliant spots of green against milk-white skin. "Yes."

An invisible hand closed around his heart.

"Why?" He congratulated himself silently on squeezing that single word past a throat too tight to breathe through.

The fight went out of her. He saw it in the slump of her shoulders and heard it in the soft tone of her voice. A sheen of water sparkled in her eyes and he hoped to hell she could keep those tears from falling.

"Because I'm a Lowell," she said finally. "The last of the Lowells."

"So?" What the hell did her name have to do with any of this, for God's sake?

She gave him half a smile. "The Lowells were a powerful family in the Guild. We—Eudora and I—are the last. He knows that by marrying me, he'll strengthen his own powers by being able to draw on mine." At his look of disbelief, she added, "Oh, I'm not a very good witch, I know. But as a Lowell, the talent is there—and would be passed through me to my husband. And my children."

"So you came to me," he said tightly, trying not to flinch at the words *husband* and *children*.

"Yes." She reached up and scrubbed the tears from her eyes with the tips of her fingers. "You're our last hope, Mackenzie. You're the only one strong enough to defeat Blake Wolcott."

The tree, he reminded himself and thought maybe he should tell her.

"And when we marry, my family's power will be yours, strengthening you further. And the child we conceive will have the strength of both our lines."

Again, he thought, groaning silently at her words. He remembered all too clearly the last time she'd spoken of marriage and children.

She'd been stretched out naked atop his bed, offering her virtue for the sake of this damned Guild. His fingers curled into fists to keep from reaching for her. His body tightened, thickened with the memory of her smooth skin and the desire she quickened inside him.

Briefly he gave into her fantasy, imagining her round with his child, and surprised himself by enjoying the image. But in the next instant, old memories reared up to strangle him with fear and he let that mental picture go.

She lifted her chin and stared at him, that green gaze spearing into his. Apparently, she had no trouble guessing what he was thinking, because she assured him, "A marriage between us would only help you."

"Maybe," he said and briefly touched her cheek with his fingertips before letting his hand fall to his side. "But it might kill you," he added. "And that's one chance I'm not willing to take."

"If I never *see* another train, it'll be too soon for me," Eudora muttered and brushed one hand across the wrinkled fabric of her skirt. Good heavens, by the time she finally reached Hannah, she would look no better than the poor disheveled men she saw stealing rides in the boxcars.

Temper flaring, patience almost exhausted, she half turned in her seat to look at the man she'd begun thinking of as her shadow. Ed Thistlewaite no longer bothered to hide from her. Clearly, subterfuge expended too much energy to suit Ed.

Her gaze touched his and he inclined his round head regally, like king to peasant.

Eudora's gaze narrowed. It really wasn't wise to irritate her when she was already feeling tired and cranky.

Just above Ed's head, tacked to the back wall of the train car, hung a coal scuttle, with enough black lumps inside to feed the potbellied stove in the corner. Staring at it, Eudora lifted one silver eyebrow and the bottom of the scuttle dropped out.

Coal clattered from the bucket, bouncing off Ed's fat head and scattering across his full belly amid a cloud of black dust. The lazy man was forced out of his seat with a yelp and as he brushed ineffectively at the grime covering him, Eudora smiled and turned back around to face front.

She shouldn't have done that, she told herself firmly. It was an abuse of the magic, pure and simple. But, she thought, stifling a yawn behind a dirty glove, she was, after all . . . only human.

A few more days, she thought with an inward sigh. A few more days and she would be able to join Hannah and, she hoped, leave this train behind her forever.

The dream came again.

Jonas twisted and turned in his sleep: groaning, he lost himself in the battle that raced to meet him.

"Don't try, Mackenzie," Blake Wolcott *challenged as he strode across the dark emptiness toward his enemy. "You'll fail. You're not the warlock who can defeat me."*

"Now," Jonas *taunted, glancing over his shoulder for Hannah. He had to protect her. Had to keep her safe. "We won't know that till we try, will we?"*

Wolcott laughed and the sound boomed into the stillness, creating a thunder of noise that crashed around Jonas, pushing him down into the blackness.

"I'm too strong for you," the man said and waved a *hand, plucking a lightning bolt from the sky to hurl at Jonas's head.*

It flashed past him as he bent low and rolled out of range.

"Jonas!" Hannah *shouted and ran toward him.*

"Stay back!" he yelled and glanced at Wolcott warily

before turning back to her. "Stay away from him."

"I can help," she called out, still running, hands outstretched as if offering him a gift.

Another lightning bolt speared through the perpetual night, flashing brightly, then dissolving when it missed its target.

"Hannah, run, damn it! Run!" Jonas lifted one hand, palm out, toward her, hoping to stop her before she came too close to the madman closing in on him.

But Wolcott was somehow beside her now, holding her, turning her face up to his. The warlock spared Jonas a smile before he bent his head to claim Hannah's mouth.

He took and took from her until she slumped in the man's arms. Then, slowly, she faded from sight, until she was no more than a memory.

Wolcott laughed.

Jonas screamed, "No!"

And woke up.

Hannah raced from her room, across the hall, and threw open the door to Jonas's bedroom. A wash of moonlight lay over him, bathing his skin in a silvery light and glistening on the sweat dampening his flesh.

"Jonas?" she whispered from the doorway.

His head whipped around and even in the darkness she felt the strength of his gaze, pinning her to the spot.

"Hannah?" A world of fear and panic colored his voice. An instant later, he jerked the tangled sheets from his legs and leaped off the bed naked, crossing the room in two long strides.

Grabbing her, he yanked her up close to him and buried his face in the curve of her neck. She held him, her hands smoothing up and down his back. With her touch, she tried to ease the pounding of his heart and the rapid, shallow breaths shaking him.

"Jonas, what is it?" she asked, tipping her head back to look up at him.

"A dream," he muttered thickly.

His fingers tangled in her hair, cupping the back of her head. His gaze moved over her face, defining every feature, caressing every line.

"I need you, Hannah," he whispered, his mouth just a breath away from hers. "God help us both, I need you now. Tonight."

Her heartbeat skittered and she felt the heat of him soaking through the thin fabric of her nightgown. Her breathing quickened to match his and she shivered as a liquid pool of warmth settled low in her belly.

Knees weak, pulse jumping, she trailed her hands from behind his back and brought them up to cup his face in her palms. Whatever ghosts plagued him tonight, she would ease them—and find peace herself in his arms.

Staring up into the blue eyes that haunted her every waking and sleeping moment, she whispered, "I need you, too, Jonas. So much."

Then he picked her up and carried her to the bed and, laying her down on the mattress, he began the ravishing he'd promised her so many nights ago.

Chapter fifteen

Gently, he laid her down on the bed and Hannah breathed deeply to quash the sudden rush of butterflies in her stomach. Calmly, she reminded herself that *this* was why she'd come to Wyoming. This was her destiny.

The Mackenzie.

No, she corrected herself silently. Not just the Mackenzie. Jonas.

Staring up at him, her gaze moved over his so-familiar features. His strong, whisker-stubbled jaw, dark hair falling across his forehead, and those blue eyes that reached into her soul with every look.

Moonlight bathed him in a soft, hazy light. He reached to smooth her hair back from her face and she turned her head into his touch, relishing the gentle scrub of his hard-won calluses against her skin. In the indistinct light, his eyes were haunted, his mouth tight.

Then his gaze swept lower, sliding across the high-buttoned neck of her gown, to the swell of her breasts, and down. Again, that swell of almost liquid warmth swirled wildly through her. Looking into his eyes, she saw his desire for her flickering in their depths. His mouth just a breath—a kiss away from hers. She smoothed the pad of her thumb across his bristly jaw.

His eyes closed and he rested his forehead against hers.

"Hannah," he said on a muffled groan, "I didn't want to need you."

"I know," she said and rose up, meeting his kiss.

His lips moved over hers with a hunger she'd never known before. Her hands slid around his shoulders to the back of his head and fisted in his hair, feeling the black silk slide between her fingers. Another groan rumbled from deep in his chest at her response and his tongue smoothed across the part in her lips, searching, demanding they open.

When she obliged, his tongue swept into her warmth and Hannah gasped at the intimate invasion. Her nipples puckered against his chest and a curl of need settled low within her.

Again and again, he stroked the inside of her mouth, exploring, tasting, delving into the heart of her, willing her to respond in kind. And when she returned his caress with more enthusiasm than skill, his arms tightened around her until she thought her ribs would break. Yet she didn't care.

She didn't care about anything except the next wash of sensation. Hannah held his head to her, silently demanding more of him. She tasted his mouth, the edges of his teeth, took his breath for her own, and gloried in the rush of emotion that swamped her.

This was what she'd been waiting for most of her life.

This connection. This incredible feeling of belonging.

His right hand swept down along her spine, his fingertips tracing the length of her back until he reached the swell of her bottom. He caressed her through the thin cotton fabric, kneading her soft flesh with an urgency that fed the desire rocketing around inside her.

She squirmed in his grasp, cuddling tighter, closer, and felt for the first time the hard, solid strength of him pressed against her abdomen. New heat coursed through

her along a tide of sudden nerves that were then swept
away as he tore his mouth from hers to kiss the column
of her throat.

Tiny touches of lips and tongue trailed along her
neck, leaving fire in their wake. Hannah tipped her head
back and stared unseeing at the moonlit ceiling. Light
and shadow blended together as she let herself focus
only on the touch of his mouth on her skin.

"Hannah," he muttered thickly and cradled her close,
burying his face in the curve of her neck.

"Yes, Jonas . . ." she whispered, instinctively realizing that he was giving her one last chance to change her
mind. To leave this room—and him—behind.

But even if this hadn't been her destiny—even if he
wasn't the warlock meant for her—Hannah couldn't
leave him now. Not without knowing all of it. Feeling
all of him.

Becoming, at least for this night, a part of him.

Lying alongside her, he swept one hand up the length
of her leg, drawing the hem of her nightgown up and
up and up.

The chill night air brushed her skin and was warmed
by his touch. His fingertips trailed along the outer edges
of her leg, sliding up her thigh, over her hip. And then
he tucked his hand beneath the nightgown to continue
his explorations. Fiery fingers smoothed across her rib
cage, brushed the underside of her breast. Her breath
caught and the world seemed to suddenly stand still in
that heart-stopping moment. Then he cupped the fullness
of her breast and she gasped, digging her head into the
mattress, as he stroked his thumb across a nipple already
hardened and waiting for him.

"Oh, my stars," she whispered, eyes wide open, staring at the shifting shadows that darted across the ceiling.
She moved beneath him, straining to ease the low, throbbing ache that pulsed within her.

"Hannah," he whispered, as if he couldn't say her
name enough. Pushing the hem of her nightgown higher,

he bared her breasts and pulled in a deep breath as he looked at her. Smiling to himself, he dipped his head and took first one rosy pink nipple into his mouth and then the other.

Someone whimpered.

Surprised. Hannah realized the sound was coming from her. Then she forgot about everything but the feel of his warm, wet mouth on her body. Again and again, his mouth took her nipples, his tongue tracing the pink circle surrounding them, his teeth gently scraping across their tender tips.

Sparks flew inside her.

Desire fed on itself, building, blossoming.

He suckled her, drawing deeply on her as if trying to draw her heart and soul into his. With each tug of his lips, she felt the fire within her build, soaring powerfully into the night.

Then he lifted his head and she wanted to weep. Shifting her gaze to look at him, she said brokenly, "Don't stop."

He smiled, a slow, lazy smile that eased the shadows in his eyes and touched her heart.

"Hannah, we're just gettin' started," he assured her in a voice that rumbled along the edges of her nerve endings, sending a skittering of fresh goose bumps rippling across her flesh.

She licked dry lips and tried to still the frantic pounding of her heart as he leaned over her and eased her nightgown up and over her head. He tossed it aside and looked his fill of her, his gaze setting her blood ablaze.

Again, her tongue ran across dry lips and his gaze shifted to that action. Dipping his head, he too licked her lips and flames lapped at the lining of her stomach.

"You taste good," he mumbled and ran the flat of his hand over her body, his rough skin scraping against hers.

Hannah's mind whirled.

Then he eased onto his back, drawing her over and atop him.

She lay sprawled along the length of him, her naked breasts pressed to his chest, the slight dusting of hair on his skin teasing her flesh. Her legs atop his, she felt the hard muscles coiled beneath her and caught her breath again as his erection pressed into her abdomen.

"Jonas," she whispered and shifted her hips, hoping to ease the ache that only seemed to build with every passing moment.

"It's all right, Hannah," he said softly and turned again, this time pressing her into the mattress and lying half atop her while his hands moved over her, exploring every curve and line of her body.

Stars exploded in her mind. She twisted uncomfortably on the bed, writhing beneath his touch, hoping to find ease, to find . . . whatever it was that kept a careful distance.

Jonas stared into her eyes, watched them cloud with passion, and lost himself in the hazy green depths. He needed her more than he'd ever needed another living soul. Each breath she drew fed the flames inside him. Each shift of her body drove the hunger clawing at him.

With the new knowledge of who and what he was, he'd wondered if lovemaking would be different for him now. Would everything in his life be changed? Even to the loving of a woman?

And now he had the answer to that question.

Never before had he felt such a connection with a woman. It was as though he could feel what she felt. Experience both his pleasure and hers.

Heart pounding, lungs laboring for air, he slipped his hand down, across her belly to the tangle of blond hair at the apex of her thighs. Soft. Sweet. He went on, fingertips dipping to touch the heat that awaited him.

She jumped in his arms and he felt the explosion— the jolt of surprised delight that rocked her. He closed his eyes, savoring the sensation of being a part of her even before their bodies had joined.

His fingers delved her secrets, sweeping into the

warmth of her, and his mind filled with every detail of what she experienced.

Breathless, he murmured. "Is this magic, Hannah?"

Her hips lifted against his hand. "The very best kind. Jonas."

"God help me," he whispered and smoothed his thumb across the hardened nub of her center, shooting a dart of lightning that pierced both of them with its strength.

He shuddered and struggled to control himself. He needed to be inside her, to complete the link they inexplicably shared. To look into her eyes and know that she shared what he was feeling, as well.

Hannah moaned gently as her hips rocked with the movements of his fingers. And when he withdrew from her, she sighed brokenly and opened her eyes to meet his.

"I need . . ." she said softly, "I need—"

"I know darlin'," he said and moved to cover her with his body. "I do, too."

He entered her slowly, giving her body time to accept his. With every inch he claimed, his soul swelled. To be both invader and invaded was almost more than he could stand.

Jonas held perfectly still for a long moment, savoring the sensation of joining, truly joining with Hannah. And then he pushed himself home, driving into her depths.

A short, sharp burst of her pain exploded across his brain and he looked an apology into her eyes. But as that ache faded from her and from him, pleasure reared its head, claiming them both, drawing them down together into the swirling vortex of promised relief.

Her passion mounted, driven by his.

He looked deeper into her eyes, staring into her soul. And in that moment, he knew that she wasn't sharing his feelings. She didn't know the shattering combination of sensations that were pouring through him.

Hannah felt only her passion.

Not his.

A part of him wondered why that was, even as his body took over, blanking his mind.

He watched her head tip back, her eyes slide closed, counted the pulsebeats in her throat. His own heart thundering in his chest, Jonas slipped one hand between their bodies, his fingertips reaching for the core of her. When he touched her, he looked into her eyes and felt satisfaction claim her.

Hannah clung to him and mindlessly rode the crest of the wave rising from deep within her. His body sheathed in hers, she moved with him, racing toward the conclusion she knew was waiting. She looked up into his eyes and, staring into those icy blue depths, she gasped and jumped willingly into oblivion.

Jonas survived her climax only to drown in his own a moment later.

And when he slept, with Hannah cradled in his arms, there were no more dreams.

She woke before dawn, while night shadows still filled the room. Briefly, she looked around her, trying to remember where she was. And then the memories came rushing back and Hannah smiled, cuddling in closer to the man beside her. She laid her head on his chest and listened to the steady beat of his heart.

She felt more alive than she ever had before.

Smiling into the twilight of the room, she remembered all the times she'd wondered what the marriage act would be like.

And none of her imaginings even came close to the reality.

There was no doubt in her mind now. There could be no mistaking what had happened between she and Jonas. They were meant to be married. To be together. She and the Mackenzie were linked. One.

No matter that they hadn't spoken their vows yet. This was their wedding night as surely as if they'd stood in front of friends and family proclaiming their love for each other. This was the night they'd sealed their destiny. The night they'd joined two ancient lines and perhaps created the first of their children.

As that thought circled through her mind, though, she remembered that this was Jonas's second wedding night. He'd been married before. Joined with a woman who'd known the touch and feel of his body on hers. A twinge of jealousy shimmered deep within her, despite knowing she shouldn't envy a dead woman, but rather feel sorry for her at all she'd lost.

Still, Hannah wished she had been the only woman he'd loved. The only woman who'd touched him as deeply as he had touched her.

Frowning slightly, she told herself to let go of the past. After all, if he'd never loved before, how could he know enough to cherish what they'd discovered together? Surely a man who had survived losing someone he loved would be even more likely to realize what a gift they'd been given.

What mattered was that Jonas was *her* husband now. Her mate for a lifetime. And that, together, they would stand against Wolcott and anyone else who might threaten what they'd found together.

Jonas shifted beside her and ran one hand up along her spine to tangle his fingers in her hair. The man's slightest touch turned her bones to butter.

She smiled at his tenderness and whispered, "Thank you," with a full heart.

He moved his hand, letting his fingertips trail gently across her shoulders. She trembled with anticipation, already looking forward to being loved by him again. Silently, she wondered if being "ravished" was done the same way, every time.

"Thank you?" he murmured.

Hannah kissed his chest, then tipped her head back to look at him, meeting his lake-blue eyes. "For making my wedding night so perfect."

"Wedding night?"

Instantly, the blue of his eyes darkened into a swirl of indigo. His hand fell away from her and in one smooth motion he slipped out from beneath her and off the bed. Naked, he paced off a few steps, then came back and stood staring down at her, his features hard, jaw tight.

"Jonas," she asked, missing the warmth of his body already, "what is it? What's happened?"

"*You* happened," he ground out, his voice raw. "What the hell are you talking about? There was no marriage between us, Hannah."

Frowning, she reached for the sheet, covered herself as she sat up, and pushed her hair back from her face. For heaven's sake. He'd done the deed. Why was he upset now?

"We haven't said the vows yet, no," she agreed.

"And won't," he said with a brisk nod.

"Mackenzie," she said and scooted toward the edge of the mattress, holding one hand out toward him. He looked at it like it was a snake and took a hasty step back.

Letting her hand fall to her lap, she continued. "Why are you fighting this? We joined tonight"—a rooster crowed, announcing the dawn—"*last* night," she amended. "Just as we were meant to do."

He reached up and shoved both hands through his thick dark hair. The muscles of his chest rippled with the motion and Hannah sighed briefly, recalling the feel of his skin beneath her hands. How had this gone wrong so quickly? How could he possibly be regretting what they'd shared?

"Nothing is *meant,* Hannah," he said, and his arms fell to his sides. "Just like what we did has nothing to do with getting married."

She smiled indulgently at him. "I realize this is no ordinary engagement—"

"Engagement?"

"You really should stop repeating everything I say."

"I can't believe you're saying it."

"I don't know why not."

"Because I didn't *ask* you to marry me!"

"Not in so many words . . ."

"Not in any words."

"Jonas . . ." Her tone patient, she shook her head slightly and moved to the edge of the mattress, letting her bare legs dangle. Studying his features, she reminded him, "Our first child could already be on his way."

He paled visibly and his eyes widened, displaying a distinct glimmer of panic. Dropping his gaze to her abdomen, he shook his head firmly. He scrubbed both hands across his face as though trying to awaken from a nightmare.

"Jesus," he said, cutting her off before she could speak again. "There's no baby and we're not getting married." His voice steadied some as he added, "You have to understand that, Hannah."

"We *are* married," she said quickly, with a bit more impatience than she'd wanted to let him hear, "in the eyes of God."

He snorted. "God's had His eyes closed for so long where I'm concerned, you can be sure He wasn't looking tonight, either."

"How can you say that?"

"It's not as hard as you might think," he snapped.

Hannah jumped from the bed, dragging the sheet with her. It was one thing to lay with him, feel his hands on her as they made love. It was quite another to parade around his room trying to argue while naked.

And she *did* intend to argue.

Hadn't she explained everything to him? Hadn't she told him all about Blake Wolcott and the danger to the Guild? Didn't she make it clear to him that it was *his* duty to claim his birthright?

For heaven's sake, why was the man being so stubborn?

She took a determined step toward him.

"Just keep your distance," he warned her and backed off again, looking for, then snatching up his jeans from the floor.

"Mackenzie—*Jonas*," she said as he hurriedly got dressed, "we talked about this. You know who you are. You've accepted your heritage . . ."

He snorted.

"Now you have to accept that it's our duty to marry."

"No, ma'am, I don't." He tugged his pants on and when he was finished, he turned on her, his too-long hair tumbling across his brow, giving him a dangerous look in the early morning light. "I've *been* married. I won't do it again."

"Marie," Hannah whispered, bringing the dead woman into the room with them.

He winced at the name and turned away.

A sharp tug of worry pulled at Hannah. She gave a quick glance to the bed behind her and wondered if he could have touched her so intimately while still loving a woman long dead. And though she wasn't sure she wanted to know the answer, she knew the question had to be asked.

"Do you still love her?"

Slowly, Jonas swiveled his head to look at her. White sheet wrapped around her body, her golden hair spilled over her shoulders, tempting him to touch it again, entwine his fingers in the silky length of it. Her green eyes glittered in the soft dawn light and the scent of lemon seemed to fill the room, invading his lungs, clouding his mind.

If she left the ranch today, this moment, he would spend the rest of his life remembering her. Missing her.

Did he still love Marie—when the only woman he could think about was Hannah?

Damn it, he never should have made love to this woman. He'd known from the start what she wanted from him and known, too, that he couldn't give it to her.

Marriage to him was a poor bet, and by God, Hannah deserved better. No matter what she seemed to think.

Yet, even realizing the depth of the mistake he'd made last night, he couldn't regret it completely. His body still hummed with completion like he'd never known before. His mind still raced with the memories of her response to him. Her soft breath, her sighs, her hands caressing him, her body cradling him.

Never. Not once in his life, had he known such . . . *magic*.

Hannah had invaded his life, stolen his heart, and torn his world out from under him. Nothing would ever be the same for him again.

And she wanted to know if he still loved Marie.

"No," he said simply and hoped she'd leave it at that.

He should have known better.

"Then why?" she demanded, stepping closer.

Old angers and frustrations bubbled inside him. She had a right to know, he figured. But that didn't mean the telling would be easy on him. Better to just blurt it out and have done with it.

"Because Marie died," he snapped. "She died and it was my fault."

Chapter sixteen

"I don't understand," she said.

Jonas heard the flash of temper in her voice and was grateful for it. This would be easier on them both if she stayed angry. He didn't want to hurt her, damn it. But that's just what he was about to do.

"No reason why you should," Jonas said tightly. Mad at himself for letting things between them get so out of hand, he bit back a curse.

In the distance, thunder rumbled.

Another storm.

Shoving one hand through his hair, he felt his fury mount. Had she been right about the goddamned weather, too? Were his moods really responsible? If so, then he had a hell of a lot more to feel guilty about than he'd ever imagined.

He stalked to the window and stared off into the pre-dawn dusk. Overhead, a few stars still shone brightly, but he wasn't seeing them. Instead he looked beyond them, into the past. To a small cabin in Colorado.

"She was seventeen," he said and sucked in a breath to say the rest. "Pregnant with our first child." A swell of regret shimmered through him. He shot Hannah a glance and saw disappointment dart across her features before he turned back to stare at the still-sleeping ranch yard. "There was a horse auction being held in a county about thirty miles from our place. Elias and I, we wanted to go pick up a few for the ranch." It all sounded so stupid now. Yet back then, at twenty, he'd been determined to prove to his new wife that she hadn't made a mistake in marrying him. That she'd never regret giving up her father's nice house for his little cabin.

"Was it a big ranch?" Hannah asked, bringing him out of his thoughts briefly.

"Would've been, in a few years," he said, nodding to himself. Same thing he said about this place now, he realized. And suddenly, he wanted Hannah to know the plans he'd had. For someone to know that he would have done right by his wife if he'd had the chance.

"Marie was used to fine things," he said, recalling how she'd shuddered that first night in her new home. He'd built that cabin himself and had taken real pride in it until he'd seen it through her eyes. She'd lifted the hem of her dress and stared at the chinked walls and river-stone fireplace with tears raining down her cheeks. The sharp sting of shame stabbed at him again. "I would have made it up to her."

"What?"

"Everything. All she gave up when she married me," he said, squinting into the distance, looking past his reflection in the glass. "She wasn't used to rough living. She hated that cabin," he admitted with a shake of his head. "Hated the loneliness of ranch living. Wanted to be in town again, but"—he turned and noticed Hannah had walked up to stand beside him—"all I know is horses and cattle. A man has to support his wife with what he knows."

She nodded and he saw the sheen of unshed tears in her eyes and wondered idly if they were for him or for Marie.

Taking a deep breath, he blew it out again and turned from the sympathy in her gaze. He didn't deserve it. Staring blankly at the window glass, he shoved his hands into his pockets and went on. "Anyway, before me and Elias left, she asked me not to go. She was seven months along then and scared." He closed his eyes tightly. "But I knew she'd be all right. Knew I could go to the auction and be back before she missed me."

Opening his eyes again, his jaw hardened as old images wavered in front of him. "We bought a few good horses, and then"—he frowned, remembering—"I got to feeling like I should be at home. Like there was something wrong."

Hannah laid one hand on his arm. He hardly felt it.

"Couldn't explain it—not then, not now. Just, something inside me telling me to get home. We rode out, headed back, and a storm blew in, making travel hard." Scowling now, he said, "It seemed the more I worried, the harder the snow flew. We had to hole up and wait out the worst of it, Elias telling me the whole time that nothing was wrong. Marie was fine."

He paused and half turned to look at Hannah. Through gritted teth, he added, "She should've been. But she wasn't. We got home the next day, digging our way through the snow blocking the pass." He pulled in a long, shuddering breath. "I found her in our bed."

"Jonas . . ."

He shook his head, desperate now to get it said. Then she'd know. Then she'd understand that despite what he might feel for her, he couldn't take what she offered. Couldn't give her what she wanted.

"The baby'd come early," he said, rushing the words out, unable to stop the flow of memories that were choking him. He hadn't spoken of that night, ever. And releasing the words, the images, brought it all back so clearly, he half expected to turn and find Marie's sightless eyes staring up at him from the bed.

He bit back a groan. "It was a girl," he said, remembering the tiny scrap of humanity he'd buried with her mother.

"Oh, Jonas, stop," Hannah said, stepping in close and

wrapping her arms around his middle. Her palms flat against his back, she laid her head on his chest and he felt her warmth trickling into his scarred soul.

He didn't hold her. Had no right to hold her.

"So much blood," he whispered, and for a moment, his mind was awash in the deep scarlet that had stained his bed, his wife, and the child who'd never drawn a breath. "She was alone, because of me. In a cabin instead of town, because of me. And she died birthing *my* baby. I couldn't get to her because of a storm—a storm I know now that I probably caused. She's dead. Because of me."

Hannah only snuggled in closer, tighter, her hands splayed open on his back, rubbing up and down his spine, drawing out the chill that had hidden inside him for years. Her warm breath puffed against his chest and he felt the slow roll of her tears sliding down his skin.

God, he wanted to hold on to her. He wanted to take comfort for sins long past. He wanted to feel as though he deserved the love, the sympathy she offered.

But he didn't.

Taking her upper arms in a tight grip, he set her back from him, meeting her teary gaze with stone-hard eyes.

"Do you see now? Do you understand?" He gave her a shake that sent her hair flying and loosened the sheet she'd wrapped around her naked body. Slowly, slowly it slipped free and dropped from her to pool on the floor. In the dim light, her skin glowed like fine white china. But in his mind, he saw her lying in a pool of her own blood. Just like Marie.

And the horror that thought brought rocked him to his heels.

He released her instantly and turned his back on her. "I won't get married again," he muttered thickly. "I can't."

A rustle of fabric told him she'd grabbed the sheet again and twisted it around her. Then she laid one hand on his back and he flinched at her touch.

"Mackenzie," she murmured, her voice thick with

tears and pity. "I'm so sorry for you. For her." She took his arm and turned him around again to face her. "But I'm not Marie. I *like* your ranch and living in the country. I'm not fragile. I won't break."

"You don't know that."

Cupping his face with her hands. Hannah met his eyes, stormy with years old pain, and tried to ease him past those memories into a future they could share and make their own.

"Not every woman dies in childbirth, Jonas," she said.

"Hell, I know that," he said and cast a quick, uneasy glance at her midsection as if wondering if there was a child already growing within her.

Oh, she hoped so.

"And I'm a witch," she reminded him. "Marie wasn't."

One corner of his mouth lifted into a halfhearted smile that broke her heart. "Witches die, don't they?"

"Yes," she said. "We're mortal, like everyone else."

"Then what's your point?"

"You're a powerful warlock, Mackenzie. You could keep me safe."

"Like I did Marie, you mean?"

"You didn't know then who you were."

"If I had," he asked, his gaze delving into hers, "could I have saved her?"

Hannah breathed a worried sigh and shook her head. She never should have started this line of thought. Now he would plague himself with thoughts of "what if." Choosing her words with care, she said, "I don't know. No one can."

"So your witchcraft is good for nothing."

"You helped Billy," she reminded him.

"That was a small thing." He waved his hand as if brushing the matter aside. And across the room, his hat fell from the table. He frowned at it, glanced at his hand, then shook his head. "That was a burn. He was in no danger."

"We're not miracle makers, Jonas," she said with another sigh. "We're witches, not gods. And not even magic can defeat destiny."

He scowled at her and rubbed the back of his neck viciously. "My father said that, too. Elias told me."

She smiled and moved toward him. "What is meant to be *will* be. We are meant, Jonas. Can't you feel it?"

Grabbing her hands, he held them tightly, his thumbs stroking her knuckles. "I think you know exactly what I feel, Hannah."

Her breath caught at the swift, pulsing heat that leaped from his hands into hers.

He stared into her eyes and said. "You have to know, I wish things were different."

"They could be if you'd only let me into your heart."

"You're there, Hannah," he whispered and gave her hands one last squeeze before releasing her.

But she didn't even have time to enjoy hearing his words before he added quietly, "Now all I have to do is figure a way to get you out of my heart without killing both of us."

That Afternoon

Eudora stepped off the train, her carpetbag clutched in one tight fist. Turning her head slightly, she waited for Ed Thistlewaite to alight. When he did, she marched toward him and came to a stop just inches from his overfed, even dirtier-than-usual person.

"Eudora," he said, "lovely weather we're havin', eh?"

She inhaled deeply, pulling in the cold, crisp Wyoming air. Then, muttering a brief chant for patience, she looked up into Ed's small eyes and said sharply. "Send your telegram to Creekford, you turncoat."

"Turncoat?" he echoed, clearly offended.

How did he have the nerve to stand there looking

surprised after the way he'd cozied up to Blake Wolcott?

"You turned your back on your friends and neighbors to ingratiate yourself with Wolcott, didn't you?"

He shifted uncomfortably. A natural bully with no nerve was truly a pitiable sight. "Blake's a great man," he finally managed to say.

"You turned a blind eye when he killed the innocent."

Ed scraped his whiskery jaw with one hand. "He had reasons."

Appalled, Eudora gave him a scathing look that had him backstepping quickly. *"Reasons?"*

"He's a great man," Ed said again, as if trying to convince himself, this time.

"He certainly thinks so," Eudora said. "No doubt we'll all find out soon whether he's correct or not."

Ed picked up on one particular word in her statement. "Soon?"

Straightening up, she lifted her chin and looked the disreputable man in the eye. "I'm leaving the train now."

Ed looked at her suspiciously. "How do I know you're not just trying to make me leave the train without you?"

"Because I said so, you miserable little toad."

His eyebrows lifted high on his sweat-beaded forehead. "No call to be nasty."

If he knew how badly she wanted to turn him into the toad he so resembled, he would think twice about criticizing her manners. Control, Eudora, she told herself firmly.

On that thought, she said, "I'm going to find a hotel room for the night and set out first thing in the morning to join Hannah."

Again, a sly look crossed his features. "Wouldn't care to tell me exactly where she is, would you?"

"No, I wouldn't." Glaring at him, she went on. "When Wolcott arrives, tell him to follow the magic when he's ready to meet us. If he's as great a warlock as he claims, he shouldn't have a bit of trouble."

From somewhere in that corpulent body, Ed found a tiny bit of spunk. "Blake and me'll be along directly."

Eudora lifted one silver brow and narrowed her gaze on the man. Out of patience and out of time, she stepped closer, poked him in the chest with the tip of one finger, and said tightly, "Blake Wolcott must be dealt with. You, however..."

"Now, Eudora..." His brief stab at courage failed him. Ed's panicked gaze swept the empty platform.

"If I see so much as your shadow anywhere near me or Hannah," she warned, "I *will* turn you into a toad." It would be an abuse of her power, certainly, but she had a feeling that it would also be very satisfying.

He cleared his throat and stepped back, keeping his gaze locked on her finger as if expecting a bullet to fire from its tip.

While sweat rained off his broad forehead, she asked, "You know I can do it, too, don't you?"

"Yes, ma'am." The admission pained him, but he nodded and swallowed heavily.

"Good." Then, spinning on her heel, she walked away from the man, already feeling better.

All she needed now was a hot bath, a decent meal, and a good night's sleep, in that order. First thing in the morning, she herself would follow the magic—the faint traces of power emanating from the Mackenzie's presence—and rejoin Hannah.

"What d'ya figure he's doin'?"

Billy glanced at the man beside him and shrugged. "Hard to say."

Stretch stood up in his stirrups and craned his neck for a better view of the valley below. Easing back down again, he looked at the younger man and shook his head. "He's still just standin' there wavin' at that rock yonder."

"Huh." Billy scratched his jaw. "Don't make much

sense, but then, the boss has been actin' sorta peculiar here lately."

"*Peculiar* don't just say it, boy. Ever since that gal showed up, things 'round here have gone plumb strange." The cowboy shook his head solemnly. "Like my pa always said. 'Women's fine, just so long as you don't try to talk to 'em.' "

Billy squinted into the afternoon sun. "I like her."

"Oh, me, too, son," Stretch said on a laugh. "But look what she's done to *that* poor fella."

"What're you two doin'?" Elias rode up behind the two cowboys. "Don't you have some cows to tend?"

"Reckon so," Stretch said and tugged his horse around. "Although," he went on with a wink at Billy, "you might want to have a look at the boss."

The older man scowled at him. Stretch Jones was a man with too much time to talk. Once he got down to work, there wasn't a better hand with cattle around. But he did love the sound of his own voice. "What's that supposed to mean?"

Billy spoke up instead. With a nod toward the valley, he said, "Jonas has been down there for nigh on an hour, pointin' his finger at some rocks."

Frowning to himself, Elias rode a bit closer to the edge of the slope that led down to the valley. Sure enough, there stood Jonas, his horse close by, while he waved both hands at a small pile of rocks. What in the hell was going on around here now? he wondered. But to the two cowboys watching him curiously, he only snapped, "The only way you two could know he's been down there an hour is if you been settin' here watchin' him instead of workin'."

Billy ducked his head, but Stretch only smiled until Elias's hard gaze landed on him.

"All right, then," Stretch said a moment later. "Billy, we best get to those cows and leave the boss man to Elias, here."

Once they'd gone, Elias gave his horse a nudge and

started him down the grassy slope. Jonas hadn't spoken to him in a few days now except to give orders about the ranch. It was purely time they had a talk.

Jonas glared at the small pile of stones he'd set up a hundred paces off. Except for rattling precariously a time or two, they hadn't budged an inch. Despite all of his hand waving and half-witted attempts at witchcraft.

Hell, if he couldn't dispatch a pile of rocks, how was he going to deal with this Wolcott?

And he would have to deal with him, he knew. There was a feeling rising in him of impending danger. Something was coming and he had a feeling it was the warlock. But was the man coming to fight Jonas or to take Hannah?

Didn't matter, he told himself. Wolcott would be dealt with. Just because Jonas couldn't marry her, didn't mean he'd stand by and watch that warlock have her.

But who was he trying to fool, here? He didn't want *any* other man with Hannah. His fingers curled into tight fists as he imagined her living out her life with some faceless husband who would see her smiles, hear her off-key humming, father her children, and gather her into his arms every night.

A pain so wide and deep it felt as though his soul were falling into a black pit of despair opened up inside him. Hell, he hadn't been able to stand being in the kitchen without her for half an hour. How would he manage to live a lifetime without her?

There were only two choices that he could make in this. Marry her and worry every day that he'd lose her. Or lose her now and miss her for the rest of his life.

And there was still this Blake Wolcott to face. What if he wasn't good enough or strong enough to defeat the warlock? If he was killed in the coming fight, Jonas thought, how safe would Hannah be?

A cold chill suddenly raced along his spine, shattering his thoughts and demanding his attention. The small

hairs at the back of his neck lifted and he raised his gaze
briefly to the cloud-dotted blue sky. No wind stirred the
leaves in the trees around him. A warm sun shone down
on his shoulders. So the only explanation for that chill
was the renewed sense of foreboding building inside
him.

Wolcott was coming.

He felt it as surely as he did the ground beneath his
feet. And a part of him knew that he didn't stand a
chance in defeating the enemy readying to face him.
How the hell could he? He'd only just found out he was
a warlock, for God's sake. How was he supposed to pit
his skill against a man who'd been dallying with magic
all his life?

"What's going on here, boy?"

Elias's voice broke into his thoughts and he half
turned to watch the older man ride up. When the horse
stopped just a foot or two away from him, the other man
looped the reins through his work-roughened fingers and
folded his hands atop the saddle horn. Leaning in, he
looked from Jonas to the rocks and back again. "What
are you tryin' to do, exactly?"

Jonas shifted his gaze from the man's too-knowing
gray eyes. The resentment, the anger he'd felt for Elias
seemed to have faded away in the last few days. It was
hard to remain angry with a man who'd given you
everything in your life but your name.

"Magic," he said sourly.

"Ah. And how're ya doin'?"

"Well, let me just show you what all my practicing's
done for me."

Jonas looked at the rocks and slowly pointed his finger at them for the dozenth time in the last hour. Narrowing his gaze, he concentrated on that small cache of
stones until sweat beaded on his forehead.

What he got for his trouble was one tiny pebble rolling down the stack of stones to settle in the dust.

"That tell you anything?" he muttered in disgust.

Elias tipped his hat back on his head. "That you need you some practice?"

"Practice?" Jonas repeated. "You old goat, didn't I just say I've been *practicing* all afternoon?"

"I don't figure you can learn all you need to know in a day or two."

"Or a year or two," he snapped, feeling a rush of frustration fill him. In the distance, thunder rumbled and Jonas took a moment to calm himself. They sure as hell didn't need any more rain. "This is useless," he said when he was settled again. "The only magic I know is this."

Then he pulled his pistol from its holster, held it waist high, and fired from the hip. A bullet smacked into the tiny tower of stones, scattering them, and an instant later, the brief explosion of sound echoed through the valley.

"Magic's all right for some folks I guess," he said, "but I'll take my .44." A brief smile touched his mouth before he turned to look up at Elias. "Yeah, I'm a helluva warlock, all right."

He studied his pistol for a long moment before dropping it back into the holster. "You sure my pa wasn't lying about all this magic stuff?"

"I'm sure." The older man climbed down from his horse and dropped the reins to the ground, letting the animal crop the meadow grass. "Maybe you're goin' at this wrong."

Jonas chuckled. "Is there a wrong way?"

"Hell if I know," Elias admitted. "But maybe you shouldn't be tryin' so blamed hard."

"What d'ya mean?"

"Well, try it more like you just did with your pistol."

"Huh?"

Sighing, Elias said. "Instead of aiming and thinking about it too hard, just point your finger and go."

Jonas laughed sharply. "You mean like this?" He whirled around, pointed his hand at the remaining stones, and instantly they shattered with a bang, sending jagged pebbles whistling through the air like a hail of shotgun pellets.

Both men dropped to the ground.

Looking into the other man's surprised gaze, Jonas said in a stunned whisper, "What the hell happened?"

"You're askin' *me*?"

Slowly, they stood up, brushing dry grass and dirt from their shirtfronts. Elias looked at the still-smoking rubble of stones, then shifted his gaze to Jonas again. "Seems to me you're better at this than you thought."

"You mean worse," he said. "I didn't plan that. What good am I to anybody if I have that kind of power and can't control it?"

"You can't hope to change yourself overnight."

"That's exactly what happened, though," Jonas said and let his gaze drift to the near mountains. He rested his right hand on the carved wood stock of his gun. "Overnight, everything changed."

And nothing would be the same ever again, he knew. He would never be just an ordinary rancher. With every success, he'd have to wonder if it was his skill or magic that had made the difference. With every failure, he'd wonder if he'd somehow hexed himself.

Rubbing one hand over his eyes, Jonas almost wished he could wipe out the last few weeks. Make it so that none of it had happened. But even as he considered it, he realized that if that wish came true, he never would have met Hannah.

And that he couldn't imagine.

"I'm sorry I lied to ya, boy."

He shot Elias a quick look and shook his head. "Not your fault. I finally figured that much out at least." A short, harsh laugh choked him and he cleared his throat before speaking again. "You gave your word to my father." He looked the older man in the eye. "And you taught me what that kind of promise means."

Relief colored Elias's features and he looked younger by years as the knowledge that he was forgiven sank in.

"But," Jonas went on a moment later, as he looked across the land that he loved so much, "everything is still different now and I'm not sure what to do about it."

"Change ain't always a bad thing."

"Nor a good one."

"This ain't *all* about magic, is it?"

Jonas snorted and shot him a look. "I don't know what the hell else it could be about."

"Hannah."

He inhaled sharply and deliberately turned away from the older man. But Elias wouldn't be ignored and if he had something to say, it would get said, like it or not.

"You spent the last ten years hidin' from feelin' anything for anybody."

"Leave it alone."

"I don't think so." Elias stepped in front of him, meeting his gaze, silently daring the younger man to look away. "I watched you bury yourself in work and pretend it was enough. I sat by and let you beat on yourself because you thought you failed Marie."

"I don't want to hear this," Jonas said tightly. He'd been through it all with Hannah. Jesus, couldn't these people let Marie stay buried and let him find some peace?

"That's too damn bad," Elias snapped. "I'm through keepin' quiet about things that shouldn't be secrets."

"I got work to do," Jonas told him and half turned toward his horse.

Elias grabbed his arm and held him in place with an iron grip. "First, you'll hear me out. You look at Hannah and want what every young man wants. But instead of claiming her and what you could have together, you turn your back on it all."

"That's my business, you old goat."

"Not anymore." Elias's fingers tightened around Jonas's upper arm until the younger man winced. "Not when you're doin' it because of something that wasn't your fault."

"It was my fault," he said tightly, his voice scratching the still air. "I should have been there. With her."

"It wouldn't have changed a damn thing." His voice softening slightly, Elias added, "Some things are just meant to be, boy."

Hannah'd said that, too, he remembered.

"I don't mean to speak ill of the dead," Elias continued.

"Then don't."

"But Marie," the older man went on quickly, "was a spoiled, selfish girl."

"She was my wife, Elias."

"She didn't act it."

"She was only seventeen."

"You were only twenty."

"I took her away from her family. Her home."

"You married her. And took her to your home."

"She was used to better."

"And wouldn't make do with less."

Jonas pulled in a deep breath, closing his mind to the images Elias was evoking. It hadn't been a perfect marriage, he admitted silently. But she hadn't deserved to die. Alone.

"She might have done some growin' up in time," Elias said, his tone filled with compassion. "But she didn't have the chance. That was fate, boy. Pure and simple. Nothin' to do with you. You tried to make her happy," he added. "Take comfort in that."

"It wasn't enough." The taste of old failures seemed bitter on his tongue.

"No, it wasn't," Elias agreed. "It never would have been, with her." Releasing his grip on Jonas's arm, he gave the younger man a hard slap on the back. "But you've got another chance now. With a woman grown, who loves you, boy."

Jonas's eyes closed tightly. She did love him. More than anyone else ever had. It was in her touch. Her kiss.

Her smile. And everything inside him wanted to grab what she offered and hold it close.

"Don't lose that," Elias murmured. "It's too rare and precious."

Jonas looked at him and noted the faraway gleam in his eyes. "You still think about her—the woman you loved—don't you?"

Nodding, Elias stared dead into his eyes. "Every damned day, boy. Don't you live like I have. Alone. Missing the one woman who could have made you whole."

Hannah *did* make him whole, he thought. She filled empty places inside him he hadn't even known were there. "But," he said, more to himself than to Elias, "what if it all goes to hell again?"

"Don't turn your back on love because of fears of the past." His voice lowering, Elias added, "We've both hidden from the past too long, Mac. It's time we let it go."

Maybe, Jonas thought as another chill crawled through him. And maybe the past couldn't be buried without a fight.

Massachusetts

Blake Wolcott boarded the night train west, carrying only one bag. He didn't need much baggage, after all. It would be a short trip.

With Ed Thistlewaite's telegram tucked into his suit coat pocket, Blake smiled and took a seat at the front of the car. In a few short days, he would be reunited with Hannah.

With his destiny.

The dream came again and Jonas woke up in a cold sweat, air heaving in and out of his lungs.

He sat up, stared around his darkened bedroom, and tried to tell himself that it was only a nightmare. But it was more than that. Much more, and he knew it.

A chant danced through his mind, repeating itself over and over.

He's coming, he's coming, he's coming . . .

Jonas couldn't quiet the voices any more than he could ease the chill that seemed to have settled around his heart. Then Elias's words ran through his mind again and he couldn't help wondering if *his* destiny was to always lose the women he loved.

Chapter seventeen

Elias looked at the two of them sitting on opposite sides of the breakfast table and told himself that stubborn wasn't always a good quality.

He shot a look at Jonas, whose eyes were shadowed by a lack of sleep and haunted by old memories and new fears. Hannah's eyes were clear; it was her expression that told her tale. Staring at Jonas, she looked like a soul peering through the Pearly Gates at Paradise, knowing she hadn't a prayer of stepping inside.

His fingers tightened on the handle of his coffee cup. Ordinarily, he wasn't the man to stick his nose in where it might get punched, but damned if these two didn't need a good push.

"Y'know," he started, and both of them turned to look at him. "I'm not a nosy man."

Jonas snorted.

Hannah scowled at him before turning to the older man again. "Go on, Elias."

He frowned at Jonas and said, "I intend to, missy. Now, the way I see it is—"

"I already know how you see it," Jonas interrupted and pushed up and away from the table.

"Well, I don't." Hannah snapped and stood up, too. "I'd like to hear what he has to say."

"Thank you, missy."

"This has nothing to do with him," Jonas told her.

"Of course it has," she said, leaning toward him. "He's been a father to you your whole life. Who has a better right to offer an opinion?"

Elias sat back in his chair, folded his arms across his chest, and watched the fun. For the moment, they'd forgotten all about him. They were too caught up in each other. As it should be. His gaze shifting from one to the other of them, he could have sworn he saw sparks fly.

"This is between you and me, Hannah," Jonas said flatly, his gaze spearing into hers. "We decide. Nobody else."

"Oh!" She laid one hand on her breast and widened her eyes innocently.

Elias had seen that look from females before and if he'd had a chance, he'd have shouted a warning to the boy.

But she rolled right on. "Then you're saying *I* actually have a say in what happens between us?"

"I couldn't stop you if I tried," Jonas muttered. He'd never known a more hardheaded woman. It didn't seem to matter how many times he told her he wouldn't marry her, she didn't quit.

And a part of him loved her for it.

"No, you couldn't," she agreed and stepped around the edge of the table to stand in front of him. Stabbing the tip of her index finger against his chest, she went on. "And you've been deaf to me too long."

"If I'm deaf to you, how come all I do is spend my time arguing with you?" he demanded, looming over her, hoping for intimidation.

It didn't work.

"I don't know why you're arguing with me, Mackenzie," she said, leaning in and going up on her toes. "I tell you I love you and you act as though I'd stolen one of your precious cows."

Elias chuckled and they both glared at him briefly.

"What'd you expect me to do?" he demanded.

"I expected you to say you love me, too."

"What good would *that* do?" he asked, throwing his hands wide before grabbing hold of her upper arms and dragging her up onto her toes. Her face just inches from his, he carefully schooled his features, not wanting her to know what he was feeling. Just holding her like this sent a bolt of heat lightning right through the core of him. What he'd found with her was unlike anything he'd ever known.

He looked down into her flushed cheeks and over-bright green eyes and knew in that moment that he *did* love her. Loved her more than he'd thought possible. Her passion, her joy, her damned humming. Everything about her, he loved. Yet the knowledge solved nothing. There was still a danger to her. A warlock to face. And old fears to conquer.

"Love doesn't solve a problem," he said tightly. "It just makes new ones. Bigger ones." He released her before he could wrap his arms around her and hold on for dear life. "Ours are big enough as it is."

"So we ignore what we found together?"

"We try," he said simply, even though he knew it would be like trying to ignore the beating of his own heart.

Her eyes flashed green fire that should have singed him. "So you were lying."

"What?" She changed subjects so fast, it could make a man's head swim.

"When you said I had a say in what happens between us, you were lying."

"Of course you have a say." Hell, hadn't he spent most of the last few weeks *listening* to her say?

"Oh, thank you very much," she ground out from between gritted teeth. "I get an opinion, but only yours counts."

Couldn't she see how hard this was?

"Damn it Hannah—"

A sound from outside caught Elias's attention and he

half turned in his seat to look out the window. Frowning, he said. "Someone's coming."

He's coming, he's coming, he's coming . . . The chant repeated itself in Jonas's mind and he reacted quickly. Pushing Hannah back, he stalked to the window in two quick strides. Staring through the glass, he watched a buckboard roll into the ranch yard and relief poured through him.

"It's all right." He pulled in a deep, steadying breath. "It's a woman."

A woman. Elias's throat closed up as he stared at the tall, elegant creature being helped from the bench seat by one of the ranch hands. He felt his jaw drop as he looked her over from the top of her tiny blue hat to the tips of her shining black shoes.

"Sweet Jesus," he whispered around the knot in his throat. "Thank you."

"What's wrong with you?" Jonas demanded, and his voice sounded like an annoying buzz in Elias's ears.

"Who is it?" Hannah asked and pushed both men aside for a look. Then a moment later, she squealed with delight, shouted, "Eudora!" and raced from the room.

"Eudora." Elias repeated the one word quietly, almost reverently.

"Her aunt," Jonas said and focused his gaze on the woman. She didn't look like a witch, he thought, but then, neither did he. Or Hannah. As her name flashed across his mind, she hurried through the main room, darted out the front door, ran across the yard, and hurled herself at the older woman. Laughing and clutching at her hat, Eudora returned her niece's hug, then held her at arm's length to look her over.

Another witch, Jonas thought with an inward groan. He'd gone twenty-five years without knowing a damn thing about witches and magic and whatnot, and in the space of a few weeks, he was hip deep in them. Hell, if he wasn't careful, soon the place would be crawling with them.

From a distance, he couldn't hear what was being said, but he could feel Hannah's pleasure rippling through him like a rising tide, and in spite of himself, he smiled. Gaze shifting from one to the other of them, Jonas told himself the women were as different as night and day. If he hadn't known better, he wouldn't have guessed they were related.

As he watched, though, Jonas began to see that something about the scene was . . . wrong, somehow. He couldn't put his finger on it. He was still too new to this whole witchcraft business. But this was an instinctive knowledge.

Jonas sucked in a gulp of air and kept studying the women, even as Elias stood up and took up a position alongside him.

"Her aunt, you said," the older man muttered thickly. "Hannah's aunt."

"Yeah." Jonas spared him a quick look. The man's eyes were wide and startled.

"Then she's a witch?"

"Isn't everybody?" Jonas quipped.

"That's why," Elias whispered to himself, remembering the months he'd spent searching for her. If she was a witch, then her parents were, too—and no doubt her father had done . . . *something* to keep Elias from finding his daughter. "That's why I never found her."

"Found who?" Staring at the man, Jonas turned with him to face the doorway where the women would soon appear. A moment later, he spoke again, confused awe ringing in his tone. "You mean . . . Hannah's aunt Eudora is the woman you . . ."

Elias hardly heard him. With his blood thundering in his ears, his mind filled with images past and present of the woman who would, in another moment, be walking back into his life. Would she know him? Did she remember, as he did, every minute of the time they'd had together? Did she ever think of him and wonder?

Every breath cost him. His heartbeat thudded pain-

fully in his chest. His eyes stung with a sheen of tears
that were as unexpected as they were unstoppable.

So many years, he thought. Hundreds, *thousands* of
nights, he'd dreamed of this moment. Wished for it.
Prayed for it.

Hands trembling, mouth dry, he waited, as he'd
waited the last thirty years.

The sound of her voice reached him first. It was as
familiar to him as his own. She laughed at something
Hannah said and he felt himself smiling, too.

And then she was there. In front of him. Beautiful.
More beautiful than he'd remembered. He didn't see the
silver in her hair or the fine lines stretching out from the
corners of her eyes. Instead, he saw the pretty, sparkling
young woman she had been and he knew that as long
as he lived, he would always see her thus.

She stepped into the room and the shine in her blue
eyes warmed him as thoroughly as it had when he was
young.

Elias pulled in a long, shaky breath and realized that
thirty years had just dropped from his shoulders. In an
instant, he'd become the young cowboy who'd spotted
a fine lady on a ship's deck one morning.

He cleared his throat. "Eudora . . ."

She froze.

He spoke her name again, luxuriating in the sound of
it on his lips. It had been so long.

She knew.

She remembered.

He saw it.

She turned toward him slowly, as if no more able to
believe this was happening than he. He watched her as
she lifted one hand to cover her mouth, open now in surprise. Her eyes . . . those eyes that had haunted him for a
lifetime . . . glimmered with a sudden sheen of tears. Her
breath caught and a soft, tremulous sigh escaped her.

"Elias?"

He nodded.

"Oh, my . . ."

Somehow, he moved. His unsteady legs took him across the floor. His gaze locking with hers, he drank his fill of her and knew he would never tire of staring into those eyes. The other two people in the room had ceased to exist. It was only he and Eudora now. As it was always meant to be.

"My God," she whispered brokenly as he came closer, and even the tone of her voice was like music to a man long deaf to sound. "It *is* you." Her breath left her in a rush; she tilted her head to one side and a slow, sad smile curved her lovely mouth. "Elias. My Elias."

His own breath hitched in his chest. The love was still there. As it had been so long ago. As it would always be between them. "Always yours," he told her and opened his arms to her.

She came to him, as she had then, fitting herself into his embrace, cuddling close, resting her head on his chest where she could listen to his heartbeat. And when his arms closed around her, he felt, for the first time in too many years, a whole man. Complete.

"I didn't know," she muttered quietly. "I didn't know you were still with the Mackenzie . . ."

"Still?" he asked, pulling his head back to look down at her. His fingers trailed along the edge of her jaw like a man retracing familiar steps. "Then it was you who sent his parents to me?"

She looked up at him and nodded. "I knew they could trust you."

"Why didn't you come to me then?" he asked, his heart breaking for the lost years.

Eudora reached up, cupped his cheek in the palm of one hand, and smoothed her thumb across his lined face. "I didn't know if you would still want me." She inhaled deeply and let it go again on a sigh. "It had been five years since my father sent me away."

"But . . . you're a witch," he murmured. "Couldn't you see?"

She shook her head. "Not for myself. The crystal doesn't allow that. It's why I didn't know you were still here."

"You shouldn't have doubted," he told her gently, regret rising in his chest for all the lost time. Time.

He caught her hand in his and dipped his free hand into his pocket. Pulling out the tiny gold watch she'd given him so long ago, he studied it for a long moment, then placed it in her palm.

She sniffed and smiled. "Oh, Elias, you kept it all these years?"

Elias curled her fingers over the watch, then kissed the inside of her wrist. Looking at her again, he murmured, "Five years or fifty, Eudora. You should have known I'd be waiting."

"Oh, my love," she whispered as a tear rolled down her cheek, "I've missed you so."

"And I, you," he said, bending his head for the kiss he'd dreamed of claiming.

Softly, sweetly, their lips met in a silent promise of a future they could finally share.

Jonas stared at the two older people, so oblivious of their audience. Shifting his gaze from Hannah to the couple and back again, he was only slightly relieved to see that she was as confused as he.

Destiny, he thought. Fate. Words Hannah used with regularity. Was it possible that all of this had been set into motion by some Master Planner? Were Eudora and Elias meant to bring he and Hannah together all along?

A headache roared into life behind his eyes. Jonas looked from Hannah to her aunt, studying the two women as that sense of . . . *wrongness* reared up inside him again.

What is it? he wondered as a small kernel of suspicion took root within him and blossomed. Wrong. Something . . . Narrowing his gaze until his vision was slightly out of focus, Jonas stared at the tall older woman, concentrating on her alone.

Then he saw it.

A light. Surrounding Eudora, the pale, iridescent glow seemed to shine from deep within her and halo around her body like a child's outlined drawing. Jonas's pulse rate jumped as he studied the sparkling color that defined her form. Like dust motes caught in a sunbeam, showers of tiny sparks enveloped her, moving with her, shining like the sun glancing off new snow.

Magic.

Instinctively, he knew that was what he was looking at. The proof that Eudora was a witch. The magic was a part of her. In her bones, her heart, and soul.

He looked at Elias, still holding Eudora close. There was no light . . . no color around the man. No sense of magic there at all.

Jonas's breath caught, and briefly he lifted his own hands in front of his still-out-of-focus gaze. "Damn," he whispered.

The magic was surrounding him.

A sparkle of light, shining softly in outline around his palms and fingers. Another shallow breath shuddered through him as he turned his hands this way and that, watching the light play and dance, but never leave him.

More than any words he'd heard—more than any speeches about duty and what his heritage really meant— this pale, shimmering light struck him to his soul. Witchcraft wasn't something he could pick up or put down. It was *him*. In him. With him. A part of him that he would never be free of.

Something inside him shifted, opened, and allowed a light to enter where before there had only been darkness. And for that one brief moment, Jonas felt the power of his ancestors roaring through him. For one split second, he thought he saw the shades of his parents smiling at him.

Then the world righted itself and he was once again,

standing in his kitchen. Still a bit shaken, he let his hands fall to his sides as he looked at Elias and Eudora, still celebrating their reunion. Slowly, Jonas turned his gaze on Hannah, already anticipating her reaction when he told her about what he'd seen.

She'd been right all along. And maybe, he thought with a small surge of hope, maybe she was right about the two of them, as well. Perhaps they were *meant* to be together.

Her wide, green eyes shone with happiness. Her smile dazzled him to the soles of his feet. Smiling himself, he let his gaze shift out of focus again, wanting to see the sparkle of light that defined her. He stared at her for a long minute. Then another. His smile faded. Now he knew what had struck him as being wrong. His heartbeat staggered. He looked again. Harder this time, straining to see what he now knew wasn't there.

This was what he'd sensed was wrong.

It was Hannah, blast her.

Fresh betrayal slapped at him. He'd believed her. Trusted her. Hell, he'd come damn close to admitting he loved her.

For what?

More lies?

Hannah frowned as Jonas's smile faded. What could be wrong now? Couldn't he be happy for Elias and Eudora? Couldn't he feel the love swirling through the room? How could he not be affected by something as tender and touching as the scene unfolding now in front of them?

He was looking at her as if he didn't even know her.

Flicking a quick glance at the happy couple, Hannah turned back to him. "What is it?" she asked. "What's wrong?"

He snorted a laugh at her, his icy blue eyes as frosty as a lake in midwinter. At the harsh sound, Elias and Eudora both turned to look at him.

"You ought to be on the stage, Hannah," he said, glaring at her. "You're so damn convincing, you'd be a real success as a professional liar."

"What?" Whatever she'd expected, it hadn't been this.

"How many more lies are there?" He shrugged his shoulders and his mouth turned up in a mocking smile. "Just make a guess, if you're not sure."

"What are you talking about?" She forgot all about Eudora and Elias and took a step toward Jonas.

"That's one," he said shortly. "You know damn well what I'm talking about."

"I don't," she said, her voice rising slightly. "I swear I don't."

"Another lie," he snapped. "This magic horseshit." He paused and added sarcastically, "Oh, excuse me, ladies . . . it all goes hand in hand with lies, doesn't it?"

"Here, now!" Elias said.

"Jonas—" Hannah started, but was cut off.

"Sure it does!" He answered his own question, then went on. "Magic is making somebody see something that isn't there, right? It's making something out of nothing." He threw his hands wide and let them fall to his sides again. "It's *lies*. Something you're damn good at."

It was his voice, more than his words, that slashed at her. The banked fury in his tone and the remote gleam in his eyes made her cold down to her toes.

"Damn you, Hannah!" he shouted. He took a half step toward her before he stopped himself. "You came all the way here to force me to remember a past I wanted to keep buried. You tossed my life upside down, destroyed the first chance at peace I've known in ten years, convinced me to love you, and you're not even a *witch*!"

A bright flash of lightning skittered across the sky, gilding the windowpanes with an eerie, momentary brightness. An instant later, a roll of thunder crashed down around them, rattling the crockery in the cupboards.

"What?" she said on an outraged gasp. She couldn't even take a moment to enjoy the fact that he'd admitted to loving her. Not when he was spouting such utter nonsense, too.

"You heard me, damn it!" he shouted over another clap of thunder.

"Of course I'm a witch," she argued hotly, while a part of her mind tried to understand why he was doing this.

"What are you sayin'?" Elias demanded, but no one answered.

"No, you're not," Jonas went on, his voice dropping to a low, furious growl. "I can *see* the magic in a witch. I see it in her." He jerked a thumb at Eudora. "Hell, I see it in me. But when I look at you," he finished, "all I see is a liar."

"You're wrong," Hannah whispered, her voice tearing from her throat. "I'm a Lowell. A witch. Ask anyone back home."

Jonas snapped a glance at Eudora and Hannah watched her aunt's face pale slightly.

"Tell him, Eudora," she said and heard the thread of panic in her own voice. "Tell him he's wrong."

But the tall, older woman only looked at them both through eyes glimmering with sorrow. She held tight to Elias, her arms around his thick waist, burrowing close for his support.

Jonas wasn't moved. He wouldn't be fooled again. Not by Hannah. And not by her aunt, either, damn it.

He studied Hannah again, just to be sure in his own mind. But there was no change. No halo of light enveloped her. Not the smallest spark shimmered in the air around her.

"There's no magic in you," he said flatly. "So just who the hell are you and why are you here at all?"

"Adopted?" Hannah's voice sounded oddly hollow, but she couldn't seem to help it.

She'd expected Eudora to set Jonas straight. To tell them all that Hannah was a Lowell. The last in a long, illustrious line of witches. Her lungs trembled with the heavy task of drawing air. Her heartbeat thudded painfully in her chest. Her throat closed around a knot of regret, disillusionment, and fear.

Adopted?

So not only wasn't she a witch . . . but she also wasn't the woman she'd always thought herself to be. The ancestors of whom she'd been so proud weren't hers anymore. Her family ties were being snipped neatly, leaving her floating free, uprooted. Unbound to anyone or anything.

Oh, God . . .

Breathe, Hannah, she told herself, breathe. She looked around the table at the faces of the three people watching her. Elias, his features twisted into a mask of concern even as he kept a tight grip on Eudora's hand, as though he were afraid she'd slip away from him again. And Eudora, eyes rimmed with tears and glittering with trepidation. Finally Jonas, his expression neutral. Unreadable.

They were all waiting for her to say something. But what could she say? Her mind worked frantically and came up empty. Dear God, she prayed silently, please give me the words I need.

"You two want to be alone to talk about this?" Elias asked, clearly recluctant to go.

"No." The word shot from Hannah's throat. She looked from him to Jonas. "Stay. Both of you."

"You sure about this, missy?" Elias asked.

She wasn't very sure about anything at the moment, but she felt this was the right thing to do. After all, she'd ruined Jonas's life. It was only fair that he witness the crumbling of hers.

"Yes," she said, her gaze locking briefly with Jonas's. "There've been enough lies and secrets."

"Oh, Hannah," Eudora said, her eyes shadowed with pain, "you have to understand, dear."

She was trying.

Oh, Lord, she was trying. But how could she understand having her identity shattered? Her world torn apart? And suddenly, she found a new and much deeper sympathy for Jonas over what she had done to his life simply by showing up and insisting he accept *her* truth.

Oh, Jonas, Hannah thought, I'm so sorry . . .

She'd been so sure of herself. So completely confident that she was doing the right thing. She truly hadn't realized how horrifying it was to lose everything familiar. To suddenly have *nothing* you could call your own.

Hannah groaned inwardly and turned her head toward Eudora when the older woman started speaking.

"Your parents wanted children so badly that when none came, they went in search of a child to call their own." A half smile touched the woman's lips as she used her free hand to wipe away a stray tear. "They found you, in an orphanage in New York."

"New York." And she'd been told that she was born in Boston while her parents were on a trip. A small lie, she knew, in comparison to the full, glaring truth. Yet it was one more chip taken from the solid base on which she'd built her life.

This couldn't be happening.

Hepzibah strolled into the kitchen, sniffed at Eudora's feet, then took a flying leap to land in Hannah's lap. At least she still had this. This one small cat didn't know or care if she was a witch or a Lowell.

Tears filled her eyes and she dipped her head to hide them from the others. She held the little animal close, her fingers smoothing the cat's lush white hair. When Hepzibah purred, Hannah was grateful. At least there was one thing in life that she could still count on.

"They loved you so much, Hannah," Eudora was saying, and she really tried to concentrate. But it was so hard. So hard to think, when all she wanted to do was run away screaming.

"No one in Creekford knows the truth," her aunt said quietly.

Oh, she believed that. If anyone had known she was adopted, Hannah would have heard about it long before now. No one in Creekford could keep a secret long. And a secret this big would have been impossible to hide.

She glanced up at Jonas and wished she could read the emotions glittering in his eyes. Wished he would say something. Did he still think she'd come here to trick him somehow? Did he still think her love for him had been one of the lies cloaking them?

Eudora cleared her throat and Hannah looked at the woman who'd raised her. "When your parents died in that carriage accident," she said. "I saw no reason to tell you the truth." A new sheen of tears filled her blue eyes. "You were already in so much pain . . . what purpose would it have served? You were so young, Hannah, and I loved you so much."

The truth would have prevented this hideously painful moment, she thought, absently scratching behind Hepzibah's ears.

Jonas was right, Hannah told herself. There were too many lies. One seemed piled on top of another and when they started to fall, it became a rockslide, wiping out everything and everyone in its path.

And yet, a part of her wished desperately that this one particular lie had never been revealed. A lie was a comforting thing, when the truth was a devastating blow.

Eudora stared at her, sympathy and a plea for forgiveness shining in her pale blue eyes. Hannah knew she should say something. She only wondered if her voice would work.

"How . . ." she started, and stopped again. "Why . . ."

"What, dear?" her aunt prompted gently.

Hannah laughed shortly under her breath and was

grateful the laughter didn't escalate into the hysteria she felt bubbling in her chest. Before, she couldn't speak at all. Now there were too many questions trying to pop out at once.

Taking a long, deep breath, she tried again. "If Jonas could look at me and tell I'm not a witch, why didn't anyone at home see the truth?"

Eudora's head dipped a bit and she toyed with the handle of her coffee cup before answering. "That was my doing," she said. "I surrounded you with *my* magic." She paused and heaved a long, tired sigh. "When you came west, I had to hope that the Mackenzie wouldn't look at you too closely, because Wyoming was simply too far away for me to be able to continue the subterfuge."

"Almost worked," Jonas said tightly. "I didn't see it. Not until today."

"Ah, well," Eudora said. "Fate has taken a hand."

Fate.

Destiny.

Hannah gasped and her gaze flew to Eudora's. "You said it was my destiny to marry the Mackenzie. To strengthen him."

At the end of the table, Jonas stiffened slightly.

"Yes," the older woman said.

Hannah set Hepzibah down onto the floor and scooted her chair back from the table. "But how can that be if I'm not a true Lowell?"

The silver-haired woman looked at the two men watching her before turning her gaze back to Hannah. "I said it was your destiny to love the Mackenzie. And you do, don't you?"

Oh, she did. But that didn't matter anymore. "He has to marry a witch. You know that."

"He has to find love," Eudora countered firmly.

"With a witch."

"Hannah . . ." Her aunt reached for her, but Hannah

moved back and away. She didn't want to hear any more
lies. She knew as well as anyone that the Mackenzie *must*
marry another witch in order to strengthen his powers.

She felt Jonas's gaze on her and knew he was waiting
for her to speak. To say something. But she couldn't.
She no longer had the right. She wasn't a Lowell. She
wasn't even a witch.

Hannah groaned inwardly, remembering all the times
she'd complained about the pitiful strength of her powers and how she'd longed to be a better crafter. Now . . .
what she wouldn't give to be able to lay claim to even
the smallest of witchcraft abilities.

Oh, God, she wanted to cry for the loss of everything
she'd found in these last few weeks. She wanted to wail at
the knowledge that her family wasn't really her family.

And Jonas, she thought, his name echoing over and
over again through her mind.

"All these years," Hannah whispered, more to herself
than anyone else. "Lies. My whole life was built on
lies."

"Oh, Hannah," Eudora said on a groan.

She heard the pain in the older woman's voice and
instinctively spoke to ease it. She'd loved Eudora too
long and too well to see her torture herself over doing
what she'd thought best.

"No," she said, standing up and looking down at the
silver-haired woman, "it's not your fault, Eudora. I know
you only did what you thought was right for me. But
don't you see? This changes everything."

The Guild. Her home. Her magic. Her aunt. None of
it belonged to her by rights.

None of it.

Her gaze shot to Jonas. The Mackenzie.

A deep, soul-shaking pain took hold of her until she
wanted to moan aloud. But she gritted her teeth against
that need and swallowed the bitterest pill of all.

She had no right to the Mackenzie.

No right at all to love and be loved by Jonas.

Choking on the sob lodged in her throat, Hannah spun around and lurched toward the back door. Eudora's voice stopped her as she grabbed the knob.

"Don't leave, Hannah," she said, desperation coloring the words.

Bracing one hand on the wall, Hannah didn't turn around. She didn't want them all to see the tears she hadn't been able to will away.

"I'm just going for a walk," she forced herself to say. "I need a little time to think. I'll be back." She paused before adding another lie to the mountain of falsehoods towering over them all. "I promise."

Chapter eighteen

Jonas winced when the door slammed behind Hannah. Just as he'd felt her joy at greeting Eudora, he now felt the overwhelming despair choking her. His instincts told him to run after her. To hold her in his arms until her world righted itself again.

His fault, he thought with disgust. Because he hadn't trusted her. Damn it, he should have known Hannah wouldn't knowingly betray him. Hell, it was her determination to have him face the truth of his own past that had most annoyed him over the last few weeks. A woman that dedicated to honesty wouldn't have deliberately lied to him.

Now he'd inadvertently turned the tables on her. He'd forced her aunt into telling Hannah a truth that had ripped away years of comfortable lies.

Eudora jumped to her feet and started for the door.

"Leave her alone," Jonas said, his voice a cold, steely thread.

"I have to talk to her." The older woman turned to look at him.

Jonas glanced at Elias, then shifted his gaze back to Eudora. She was fairly shaking with the need to find Hannah. To apologize again. To try and repair the damage done by a hastily told truth.

But from personal experience, he knew the one thing Hannah needed right now was time to herself. To think about her changed world and how she fit into it.

It wasn't so long ago, after all, that he'd been the one forced to face a long-buried truth. He knew all too well what she was feeling. The destruction of everything she'd ever known. The tearing away of the floorboards she'd spent her life standing on.

Looking at the two people opposite him, Jonas tried to find that flash of anger he'd felt when he'd believed Hannah had betrayed him—and then the simmering temper he'd felt on her behalf as Eudora had started talking.

But he couldn't.

These two. Elias and Eudora, in the name of love, had woven such a net of lies around he and Hannah, it was a wonder that either of them could breathe. And though they'd meant it all for the best, that didn't take the sting out of the truth when it was finally shoved in front of them.

"Jonas'll go after her," Elias said, turning in his chair to look at the woman behind him.

Her expression worried, her eyes frantic, she nodded. "All right," she said. "But tell her, Mackenzie, that I meant no harm to her."

"No harm," he repeated thoughtfully.

"I only wanted to protect her."

"From the truth," he pointed out.

"Yes." She lifted her chin and focused her pale blue gaze on him defiantly.

Jonas shook his head and looked at Elias. "Just about what you did to me, isn't it?"

"Reckon so," he admitted.

Jonas had kept quiet through that whole earlier conversation, though at times he'd had to bite his tongue to do it. He'd watched Hannah's eyes and seen the desolation shining from her soul.

He shouldn't have said anything about her not being a witch. Should have waited. Thought about it more before blurting it out. But it was too late now for "should haves." Standing up, he looked at Hannah's aunt. "You sent her to me. Why?"

"You know why, Mackenzie," she said. "Hannah's told you about Wolcott."

Not only did he know about him, he'd fought and lost to the warlock almost nightly in his dreams.

But there was something he had to understand here. "Hannah told me that Wolcott wanted to marry her to strengthen his own powers."

"Yes." Eudora threw a look out the window, then returned her gaze to Jonas. "He knows that by joining his line with the Lowells', his power will be nearly untouchable."

"But she's not a witch," he said, straining to keep his anger reined in tightly. "You could have told him that and kept her safe yourself."

In the dim light of a cloudy morning, Eudora seemed to pale and then, just as quickly, two bright spots of color filled her cheeks. Straightening up, she glanced at Elias before looking Jonas dead in the eye. "I *couldn't* tell him. You don't know this warlock. He's . . . demented."

His dreams roared through his mind and still he needed to know more. "Tell me."

She sucked in a gulp of air and, twisting her hands together, she said, "If he'd known Hannah wasn't a witch, he would have gotten rid of her."

A deep, heavy cold settled in his chest. "Killed her?"

"Nothing so straightforward," Eudora muttered, shaking her head. "He has no respect for any ordinary creature—human or otherwise. Whenever a nonwitch stumbled across Creekford, Blake 'removed' them."

"How?"

She shivered and wrapped her arms around herself. Elias stood up, went to her, and pulled her tight against him. From the safety of love's harbor, she looked at Jonas. "They simply . . . disappeared. Ceased to exist."

"Jesus," Jonas whispered, shooting a quick look at the door through which Hannah had escaped.

"You were my only chance, Mackenzie."

Her voice brought his attention back to her.

"Once Hannah was married to you, she would have been safe from Blake. Your strength is enough to protect her."

"Then all this other stuff about my powers growing through marriage is just so much crap."

"No." She shook her head again firmly. "When witches marry, their combined strength always grows."

"But she's not a witch."

"It's not the witchcraft that strengthens their bond," Eudora said simply. "It's the love they share. Love is the one thread that cannot be broken. The one strength that builds on itself, growing stronger with each passing day."

Love. He felt it. He knew Hannah felt it. But would it really be enough to protect them all from the warlock he knew was coming?

He looked at the two older people and realized that most of his anger was gone. "You two have done a helluva lot of damage in the name of love."

"I know it seems that way now," Eudora said quietly. "But everything happens for a reason, Jonas. And fate cannot be avoided." She looked up at Elias and he smiled down at her. "What is meant to be, will be. No matter what. And I saw that you and Hannah were meant for each other."

His gaze narrowed. "You *saw* it."

"Yes." She smiled now, as she would at a particularly slow-witted child. "I knew your parents, Jonas. Very well."

He shifted uncomfortably.

"I knew that if you were half the man your father was, you and Hannah would make a fine life together." She drew a long, deep breath. "I looked into the crystal and saw the two of you, linked, joined. But there are challenges yet to be met. And Blake Wolcott will be furious at having his plans thwarted." A flicker of warning darted across her eyes. "He's a dangerous man. Your strength will defeat him."

"If you'd seen me trying to practice some magic," he said, "you wouldn't be so sure of that."

"He has a point," Elias told her. "I seen him."

"Thanks," Jonas said.

Eudora shook her head at both of them. "Neither one of you has realized the most important thing in this. Magic can't be 'practiced.' It simply *is*." Staring up at Jonas, she went on. "It's as much a part of you as breathing."

He didn't think so. Memories of his dream battles with the warlock came rushing back, filling him with a dread he'd never known before. Wolcott had defeated him every time. If he did so in real life, then Hannah would be unprotected from a man ready to wreak a little vengeance.

Jonas pulled his hands from his pockets, reached up, and shoved them both through his hair. A month ago, he would have laughed himself sick over talk of witchcraft and warlocks. Now it was all too real. And his main concern was finding a way to survive the coming battle so Hannah wouldn't be left unprotected.

Years of lies had brought them all to this point. If he'd been raised knowing who and what he was, he'd be more prepared. He'd know what to do and how to do it. And Hannah would never have been put into danger.

Letting his hands fall to his sides again, he said, "You had no right to meddle in our lives." He paused and spared a glance for Elias, as well. "Either of you."

The older man's arm tightened around Eudora's shoulders and the two of them faced him down.

"We had the right of those who love," she told him. "We meant only to protect you."

"She's got the right of it," Elias put in. "And we're

not goin' anywhere, either. We'll both be right here, ready to help any way we can."

Jonas shoved both hands through his hair again. "Love is sure being used to explain a lot around here."

Eudora chuckled, despite the situation. "Love explains everything, Mackenzie."

From where he stood, it only seemed to complicate matters, but he didn't bother to say so. What would be the point in arguing her position now? What's done was done. Jonas turned his head and glanced out the window. The thunder and lightning had faded away, but a light rain still fell. He scowled to himself as he thought of Hannah running blindly into that rain, and a new swell of anxiousness rose up inside him.

The hell with giving her time to think. He couldn't rest knowing she was out there, in the darkness. Alone. He wanted—*needed*—to be with her. "I'm going after her," he said, then shot a look at Elias. "Throw some food together, will you?"

The older man jerked him a nod, gave Eudora a quick kiss on the cheek, then turned, already bustling about the kitchen, apparently grateful for something constructive to do.

"When you find her," Eudora said, reaching out to squeeze Jonas's arm gently, "tell her I love her."

He looked down into those soft blue eyes and nodded. "I will," he promised. But first, he was going to tell Hannah that *he* loved her. As he should have done first thing this morning. He'd realized the depth of his feelings days ago. Hell, he'd probably known for weeks now. But he'd been so busy trying to ignore her and what she made him feel, he hadn't seen that he was being offered a gift. Well, he was tired of pretending that living alone was enough. He was tired of running from the past.

He wanted a future, damn it.

With Hannah.

Old fears and haunting memories still crowded his

mind and he knew he'd never be completely free of them. But if he had a choice between living without Hannah and living with her, there was really no choice at all. Going through the next forty years without her wouldn't really be living, anyway.

But even as that thought raced through his mind, a rising tide of darkness hovered at the edges of his brain, reminding him that their future was still at risk.

As if reading his thoughts, Eudora said quietly, "Wolcott *is* coming."

Nodding, Jonas shifted his gaze to the gray day outside. A crawling sense of approaching trouble moved along his spine. "I know. I can feel him."

"And you will have to face him."

"I know that, too," he said on a rush of breath. Fear coiled in the pit of his stomach. Not so much for himself, but for Hannah, if he should fail.

His doubts must have registered on his face because Eudora glanced over her shoulder at Elias, then spoke up again.

"It isn't only a talent for witchcraft that will win the battle, Mackenzie," she said, and he turned to give her his full attention. "The real power in this world is love. When a man's heart is full, he can do anything."

Again he remembered the dream blackness swallowing him down and he hoped to hell she was right. For all their sakes.

"But," she added, "you must believe. You must listen to yourself and open your mind to the power surrounding you."

What he *believed* was that he and Hannah belonged together. Just as she'd been saying from the start. He just wasn't sure that either of them would survive long enough to put that thought to the test.

Elias and Eudora stood side by side in the drizzling rain, watching Jonas ride out of the ranch yard toward the tree line at the base of the mountains.

"It'll be all right," he said, his gaze locked on the woman he'd never forgotten. "My boy'll find her."

She turned her head to smile at him. "I'm sure he will."

"You still seem worried," he said.

She nodded and laid one hand on his. Then she let her gaze drift to the sea of meadow grass and the gray thunderheads piled up against the mountain tops. "Trouble is coming," she whispered, more to herself than to him.

"We'll handle it," he promised and gave her hand a pat.

Turning toward him again, Eudora said, "Hannah and the Mackenzie must show a united front to Wolcott when he arrives. Or all will be lost."

Smiling, Elias assured her, "They're united already, Eudora. Just neither of them knows it yet. Jonas loves the girl. Don't you worry about that."

Eudora looked up into silver-gray eyes and found peace shining there, waiting for her. Leaning on him slightly, she whispered. "I hope it's enough."

"Love is always enough," he said, closing his arms around her just for the pure pleasure of it. The cold, misting rain didn't affect him. Nothing could. Silently, he said a short prayer of thanks for whoever had sent her back to him.

"I've missed you so," she whispered.

Elias's heart swelled until he thought it might fly from his chest. He blinked back a sheen of tears and struggled to speak. "Why did you stay away so long?" he finally asked, his voice a hush filled with years of loneliness.

"At first," she said, "because of my father. He refused to allow me to marry a nonwitch. He whisked me away from England and kept me in Creekford, away from everyone so that I would forget you."

"Did it work?"

"Of course not," she told him softly. "You were my heart."

He closed his eyes, then bent to rest his chin on top of her head.

"But as the years passed, I told myself that you had forgotten me."

He straightened up again. "How could you think that?"

"Forgive me," she whispered, leaning her head back to look up at him. "I should have trusted our love. *Your* love."

His work-hardened hand came up to cup her cheek. "I looked for you, everywhere."

She smiled and leaned into his touch. "I tried to see you in the crystal, but it won't allow me to use its magic for myself."

Years gone. The life they might have had. The family they might have made together, no more than an empty dream. And yet . . .

"It doesn't matter now," Elias said, his voice trembling. "We have the future and we have *our* children. Jonas and Hannah."

"Yes," she whispered. "Our family. Our future."

"Together," he said, and it was more than a wish, it was a question that needed to be answered.

"Together," she told him. "Always and forever."

Elias released a sigh, then bent his head to claim a kiss.

The Train

"Well, excuse the hell outa me!" the drunk said when he fell against Wolcott.

The overpowering fumes of cheap whiskey rolled around his head and Blake's nostrils twitched. Really, traveling in this manner was enough to test the patience of a saint, let alone a man of his refined temprament.

Sooty smoke filtered in through windows he was

forced to keep open because of the smells emanating from his fellow passengers. The constant clattering of steel wheels against the rails became a thrumming headache behind his eyes. And complete strangers felt compelled to involve him in conversations concerning their relatives of whom he had been previously, blissfully unaware.

But when a man in a drunken stupor collapsed against him, spilling his noxious brew onto an exquisitely tailored suit, he realized the line must be drawn.

Narrowing his gaze, his dark brown eyebrows lowering, Blake Wolcott looked at his accoster. With a flick of his wrist, he sent the man sprawling backward, tottering helplessly toward a suddenly wide-open window. And before anyone could react to this surprising situation, the drunk had gone through the window and the train rolled on, leaving him behind.

"Did you see that?" someone asked.

"Damnedest thing I ever saw," another voice answered.

Blake smiled to himself, wiped the whiskey spot dry with a spotless white handkerchief, and eased back in the uncomfortable seat. Then, closing his eyes, he quietly doubled the speed of the ramshackle train.

It amused him to think that months from now, engineers and firemen would still be wondering how they'd managed to travel so quickly. No doubt they'd spend years trying to repeat their success.

Still smiling, Blake told himself that in less than two days now, he would be at Hannah's side. And he would be sure to let Eudora know how unhappy he was to have had to make such a journey.

Jonas tugged the brim of his hat down low over his eyes and shrugged deeper into the folds of his coat. Cold and wet, he couldn't even allow himself to be angry at the weather, for fear a bigger storm would set in.

Hours he'd been riding in circles, searching for her

trail. But whether it was the rain muddying the signs or his own anxiety, he hadn't found a trace of her.

There was only one thing left to try, and right now Jonas was willing to try anything. He hadn't attempted the magic Eudora insisted was such a part of him before this because he trusted his abilities as a tracker more. But since nothing else was working . . .

Closing his eyes, he concentrated on Hannah. Her features rose up in front of him and he held his breath as he saw her, hunched beneath a tree, cold and wet and so unbearably sad his heart ached for her.

Steeling himself against the waves of emotion crowding him, he looked beyond Hannah to the land around her, searching for something familiar. Something to guide him to her. When he found it, he smiled.

Spurring his horse, he rode off to the left, toward the cliffside.

Hannah wrapped her arms around her waist and tried to stop shivering. Her wet hair straggled down on either side of her face like soggy ropes and her clothes were so soaked, the cold drove needle like stabs right down into her bones.

She leaned her head back against the tree trunk and stared straight up into the canopy of branches and leaves above her. Droplets of water splashed against her cheeks and from far away came the rumble of thunder. She groaned. "What's he mad about now, I wonder?" she muttered and wished Jonas would curb his temper before she drowned.

Her eyes closed on the thought of his name and a moan from deep within her slid from her throat. How could she face him now that he knew the truth about her? All of her fine talk about marriage and children and joining the lines of two great families.

She'd felt so sorry for him when he'd had to face the fact that his life had been built on lies. And now she was the one whose world had exploded. But where he'd gained a family, a heritage . . . she'd lost.

Who was she, if she wasn't Hannah Lowell? If she wasn't a witch?

"And what am I supposed to do now?" she asked aloud.

"You could dry off," a deep, familiar voice answered.

Oh, God. Her chin hit her chest. She grabbed handsful of wet, lank hair and dragged them along the sides of her face. Why hadn't he just stayed away? Why did he have to follow her? She sneaked a peek at him through the wet, blond strands of her hair. He looked wonderful, naturally. And she looked . . . as hideous as she felt.

"Hannah . . ."

Muttering curses under her breath, she realized he wasn't going to leave until she talked to him. Scrambling to her feet, she tossed her wet hair behind her shoulders and looked at him. "I didn't know you were here."

"I figured that." He swung down from the saddle and started walking toward her.

"Go away, Jonas." Her gaze swept from his determined, long-legged stride to the surrounding countryside, looking for an escape route.

"If you're looking for a different place to hide," he said and lifted one hand to point to a spot behind her, "there's a cave just over there. It'll be a lot drier."

"I'm not hiding," she countered, then said, "a *cave?*"

He nodded.

Of course, she thought. She'd been sitting in the rain for hours with a nice warm cave going unnoticed. Dismay rippled through her. If she'd been a witch, she would have found it.

"Quit feeling sorry for yourself," he said in a voice low and deep enough to plumb the depths of the ocean.

She sniffed and squared her shoulders. "Sorry for myself? Is that what you think I'm doing? Feeling sorry for myself?"

He cocked his head to one side and stared at her, his blue eyes a piercing bright light in the surrounding gloom. "Aren't ya?"

Maybe. But then, she thought silently, who had a better right? Still, she wouldn't admit to self-pity. She'd had enough humiliation for one day, thank you very much.

"Certainly not," she said on a sniff. Then, rubbing her hands up and down her arms, she added, "I just needed some time to think. That's all."

"Well," he said, stepping forward and taking her arm in a firm grip, "you can do the rest of your thinking in the cave."

"Let go of me," she snapped and tried to yank free.

"Nope."

"Jonas, I don't want to talk to anyone right now, especially you."

"Too bad," he said simply and started walking toward the cliff face just a few yards off through the trees. His horse followed them, its hooves clomping against the sodden ground like a heartbeat.

His touch on her arm brought her more warmth than she'd felt all day. But even as she relished it, she reminded herself that she had no right to him. Love wasn't enough. He was the Mackenzie.

And she was . . . no one.

At the cave mouth, he said, "Duck your head. The ceiling's a bit low until farther back."

With no other choice, she did what she was told. He led his horse all the way to the back of the cave, where he unsaddled the beast and left it to munch on some straw that had been left there.

Out of the cold, wet air, Hannah glanced around the darkened shelter and started when a match was struck. The tiny flame sputtered into life and fanned eerie shadows across Jonas's features. His eyes gleamed at her as he touched the flame to the wick of a candle set on a rock ledge.

"I've used this cave before to wait out storms," he explained as he crouched and set about building a camp-fire. "After the last one, I brought some supplies and left 'em here just in case I might need 'em again sometime."

"Very wise," she said and forced the words past chattering teeth.

Another match flared up and a moment later, the flames grew as the tiny fire blossomed on the fuel of wood and straw. Shadows leaped into life on the cave walls, flickering and dancing as the fire snapped and hissed in the strained silence.

Instinctively, Hannah moved toward the blaze, holding chilled hands out to capture the heat. But the cold she felt went far deeper than the fire could reach.

"You worried everyone," he said quietly from his crouched position near the fire.

That shamed her. After hearing Eudora's startling confession, she hadn't given a thought to anyone but herself and her need to run. From the truth. From Jonas's knowing eyes.

Hannah went down on one knee and looked up at him from beneath lowered lashes. "I'm sorry for that," she said, then shook her head. "But once I'd run, I couldn't go back."

"Why?"

She laughed shortly and was horrified at the shaky sound of it. "I didn't know what to say."

"How about," he suggested, "don't worry. I'm alive."

He was right. Poor Eudora. How she must have worried when Hannah ran off without a word. Hot, sudden tears filled her eyes and spilled over to rain down her cheeks. When she looked up at him, he seemed to blur and weave in her clouded vision.

He pushed himself to his feet, then took hold of her and pulled her into the circle of his arms. "I couldn't find you," he whispered, burying his face in the curve of her neck.

"I didn't want you to," she admitted. "At first . . ."

"Damn, Hannah." His arms tightened around her.

She sighed and just for a moment gave in to the urge to lean on him completely.

"I'm sorry, Jonas."

"No reason for you to be sorry," he told her, lifting his head to look down at her, "except for runnin' off and scaring me to death."

She wrapped her arms around his waist and kicked at the wet, clingy folds of her skirt. "Scared? I thought you were mad."

"Why?"

"It's raining."

He snorted a laugh. "I don't make *all* storms, you know."

Shifting his hold on her, Jonas cupped her face in his palms and looked his fill of her. Relief swamped him. She was safe. And in his arms. Where she belonged. Where she would stay if he had anything to say about it. Just holding her like this made everything feel all right. He wouldn't lose that. Or her.

"There's something I wanted to tell you this morning," he said. "Before everything went to hell."

Apparently what he was feeling showed on his face. "Maybe," she said, "it's better that you didn't."

"No," he told her. "No more running. No more pretending. And no more lies."

"Jonas . . ."

"I love you, Hannah." How easy that was, he thought. How right.

"No," she said, shaking her head. "Don't say that now."

"I have to say it," he told her. "You have to know that no matter what else happens around here . . ." His mind slipped to the still looming problem of Wolcott. "I love you."

She stepped back from him, eyes wide and swimming in fresh tears. He hadn't expected his declaration to have this effect on her, but Lord knew, with Hannah he should have been prepared for anything.

"You can't love me," she said.

"You can't stop me," he assured her with a soft smile.

"Mackenzie . . ."

"Look," he said, "we'll argue all you want later." His gaze swept her up and down and he knew that he had to get her dry and warm. "First you get out of that dress and we'll warm you up. Then we'll fight."

A brief, sad smile touched one corner of her mouth and he wanted to kiss it away. He wanted to take this whole damn day and wipe it from her mind. But since he couldn't, he figured to give her a memory that would be so good, she'd never look back on this day without smiling.

As her fingers fumbled with the top buttons of her dress, he turned and retrieved the blankets tied up in his bedroll behind his saddle. Then, grabbing up the coffee-pot he always carried, he took it to the mouth of the cave and let it fill with rainwater.

He set the pot near the edge of the fire to heat and turned to Hannah in time to see her wrap the rough wool blanket around her still-shivering body. Standing up, he went to her and rubbed his hands up and down her back and over her arms briskly. She sighed against him and when he knelt down, dragging her with him, she came willingly.

"I need you, Hannah," he whispered and the crackle of the fire nearly swallowed his words. "I need to be with you."

"Jonas," she said as she reached up and cupped his cheek, "I need that, too, but—"

"No buts," he interrupted, smoothing her hair back from her face. "Just for today," he went on, "there's no one else in this world but you and me."

"You and me," she repeated, her green eyes already hazing with the passion blossoming between them.

Laying her down on the rocky floor, he quickly got

rid of his own clothing and joined her in the folds of the blanket. Her skin was like ice and he drew the cold from her with his own body, giving her his warmth, his desire, his love.

Her lips met his in a kiss filled with sweetness and the promise of a tomorrow that might never come. The bittersweet ache in her heart threatened to choke her. She held him to her and wished that things were different. Wished that she was the woman she'd always thought herself to be. She had his love and now, for his sake, she couldn't accept it.

But this one moment she would claim for herself. And in the years to come, she would remember every second of it. The feel of him. The taste of him. The wonder of his touch.

Hearts beating in time, hands caressing, they joined in an age-old dance, celebrating life and the gift of two souls finding each other.

He touched her gently, his fingertips smoothing across her skin with a feather-light touch that sent sparks of heat dazzling through them both. He looked into her eyes and stared straight into her soul—into the shining, pure heart of her, and knew that this woman was his past, his present, and his future.

And without her, he was nothing.

As their bodies joined, their souls met. In a hush of whispers and sighs, Jonas felt her love fill him and he gave her all that he was and all that he ever hoped to be.

Chapter nineteen

Hours later, they dressed and readied to head back to the ranch. Hannah glanced at him as he carefully put out the fire and stacked the supplies he would leave behind.

He was so much a man of this place, she thought. His broad shoulders and work-hardened hands, the squint between his eyes that came from hours of staring into the sun. The Mackenzie he might be, but he didn't belong in Creekford as the head of the Guild any more than she did.

He belonged here. On his ranch in the life he'd built for himself. Hannah only wished she could share that life.

She shifted her gaze to the slash of late afternoon sun pouring through the cave's entrance. The rain had ended, just as her time with him had. It was time to admit it, out loud.

"I'm sorry I came here, Jonas," she said softly, though she wasn't really. She would treasure these few weeks with him for as long as she lived. He turned around to face her and she continued. "I'm sorry I disrupted your life."

"Don't be," he said and walked toward her. "I'm not. I'll admit, I wasn't real happy with you at first. But

Hannah, if you hadn't come . . . if you hadn't brought me back to life . . ."

He reached out for her, but she stepped back, afraid that if he touched her again, she might forget what was right.

"What's wrong?"

"Nothing . . ." she said, then muttered, "everything."

"What are you talking about?" Eyes narrowed, he watched her suspiciously.

"Us, Mackenzie."

"Hannah," he said and grabbed her before she could sidestep him. Pulling her close, he looked down into her eyes, forcing her to meet the cool blue gaze directed at her. "I don't know where you're going with this, but I sure as hell don't like the look in your eyes."

She looked up into his so-familiar features and realized how deeply she would miss seeing his face every day. Hearing his voice. Feeling his touch.

"Hannah . . . I *love* you."

"Oh, God . . ." She shook her head and swallowed hard. Panic and regret and an aching loneliness opened up inside her. "Don't say that anymore. Not now."

"Now and every day for the rest of our lives," he muttered thickly, his gaze moving over her features like a dying man glimpsing paradise.

"Don't you see?" she whispered, her voice breaking on a choked-off sob. "It doesn't matter now. *We* don't matter now."

"Love's all that matters." His fingers dug deeper into her upper arms. "You taught me that."

"But I'm not a witch," she said and again felt the pain of those words stab at her.

"I don't give a good goddamn if you're a witch or not. Hell, you ought to know that by now!"

He didn't care. She knew that. Witchcraft meant nothing to him and it had meant so much to her. What a joke the gods had played on them. She had to try to make him see how the truths they'd discovered in the last few days had irrevocably destroyed what might have been.

"When you found out the truth about yourself," she said in a tumble of words, "you discovered your family. A heritage."

"That doesn't mean anything. It doesn't change who and what I am."

Furious that he could so glibly toss aside what had been ripped from her, she countered, "When *my* truth was revealed, I *lost* everything. My family. My name." She shoved at his chest, but it was like trying to push a boulder uphill. "I don't even know who I am!"

He dragged her even closer, until their bodies brushed, igniting small fires in her blood that she determinedly tried to stamp out.

"You're Hannah Lowell. Soon to be Hannah Mackenzie," he muttered darkly. "The woman I love."

"I'm no one," she whispered, shaking her head. "An orphan, plucked out of an asylum and given a name she had no right to."

"No right?" astonishment colored his voice. "Your parents gave you that name when they chose you to love. To raise."

"I'm not a witch," she repeated, hearing the words sound over and over in her mind. "I'm not a real member of the Lowells. I have no powers. I have no claim to generations of magic. I'm . . . ordinary."

A harsh, short laugh shot from his throat. He shook his head and said, "If there's one thing you're not, Hannah, it's ordinary."

She wished that were true . . . but it wasn't.

"Let me go, Jonas," she said, staring up into his eyes.

"Why do you care so damn much about our pasts?" he asked. "I don't. I didn't ask to be a warlock and I damn sure don't *want* to be one."

"Unfortunately," she whispered, "we don't get a choice." If they did, she would still be the pitifully poor witch she'd always thought herself to be.

"Why are you being so damned stubborn about this?"

"You're the Mackenzie."

"I'm Jonas."

"The hereditary head of the Guild."

"A rancher in Wyoming."

"*Now* who's being stubborn?" she shouted.

"It's not stubborn to put up a fight against nonsense. You taught me that, too."

"Who you are isn't nonsense. Your duties, your responsibilities aren't nonsense."

"*My* responsibilities?" he asked. "What about yours?"

"I'm not the Mackenzie."

"No, you're not. But you *might* already be carrying the *next* Mackenzie."

Her eyes widened and one hand dropped to her flat abdomen.

"What about your responsibilities to that baby? To me?"

"We don't know that there is a baby," she said, though a part of her hoped to heaven that there was. At least then she would have something of him, of their love, with her always.

"That's not the point."

"Jonas . . ."

"No," he said, tightening his grip on her until she felt each of his fingers branding her skin right through the fabric of her dress. "What are you trying to say? That because you're not a witch, any child we might create together wouldn't be *worthy* of living?"

"Of course not," she snapped. "Every child is a blessing. A gift."

"Even orphans?" he asked quietly.

She sucked in a breath. My, he was a tricky warlock. Oh, she knew what he was doing. And it wasn't fair. She'd resigned herself to living without him. How could he throw hope at her when she knew it was useless?

"You *must* marry another witch," she told him, though the thought of another woman loving him, taking his name, bearing his children made her want to sink to her knees and weep. Hardening her heart and her voice, she continued, "A woman who can strengthen your powers and enrich your bloodline."

"I *must* marry the woman I love or nobody at all." He scowled at her. "And bloodlines should only be worried about in horses."

"Why are you making this so hard?" she demanded.

"This isn't hard, Hannah. Just like running away isn't hard. It's the staying and fighting for what you want that's hard."

"I don't want to leave you. I have to. I'm not a witch!"

"I don't care who you are," he roared and his voice echoed in the cave. "I love *you*." He threw his hands wide and let them fall again. "You. The woman who piled food in the middle of my table to teach me a lesson. The woman who wore feathers in her hair for who knows what reason. The woman who touches me and brings me to life again after too many years of darkness."

She choked back a sob.

"The woman who can bring me to my knees with a single glance out of her green eyes." He paused, then said, "There's only one important thing here. Do you love me or not?"

Oh, Lord, what she would have given a week ago to hear him say these things. Why was this happening? Why did she have to love him so desperately and give him up?

And why couldn't he see how difficult this was? How it was tearing at her heart?

She'd never be able to make him understand, and mentally she decided to quit trying. She knew what had to be done and she would do it. When the trouble with Wolcott was over, she'd leave Wyoming and allow Jonas to find his true destiny. And until then. Hannah would let him think he'd convinced her. It would make their last few days together so much easier to bear.

And what was one more lie between them now?

Looking at him, she saw the pain in his eyes that so echoed the ache in her heart. How she would miss him, she thought and silently prayed that he'd given her a child to cherish in the lonely years ahead of her. "I do love you, Jonas," she said. "I always will."

He looked at her warily for another moment before asking. "So it's settled?"

"Settled," she lied.

He sighed and shook his head, grinning at her. "Have to admit," he said, "you had me worried there for a while."

She forced a smile she hoped looked genuine.

"Then we'll get married as soon as Wolcott's been dealt with."

She inhaled sharply and lied again. "Perfect," she said and let herself be drawn into the circle of his arms.

The next two days passed quickly.

Too quickly for Jonas. He sensed trouble in the air and it wasn't just because his nightly dream battles with the warlock were becoming darker, clearer. He felt Wolcott drawing closer. Danger became a tangible thing, choking him, strangling him nightly.

His eyes gritty from a lack of sleep, his temper constantly near the flash point, Jonas kept to himself as much as he could, sensing that he needed this time to prepare for the approaching battle.

And it was coming. Soon.

"You all right?"

He spun around to face Elias, silently cursing himself for not paying attention to his surroundings. Hell, if an old man could sneak up on him, the warlock should have no problem catching him off guard.

Then the battle would be lost before he could make a try for victory.

And Hannah would be defenseless.

Taking off his hat, Jonas wiped his forehead with his sleeve, then resettled the hat again. "I'm fine," he snapped. "Or I would be if folks didn't pop up out of nowhere at me."

"Nowhere?" Elias swung down from his horse and picked up a strand of barbed wire laying on the ground. Holding it in place for Jonas to hammer it into the fence post, he said, "Hell, boy. I rode straight at ya across the meadow. You'd have to be blind not to notice me."

Blind or thinking, Jonas thought. And God knew, he had plenty for his mind to chew on. Not even counting Wolcott, there was Hannah. Something was wrong. Oh, she'd been doing and saying all the right things. But he felt her distancing herself from him.

Her sadness reached out to him, putting the lie to the smile she gave him whenever he looked at her.

He wished again that they'd been able to spend these last couple of nights together, in the same bed. Then at least he could have loved her and held her, made her see how much she meant to him. But with her aunt in the house, they'd had to behave respectably.

And every day, despite her smiles and her kisses, he felt her pulling back from him. It was almost as though she were already gone.

"She's leaving," he said bitterly, suddenly sure of it. He slammed the hammer onto the nail head.

"Who?" Elias asked. "Hannah?"

"Who the hell else would I be talking about?" Jonas glanced at him and briefly he envied his old friend's renewed romance with Eudora. Elias looked twenty years younger and Jonas had a feeling the couple would be married before he and Hannah were.

The curl of envy twisting in his gut shamed him.

"That's nonsense, Mac. Hell, her and Eudora's planning your wedding."

A wedding that would never happen, he told himself, silently mourning. Damn it, she was still trying to step aside so he could marry a blasted witch. Wasn't one damned witch in a marriage enough?

"Why would she leave?" the older man asked.

Jonas looked at him. Hell, maybe Elias could find an answer to the situation. Briefly, he explained Hannah's determination to marry him off to some other witch.

Elias frowned and shook his head. "Don't make sense. Eudora herself told the girl that you two were meant."

"Eudora lied to her before," Jonas pointed out.

Instantly defensive, Elias said, "She explained all that."

"I'm just saying that Hannah might figure Eudora's lying about this, too."

"Well, she ain't."

"It doesn't matter to me if she is or not." Jonas said flatly. "I don't care if we're *meant* or not. I know Hannah's the woman I want. And to hell with all this witchcraft horseshit."

"Then tell her so."

"You think I haven't?" He tossed the hammer to the ground and stalked off a few paces. Frustration brewed in the pit of his stomach and absently he noted the distant roll of thunder, but he didn't care. "That woman is as hardheaded as they come." And she was determined to leave him, for his own good. Half turning, he looked at his old friend through eyes filled with misery. "She's going to leave me Elias. First chance she gets."

The older man walked toward him and laid a hand on his shoulder. Jonas shifted his gaze to the far mountains. "I can feel it in her. She's waiting until this warlock business is finished. Then she's gonna run."

"And you'll find her."

Jonas laughed shortly. "You looked for Eudora for years and didn't find her."

Elias slapped him on the back. "But witchcraft hid her from me. Hannah won't be able to hide from the Mackenzie."

A single, fragile thread of hope unwound inside him and for the first time in days, Jonas's heart stopped aching. It was true, he thought. Witchcraft could turn out to be his strongest ally.

"You'll find her, wherever she goes," Elias told him gently. "And you'll bring her home."

Jonas smiled thoughtfully, turned to speak, and was stopped by a distant shout.

"Boss!"

Both men turned to watch Stretch Jones, riding his horse at a hard gallop, head straight for them. Practically standing up in the stirrups, he was waving his hat over his head like a wild man.

"Now, what d'ya suppose has got him so worked up?"

Jonas didn't answer. Staring hard at the approaching cowboy, he felt a strong sense of danger crowding in around him. A chill snaked along his spine and lifted the small hairs at the back of his neck. Whatever it was that had Stretch in such an uproar couldn't be good news.

Shifting his gaze slightly, Jonas looked in the direction of the ranch and squinted, deliberately blurring his vision slightly as he had to see the magic surrounding Eudora.

But what he saw now was different.

Different enough to stagger him and shatter what was left of that small bud of hope.

His breath hitched hard in his chest. His throat tightened and an invisible fist closed around his heart. Every instinct he possessed kicked into life, and unconsciously he stood up straighter, moving his right hand to rest atop the butt of his pistol.

Darkness hovered in the air over the ranch house. As he watched that blackness spread, like a spill of ink across a blue tablecloth, snaking out arms as if dragging itself across the sky. Alive and moving, the shadows shifted in a wind he couldn't feel, then dipped toward the house and the women Jonas knew were inside.

His dreams hadn't prepared him enough, he thought as the darkness seemed to hover around him, prodding him, goading him.

Fury roared through him and he stamped it down into a tiny corner of his heart. He'd need to keep calm, he told himself. Steady. If there was danger, he'd face it; but, he thought, it had better keep well away from Hannah or there would be hell to pay.

The darkness continued to grow even as it thickened, blackened, writhing in fits and starts like a soul caught in the torments of damnation.

He couldn't tear his gaze away from it.

It beckoned him even as it warned him off.

"Jonas!" Elias shouted, giving him a shove that shattered his attention.

He saw the flash of fear in Elias's eyes and wished he could say something to ease it. But he had a feeling that things were about to get a whole lot worse.

Jonas turned to face the incoming rider.

Stretch's horse reared to a stop and the winded cowboy leaped down, gasping for breath. Around great gulps of air, he managed to say, "The corral . . . ground . . . opened up . . ."

"What?" Elias gave him a shake, impatient to hear what the man had to say.

Jonas waited, too. Like a mounted cavalryman waiting for the sound of the bugle sending him into a charge.

The cowboy shook his head, drew one long, deep breath, and said, "The ground in the corral. It just . . . kind of broke open. Took down one or two horses before we could get the others out."

"Earthquake?" Elias said, disbelief coloring his voice. "I seen a couple in California, but never out here."

Jonas half turned and looked again toward the blackness now sliding down to cover the ranch like an evil blanket.

"It was no earthquake," he said stiffly, already moving toward his mount.

"Then what?" Stretch shook his head. "Damnedest thing I ever saw. That hole looks deep enough to reach into hell."

"It probably does," Jonas muttered, snatching at the reins and swinging into the saddle.

It had finally come. The day he'd been dreading and anticipating. And though he doubted he had the strength to win, he knew he had to try. He had to keep Hannah safe.

"Mac?" Elias walked to him and laid one hand on his horse's bridle. "What is it? What's happening?"

Jaw tight, eyes grim, Jonas looked down at him and said simply, "Wolcott's here."

The screams from the horses drew Hannah out of the kitchen, still clutching her dish towel. Racing across the yard, Eudora hot on her heels, Hannah stopped at the fence and stared into a yawning chasm that had opened in the middle of the paddock.

Frantic animals fought to escape the still-growing slash in the ground and two of the men skirted the lip of the gash in their attempt to save the remaining horses.

"Get back, ma'am," Billy shouted above the screaming animals.

Hannah took a half step back from the fence, but kept her horrified gaze on the yawning gap in the earth. "What in heaven . . . ?" She'd never seen anything like it. Oh, she'd heard of earthquakes, but if the earth had shaken badly enough to cause *this,* surely they would have felt it in the house, too.

"May the gods help us," Eudora muttered as she came up behind her. Then, grabbing her arm and spinning her around, she gave Hannah a mighty shove toward the house. "Get inside. Now."

"Eudora," she said, staggering slightly to regain her balance. "I have to help."

"There's nothing you can do," her aunt said, gaze lifting to the dark, encroaching clouds overhead.

Hannah looked up, too, and gasped at the storm-tossed sky. Dusky, wind-driven clouds covered the sun and instantly the ranch yard was plunged into an eerie twilight that seemed more like evening than late morning. She shivered and turned in place, letting her gaze sweep across the familiar landscape until finally it came to rest on Eudora's tight features.

The tear in the ground. The black clouds blotting out the sun. This was no earthquake or an ordinary shift in the weather.

This was the beginning of what she'd been dreading for weeks.

"It's Blake Wolcott, isn't it?" she whispered, feeling the bottom drop out of her stomach.

Her aunt nodded and closed her eyes, apparently trying to feel his presence. "He's here."

Jonas.

Oh, God, where was he? Had Wolcott already found him out on the range? Was the battle over and Jonas dead? Even as that fear reared up, she told herself desperately it wasn't true. If he was gone, she'd feel it. Know it, deep inside her.

Jonas was still alive. And she would do whatever she had to, to ensure he stayed that way.

"Where?" she demanded.

"Close," Eudora whispered, swaying slightly.

"Closer than you might think, Eudora," the warlock said as he stepped out from behind a corner of the barn.

Hannah gasped and grabbed hold of her aunt to steady her as they turned to look at him.

Smiling broadly, Blake Wolcott strolled across the yard toward them. Hannah looked into his sharp blue eyes and felt a quiver of apprehension shake her to her soul. Power seemed to ripple from the man. Arrogant in his own confidence, he walked with a swagger that invited a challenge.

One of the cowboys shouted at him. Wolcott waved a hand and the men in the corral—along with the surviving horses—dropped where they stood.

Fear clutched at Hannah's throat as she stared helplessly at the fallen men. This was all her fault. She never should have come here. My God, how could she have been so willing to throw Jonas into a pitched battle with a warlock like Wolcott?

"You killed them," Hannah yelled, outraged enough to momentarily forget the danger surrounding the man.

"Not yet," Blake said as he stopped just a foot or two away from her. "They'll wake in a few hours, unless I change my mind. For now, I simply wanted no distractions." He turned to look at the older woman. "Eudora," he said, eyes narrowing. "You've caused me quite a bit of trouble."

"Do forgive me," the woman said, not a trace of an apology in her voice.

Smiling tightly, Blake looked at her and told himself there would be plenty of time later to take his revenge on the woman who had tried to thwart him. It was enough for the moment to simply let her know that her plan had failed.

"I know now why you came to this godforsaken place," he said quietly. "Why you sent Hannah here."

"Is that right?"

"Oh, yes," he said, beginning to enjoy himself. "I've known for days." His eyes narrowed as he watched her for signs of worry. "You've found another warlock."

Hannah inhaled sharply and he whipped her a glance. "Who is he?" he asked.

"Don't you know?" The older woman smiled.

He bit back the frustration he'd felt since first sensing the presence of another warlock. He didn't have any idea who he would be facing. But, though the level of power emanating from this place was higher than he'd expected, he didn't doubt for a moment that he would be victorious.

"It doesn't really matter, Eudora," he said, enjoying shattering the old witch's hopes. "Whoever he is, he isn't strong enough to defeat me."

"I wouldn't count on that, Blake," she said.

Was she so sure, then? Who could it be?

"There doesn't have to be a fight," Hannah interrupted, forcing herself to take a step closer to the man she loathed.

He gave her his full attention.

"Hannah . . ."

She ignored her aunt and looked up into icy blue eyes. "There's no reason we have to wait for the Solstice to be married, Blake."

"Hannah!" Eudora's voice sharpened.

"We can leave now," Hannah went on, determined to get Wolcott away from the ranch before Jonas returned. She wouldn't risk his life. Even if she couldn't be with him, at least she would know that he was alive. And safe.

"That's very touching, my dear," the warlock said and ran the tips of his fingers along her jaw.

Hannah shivered.

He saw it and stiffened before pushing her away from him. "But even if we married, I wouldn't leave this place until dealing with the warlock. I won't have a challenger for my place at the head of the Guild."

"But when we're married," Hannah said, shuddering slightly, "you'll have the strength of the Lowells to draw on. There won't be a need to fight anyone for control. It will be yours. By right."

But he wasn't listening. His gaze swept over her, narrowed slightly, then repeated the long, searching look. His lips twisted and he took a step back from her. "There'll be no marriage between us."

"But Blake—"

"You're not a witch!" he cried, fury coloring his voice. "I can't imagine how I missed seeing the truth all this time. Ah . . ." He paused and flicked a glance at Eudora. "Another of your *games*?"

"Hannah," her aunt said, stepping in front of her, "stop. Say nothing else."

"No! I can still be a help to you, Blake." Hannah argued, panic nipping at the edges of her soul. If he didn't want her, she would have no way to bargain for Jonas's safety. She felt her last chance slipping from her as she yelled. "I'm still a Lowell."

He stared at her for a long minute and Hannah watched his features darken.

"You're *nothing*!" he shouted suddenly and shoved Eudora to the ground as he advanced on Hannah. Eyes blazing, hands fisted, he walked toward her and she instinctively backed away from the fury on his face. "Nothing!" he shouted again, and a cold, strong wind rose up, buffeting her, pushing her closer to him. "Without the witchcraft, you have nothing to offer me! Do you think I wanted *you*?"

The wind whipped her hair across her eyes and Hannah clawed at it, desperately trying to clear her vision.

"Power, that's what I wanted," he said, his voice rising to be heard above the keening of the wind. Grabbing hold of her shoulders, he shook her fiercely. Hannah cried out from the blast of cold driving from his hands into the heart of her. Then he tossed her to the ground and loomed over her, glaring down into her eyes. "The power and strength of the Lowells."

The wind lifted his dark brown hair and tugged at the edges of his coat until the material stood out from his sides and he looked like some evil winged creature about to take flight.

Mouth dry, heart racing, Hannah feared Jonas could never defeat this man. His power was too strong. His rage too deep. Terrified, she realized that there was no way for her to prevent the confrontation from happening. The two warlocks would meet.

And only one of them would survive.

"Once I've finished with your warlock," Blake promised, as if reading her mind. "I'll see to it you and your aunt pay for your deception."

"That's what you use magic for?" a deep voice taunted. "To threaten women?"

Wolcott whirled around to face his accuser.

Hannah struggled against the wind pinning her to the ground. Levering herself up on one elbow, she watched Jonas swing down from his horse and walk toward Blake.

Then she closed her eyes and prayed.

Chapter twenty

Jonas threw a brief glance at the corral. Two men and four horses down. He couldn't tell if they were dead or alive. A gaping chasm stretched across the center of the paddock and he bit back an oath as he thought of the animals already lost to that slash of emptiness.

But he couldn't think about that loss now. His focused gaze locked on Hannah, laying sprawled at the feet of the warlock.

Against the pallor of her face, her green eyes looked wide and overbright. His chest tightened and again he felt the swell of rage that had claimed him when he saw Wolcott toss her to the ground.

Hannah's fear invaded him and for the first time in his life, Jonas wanted desperately to kill a man. But he couldn't risk giving in to the fury rising inside him.

Hands fisted at his sides, Jonas faced into the wind, a cold, bruising force that pushed and shoved at him. He widened his stance, instinctively preparing for the coming fight.

Behind him, he heard Elias mutter a curse, but he couldn't afford to be distracted. Now he needed to concentrate on the man turning to face him.

"So, you're Eudora's hope," the warlock said above the rising wind. "The man she sent Hannah to find."

"I'm Jonas Mackeznie," he said through gritted teeth. "And you're on my land."

Wolcott's dark eyes widened slightly and for one split second, complete surprise colored his features. "Mackenzie?"

"That's right."

"Well . . ." The warlock recovered quickly and moved, walking off to his right, circling his opponent. "I thought the Mackenzie was dead."

"You thought wrong." Jonas didn't turn, but his gaze followed the other man as he moved.

"Mac—" Elias's voice, worried.

"Take care of Hannah," he said, never taking his eyes off Wolcott.

"Oh, yes." the warlock agreed. "We wouldn't want anything to . . . happen to either of the ladies. Would we?"

"Touch her again, Wolcott," Jonas promised him, "and I swear there's not enough magic in the world to cure what will ail you."

Dark brown eyebrows lifted and one corner of the man's mouth tugged into a mockery of a smile. "My, my. It's love, is it?" His lips flattened into a grim slash across his face. "How sad for you both."

The implied threat only fueled the anger blazing in Jonas's heart. He felt as though his insides were on fire. Rage fanned the flames licking at his soul and he had to fight to maintain control.

Above him, thunder crashed and lightning shimmered weirdly against the black, roiling clouds, brightening the gloom-filled yard with brief flashes of brilliance. The wind churned, tearing at his clothes, roaring like lost souls on the road to hell. The strength of the storm invaded Jonas and he wasn't sure if his power was feeding it or if it was the other way around. And a part of him realized it didn't matter.

Nothing mattered except ridding Hannah, the Guild, and the world of this warlock. She'd been right when she'd said that Wolcott had to be defeated. The man was wild-eyed and dangerous. As an ordinary man, he could cause plenty of problems. As a warlock, the damage he could do with even *more* power was staggering to consider.

If he had to use his last ounce of strength and will to accomplish this man's defeat, that's what Jonas would do.

And in that moment of realization, he silently accepted the weight of his heritage and the mantle of responsibilities that defined it.

"You shouldn't have come here, mister," Jonas told him, turning a slow circle, keeping a wary eye on the man as he watched for any sudden movements that might signal the start of the battle.

Wolcott shook his head and the wind swept his long, dark hair up and around his head like a dark halo. His gaze dropped briefly to the gleam of burnished brass shining at Jonas's waist. "You *are* the Mackenzie," he said with a little less bravado than before. "I see you have the circlet."

Was that hesitation—even uneasiness—in the warlock's voice? Jonas felt a momentary surge of optimism.

But a moment later, the man covered his brief lapse and said firmly, "But owning the circlet and being worthy of it are two different things, aren't they?"

Pay no attention, Jonas told himself. Don't listen to him. Just watch him. Watch his movements. Watch where he looks. Watch his eyes. The eyes were always the key in any fight. A man ready to make his move usually telegraphed the notion by blinking, or twitching, or . . . *something*.

Jonas bent his knees slightly and balanced himself on the balls of his feet—doing what Elias had taught him—looking for a weakness in his opponent. An opening. Something he could use to destroy the man who threatened everything he loved.

Wolcott was a tall, strongly built man, but he moved

unsteadily across the ground. Like a man too used to relying on magic to get things done. And that might be the weakness Jonas needed. If he could force this fight into the ordinary world, *he* would have the advantage.

From the corner of his eye, he caught a flicker of movement that *did* distract him. Long, blond hair, swept by the wind into a froth of brightness in the unnatural gloom. He glanced her way quickly and watched as Hannah fought and struggled against the powerful wind pushing her down into the dirt.

Anger, fear for her safety, and an all-encompassing love filled him.

He wouldn't lose her, he told himself firmly. He wouldn't lose his last, best chance at love. Not to some warlock with a lust for power. Not because he wasn't good enough at magic to best an enemy like he'd never faced before.

No matter what, he would win. He had to.

On the other side of the yard, Elias slowly made his way to Eudora. Jonas could only hope the two people would be able to protect Hannah until this was over. Eudora's magic was no match for the warlock's, but it might be enough to shield Hannah just enough.

"I'll have that circlet, Mackenzie," Wolcott crowed, and Jonas's eyes narrowed. "When I've finished with you, all that you have will be mine."

The wind howled, screeching around them like a demon, and the fires inside Jonas burned brighter. Hotter.

He glanced at Hannah again before saying, "You'll have nothing from this place. Wolcott."

"You'll stop me, I suppose?"

"With my last breath," Jonas assured him.

"Just as I'd planned."

"Jonas, no!" Hannah's voice trembled in the rush of wind, but he felt her terror.

He blanked his mind to it. He couldn't do anything to ease her worries and couldn't afford to think of them now. "Stay out of this, Hannah," he yelled, his gaze still centered on the warlock.

"Yes, do," Wolcott said tightly.

"Let's get to it, witch," Jonas told him as he took a step closer.

"Warlock," the other man corrected.

And Jonas dove at him, his arms wrapping around the other man's knees and toppling him into the dirt. Air exploded from the warlock's lungs and rather than reaching for the help of magic, he reacted as Jonas had hoped he would.

Bringing his right fist up, Wolcott swung a punch that missed Jonas's jaw by inches. He responded with a solid right to the man's midsection that purpled the warlock's features as he struggled for air.

Again and again, Jonas landed punches squarely, battering the man's face and body with work-hardened fists driven by muscles earned with years of backbreaking labor. He felt a satisfying crunch of bone as the warlock's nose broke and blood flowed from him. Wolcott screamed in pain and rage, but Jonas didn't hesitate. His fists flew at the enemy, over and over again. Desperation drove him. He fought for those he loved. He fought for his life.

And the future he wanted so badly.

Wolcott hit him with a punch that snapped his head back, then another that made him see stars. But the next few were Jonas's and those hits hurt the warlock badly.

Overhead, the skies exploded in a blast of noise and light. The rolls of thunder became a continuous roar and the weird snatches of illumination from the bolts streaking across the heavens shone through the darkness clawing at Jonas.

Like his dreams, that blackness loomed closer, heavier, threatening to swallow him. He remembered the fear and slammed it down, refusing to give it life. Jonas fought, harder than he had in those nightmare struggles. More fiercely. More desperately. It was as if those nightly battles had been honing his skills . . . driving him to realize that when the fight came, it would be all or nothing. No half way measures would end this.

Either he, or Wolcott, would die.

And he was winning. He felt it. Felt the warlock's confidence shatter as he lay helpless beneath Jonas's fists.

So he should have expected the fight to change. But he didn't.

In an instant, he was catapulted from atop Wolcott to sail across the yard. He landed with a solid thump that knocked the wind from his chest and set his ears ringing. Clambering to his feet again, he shook his head to clear it, stood up, and faced the warlock from twenty paces off.

Swaying slightly in the wind, Wolcott reached up and wiped a streak of blood from his split lip, then tenderly explored the shattered remnant that was his nose. "You fight like an ordinary man," he sneered. "You're no warlock."

"Bloodied you," Jonas managed to say.

"First blood is not always *last* blood," the warlock reminded him.

In the next flash of lightning, Jonas saw the man's black gaze flick briefly to Hannah. The warlock raised one hand . . .

"Jonas, look out!" she yelled above the keening wind, obviously convinced the man was about to strike him down.

A sudden spurt of dread rocked Jonas on his heels. Not for himself, though, because he knew without a doubt the warlock's next move would be against Hannah.

Beneath her, the ground opened up with a terrible tearing and ripping that carried over the wind and the roar of the storm.

"Hannah!" Jonas shouted as he watched her legs slide into the yawning black gash in the earth. She screamed once and dug her fingers into the muddy dirt, clawing for purchase. Eyes wide, she looked at him, and in a flash of lightning he saw acceptance of her fate gleaming in her green eyes.

"No!" he shouted, panic stabbing at his heart.

"By killing her," Wolcott yelled to him, "I kill you."

The earth moved again and she fell deeper into the abyss opening beneath her.

"Oh, God!" Eudora's voice, frantic. She lifted both hands toward her niece, but her magic was no match for the warlock's.

"I'll get her," Elias shouted.

But Jonas knew the older man couldn't save her. He wasn't strong enough or quick enough to best the magic hurtling through the yard. Even Eudora's power wouldn't be enough. Wolcott might be crazy, but he was damned strong, too.

"Hang on, Hannah," Jonas murmured. Focusing his mind on the woman he loved, he used his formidable will to hold her, keep firm her precarious grip on safety.

And as the wind buffeted him and the thunder crashed and boomed around him, Jonas looked deep within himself. A corner of his mind noted that Wolcott stood patiently, waiting for Hannah to die so that he might finish Jonas off at his leisure.

But he steeled himself against thoughts of failure.

He wouldn't lose. Not this time. Not when so much was at stake.

Closing his eyes, Jonas heard Eudora's voice echoing in his mind: *The real power in the world is love, Mackenzie . . . When a man's heart is full, he can do anything . . . But he must listen to himself and open his mind . . .*

Wolcott knew only the lust for power and the need to destroy. He had no love to draw on, to gather strength from.

Jonas slowly lifted both arms wide as he had the night of the stampede, when everything in his world had changed. Opening his eyes, he stared into the dark brown gaze of the warlock bent on destruction, then threw his head back to look at the sky and whatever lay beyond.

Calling out to whoever might be listening, Jonas shouted and his words were snatched up by the wind and carried to the heart of the storm.

"I am the Mackenzie," he called out, and the thunder rolled. Later, he would wonder where he found the words, but as they poured from him, they sounded right. And proper.

"Save her and end this. I call on the magic that lies within us all." He pulled in a breath and shouted, "I call on the power of love. I call on those who would have us win this day!"

And generations of Mackenzies lined up on either side of him. He felt their presence, though even he couldn't see them. Hundreds of them. Spirits, souls, ghosts. It didn't matter what they were called. All that mattered was that they were real. And standing with him. From the first Druid priest to his parents, the members of the Mackenzie family surrounded him, strengthening him, pouring centuries of knowledge and love into the well of his soul.

They filled him with light, with magic, with the power that was his birthright.

Blake Wolcott paled. His raised fists shook. And when the first lightning bolt struck the earth at his feet, he screamed.

Too late, he'd discovered what Jonas had finally accepted. The strength of centuries—of families, of *love*—cannot be denied.

Jonas watched as bolt after bolt stabbed the ground in a widening circle around the warlock who would have destroyed him. Again and again, white-hot, jagged spears slammed into the dirt. Jonas felt the hammering blows but stood untouched by the wild electrical charge rising around him. A cloud of dust and smoke and a thick gray haze rose up, shrouding Wolcott from sight.

His screams tore from his throat.

Lightning hailed from the sky.

And in a final, horrendous crash of thunder, lightning, and wind, the battle was finished.

A silence so thick it seemed to have a life of its own dropped over the yard.

Jonas slumped, drained, and half fell to one knee. The quiet pounded at him. He fought for air and, when he could breathe again, whipped his head around to look for the one person he needed to see.

"Hannah?" He pushed himself to his feet and, staggering, made his way to where she lay, unharmed. Beneath her, the earth had somehow healed itself, closing up the gaping black chasm that had nearly taken her down.

Hannah smiled up at him. "Jonas," she whispered, and his own name had never sounded sweeter.

Pulling her to her feet, he yanked her into his arms, holding her pressed so tightly to him, he couldn't have said where her body ended and his began. Burying his face in her hair, he inhaled the fresh scent of lemons and reveled in the warm, solid feel of her in his arms. Alive. Safe. *His.*

"Are you all right?" she asked, her voice muffled against his shirtfront.

"I am now," he said, just before he swayed unsteadily.

"Jonas?" She tipped her head back to look at him.

"It's all right," he told her, trying to ease his racing heart. "It's that rush of magic that's left me shaking a bit. Wolcott didn't hurt me."

She lifted one hand and touched a darkening bruise beneath his eye.

He winced and choked out a laugh. "One lucky punch."

Hannah didn't smile, though. Instead, she half turned her head to look toward the spot where she'd last seen Wolcott. A heavy pall of smoke still swirled there, twisting and shifting in the now-soft breeze. "Is he . . . ?"

"Yeah." Jonas didn't need to see a body to know that Blake Wolcott had been destroyed. If the warlock had still been alive, Jonas would have been able to sense it.

Holding on to each other, they walked across the yard and came to stop at the edge of a wide circle of blackened grass. As the smoke cleared, they saw the earth, still smoldering from the lightning strikes, and all that was left of Blake Wolcott. Ashes.

Jonas tightened his grip on Hannah's shoulder and watched as a quick surge of wind lifted those ashes and scattered them.

"It's over," he whispered, more to himself than to her.

"It is, Mackenzie," Eudora said from behind him.

He turned his head to watch the older couple approach.

"A helluva fight," Elias told him with a smile that didn't quite hide the worry still shining in his gray eyes.

"It was that," Jonas agreed. One he didn't want to think about repeating anytime soon.

"You did well," Eudora said.

He met her gaze and silently thanked her for giving him the clue he'd needed to defeat Wolcott. It had been a close thing, that fight. Tipping his head back, he watched as the storm clouds rolled away, revealing a sky so blue it hurt to look at it. "Thank you," he whispered and knew his family had heard him.

The neigh of a horse caught his attention and he glanced at the corral, where the cowhands and horses were awakening to stumble around the paddock. How he'd explain to *them* what had happened, he didn't know yet. Smiling to himself, he realized he was too tired to think at the moment anyway.

Speaking quietly, Jonas said to no one in particular, "I need a drink."

Then the world went black, his legs gave out, and he fell face forward into the dirt.

*   *   *

"This ain't right," Elias said for the hundredth time in the last hour.

Hannah handed her carpetbag to the stagecoach driver, who stowed it atop the coach. Looking around the little town, she said a silent good-bye before turning to face the older man scowling at her.

"It is right," she told him and wiped a stray tear off her cheek. Her brain knew this was the only answer. It was just her heart that hadn't accepted it yet.

"You could at least wait till he wakes up."

Hannah shook her head and swallowed heavily. No, she couldn't. It was better that she leave now, while Jonas was still sleeping.

After he'd collapsed in the yard, the men had carried him to bed. Eudora had calmed Hannah's fears, telling her that Jonas was simply exhausted. After serving as a funnel, delivering such an enormous amount of power, his body was drained and he would probably sleep around the clock.

Perhaps it was cowardly of her to slip away before he awakened. But she couldn't bear the thought of looking into his eyes and saying good-bye. This way, while Jonas slept, she would ride the stage to the train station. And by the time he woke, she would be miles from here. From him.

"It's easier on both of us if I leave now," she said and tried to smile up at him.

"He won't let you go," Elias said gently.

"He has to."

"But you're all alone."

True. For the first time in her life, Hannah was completely alone. Eudora was staying behind to be with Elias and though the older woman had wanted to at least see her off on the stage, Hannah had insisted that she remain with Jonas.

She'd left Hepzibah behind, too, knowing it wouldn't be fair to drag the little animal across the country again.

"I'll be fine," she told him and hoped her voice

sounded steadier to him than it did to her. "Creekford is my home." Though she didn't think she would stay there long. Without Eudora's protective spell, everyone there would know she wasn't a witch. And frankly, she simply couldn't bear the thought of being an object of pity.

"Don't go, Hannah," Elias said quietly. "Stay here. With him. With us. Where you belong."

Such a dear man, she thought, looking up into gray eyes filled with sadness, regret. How she would miss him. Miss them all. Pain rippled through her and Hannah bit back a gasp at the near-crippling sensation.

Elias shook his head, then reached down and grabbed one of her hands.

"Time to go, ma'am," the stage driver announced from his bench seat.

Elias shot him a glare, then turned back to Hannah. "You have to know something," he said, keeping a tight grip on her fingers when she would have pulled away.

"Elias, please don't make this harder . . ."

"He's never loved anyone like he loves you," the man said, his voice gruff and thick with choked-off emotion. "You're his heart. Hannah. You leavin' will kill him."

Her heartbeat raced and every beat stabbed at her chest. The ache swelled and blossomed inside her until Hannah felt as fragile as fine crystal. One more word would shatter her.

Quickly, she pulled her hand free of his grip, went up on her toes, and gave him a brief kiss. "Help him understand, Elias," she whispered. "Help him know that I'm doing this because I love him so much."

He frowned at her. "Can't help him understand what I can't figure out myself, missy."

Fresh tears welled up in her eyes and Hannah turned quickly away. Climbing into the coach, she winced when the door was slammed shut, and kept her eyes closed as the horses lurched into motion and she left Jonas—and her heart—behind.

*   *   *

"All aboard!"

The train whistle blew and Hannah stood back as her dozen or so fellow passengers hustled forward to board the train. Clouds of steam whooshed up into the air from the engine and swirled across the platform like a wayward fog.

Another blast of the whistle prodded her forward and, clutching her bag tightly, she lifted the hem of her skirt to mount the iron steps.

And stopped dead.

As if she'd run into an invisible wall, she could not put her foot on that step. Scowling, she tried again. And again. First her right foot, then her left.

Nothing.

Irritated, she swung her carpetbag toward the steps, only to have it bounce off something she couldn't see and smack into her chest.

Hannah staggered backward and watched dumbfounded as a little boy raced past her, jumped up the steps, and entered the car. Quickly, she ran forward and tried to board in the same way. She smacked headlong into that invisible barrier, knocking her hat off to hang behind her back, dangling from its pale green ribbons.

Witchcraft, she thought, rubbing a sore spot on her forehead, and wondered how Eudora had managed to cast a spell from such a distance.

"For heaven's sake," she muttered, then gasped as the train started rolling. Shooting a look toward the engine, she shouted, "Wait for me!" But a blast of the whistle drowned her out and the rising cloud of steam sent her scurrying back from the edge of the platform.

Tears stung her eyes as she dropped her carpetbag and watched the train pull out of the station. Iron wheels clanked, steam huffed, and in minutes the train was gone, its passage marked by a towering rise of black smoke from its chimney stack.

Frustrated misery bubbled inside her. Couldn't her aunt see that she was only making the leaving that much harder? Delaying the inevitable only lengthened the pain. "I'll just wait for the next train," she said aloud on a sniff. "Or the one after that."

"I'll stop you every time," a deep, oh-so-familiar voice said from close behind her.

She closed her eyes briefly and struggled to still her suddenly racing heart. Then, slowly, she inhaled and turned around to meet Jonas's deep blue eyes. "You're supposed to be asleep," she accused.

He shook his head. "Sorry to disappoint you."

"That's not what I meant." Oh, God, it was so good to see him again. To have one last chance to look into his eyes, watch the sunshine slanting off the midnight of his hair.

"I won't let you leave me. Hannah," he said softly.

"You have to, Jonas," she told him and heard the catch in her voice.

"Why?" he asked. "So we can both be miserable apart instead of happy together?"

"So you can find the right woman to love. To marry."

"I already have."

A lone tear slipped from the corner of her eye and rolled along her cheek. She wished it were that simple. "You have to marry a witch, Jonas." She had to make him understand. For both their sakes. "Don't you see? Blake Wolcott isn't the only dark warlock in the world. Any one of them might come here to challenge you."

"Let 'em come," he said, reaching out to tuck a stray lock of her hair behind her ear.

She batted his hand away, determined to reach him. "You have to marry a witch . . . strengthen your powers, so you're ready for them."

"You make me strong enough to take on the world." he told her with a smile.

Her heart fluttered wildly in her chest, but she still argued. "You're the Mackenzie. Your children must be able to follow in your footsteps."

His eyebrows lifted and his smile shifted into a grin.

"You mean be ranchers?" Shaking his head, he said, "Only if they want to be."

"You know what I mean, Jonas."

"Yeah, I do," he said and took a step closer to her, closing the space between them to no more than a breath of distance. "You're worried about the Guild. Well, I've figured that out. We can take a honeymoon trip back East, put somebody else in charge, then come back here. This is my home, Hannah. I couldn't stay back East."

"I wouldn't expect you to," she said. She could no more imagine Jonas living in the quiet, refined little town than she could picture Elias flying. "But that's not the point."

"Then tell me what's important enough to make you want to leave."

"Joining with another witch would keep you safe."

"Losing you would kill me."

Simple words, said so quietly, they rang with the clear bell of truth.

And still she tried. "What if, by marrying me, you cheat your children out of their heritage?" Lord, she could hardly think with him this close. "What if they're not witches?"

He shook his head, letting his gaze sweep across her features. "Witchcraft isn't what matters, Hannah." Reaching out for her, he cupped her cheek and reminded her of what Eudora had told him only days ago. "*Love* is the greatest power in the universe. And with love," he added with a smile, "anything is possible."

Jonas looked into her eyes and saw that she was still only half convinced. How had he lived before this woman had come into his life? A woman who was willing to walk away from what they'd found together, in the hopes of keeping him safe. He had to make her understand that it was her and her alone who had given him the strength to defeat their common enemy.

"*You're* the reason I was able to defeat Wolcott." he said, willing her to trust him. "*Your* love gave me more power than any simple witchcraft could have."

"I want to believe that," she said, and the tears in her voice caught at his heart.

"Believe, Hannah," he whispered. "Our children could only be strong and happy coming from our love. Witches or not, they'll be perfect. Every one of them." Including, he thought as he stared hard at her, the tiny witch she carried inside her even now. Jonas smiled at the almost invisible shimmer of color he saw cradled within her and knew that their first child, a girl, would be as strong and beautiful as her mother, with the crafting abilities of her father.

A baby girl, he thought and waited for the old flash of fear and pain to rise up inside him. But instead, he felt only thankful for this second chance at fatherhood.

And tonight, he'd tell Hannah all about the coming baby.

Now, though, he reached into his coat pocket and slowly pulled out the belt buckle he'd only that morning changed back into the brooch it was always meant to be.

The circlet that had been handed down from generation to generation in his family lay in the center of his palm. He held it up, silently paying his respects to the Mackenzies who had gone before him, while letting the sunshine glint off the ancient brass.

Then, slowly, he lowered it again, looked at Hannah, and solemnly said, "I *am* the Mackenzie. And you are the woman I've chosen. The woman I love."

"Jonas . . ."

Still arguing, he thought with an inward smile, but with less determination.

He pinned the circlet to her coat, just above her heart, then laid his hand atop it gently.

Hannah's eyes widened and she gasped as she felt the rush of his power roar through her veins. Jonas smiled and gave her more, letting her feel every beat of his heart. Every whisper of magic that filled him. Every trace of strength and power that he had was now also hers.

"I don't understand," she said and leaned into him, still reeling from the tingling sensations coursing through her.

He caught her face between his palms and stroked her cheeks with the pads of his thumbs. Smiling into the green eyes that had captured him from the first, he said, "Love is the real magic, Hannah. And you are the love."

Then he kissed her and the sparkle of magic that surrounded him enveloped her as well, enclosing them in a world all their own.

And the circlet gleamed as when it was new.